PRAISE
AND

"Sensual and thrilling, a wonderful combination of vampire myths old and new. You cannot miss this novel!"
—Michele Bardsley, national bestselling author of the Broken Heart series

"Wow! Steamy-hot fantasy, sizzling sex, and a story that makes you think . . . Marie Treanor really packs a lot into these pages."
—Fallen Angel Reviews

"Prepare to be scorched, alarmed, illuminated, and fired up!"
—TwoLips Reviews

"Witty and sensuous." —Romance Reviews Today

"My first impression of this work was *wow* . . . highly recommended read from an author to watch."
—The Romance Studio

"A very unique fantasy. The passion and heat . . . was Pure Erotic but with a loving passion that made me feel all warm inside." —Paranormal Romance Reviews

"A fantastic story . . . superhot sex. I cannot wait for future books." —Joyfully Reviewed

"A provocative read . . . witty, sensual, and sometimes dark. . . . Brimming with complex and compelling characters, sexual tension, danger, betrayal, emotional turmoil . . . this erotic gothic story grabs your attention and holds it right up to the very last page." —Romance Junkies

"Funny, sizzling, and tender." —Bitten by Books

"Marie Treanor always delivers a book that you'll be talking about long after reading it." —Love Romances and More

"Hauntingly beautiful and entirely sensual." —eCataromance

"In a sea of vampire stories, her creation stands out as one of the best." —Brazen Broads Book Bash

"A superbly written story filled with suspense, action, and steamy, passionate encounters." —Literary Nymphs

ALSO BY MARIE TREANOR

Blood Sin
Blood on Silk

Blood Eternal

AN AWAKENED BY BLOOD NOVEL

MARIE TREANOR

A SIGNET ECLIPSE BOOK

SIGNET ECLIPSE
Published by New American Library, a division of
Penguin Group (USA) Inc., 375 Hudson Street,
New York, New York 10014, USA
Penguin Group (Canada), 90 Eglinton Avenue East, Suite 700, Toronto,
Ontario M4P 2Y3, Canada (a division of Pearson Penguin Canada Inc.)
Penguin Books Ltd., 80 Strand, London WC2R 0RL, England
Penguin Ireland, 25 St. Stephen's Green, Dublin 2,
Ireland (a division of Penguin Books Ltd.)
Penguin Group (Australia), 250 Camberwell Road, Camberwell, Victoria 3124,
Australia (a division of Pearson Australia Group Pty. Ltd.)
Penguin Books India Pvt. Ltd., 11 Community Centre, Panchsheel Park,
New Delhi - 110 017, India
Penguin Group (NZ), 67 Apollo Drive, Rosedale, Auckland 0632,
New Zealand (a division of Pearson New Zealand Ltd.)
Penguin Books (South Africa) (Pty.) Ltd., 24 Sturdee Avenue,
Rosebank, Johannesburg 2196, South Africa

Penguin Books Ltd., Registered Offices:
80 Strand, London WC2R 0RL, England

First published by Signet Eclipse, an imprint of New American Library,
a division of Penguin Group (USA) Inc.

First Printing, October 2011
10 9 8 7 6 5 4 3 2 1

Printed in the United States of America

PUBLISHER'S NOTE

This is a work of fiction. Names, characters, places, and incidents either are the product of the author's imagination or are used fictitiously, and any resemblance to actual persons, living or dead, business establishments, events, or locales is entirely coincidental.

The publisher does not have any control over and does not assume any responsibility for author or third-party Web sites or their content.

To this book's editor, Jesse Feldman, who took on an unexpected job with grace and kindness! Thank you!

She who stirs the Ancient will end his power and make way for the rebirth of the world, for the dawn of the new vampire age. She will smite his friends and cleave to his enemies, who would end all undead existence. To see the new age, she must give up the world.

—The prophecy of the Ancient vampire Luk, as witnessed by a sixteenth-century vampire hunter

Cast of Characters

The Humans

Cynthia (Cyn) Venolia: An untrained psychic who senses the presence of the paranormal. Friend of Rudy Meyer, her partner in killing vampires.
Dr. Elizabeth Silk: The Awakener; descendant of Saloman's killer, Tsigana; Saloman's companion. An academic recently awarded her PhD, she accidentally awakened Saloman more than a year ago. Her blood is necessary to Saloman if he's to reach his full strength.
Senator Grayson Dante: A powerful U.S. politician and onetime Grand Master of the American Order of Vampire Hunters. Disgraced and replaced as Grand Master following his pursuit of Saloman's sword and his quest for immortality, which involved kidnapping Dmitriu and Josh Alexander. Elizabeth prevented Saloman from killing him during the rescue at Buda Castle.
Rudolph (Rudy) Meyer: New Yorker, descendant of Saloman's killer, Ferenc. Survivor of a vampire attack, he has allied with Cyn to hunt and kill vampires.

The Vampire Hunters

István: An expert in the science and technology of hunting. A strong hunter; having killed many vampires, he's absorbed their strength. Member of the Budapest vampire hunter network.
Konrad: Leader of the first hunter team. Elizabeth's friend. A descendant of Saloman's killer, Ferenc, which gives him extra strength. Member of the Budapest vampire hunter network.

Lazar: Operations manager, supervising the hunter teams. Ex–field hunter. Member of the Budapest vampire hunter network.
Mihaela: She and Elizabeth formed a close friendship during the original campaign to kill Saloman. Also a veteran hunter with the strength of many kills. Member of the Budapest vampire hunter network.
Miklós: Librarian and second in command of the Budapest hunters, under the Grand Master of the Hungarian order. Inclined to secrecy and preservation of traditional ways.
Mustafa: Leader of the Turkish hunters.

The Vampires

Angyalka: Owns the Angel Club in Budapest.
Dmitriu: The younger of the two vampires created by Saloman. More powerful than most modern vampires, he's nevertheless always avoided power struggles and sought a peaceful life among humans. A year ago, he directed Elizabeth Silk to the crypt where she awoke Saloman.
Luk: Saloman's cousin, the friend and mentor who turned him into a vampire. He fell into insanity toward the end of his existence, growing jealous of Saloman's power and of his relationship with the beautiful Tsigana. He then attacked Saloman, who slew him.
Maximilian: Saloman's elder creation. After betraying Saloman, he seized power and lost it a century later to the more brutal Zoltán. He lives now in isolation, hidden on an uninhabited Scottish island, from which he emerged a year ago to support Saloman in his battle against an alliance of Zoltán, Elizabeth, and the vampire hunters.
Saloman: The last of the Ancients. Their race is older than humanity and had the ability to achieve immortality by reviving their dead and drinking living blood. His body was hidden in a Romanian crypt until revived accidentally by Elizabeth Silk a year ago. Having taken his revenge, his remaining ambition is to rule both the human and vampire worlds.
Travis: Leader of the vampires in North America. Based in New York, he managed to take over the leadership of the whole continent after Elizabeth killed his rival Severin. A recent ally of Saloman's.

Blood Eternal

Chapter One

When the earth moved, the vampire Saloman felt a surge of exquisite pleasure almost akin to sexual release. The tension in him snapped, broken by the rush of rare, intoxicating fear.

Dawn approached, and he was too close to the earthquake's center for safety, too isolated in these Peruvian mountains to be discovered should he become buried under an immovable fall of rock. Already he could hear the thunder of incipient avalanches and landslides drowning out the lesser destruction of man-made edifices, but if he honed his supernatural hearing, he could just about make out the distinctive thuds of collapsing wood and masonry in the distant villages. The sounds of wreckage brought him a certain amount of satisfaction. The villages were already empty of life—he'd seen to that over the past couple of weeks.

He, Saloman, was one of the very few able-bodied beings left on this mountain. Even the animals had fled, their instincts warning them that the earth was angry. Unlike them, Saloman savored that anger, that knowledge of a unique power far superior to his own, a power before which even his strength could do nothing. And so he lay on this hard mountain ledge in the dark, reveling in his rare moment of helplessness, smiling up at the black, wavering sky while the earth under him heaved and cracked, splitting rocks and trees, hurling down the flimsy village buildings.

He knew the risk; he didn't want to end his existence or to return to the tortured sleep of death. He didn't want to leave this world. He didn't want to leave Elizabeth. And yet still he had come closer than he should to wait for the earth to shake—partly because he wanted to feel the massive power of it, partly because, like the rebellious boy he'd once been, he wanted to dare the danger.

It was an indulgence he shouldn't have allowed himself. He acknowledged that as the ledge of rock split under his back, hurling him off the edge. At the last moment, he grasped onto the one stable corner, giving himself a modicum of control as he jumped the fifty feet or so onto the hard, jagged ground below—more from memory than sight, since the tumbling boulders and dust impaired his night vision.

By the time he'd found a flatter foothold sheltered enough to prevent any more stones from landing on his head and shoulders, the quake had stopped. The mountain, however, hadn't. It continued to spit rocks down toward him, and below he could hear them gathering pace and volume. By morning, the mountain would have changed its shape.

Fear was good. He was glad he'd come up here to remember what it was like to be afraid. *Confront your fears,* his cousin Luk had told him, even before Saloman had died and been reborn a vampire. Luk had turned him, and had taught him well, just as if he'd known that Saloman would be the last of their Ancient race. Saloman had learned to face soul-destroying loneliness; he'd fought and defeated everyone who threatened him. There was no one left who could invade his mind and find him wanting—which had been his first and most intense fear, the one that had formed his boyhood and never quite left him. And yet he could think of his father now without pain or hurt or terror, and he knew that if it had been possible for them to meet again, he would not be afraid. He had no reason to be.

Saloman lay down once more, gazing up at the steady sky while the mountain rearranged itself with noisy, dust-filled aggression. He smiled, because no one else could possibly have done what he just had. No one had ever done what he was doing now.

Watch me, Elizabeth. I will prevail. The world will do my bidding. You can't doubt it.

It was his own thought. He didn't send it to her. He wouldn't even tell her about this; he would let her find out for herself. Perhaps he'd even go to her, so he was with her when she made the discovery. Hunger tore through him. Blood and sex and Elizabeth. A reward before the next stage began.

He sat up, unable to be still any longer. His lesson in humility had, in the end, fed his self-belief. Only he could have survived the earthquake from here; he alone could unite and direct the world. No one could stop him. And as the world learned his power, who would want to? He'd find his way down the mountain and drink some human blood before he began his journey across the world to Scotland.

But as he rose, a scream of rage and terror slammed into his mind. Saloman let out an involuntary cry, grasping his head in both hands to prevent the pain, the anguish, instinctively trying to squeeze out the howling voice that should have been mere memory and yet felt as real as the rocks sliding and crashing their way down the mountainside. The flash of impossible presence surged and then vanished as swiftly as it had come, leaving Saloman to drop his hands slowly from his face.

Which was when he realized he had no time to analyze himself for sanity or injury. In a moment, he was going to be buried deep under an avalanche. Saloman hurled himself forward and leapt into darkness.

Six thousand miles away, in a Scottish café, Elizabeth Silk caught her breath and shivered uncontrollably.

"What's the matter?" her friend Joanne demanded, placing two large mugs of coffee on the café table before resuming her seat beside Elizabeth.

"Oh, nothing," Elizabeth said evasively. *There's a vampire in my head. Or at least there was for an instant.* What would Joanne make of that? "Someone walked over my grave."

The trouble was, it felt like Saloman, although her instant telepathic reach to him hit nothing. Not surprising. Her abilities had grown by leaps and bounds in the past few months, but she still operated best with peace to concentrate, even when Saloman chose to receive her. Something had happened, she was sure, though whether it involved physical danger or emotional upheaval, she had no way of knowing. Once, she would have denied the possibility of the latter. Now she knew him better, knew him as a being of profound feelings, even though they were often beyond her ability to understand. If something had occurred, if he needed her . . .

Thrusting her unease aside, she smiled and lifted her cup to her lips.

"I meant in general," Joanne said dryly. She was a short, eye-catching woman with purple-tinged, frizzy hair and a razor-sharp mind. "You seem a bit glum."

"It's only ten in the morning and I was up until three."

"Doing what?" Joanne asked.

"Writing. I think I've finished the book based on my thesis. I'll send it off to your agent tomorrow."

"He'll be your agent too the day after," Joanne said with a confident grin.

"I hope so. I'm finally happy I've struck the right balance between academic and popular—which is pretty important with a subject like vampires and superstitions!"

"You're right there," Joanne said, raising her mug in a toast. "Hats off to you. So that's out of the way—what now? Glasgow?"

"Ah. Maybe that's why I look glum. I didn't get the job in Glasgow." It had been a rare opportunity, a permanent, full-time post at Glasgow University. Elizabeth had applied, knowing she would have to be stupid not to, and yet her heart hadn't been in it. Perhaps this had come across at her interview.

"Idiots," Joanne said roundly.

Elizabeth gave her a lopsided smile. "Thanks for the support. I wasn't even certain I wanted it, so I've no right to whine about not getting it."

"I'm pretty sure there'll be a vacancy here at St. Andrews next year," Joanne said. "What else is still in the pipeline for now?"

Elizabeth shrugged. "Nothing truly inspiring. A college in London, part-time. And a maternity leave post at the University of Aberdeen."

She hesitated, until Joanne nudged her and commanded, "Spill!"

Elizabeth laughed. "Well, there's a one-year appointment at the University of Budapest."

Joanne sat up straight. "Budapest!"

"It's more my thing, includes teaching a special course in the historic value of superstitions, and there'll be research opportunities in other areas. Also, I do speak the language, more or less. . . ."

"And your man's there," Joanne finished with unnecessary relish.

Elizabeth felt her skin color, and took a hasty gulp of coffee to try to cover it. "Only sometimes," she mumbled. "He travels a lot." Then, since Joanne continued to stare at her, she lowered the cup and sighed. "I don't want him to think I'm pursuing him."

"He might like that you are."

"But I'm not!"

Joanne blinked. "Aren't you? I bloody would be."

Elizabeth couldn't help laughing at her friend's fervor. She still regarded the evening that she'd been obliged to introduce Joanne to her vampire lover as the weirdest moment of her increasingly bizarre life. Saloman had arrived in her flat without warning two months ago, while she and Joanne had been putting the world to rights in the sitting room over a bottle of wine. He'd come through the kitchen window, but neither he nor Elizabeth had corrected Joanne's assumption that he had his own key.

Joanne had watched their reunion with interest, clearly torn by conflicting desires to leave them alone and to discover more about Elizabeth's mysterious lover. She'd compromised by subjecting Saloman to half an hour of penetrating questions—which he'd answered or deflected with equal amusement as the notion took him—and then departing earlier than she normally would.

"Fuck me, he's gorgeous," she'd informed Elizabeth at the front door. "No wonder you're messed up."

At the time, Elizabeth had jeered at the term "messed up," for Saloman's arrival had filled her with the complete happiness only he had ever brought her. But now, in his absence, she acknowledged her friend's perception. She *was* messed up, had been since she'd first met him. But if Joanne knew the truth—that Elizabeth's handsome and charming lover wasn't merely mysterious, but also the most powerful vampire who'd ever existed—she wouldn't put the cause down to his looks.

Joanne said, "So you're hesitating over whether to apply for the job? Apply now and worry later."

Elizabeth shifted in her seat. "Actually, I already applied. They've offered me the post. I just have to decide whether to take it."

Joanne finished her coffee and set down her mug before rising to her feet. "Bite their hands off," she advised, swinging her bag off the floor and onto her shoulder, to the imminent danger of the mugs that would undoubtedly have been knocked to the floor if Elizabeth hadn't seized them out of harm's way. Behind Joanne, a passing waiter stared at Elizabeth, wide-eyed. She must have moved too fast.

"I'll miss you, of course," Joanne added, oblivious to the entire incident.

"No, you won't; you'll come and visit me or I'll never speak to you again." Which was another point against accepting. In Budapest, Saloman's own city, there would be untold distractions from the world of academia—leaving love out of it, there were vampires and hunters and an inevitable conflict waiting to erupt, which would place her squarely in the middle. Could she really hope to keep Joanne out of that?

But traipsing downstairs in her friend's wake, Elizabeth couldn't help feeling a secret leap of excitement at the prospect of moving to Hungary. Outside the Victoria Café, it was raining, a fine, misty drizzle that seemed to exemplify the Scottish summer. Dull.

"Well, back to the grindstone," Joanne said happily enough. "What are you up to for the rest of the day?"

"I said I'd do a favor for a friend—visit this wounded soldier in Glasgow."

"Badly wounded?" Joanne asked in quick sympathy.

"Badly enough, but he's pretty well recovered physically. Apparently he's still traumatized."

"Sounds like a worthy but fraught day for you, then," Joanne observed, lifting her hand in farewell. She was clearly anxious to get back to her books. Elizabeth watched her scuttle across Market Street with a feeling that came close to envy. Once, being lost in academia had been enough for Elizabeth too. And visiting an injured soldier would have aroused a much simpler compassion in her, without this guilty, nagging hope that because the British vampire hunters had asked her to go, he'd have something paranormally intriguing to say.

She was bored, she realized with some surprise.

Achieving her doctorate had been satisfying; writing the book had been fun; research and teaching at some academic institution were still a necessary part of her ambitions, to say nothing about putting food on the table. Six months ago, desperately trying to keep her life stable and normal in the midst of unasked-for and unwanted new responsibilities and dangers, she wouldn't have believed this was possible; yet now, perhaps influenced by her earlier shiver of anxiety, she actually *missed* the menacing world of darkness and vampires: a world in which her mind and body could both stretch without hindrance, and succeed.

She missed Saloman.

With the sound of the vampire's preternatural scream splitting his ears, Senator Grayson Dante knew it had all gone horribly wrong. Dante thought back to the accounts he'd read of Saloman's awakening, taken from Elizabeth Silk's testimony. She too had found an empty underground chamber, except it had turned out not to be so empty. She'd been bleeding from a thorn prick and surmised that it was the drops of her blood that had first made the dead Saloman visible to her. She'd mistaken him for a stone sarcophagus.

Dante crouched down and delved into his bag to retrieve the vial of blood. It was a tiny amount, distilled from the stain of Saloman's blood left on his shirt during their last violent encounter. He couldn't afford to waste any. He was sure this room was enchanted, as the outer cave had been, to deter visitors. But simply staring wouldn't break through this spell.

Dante unscrewed the lid with great care.

"What is that?" Mehmet, his Turkish guide, whispered.

It's the blood of the Ancient vampire Saloman, with which I hope to awaken his cousin and enemy Luk, whom Saloman killed over three hundred years ago. Would Mehmet run or laugh if he said such a thing aloud? Instinctively, Dante knew his need for Mehmet was almost over. But only almost. The Turk had one more purpose to fulfill.

Dante crept around the dark chamber. The beam from his flashlight bobbed erratically around the rough stone floors and walls, barely penetrating the profound blackness more than a couple of feet beyond his unsteady fingers. He hoped that if he couldn't see the body, at least he might feel it with his hands or feet. Even so, when his foot struck something it felt like stone, part of the floor's uneven surface, and he almost paid it no attention. Then he paused and placed his finger over the vial's opening before he shook it and removed his finger.

Drawing in his breath with a quick, silent prayer to no one in particular that it would be enough, he shook his whole hand out in front of him. His finger tingled as the tiny spatter of blood sprayed downward. And there in the darkness, without suddenness or shock, was what he'd been looking for all these weeks.

A stone table on which lay a sculpted body. Almost exactly as Elizabeth Silk had found the body of Saloman a year earlier.

Mehmet's breath sounded like a wheeze. "My God, I almost didn't see it. I thought there was nothing. . . . Is this it? Is this your nobleman's tomb?"

"Almost certainly." Dante felt dizzy. His whole body trembled, not just with reaction to his first glimpse of the deeply sinister figure illuminated by their flashlights, but with the enormity of what he was doing. He found it difficult to get the words out, and yet he had to concentrate, to ignore his sudden fears and stick to his plan. Mehmet had to continue to believe in the fiction that this was merely the lost tomb of a historic nobleman. And then, finally, Dante would reach his goal. Eternal life. Eternal power. Damnation, if it existed, was a small price to pay.

With carefully judged casualness, he passed the vial to Mehmet. "Here. I want to photograph this."

Even shining his flashlight on the tiny drop of dark liquid, Mehmet could have no idea what it was. He seemed happy that Dante had found what he sought—even if only so that he could get back into the fresh air and climb down the mountain again.

Dante produced his camera and pointed it at the tomb. "When I say 'now,'" he directed, "pour the contents of the vial over the carving."

"Why, what is it?"

"It'll make the tomb stand out more in the picture." Dante lied easily. He wasn't a politician for nothing. "Okay . . . Now!"

Dante held his breath as Mehmet shook the tiny drops of liquid over the carved face. This was it, the moment of greatest risk and greatest hope, on which all Dante's ambitions rested. Religion, decency, nature itself—none of those things counted beside the huge power Dante was about to take. . . .

At this point in the earlier awakening, Saloman had clamped his teeth into Elizabeth's neck. Dante had been torn over this part of his plan. The blood used in the awakening had to be Saloman's—Luk's killer's—or it wouldn't work, but Dante didn't know whether any of the mystical attributes of awakening would be bestowed on whoever did the pouring. No one had ever done it like this before, to his knowledge. If there was power to be had from awakening, he naturally wanted it for himself; but on the other hand, he needed Luk to be as strong as possible, which meant drinking the blood of his Awakener and killing him to absorb his life force. So far, Saloman had failed to kill Elizabeth, and therein lay his weakness. Dante did not intend for Luk to make the same mistake.

It was a pity for Mehmet.

Dante shone his flashlight unwaveringly on Luk's dead face. It did indeed look like stone. He'd expected it to be more lifelike, to give some hint of his Ancient strength, a clue that he could be awakened. Tiny droplets of blood splashed on Luk's cheek, his nose, lips, and chin. Nothing happened.

Oh fuck. It isn't enough. After all this, I needed more blood. . . .

"Did you take it?" Mehmet asked.

"What? Oh, the photograph—yes, I got it. Thanks." He took a step forward, meaning to take back the vial and see if there was anything at all left in it. But before he could touch it, a sound like a faint groan issued from the carving.

Oh, yes. Hallelujah.

Under Dante's riveted gaze, the dead eyes of the sculpture opened; the lips parted. The skin moved, shifting slowly into an expression not of triumph but of shock. Even . . . fear. Luk sat up and Mehmet fell back with a low moan of terror. Luk's twisted mouth opened wider, revealing his long, terrifying incisors as he stared at Mehmet.

The vampire's scream started low, like a rattle in his throat, then rose quickly into the most horrific, gut-wrenching howl Dante had ever heard. Like all the pain of everyone in the world rolled into one pure, dreadful sound.

This isn't meant to happen, Dante thought in panic. *Something's gone terribly wrong. I must have gotten the wrong vampire. . . .*

Then, in fury, the creature who may or may not have been Luk swung himself off the stone table, and Dante stepped circumspectly behind Mehmet before giving the Turk a sharp, ungentle shove into the reaching arms of whatever they'd awakened.

Chapter Two

A pale, watery sunshine shone feebly down on the grounds of Glasgow's Southern General Hospital, flickering intermittently through the ward windows and across the floor in front of Elizabeth as she made her way to Private John Ramsay's room.

The British hunter, tied down in Cornwall tracking a bizarre but elusive vampire who seemed determined to introduce himself to every member of a village community, had sounded harassed when he'd asked her to get Ramsay's story.

"It sounds like a mixture of fever dreams and trauma to me, but we've been asked to look into it, so see what you think."

She'd been aware, then as now, that she was being used as a filter. The hunters, who were based in London, didn't want to come all the way up here for nothing. If there was anything in Ramsay's story, they'd make it their next assignment once the Cornish vampire was dealt with. If there wasn't, they would simply report Elizabeth's findings.

And Elizabeth was glad to help, not just because she

was bored, but because she valued their trust, perhaps as a counterbalance to the growing *dis*trust of her friends the Hungarian hunters, who'd recently discovered her relationship with Saloman, their greatest enemy.

The final room in the ward, to which she'd been directed, contained three beds. Two were empty, and the third was occupied by a fully dressed young man stretched out on the top of it, staring into space. His shaved head revealed a long red scar above his left ear. He wore a short-sleeved khaki T-shirt; no arm protruded from the left sleeve.

When Elizabeth gave a tentative knock on the open door, the young man's eyes drifted toward her without much interest.

"Are you John Ramsay?" she asked hopefully.

"Aye."

Ignoring the lack of encouragement in his curt response, she stepped inside the room and held out her hand.

"Hello. I'm Elizabeth Silk."

The soldier glanced at her hand, and for a moment she thought he wouldn't trouble to shake it. His eyes were unfriendly and cold as flint. In the end, he did lean forward and reach up with his remaining hand to take hers. It was firm but brief, and he fell back against the pillows with an odd expression of mocking tolerance on his young face.

"You another shrink?"

"Oh, no. I'm not a doctor at all."

"Really? That why it says 'Doctor' on your label?"

Elizabeth frowned, trying to think what he meant, before she remembered the name tag she'd been given at reception. It hung around her neck, and when she picked it up and read it, she realized it did proclaim her to be Dr. E. Silk. Perhaps that was how the hunters had made the appointment for her so easily. There was clearly nothing wrong with Private Ramsay's powers of observation.

"Ah. Well, I have a PhD, which gives me the title, but I'm not a medical doctor. I'm a historian."

John Ramsay curled his lip. "I'm not history yet," he observed, but a faint spark of interest did cross his face. "What do you want with me, then?"

"I was hoping you wouldn't mind talking to me about what happened after the ambush."

"So much for medical confidentiality."

"I represent an organization that takes paranormal experiences very seriously."

"Aye? Sure you don't represent the *News of the World*?"

"Or any other newspaper," Elizabeth said steadily. "I wouldn't have been allowed to see you if I did."

Ramsay shrugged. "Doesn't matter anyway. My 'experiences' are post-traumatic stress and fever-induced dreams. Ask anyone."

"I'd rather ask you. Will you tell me what happened?"

"I got posted to Afghanistan. Helmand. We got ambushed, and I got my arm and half my head shot off. But I'm fine now. Waiting on redeployment." He winked. "Helmand's still favorite."

Elizabeth sat down without invitation. "Will they really send you back there?"

Ramsay shrugged. "Why not? I'm a soldier."

True, but surely they wouldn't return him to the front line? The truly baffling thing was that he obviously wanted to go back. "How old are you, John?"

His eyes changed. "Twenty. What difference does that make?"

He was younger than some of her students last term. "None," she said. "None at all. So what did you see after the attack? What do you remember?"

He looked at her, then let out a quick breath of laughter that lightened his too-harsh young face.

"What?" Elizabeth asked.

"I was just thinking: I'm used to telling this story to

people who think I'm a nutter. Now I'm telling it to someone *I* think is a nutter."

"Maybe neither of us is."

"Maybe." He shifted position with a twinge of pain that Elizabeth seemed to feel physically in her left arm. Irritated, she shook it, while John said, "What is this organization you represent? What do you do?"

"Primarily," Elizabeth said, "we hunt down and kill vampires."

With undisguised mockery, John looked her up and down, no doubt taking in the deceptively frail body and her careless, academic appearance: long red-blond hair imperfectly confined behind her head, well-worn jeans, and a comfortable if pretty secondhand top. She knew she didn't look threatening, and John confirmed it.

"Get many kills, aye?"

"Aye," said Elizabeth, and unexpectedly, John grinned.

"Buggered if I know why, but I believe you," he said. "You remind me of my English teacher in third year. She scared the shite out of me too."

"Did *she* kill vampires?" Elizabeth asked lightly, playing along.

"Nah. I fancied her something rotten."

Surprise at the implied compliment brought an annoying blush to Elizabeth's cheeks. However, this seemed to give John some kind of reassurance, for without any further warning, he began to talk.

He spoke matter-of-factly, relating how he'd been on patrol when the ambush occurred. He'd been injured right away, his left arm shattered and his head bleeding profusely, but attempts to crawl to safety had been thwarted by his own dizziness as well as the intense firefight going on around him. By the time his comrades got to him, the Taliban were running, though from whom John hadn't known—not until the majority of the British force had set off in pursuit and the comrades who'd stayed with him both lay dead.

"I saw them die. Two blokes in turbans just disarmed them, picked them up as if they were kids, bit them in the throat like dogs, and then threw them back on the ground. One said to the other, 'Good blood.' Only, the funny thing was, his lips didn't move."

Elizabeth leaned forward, frowning. "What language did he speak?"

John grimaced. "I don't know. I can't remember. I only remember the meaning. The shrinks reckon that proves I was dreaming."

"It could mean he wasn't speaking in words," Elizabeth said slowly. "You could have heard him telepathically. Was he speaking to you?"

"Don't know. His pal answered. I wasn't in any condition for conversation. I don't even remember exactly what they said after that. I just remember their voices going on all the time, arguing over me. One of them was scooping my blood off the ground with his fingers and licking them. I thought they were going to torture me before I died. Then . . ."

His gaze slid away. He tugged irritably at the empty, flapping sleeve of his shirt.

"I'm sorry," Elizabeth said, low. "I know this must be painful—"

"It wasn't," John interrupted. "It wasn't painful. Maybe I was already out of it. Or my arm and my head hurt too much for me to notice the rest. But when he bent over me and bit my neck—still bloody talking—I didn't feel anything except curiosity. It was only later I thought it was fucking disgusting. Sorry."

The apology for his bad language touched her. Perhaps she was reminding him of his English teacher again. "Show me where he bit you," she managed.

He reached up quickly, pinching at the vein on the side of his neck. There was no sign of any wound. Elizabeth shivered.

Shaking off her own disturbing memories, she said, "Did you get the impression he meant to kill you?"

John shrugged, an unbalanced gesture that seemed to irritate him, for his frown deepened. "They were still arguing over whether or not to share my blood when the other guy arrived."

"Another vampire?"

A sardonic smile stretched his lips. "You're the first who's actually used that word. Yes, I'd say he was another vampire. He seemed to fall out of the sky, tore the guy off me, and bit him until he sort of . . . disappeared. The other one had started to run, but the new guy caught him and then he vanished too. All I could see was dust. But I know he bit him as well. I *saw* it, even though they were out of my line of vision—dreaming again, right?" His laugh turned into a shudder. "And then he came for me and I . . ."

"What?" Elizabeth urged gently.

"I started to cry. I don't know why, except my pals were dead beside me. I was dying too. It didn't hurt. Just the idea that another of *them* would . . . Aw, fuck."

John twisted away from her. Desperately, Elizabeth tried to think of something to say, anything that might help. But he began to speak again, once more curt and matter-of-fact.

"The big guy, this über-vamp, seemed to be some kind of boss. Scary bastard. He was telling them off; he seemed to be telling everyone off, people I couldn't even see."

Saloman?

"When he knelt and bent over my throat, I couldn't move. I was so ashamed I wanted to die—because I was crying, you know? But he didn't bite me. He *licked* the wound in my neck, and then he just looked at me. He had these huge, black eyes, like they were all pupils. He told me it was over, that my people were coming for me. Then he looked over my head. I could hear trucks and helicopters. He said he was sorry he couldn't wait and make it all go away. And then he stood up and vanished."

He turned his head back and faced Elizabeth with defiance. "And the next people I saw were big Tam McGowan and Charlie Harrison. They filled me full of meds, which at least stopped me havering. For a while."

He crossed his ankles and regarded her with unnecessary aggression. "Well?"

Elizabeth licked her dry lips. She desperately wanted not to make things worse for this damaged young man. Honesty was what she would have wanted. "I don't think you're havering," she said. "I don't think you're talking rubbish at all."

"Aye, but you're the nutter here, remember?"

She smiled. "I remember. Look, John, I can't explain everything that happened to you, but I can tell you some things that might make it easier to understand. It doesn't matter what other people say, or even what we tell ourselves to feel normal; we both know that vampires exist. They exist all over the world, in every country, to a greater or lesser degree. Recently, a very powerful and Ancient vampire—possibly this 'über-vampire' you saw—has made himself overlord and extracted submission from most vampires in the world. But about three months ago, the Afghan vampires rebelled, using the war there to cover their own violence. They went on the rampage, threatening everyone—local civilians, police, Taliban fighters, foreign troops, aid workers. The revolt's more or less quelled now, but it sounds like you and your comrades were caught in the killing spree."

He regarded her with curiosity, but otherwise his expression was unreadable. "I suppose *you* quelled it." That was definitely a sneer, but Elizabeth chose to take the words at face value.

"Oh, no," she said ruefully. "I believe the local hunters took out a few, but on their own, they were struggling. Badly. It was largely S—the vampire overlord and his followers who put down the revolt and calmed the violence. There are still rumblings of discontent, of course, but I'm told they're under control."

So why isn't he home? With me? What happened *this morning?*

Shoving her personal worries aside, she said awkwardly, "I do understand your issues with belief." And survivor guilt and shame, because it wasn't all bad, especially with Saloman. She was sure John Ramsay felt all of that and more, but she knew better than to put it into words. He was a very proud young man and he'd already said more than he'd be happy with when he was fully recovered.

"I'm pretty new to this stuff as well," she confessed. "Obviously I've got no experience of war, but I do know the vampire thing gets easier to deal with in your head as time goes by. The first encounter—and I hope it's your last—is always the worst. You don't need to admit it to anyone but yourself if you don't want to, but you're not crazy."

John pushed himself up into a sitting position and swung his legs over the side of the bed to face her. "First encounter," he repeated. "Sounds like a film or something." He touched the side of his neck and let his fingers linger there. "So you've done all this too?"

"Oh, I did something much w—" She broke off. "I did something that was *considered* much worse. I got bitten, yes, but I also awakened an Ancient vampire who was supposed to be dead forever." She gave a quick, self-deprecating grin. "Victim *and* perpetrator, that's me, Consider yourself lucky."

His lips twitched in response, but his hungry eyes didn't leave hers. It was as if her belief had opened some kind of a floodgate. "And was it?"

"Was it what?" she asked.

"Worse."

She parted her lips to answer and closed them again. Was it? Awakening Saloman had been an accident brought about by a combination of her own research and the vampire Dmitriu's specific information, added to Dmitriu's carefully planted rose thorn, which had caused her to bleed all over Saloman's beautiful tomb. Her ancestry was the key; the blood of Tsigana, one of Saloman's original killers, flowed in her veins. She was one of the few people in the world who *could* have awakened him, but she'd done it without meaning to, without even believing in vampires. And in return received a whole a lot of trouble, plus the strength of an Awakener, which made her potentially more powerful than any vampire hunter and a match for even the strongest of the undead. She'd unleashed Saloman on the world and found a love she'd never imagined.

Her life was enriched, not worsened, by what she'd done. As for the world . . . But she had to speak or she could ruin everything she'd been trying to mend for John Ramsay. Her head began to ache and she rubbed it distractedly while she let a rueful smile form on her lips. "I don't know," she admitted. "I haven't decided yet."

John said, "When I'm better, do you want to go out for a drink?"

Elizabeth blinked and must have looked startled, because he said hastily, "Just as friends. I'm not daft. I know you've got a husband and twelve kids. But I'm glad you came to see me."

Elizabeth smiled. "So am I. And I'd love to go for a drink as friends, even though I don't have any kids. When will they let you go home?"

"Soon," he said with new confidence, and Elizabeth thought that it was probably true now.

She rummaged in her bag for a pen and a scrap of paper. "I live in St. Andrews," she said, "but I'm away a lot. I'll give you my number and my e-mail address. If you write yours down for me too, then we can stay in touch. If you want."

"I want."

Leaving his room, she felt buoyantly hopeful for him. Though she wasn't quite sure what the hunters had expected her to do, she suspected that if his story was real, they wanted it quashed. It was one of the basic hunter principles: to keep the existence of vampires secret in order to prevent human panic, chaos, and a vampire war that humans couldn't possibly win. If an encounter couldn't be kept secret from the victim, then the victim was sworn to secrecy and occasionally even recruited into the hunter network. John Ramsay was in no condition to be recruited, but everything in Elizabeth had rebelled against denying the possibility of his story. He needed to believe in it and his own sanity in order to move beyond it and recover.

Which, she thought tiredly, as she trailed back along the long ward corridor, he would do now. A wave of nausea hit her and she had to pause with her hand on the wall, waiting for the moment to pass.

She should have eaten today, but she'd been too busy rushing off to meet Joanne, and then traveling over to Glasgow. She stared hard at the wall, as if that would throw off the dizziness, but she knew from previous episodes that it would go only in its own good time. In her heart, she knew too that food intake had nothing to do with it. Repressing the familiar surge of panic, willing herself not to faint, she tried to concentrate on her surroundings rather than on the weird, unspecific pain that seemed to grip her entire body, or the exhaustion that made her want to slump to the floor.

She was standing outside the patients' dayroom. A few people in dressing gowns and a few more fully dressed sat around reading newspapers and watching the television. The screen was full of a fuzzy, shaking mountain, while the announcer reported a major earthquake in a mountainous region of Peru.

That *is suffering,* Elizabeth told herself severely. *Feeling tired and sick because you forgot to eat breakfast is just pathetic. Pull yourself together, Silk.*

The pain began to dissipate, the veil of mist to lift from her mind. She was glad to hear, as she eased off the wall and walked shakily down the corridor, that no casualties had yet been reported. It wouldn't stay that way, of course. In any major disaster, the figures had a horrible tendency to go up and up until they stopped meaning anything comprehensible in terms of human tragedy.

It was raining again by evening, and the gathering gale hurled it at Elizabeth's living room window with enough force to drown out the sound of the television. Perhaps that was why she kept losing the plot of the convoluted crime drama.

Elizabeth shifted restlessly and wondered how the detective could possibly have come up with so implausible a theory. It didn't match the evidence, so far as she could recall, anyway, and it was, besides, bloody stupid.

Her hand brushed the envelope lying on the sofa beside her, and she glanced at it in annoyance. Why wouldn't it just go away? It was addressed to the University of Budapest and contained her acceptance of the lecturing post. She just couldn't bring herself to send it.

What the hell am I afraid of? Frightening him off? Cramping his style? Appearing too needy and clingy?

Oh, yes.

The trouble was, she hadn't seen him since the job came up. It had been a recent and totally unexpected approach by the university, followed by several e-mails and a telephone call before the offer was made. And it wasn't something she could tell him about telepathically. He was too much in command of that form of communication. He could read everything from her while revealing only as much as he wanted to, and she needed, she really needed, to *see* his reaction to the idea of her being in Budapest for a whole year, possibly longer if the post was extended. He moved around a lot, but if anywhere was home for him, it was Budapest.

The credits began to roll on the crime drama, adding to Elizabeth's sense of dissatisfaction. She stood and wandered over to the window. Thick clouds had darkened the night sky further, and the wild, white froth on the heaving sea shone like neon. Waves crashed over the harbor wall, a reminder of the frailty of man and all his works before the awesome power of nature.

Her throat began to ache. She wished she'd gone with Saloman when he'd left Scotland. He'd asked her to and she'd refused, mainly because she wouldn't reduce herself—in her eyes or in his—to the position of mere follower. She was his companion, but not a blind acolyte, and if she was to do anything useful, if she was to be everything to him as he was to her, he had to acknowledge her as . . . as . . . *more*. More than an extension of himself, more than his lover.

"But there *is* no more than that," she whispered to the rain-lashed window. "How can I reach you if I'm never with you?" It had seemed so simple, that decision she'd made in his arms three months ago to win his eternal love, to do something good for the world, but sometimes it seemed that nothing had changed. They were companions, yet too much apart.

She couldn't let herself become his slave, which Mihaela had accused her of being already. Was she just proving the hunter wrong? Was this the real reason she didn't travel with him, why she hesitated over the job in Budapest? Because she couldn't bear the accusing glares of her friends, to whom she was a traitor?

You chose your path, Silk. See it through; live with it. He'll come soon. Or at least contact you soon, and then it will be easier.

An echo of the morning's twinge of alarm came back to her and she shivered. Surely there was no point in worrying over the safety of the most powerful being on earth? Turning away from the window, she threw herself back down on the sofa and changed the channel to BBC News.

Government scandal—yawn. And the earthquake in Peru. Instantly, Elizabeth felt guilty for her self-pity and made a determined effort to throw it off. Compared with an earthquake disaster, her problems were puny.

"However," the announcer read, "no casualties have

yet been reported. The epicenter of the quake was in a remote, mountainous region of the country which is very sparsely populated. Peruvian sources say several scattered villages have been destroyed by the shock itself and by subsequent landslides and avalanches, and it's possible casualties will still be discovered beneath the rubble by the rescue workers already on the scene. But, as our correspondent in Peru reports, there may be more than a miracle involved for the survivors of this earthquake."

The screen switched to a shot of carnage, dusty men digging through rubble that appeared to be all that remained of a village. Although a few poorly dressed people stood by, some picking through their demolished homes as if looking for valued possessions, there was, strangely, no grief-stricken wailing, no urgency or desperation about these people's searches. They were almost frighteningly calm, considering what had just occurred to their village, their families and neighbors.

How could there possibly be no casualties?

The camera homed in on a woman smiling and nodding, with a thin child in her arms. *Smug,* Elizabeth thought. *She actually looks* smug.

"The few villagers we've met here tell us that no one was left in the village when the earthquake occurred," the reporter went on. "And the reason for that, they say, is this man."

A photograph flashed up on the screen, causing Elizabeth's heart to lurch into her throat. After which it seemed to cease beating altogether. The photograph was of a young, extraordinarily handsome man with long, thick black hair and stunning dark eyes. A faint, sardonic smile played about his full, sensual lips. He looked as if he knew everything and cared for nothing.

"Saloman," she whispered. "Oh, God . . ."

There were no casualties left in the village because he'd killed them all beforehand? Would he really regard them as of so little account? Her alien, unpredictable lover . . . Jesus, could she really love him after this? Gagging, she covered her mouth with her hand.

"Eccentric Hungarian millionaire Adam Simon," the reporter said. "He appeared in these remote mountain villages a week ago and somehow persuaded everyone in them to leave before the earthquake struck. One of the young men from this village took video footage at the time, using his mobile phone."

Saloman disappeared from the screen, and, as if this granted her permission, Elizabeth began to breathe again. Now a grainy, shaky picture filled the television, showing a ragged line of people, many of them in native Peruvian dress, all carrying small bags, trailing down a mountain track. And there, carrying an old lady on his back and several rucksacks over one arm, was Saloman.

Stupidly, it took several moments to penetrate.

"You didn't kill them," she whispered. She wanted to sing; she wanted to throw her arms around the television and hug it. Tears forced their way up her throat, spilled from the corners of her eyes, and trickled over her smiling lips. "You didn't kill them; you saved them. You saved all of them. My God . . ."

My people had an affinity with the earth that gave them senses way beyond those of humans. . . . The world could use that.

He'd spoken those words in New York during their pursuit of Dante, and only now, at last, did she understand at least some of what they meant. *An affinity with the earth.* He'd predicted this earthquake and somehow persuaded the people to believe in him and flee their homes.

The reporter's words broke briefly into her chaotic understanding. "A spokesman for Mr. Simon, whose whereabouts now are unknown, said his boss has opened a charitable fund to help rebuild these people's homes. Apparently he has also donated a large sum to seismic research."

This was huge. Bigger than anything that had come

before. Saloman was ruthless, pitiless in his extermination of those whose deaths he perceived to be necessary for one reason or another. The reasons weren't always clear to Elizabeth, but she should have known by now that he would care for the innocent, not exterminate them.

And she'd foolishly imagined she could help the world by *limiting* him in some way! My God, what she had ever done, what *could* she ever do, that would even come close to this? And he'd achieved it so casually, fitting it in between a punitive expedition to Afghanistan and a propaganda exercise with the vampire Travis in the United States. To say nothing of his business interests and his befriending of powerful politicians all over the world.

But her sudden humility was of as little importance as her shame. Pride in him, happiness at this outcome of his work, swamped everything else. What mattered was that she could help him now, that she was wholeheartedly behind him and needed to tell him so.

Peru. He must still be in Peru, lying low. Did she need a visa to go there?

Saloman! she called urgently.

No response. No matter. She'd buy her ticket and then phone him. Her reasons for not contacting him before now seemed so trivial as to be laughable. Grabbing the laptop, Elizabeth set about finding the cheapest ticket, using one hand for the mouse and keyboard and the other to dig her battered credit card out of her purse.

When the phone rang, her heart soared. She seized the handset, stabbing the "receive" button, and, gasping, said, "Hello!" She braced herself for his voice, for all the melting, delicious things the sound of it did to her body and mind.

There was a slight pause; then a very different voice said hesitantly, "Elizabeth?"

She hadn't even glanced at the number. Wrestling

with unworthy disappointment that her friend Mihaela certainly didn't deserve from her, she said, "Of course it is. Who else would answer my phone?"

"Sorry. You sounded different. Are you running for a train or something?"

Elizabeth quashed her rising laughter. "A plane, actually. No, I'm at home. What's happening? Nothing bad, I hope?"

Over the last three months, since Mihaela had learned of her relationship with Saloman, their communications had been less frequent than before. Elizabeth always had the feeling that when Mihaela called she was checking that Elizabeth was still alive, while Elizabeth herself found conversation difficult now that she knew she faced the hunter's unspoken but constant disapproval. It saddened her, as she'd always known it would, but she still hoped Mihaela would come to understand.

"Actually," Mihaela was saying, "it *is* bad. Very bad. There have been mass killings in Turkey tonight—a vampire on the rampage, completely out of control."

"Oh, dear. Are you over there? Are there not hunters in Turkey?"

"Yes, but they're a little tied up, since the vampire revolt seems to have spread into Turkey now that Afghanistan is quiet again. They asked for our help, as I'm now asking for yours. You see, we think the rampaging vampire is an Ancient."

Elizabeth closed her mouth and swallowed. "It can't be. I'm sure Saloman's in Peru."

"Not Saloman. Luk."

"Luk?" Elizabeth stared at the phone as if it weren't working properly, then clamped it back to her ear. "Saloman's cousin? How could it be Luk?"

"He was buried in the Turkish hills. The exact location wasn't known to any hunters—it was never well enough described in the sources—but it could conceivably have been tracked via local folklore. Much as you did with Saloman."

"You mean he's been awakened? My God, who would . . . ? Oh, shit."

"'Oh, shit' indeed," said Mihaela heavily.

"Not Dante," Elizabeth begged.

"We should have let Saloman kill him."

"*I* should have let Saloman kill him."

"We were all on your side," Mihaela said impatiently. "We just didn't have the guts to step in. No point in casting blame now."

"But how could Dante or anyone else awaken Luk? It would have to be Saloman, wouldn't it? The blood of his killer."

"Yes," said Mihaela in an odd, distant voice. "It would. Look, Elizabeth, you awakened the last Ancient and so you know the most about the early stages of his revival. We could use your help."

And Saloman's?

The words hung unspoken between them. Neither would bring it up. But if Luk was really awakened, Saloman would already know. . . . Or would he? Could he "feel" the awakening over the huge distance between Peru and Turkey?

"Can you come?" Mihaela asked.

Elizabeth's eyes strayed to the computer screen. Slowly, she reached out and hovered the mouse over the "Buy Ticket" button, like a caress. *Soon.* She shifted it to "Cancel" and clicked. "Of course. I'll book the next flight I can and call you back."

Dante said, "Luk."

The vampire glanced up from his bonds, which he'd been studying with dispassionate interest. When Dante had finally managed to persuade him to leave the terror-stricken village, Luk had walked passively at his side to the hidden car and sat silently through the remains of the night until they'd reached this ruined hut. Here, he'd submitted to be being retied too, just as if the ravening monster who'd spread horror and carnage through an entire village were another being altogether.

Dante said gently, "That *is* your name, isn't it?"

"Luk," the vampire repeated.

"Luk, the Ancient vampire."

"I wanted blood," the vampire said vaguely.

"Well, you got it," Dante said grimly. "And now we'll have a plague of angry villagers, police, and probably vampire hunters down on us before we can do what we have to do. You were only meant to bite the one man."

"I was hungry."

"Why didn't you come back when I called you?"

"I was hungry."

Dante sighed in frustration and crouched down to face his companion at a safe distance. According to Elizabeth Silk, Saloman had been physically weak on first awakening, but had talked with perfect lucidity. What was more, he had possessed enough self-control to pace his feeding until he was strong enough to take it. Luk, if this was indeed Luk, had drained Mehmet dry and then slumped down the wall like a drunk passing out. Dante had brought him another unsuspecting victim later on, but then what was supposed to be Luk's first hunting expedition had gone disastrously wrong.

The vampire had seemed to be intoxicated with blood or the desire for it, with no concept of discretion or moderation. In fact, he behaved more like Dante imagined a fledgling might than an awakened Ancient. The senator was just grateful Luk hadn't turned on him. Yet. Of course, treating the vampire like a pet animal who had to be tied and dominated had helped instill in Luk a sense of Dante's superiority and, hopefully, untouchability. But Dante was a worried man.

"How did you die, Luk?" Dante asked.

Luk stared at him without obvious comprehension. Although he was a good-looking man, and dark in coloring, there wasn't any other resemblance to Saloman that Dante could discover. A little older in appearance, his face was broader, squarer at the chin, which was partially covered by a hint of a dark goatee. His shaggy hair bore streaks of gray at the temples, and his eyes were more hazel than black.

"Who killed you?" Dante persisted. Until now, he'd refrained from asking the questions that might upset his unpredictable potential ally, but the matter had just become urgent.

The vampire frowned, shaking his head like a dog in the rain.

"Was it a stake through the heart?" Dante prompted. So far as he knew it was the only possible way to kill a vampire, and yet there had been no stake in Luk when they'd found him.

Luk's frown deepened. After a moment, he took hold of his shirt in both hands and tore. Both he and Dante gazed at the crack in his chest. Some vaguely red fluid that wasn't quite blood seeped out of it.

"Is that why you need so much blood?" Dante asked. "Because you just bleed it out again?"

Luk laughed, a wild, eerie sound that set Dante's tight nerves on edge. Dante rose and fetched a first-aid kit from his rucksack, but when he tried to bandage Luk's wound, the vampire jerked in his bonds, flinging Dante and the dressing off with a bewildering speed of movement that nevertheless filled Dante with much-needed fresh hope, because whatever else he was, Luk was damned strong.

"Okay, no bandage," he allowed.

Luk began to hum a vague, mournful tune from which he suddenly broke off in order to let out another of his wild laughs.

Not for the first time, it crossed Dante's mind that Luk truly was insane. Although the sources had claimed this to be the case, they'd said the same thing about Saloman, who certainly was not. At least, not once he was awakened. Somehow, Dante had assumed Luk would follow the same pattern. But Luk didn't even seem to know who he was. Mostly, he seemed frightened and miserable. He rarely said anything that wasn't simply a repetition of Dante's own words. Except, "I'm hungry." He said that a lot.

Dante thought hard. Perhaps when Saloman had killed him, for whatever reason it truly had been Luk's time to die. In which case it was possible Luk would be of very little further use.

Experimenting, he spoke the name of Luk's killer. "Saloman."

The vampire's head jerked up. Another of those weird, preternatural wails escaped his lips, turning Dante's blood to ice in his veins. There was fury there, and pain. But what interested Dante was the recognition. Only Saloman's name had produced this reaction since the vampire had awakened. It *must* be Luk. . . .

"What is *your* name?" Dante asked. "Who are you? What are you?"

The wailing stopped. The vampire bowed his head. "I am Luk. I am the Guardian."

"Guardian of what?" Dante asked.

"I am the Guardian. I am Luk."

"Okay. Luk . . ." Time could be running out. The only thing he knew definitely was that this truly was Luk. "Luk, have you ever made a vampire?"

"Of course." Although the words sounded certain, the doubtful look that went with them was not encouraging.

"Do you remember how? Would you turn me?"

Luk laughed again, this time with more obvious amusement, which piqued Dante into uncharacteristic anger. "What's so funny? I can look after you. We can be buddies, feed together, rule together."

Something changed in Luk's face at that. His head paused in midshake, and he lifted one hand to his beard, stroking it as if to remind himself what it felt like. Dante caught himself wondering whether it grew, if vampires had to shave, before pulling himself up to concentrate on more important matters.

"Friends," Luk said sadly.

Dante smiled encouragement. "That's it, Luk. Friends. I need to be strong, like you." Aware of the risk, yet sure now that he had to take it and take it quickly, before the world in general and the hunters in particular descended upon them, Dante inched closer and turned his head to one side.

Luk's gaze became riveted on the region of his jugular.

"Please," Dante whispered. "Will you turn me?"

He intended to tempt the vampire, explain his needs with this bit of visual impact. For some reason, he thought there would be discussion, a time of preparation, maybe even more persuasion. When Luk fell on his neck, he cried out in alarm, but Luk did not stop. There was piercing, agonizing pain as the vampire tore his flesh. Instinctively, although he'd wanted this for so long, Dante reached up in pure panic to shove him off, but even with his arms bound and useless, the vampire simply hung on with his teeth. His strength was overwhelming, utterly terrifying.

Oh, fuck. Now I'm really *going to die. He's going to kill me outright without turning me.*

Maybe he should have stuck to politics, mixed with a bit of business. It was only when he'd begun his serious research into the occult, into immortality, that everything had started to go wrong for him. . . .

The vampire drank his blood in loud, massive gulps. Dante's consciousness, his very life, ebbed faster than he'd ever believed possible. He couldn't feel pain anymore. But neither did he experience the pleasure that some victims of vampire bites confessed to. He felt only rage because he was going to die after all, and stay dead. Dizziness consumed him. He was going to sleep, dying, God damn it. *God damn the whole fucking world. All I wanted was a little longer, a little more. . . .*

"Drink." The voice seemed to come from very far

away, yet echoed so deeply inside him that he imagined it was God himself. His vision was clouded, almost foggy. He could barely make out the shape of the vampire, who had clearly burst free of his bonds, for he pushed Dante's face into cold, bony, slippery flesh.

Dante tasted the salt of cool blood on his lips and with stunned exaltation licked at the wound, then sucked without conscious volition. The vampire's teeth buried themselves once more in his neck as Dante drank from Luk's wrist. His heart thundered in his ears as if it would burst, but he couldn't stop sucking. Instead the compulsion overwhelmed him—almost like his late wife had once described the urge to "push" during the final stages of labor—forcing him to stronger and stronger pulls. He couldn't locate the pain; it was all over his body, excruciating, unbearable. And yet he did bear it, couldn't bring himself to stop drinking the thick, cold blood that was drowning the pain in weird, triumphant physical pleasure.

There were two heartbeats now, out of time and rhythm, growing louder and louder in his head, vibrating through his body like a pile driver, and then slowing, slowing until the beats matched perfectly, and they were both the same.

Chapter Three

It was just another New York bar: noisy, crowded with people from all walks of life; customers shouting their orders over the din of the music; couples holding hands in booths; groups of increasingly loud friends solving the world's problems around a table full of beer; a small, crowded square of dancers at the back, lit by erratic, flashing spotlights; a vampire in the corner enjoying a quiet meal.

Cyn leapt forward. The light flickered, but she could still see the red-haired vampire bent over the throat of a smartly dressed young man who held his suit jacket casually over one shoulder.

"Got him, Rudy!" Cyn said into the microphone pinned under her lapel. "He's right at the back, and he already has a victim."

She wasn't used to doing this in public. Normally, she and Rudy followed vampires to their lairs or dispatched them in deserted dark alleyways. But it shouldn't make any difference. The vampire would turn to dust and no one would be any wiser. She just hoped the victim would still be alive enough to get to a hospital.

As always, Cyn's blood ran cold as she came up close to the vampire. Every sense screamed at her. She ignored the feeling as she always did, simply drew the stake from her pocket and without pause plunged it hard toward the vampire's back. Her aim was good; the wood should pierce his heart.

It didn't. In the last instant, the vampire moved, spinning faster than Cyn could see, and snatched the stake from her hand. For an instant, blazing amber eyes like a wolf's stared into hers before she kicked his legs from under him, grabbed the victim by the hand, and ran for the door.

Startled people jumped back out of her way, desperate to avoid whatever trouble this turned out to be. As Cyn zigzagged between the tables, she could feel the vampire's watching eyes on the back of her neck like pricks of fire. Worse, she could have sworn she heard him laugh.

Rudy, who'd have been frightened by her long silence, was already at the door, reaching out to take the victim's weight from her.

"He's still in there." Cyn gasped as the door swung shut behind them. "I couldn't get him. He might be following us."

Rudy grunted, heading into the next street—the bar occupied the whole corner—where the pickup truck was parked. "You get this guy to the hospital and I'll go meet the vamp."

"He's fast, Rudy," Cyn warned. "You can't take him alone. And we don't—"

"What the hell's going on here?" the victim interrupted, straightening in Rudy's hold and making a vague movement to shake him off. "Who are you? And who in God's name was *that*?"

Rudy propped him up against the bar window as he stared from one of them to the other. He'd seemed dazed as she'd dragged him through the bar, but not unduly weak.

"Do you remember what happened to you in there?" Cyn asked cautiously.

The man touched his neck. It looked involuntary. By the streetlight, when his fingers fell away again, she could see only faint red marks, like a minor injury that had already healed.

"I remember what almost happened." The man's eyes fixed on her. "You think he's a vampire," he said incredulously.

"He bit you," Cyn pointed out. "You're only alive because I interrupted his meal."

"Not true," said an amused voice close by. Cyn's head snapped around. The red-haired vampire leaned one shoulder negligently against the bar window, so close to the corner that passersby actually brushed against his back. Cyn fumbled a fresh stake from her pocket. Rudy already had one in each hand.

The vampire eased his shoulder off the window and took two paces nearer. "I had no intention of killing him. If you'll notice, I even troubled to heal his wound before I disarmed *you*."

Cyn exchanged baffled glances with Rudy, and this time the vampire definitely laughed.

"You don't have a clue what you're doing, do you? You're not even hunters. You've no idea what's going on. Let me give you a piece of advice before I leave you: Find out who your enemies are before you start killing."

"Oh, we have no problem there," Rudy said grimly, advancing on the vampire, but Cyn caught his arm.

"Wait," she said urgently. "There're more of them, lots more, coming this way."

"How do you know?" Rudy demanded, but at least he did pause, because he knew she felt things he didn't. But Cyn had never felt anything this strongly before. The chill of vampire presence magnified so strongly that her knees began to shake.

"I feel them," she whispered. "Too many. We've got to get out of here."

The vampire gave a lopsided smile and turned on his heel. He walked back around the corner and disappeared.

Rudy was already opening the truck door.

"We'll drop you at the hospital," Cyn said to the victim, who looked more baffled than scared.

"I'm fine," he said vaguely. "Vampires? This is crazy. I'm going to follow that guy, see where he goes."

"That's what we're doing," Rudy said, starting the engine. "That many vampires getting together is worse than dangerous. Hop in with us. If you want to live."

The man climbed aboard with alacrity and Cyn squashed in beside him, slamming the door as the truck took off.

"Right," Cyn ordered.

"Pete Carlile," said the man, offering his hand to Cyn.

"Cynthia Venolia. You can call me Cyn. And this is Rudy Meyer."

"And this is what you do? Kill vampires? Like Blade?"

"I always preferred Buffy. Blade *is* a vampire, isn't he?"

"He isn't real," Pete Carlile said cautiously, and across his body Cyn exchanged grins with Rudy.

"It's okay," Cyn assured him. "We get that. Shit, Rudy, look."

Rudy slowed the truck just as a bunch of men spilled out of the alley beside them. They were fighting in eerie silence, with movements that went way beyond the speed of human fights. But among them, Cyn could make out the bright red hair of the vampire they'd been hunting all evening, the one who'd bitten Pete. Worse, it seemed to be an unequal fight, with their vampire among the majority.

"Fuck," Rudy exclaimed. "We have to help."

Cyn lunged over Pete and caught Rudy's hand on the door. "They're all vampires," she said.

Rudy paused and looked at her. "*All* of them?"

"All of them."

Rudy frowned. "What the hell are they fighting over? Scraps of human?"

"It's happened before," Cyn pointed out. "Three months ago. The so-called gang fights all over the city, remember?"

A vampire in the melee exploded into dust.

"Jesus Christ," Pete whispered.

The red-haired vampire straightened and looked directly at the halted truck. He said something and another vampire turned to follow his gaze: a tall, fair being with a trilby hat pushed to the back of his head. Wild blue eyes seemed to cut through the glass and burn her.

"Drive!" she was able to get out, but Rudy had already slammed the truck in gear and they jolted off down the road.

As the oppressive vampire presence began to fade, Cyn released the breath she hadn't realized she was holding.

"Shit, this is weird," Pete observed.

"You're telling me," Rudy agreed.

You're not even hunters. . . . "What if Elizabeth's right?" Cyn said suddenly.

"Elizabeth?"

"Elizabeth Silk. Mrs. Sherlock. The British chick."

"About what?"

"Everything. The vampire war caused by this Ancient your ancestor is meant to have staked. The 'official' vampire hunters. The different strengths and personalities of vampires. That blond one, with our target—he was strong, stronger than any I've ever felt."

Cyn's hand shook slightly as she dragged it through her tight curls, and she felt Rudy's anxious glance.

"That redheaded bastard was right too," she added, with a jerk of her head behind her. "We started this to do some good, to prevent what happened to you from happening to anyone else. But we really *don't* know what's going on. We don't know why our target left Pete alive. We don't know what side he's on, or how the outcome of this war is going to affect humanity. Maybe we should find out before we go any farther."

Finally, she turned and looked beyond Pete to Rudy's profile. "Otherwise, we're blundering about in the dark. And may well do more harm than good."

Rudy's mouth thinned to a hard, angry line. He cast her another quick glance, then looked back to the road. After a moment negotiating a sudden flood of traffic, he banished his frown.

"What do you want to do?" he asked.

"Get in touch with those people who contacted you last year. The 'official' vampire hunters. E-mail Elizabeth; find out what she knows. Find out if there're any other guys like you, and Pete here, who've survived vampire attacks. And once we have a bigger picture, we can work out what our next step should be."

Pete nodded. "Sounds sensible."

Cyn stared at him. "Who asked you?"

With time to kill at Glasgow airport, Elizabeth made use of the Internet facilities. There were a few more news stories about Adam Simon's background, about earthquakes in general and the latest Peruvian one in particular, together with some intense speculation, but nothing new appeared to have come out of it all.

Impatiently, Elizabeth cleared the search and glanced again at the departure board. She should be researching Luk's killings in Turkey, not his cousin's rescues in Peru. Except there was no point; the Hungarian and Turkish hunters already knew more than she'd ever get from the Internet.

Instead, John Ramsay nagged at the fringes of her mind, even through the more overwhelming events in Peru and Turkey. She e-mailed him to say she was away but still contactable. And then tried to find references to his story in the news reports and blogs. She found the announcement of the attack easily enough, although, obviously, there was no mention of vampires killing his comrades. She had to look at much more esoteric sites to discover those kinds of rumors.

But what grabbed her attention—and nearly made her miss her flight—was the fact that the rumors *were* there. And not just John Ramsay's experience. They seemed to grow out of earlier murmurings, from the time the vampire revolt first broke out, of some mysterious "third force" in the Afghan war that attacked both sides without partiality. And then came hints of the bizarre nature of those attacks. Elizabeth found translations of civilian Afghan accounts, and rumors purporting to come from American forces, of "weird," "unholy," and "ritual" attacks, and was left with the impression that in Afghanistan, at least, the vampire secret was jumping out of the bag. And it could only spread. Vampire hunters across the world would have their work cut out quelling it. However, they would undoubtedly make the effort: They considered concealment as important as vampire killing in their overall goal of saving humans from the undead.

As the last call for her flight penetrated her distracted mind, Elizabeth hastily shut down her laptop and shoved it into its case. She didn't doubt that the hunters could deal with these rumors; they had a worldwide network of vast influence and almost limitless funding; and besides, sane, educated people simply didn't believe in vampires.

However, as she grabbed her bags and dashed for the gate, it did strike her that perhaps the hunters should have a plan for dealing with this expanding knowledge. Surely the majority of people would never believe, but the numbers who did would grow. And that was what Saloman wanted.

"Elizabeth!"

Emerging from arrivals at Dalaman Airport, Elizabeth swerved in the direction of the familiar voice. István waved to her. One of the three Hungarian vampire hunters who'd become her good friends in the last year, István looked much as he always did, casually dressed in light trousers and a T-shirt, his light brown hair falling untidily across his high, intelligent forehead. Elizabeth had always thought it a quiet, sensitive face—like its owner, perhaps a little too serious, but she was used to seeing it light up with open pleasure whenever they met.

Her heart sank. Coming to take her bag, István certainly smiled, but there was something guarded about it. And though he kissed her on both cheeks as always, there seemed to be no warmth in the embrace.

They don't trust me anymore. They need my help, but they don't trust me.

Although she'd been prepared for it, had known in her heart it couldn't be any other way now, she hadn't expected it to hurt so much. In this weirdness that her life had become over the last year, she'd grown too reliant on their friendship.

"So you drew the short straw," she said lightly as they made their way through a crowd of chained-up luggage trolleys and a very young man haggling with some tourists for coins to detach one.

"Hey, I'm a volunteer," he protested.

As he pushed open the door of the terminal building, a wall of heat seemed to hit her.

"So where are the others?" she asked, appreciating the uninterrupted blue of the sky, loving the warmth of the sun on her upturned face, even as she wished she were wearing fewer clothes.

István jerked his head to indicate direction. "Over there. In the hills."

"Have you found him?"

"Luk? No, not yet. We pick up readings, but by the time we get there, he's gone, and we have to start scanning all over again."

Elizabeth frowned. "I thought you couldn't get readings from an Ancient?" So far as she knew, the pocket-sized vampire detectors that had become standard equipment for today's hunters had proved useless against Saloman, who, as the last of the pure-blooded Ancient race, had different body temperatures and biochemistry from modern hybrid vampires.

"We can now," István said, with just a hint of satisfaction, so she knew he had probably had something to do with the discovery. She wondered what it meant for Saloman. Very little, probably, since they were telling her about it.

"So it's definitely an Ancient, and it's definitely Luk?"

"We think so."

"And Dante?"

"Entered the country under his Grayson passport four weeks ago."

"Shit." Elizabeth swept her hand through her hair, tugging half of it loose from the elastic that bound it behind her head. "So all that effort in Budapest was for nothing."

István shrugged. "We postponed it. And we saved Josh Alexander. The world must be grateful for that."

True. After they'd rescued him from Dante and his vampire allies, Josh had bounced very quickly back into his movie-star life. *Psychics 2*, which he'd just finished filming when Elizabeth first met him, was hailed as another resounding success.

Elizabeth answered István's hint of humor with a distracted smile. "*Psychics 3* is now inevitable. Do we know whether Luk has killed Dante?"

"He's left no body behind," István replied, unlocking a grubby and unfamiliar car. "On the other hand, there are other vampire readings around the Ancient from time to time. The local vampires are clearly gathering around Luk. Whether or not one of those readings is Dante remains to be seen."

After they'd gotten into the car and fastened their seat belts, István paused. "I don't think Dante is our main problem anymore. Luk is. Revolt against Saloman has been simmering here for a while now, and Luk is the precise focus it needs to explode into the sort of war we really don't want. He's been awake three nights, and he's fed a lot. How strong is he right now?" He looked directly at Elizabeth. "How strong was Saloman in that time?"

"You saw him. Strong enough to face down Zoltán and his cohorts in the farmhouse incident. Strong enough to kill other vampires with one hand."

She didn't bring up the bedroom scene, when István and Konrad had broken in to discover her naked in Saloman's arms about to be seduced and bitten. The "seduced" part had been more than half accomplished, and even now the memory of it made her body flush hot. It might have been embarrassment. "But Saloman had drunk some of his killers' blood," she said hastily. "Luk can't possibly. Which makes me think it can't even be Luk! How the hell could Dante have awakened him? It would *have* to be Saloman, wouldn't it?"

István started the car. "According to every source we have, Saloman killed him. It should have taken Saloman to revive him." Pulling out of the car park, he glanced at her. "Only, why would he do that?"

"He didn't," Elizabeth said positively. "He's in Peru."

"Are you sure about that?"

Elizabeth stared at his profile. He was, she reflected, a handsome as well as a kind man. But it didn't seem kind to churn her up like this. Although she'd been sure enough to try to buy a plane ticket to Peru, did she *really* know? Saloman hadn't answered her messages, telepathic or otherwise. He'd certainly been in Peru *before* the earthquake, but according to last night's news report, no one knew where he was now.

"Why would he waken Luk?" István repeated.

Because he never got over the guilt or the loneliness.

"He wouldn't," she said, pressing the back of her head into the seat. "Luk was insane and jealous of him. He wouldn't waken an enemy."

You want a keepsake of your enemy? she'd said to him about the sword that Luk had given him aeons ago.

I want the keepsake of my friend.

István sighed. "No, we couldn't make sense of that either. Do you know of any other way to awaken an Ancient? Apart from his drinking the blood of his killer?"

Elizabeth blinked. "*You*'re asking *me*?"

István's smile was twisted. "We've got the books. You've got the horse's mouth."

For a second longer she continued to stare at him blindly. *Just like Dmitriu . . . I'm just an informant to them now.*

Live with it, Elizabeth. You chose it.

It was dark by the time they caught up with the others. Under the amazingly bright, unpolluted night sky, alight with its millions of stars, the beauty of the deep, jagged hills would have deprived Elizabeth of breath had she not had so many other problems on her mind. As it was, she found it hard to look away.

After several phone calls and a long drive up steep hillsides that made her ears pop, István finally stopped the car in a roadside parking place with a water tap jutting out from the rock beside it.

"I think they're quite close now," he said comfortingly, just as his phone rang again. He answered it as he climbed out of the car, then listened while he locked the car and began to walk. Elizabeth trotted anxiously beside him until he said, "Good, we're right behind you."

Replacing the phone in his pocket, he said, "They've got a reading."

Elizabeth nodded, and as he strode away from the road toward a large, wooded area, she fell into step beside him. István reached into his backpack and withdrew a handful of lethally sharpened sticks. He passed three to Elizabeth, who took them with a murmur of thanks, stuck two in her jeans belt, and held on to the last.

The hunter mantle seemed to fall about her shoulders and enfold her. Her heart began to beat faster as she strained every sense to pick up the sounds and smells of danger. She welcomed the rising excitement like an old friend. A fight was something she could deal with now. God, she'd even missed it.

"Are they headed for a village?" she murmured. "How many?"

"Not sure. The others will have the details. But we think there are several."

They found the others in a huddle near the edge of the wood—Konrad, Mihaela, and three Turkish hunters. Although they all glanced up as Elizabeth and István approached, there was little time for civilities or even greetings.

"They're on the move," Konrad said at once. "One Ancient, three other vampires. And they're going uphill for some reason, away from the nearest village."

"So what's up there?" Elizabeth asked, crouching down by Konrad to examine a detection device she'd never seen before. Its main body resembled the usual vampire detectors, but from this one a number of spikes fanned outward. And as well as a small LED, it had a dial like a compass.

"Nothing," Mihaela said discontentedly. "They must be traveling."

One of the Turks said, "There is a vampire commune around ten miles east of here. A vampire could easily travel there over the mountains."

"Gathering support?" Elizabeth suggested.

"It's a long-standing commune," the man explained. "Gives us little trouble. Occasionally it grows too large and we go in and clean it out. It re-forms around the older vampires, and operates more discreetly for the next few years. Your vampires will want to join with them."

"Dante and Luk, plus a resilient commune that survives frequent attacks?" Mihaela murmured. "I don't like the sound of that."

Konrad nodded. "We need to stop them before they reach this commune."

"We can't attack them in the mountains," one of the Turks said. "A vampire has too much advantage there. Ideally, we should have trapped them in the cave and killed them as they broke out."

"Too late for that. We didn't find them in time." Konrad drummed his fingers on his backpack. "Distraction. Is there some way we can persuade them to turn around and come back?"

"Do they know you're here?" Elizabeth asked. "Are they running from you?"

"The wood should have masked us from the ordinary vampires. What Luk can sense is anyone's guess." Konrad cast her a glance. "Can Saloman sense through forest?"

"He can sense just about anywhere in the world if he has a connection to the subject," Elizabeth said. "Luk has no connection, no knowledge of any of us, so he has no reason even to try. His—" She broke off, refocusing her gaze on Konrad while she drew in her breath. "I was wrong. There is a connection. You and I are descendants of Saloman's killers; to vampires, we 'read' more strongly than other humans. In addition, my blood is partly Tsigana's, his old lover's."

"I don't see how that helps us," Konrad objected. "If they're running from us—"

"I don't think they are. We need to make them come back for us."

The others all turned to stare at her in the darkness. She could feel their eyes, even if she couldn't see them.

"Attract them with an easy but powerful kill," Elizabeth urged. "You and I break cover, Konrad, in different directions so that we seem alone and easier meat, and we wait for them to follow one or the other. Everyone else stays in the wood, tracking the vampires until it's clear where they're going; then we join up and trap them."

There was silence. "It's a plan," Konrad said cautiously.

"It's our only plan," Mihaela said. "Let's do it. Only . . ." Her head was turned toward Elizabeth.

Here it comes, the suspicion, the distrust.

"Can you kill Saloman's cousin?" Mihaela asked baldly.

Oh, yes. Because I know what you don't. That Luk died because he attacked Saloman, not the other way around. It makes him easier to hate.

And there she was again, caught between Saloman's confidence and the hunters' safety. The hunters' documents put Luk's murder down to Saloman's insane quest for total power, together with the side issue of jealousy after Tsigana, Saloman's human mistress, had gone to Luk. The surviving texts gave no hint of the love that had once bound the cousins, or the pain that had consumed Saloman since he'd killed Luk. And those things weren't Elizabeth's story to tell.

She said, "I *may* need help pushing the stake right in, but I have no other problem with killing Luk." She sounded too haughty, too defensive, but there was nothing she could do about that.

"He isn't like Saloman," she blurted. "Saloman wasn't insane when they staked him, whatever your sources say. Luk was."

The Hungarian hunters exchanged glances.

"Horse's mouth?" István asked.

"Horse's mouth."

"Let's do it," Konrad said impatiently. "Elizabeth, take these. This is the Ancient detector," he added, shoving the strange, spiked instrument into her hands. "Look, I've just reset it, so it's as accurate as possible. The needle shows the direction of the Ancient; the display shows the distance."

"How did you come up with this?" Elizabeth asked.

"István took temperature and other readings from Saloman during the rescue at Buda Castle," Konrad said smugly. "And if you recall, Saloman bled in that room."

Elizabeth's mingled admiration and annoyance at being kept in the dark vanished in the face of a sudden, blinding memory: Saloman's bloody hand shoving Dante across that bare, stone room into the wall, and Dante sitting slumped on the floor with the scarlet handprint on his yellow shirt. "Shit. That's how he did it!"

Rising to their feet, the others paused.

"Dante," she explained. "He had Saloman's blood on his shirt—could he have used that?"

"I suppose he could," István said thoughtfully. "But there can't have been much of it."

"Enough to smear a taste on his lips," Elizabeth said without thought, then felt her body flush with quick embarrassment. Somehow it was too late to explain that when she'd done this to Saloman it was because she'd accidentally dripped blood on what she thought was a valuable statue and was trying to wipe it off.

She stood, still clutching both small detectors and her wooden stake. "I'll go this way," she muttered.

"Elizabeth." It was Mihaela, dropping something else into her pocket. "Buzzer. Attach it your phone. And don't go too far."

The buzzer connected directly to those the hunters carried and was a quick means of raising or receiving an alarm. As a sign of warm friendship, it might not have been much, but Elizabeth found she was grateful even for that. It would take time to win the others around to her adjusted views about not all vampires being evil. She'd always known that. But it wasn't impossible.

She smiled her thanks and sauntered out of the wood into the open.

Luk placed one heavy foot in front of the other, blindly following. Somewhere, between the strands of mist that clouded his mind, he was aware it should be him leading those weak fools, that he could outstrip them easily in any contest he cared to. He simply didn't care to. He didn't want to be here. He wanted to be . . . wherever he'd been before.

Grief consumed him, drowning his rage, because the memory of before had faded almost entirely and he wanted it back. That was what he wanted, not the existence Grayson kept reminding him of, Luk the Guardian, whatever that was. He wanted peace. Not this hunger, this fury, this unutterable boredom with the present or the reasonless knowledge that this reality was somehow *wrong*.

Ahead of him, sprinting up the hill, was Grayson, his fledgling, his "child." Even that act made him uneasy, though he didn't understand why. He'd just been lonely and Grayson his only companion, his helper who found him human blood. Now they'd found two more "friends," bestial idiots living like wild beggars in the hills. In fact, the idiots had found Luk and Grayson, as if drawn by some invisible rope over a considerable distance. Luk had had to stop them from killing Grayson at their first encounter, but now they behaved, accepting the leadership of Luk's "child."

The idiots, new vampires not so much older than Grayson, had clearly been made by some ignoramus who'd applied neither the correct enchantments nor the right teachings. Luk frowned. He couldn't actually remember what the right teachings were, nor what they were for, but he knew there were some. Instinct more than knowledge had turned Grayson. Now Luk wondered, vaguely, where he'd learned the enchantments.

He sat down on a convenient rock to think about it. He should teach Grayson, teach all of them. But he couldn't be bothered. He wanted to feed; he wanted to go back.

"Luk!" Grayson called, using his newly acquired, much louder vampire voice. Luk frowned. Why didn't he just use telepathy? Because he didn't know how. *How do I know?* "Luk!" Grayson yelled again. "Come on!"

Sighing, Luk stood up. He could refuse to go, but if they left him, he couldn't bear the loneliness. In any case, it didn't really matter where he was. Did it?

Before he could take a step forward, a scent assailed his nostrils that held him frozen.

Blood. Human blood. *Her* blood . . .

He didn't know what that meant, didn't even know who she was. But the echo of some powerful longing curled inside him, a memory lost in time and sleep. For an instant, he struggled to remember, then gave up because that didn't matter either. He turned on his heel and walked away from the others, in the direction of the irresistible female scent.

"Luk!" Grayson called after him in frustration. "Where the hell are you going?"

Go on. I'll catch up. His telepathic instruction clearly took Grayson by as much surprise as it did Luk himself. For an instant, Grayson's struggle to accept and reply filled Luk's mind, before Luk shut him out, uncaring whether he was obeyed. The important thing was to find the source of the smell.

Luk began to run, and as his limbs stretched out, he remembered their strength and what they could do. A surge of excitement urged him to speed up, to run around the entire world and never stop. But her scent was close and sweet, and as he leapt down the final fifty feet to land right in front of her, he grew dizzy.

Startled, the woman fell back, her dark hazel eyes huge in her beautiful face. Hair the color of a long-forgotten sunrise whipped against her soft cheeks in the breeze. Blood pumped through her delicate veins. The sound and smell of it drove him to new hunger, but this was one human he'd never kill.

"Tsigana," he whispered.

The name held Elizabeth frozen. She'd had an instant's warning from the Ancient detector, which suddenly, after indicating his slow plod away from her, went nuts, the readings obviously failing to keep up with the speed of the vampire who leapt out in front of her a bare instant after she'd known he would.

She'd had time to press her buzzer, at the same moment it had gone off in warning. The others knew. So she backed off, giving them time to get here, holding the stake poised for the vampire's attack that didn't come. He stood unmoving, staring at her.

The ordinary vampire detector in her pocket was still and silent. So the Ancient was alone. She prepared to attack, targeting the spot in his chest that she needed, but before she could fly at him, he said, "Tsigana."

If he'd said her own name, if he'd called her Jane or Esmeralda or Buffy the Vampire Slayer, she wouldn't have hesitated in the slightest. But he said Tsigana, as if he'd seen straight to her one weakness, a jealousy that amounted almost to fear of the long-dead human woman who had once held Saloman's heart.

Her fingers curled convulsively on the stake, altering its aim by accident, and she had to readjust it. The Ancient who was Saloman's cousin, his onetime friend and his betrayer, one of Tsigana's three vampire lovers, continued to stare at her. She had the impression that if he breathed, he'd have been panting, but weirdly, she sensed no threat from him. He lifted his arms slowly, reaching out to her with intense, weirdly unfocused longing. Understanding slammed into her like a blow.

"I'm not Tsigana," she said between her teeth. "I'm Elizabeth, the Awakener." And she flew at him, aware her aim was true. She summoned every ounce of strength, every ounce of power she believed in. Because she didn't know how long the hunters would take to get here, she had to try to do it alone, as she'd once tried to kill Saloman alone. She still believed she could have slain him, using her power as his Awakener, but she'd never found out for sure, because her heart, not her body, had prevented it. There was no such prevention here; Luk was the cause of most of the unbearable pain that had haunted Saloman for centuries. He was as good as dead, and she couldn't even regret her lack of compassion.

But he didn't wait for her. He leapt back so fast she didn't even see him move. Her stake sliced through air, almost overbalancing her.

"Not Tsigana," Luk repeated. He sniffed the air.

"Tsigana is dead." Again she leapt, this time before she finished speaking, but again he evaded her. A howl rent the air, like a dog or a wolf in agony. It had to be coming from Luk, as his distant figure leapt back up the hillside at impossible speed, the bloodcurdling wail fading with him into the night. Not because he'd stopped crying, but because he was too far away to be heard.

"Shit," Elizabeth whispered. With shaking hand she retrieved the Ancient detector from her pocket. The pointer indicated the hill up which Luk had vanished, the display counting madly as the distance increased. Then it went dead. Elizabeth delved for her phone, just as the needle swung rapidly several degrees to the west, and the display galloped forward.

Oh, hell, he's doubling back. He's gotten over Tsigana and now I'm dinner.

There was no time to phone. She jabbed the buzzer again and hoped fervently that the hunters were getting this reading too, before running over the jagged ground to flatten her back against a large rock outcropping.

Her heart thundered, but at least she'd stopped shaking. Jealousy of a woman who'd been dead for three hundred years was an unworthy as well as an inconvenient emotion. What the hell was it about Tsigana that tore up all those powerful vampires?

Focus, Silk! Change your tactics. He moves too fast. You have to wait for him to get close enough. Then stake the bastard, and stay the hell away from his teeth. . . .

She gripped the stake, bracing her free hand against the rock. She didn't need the detector anymore. She could *sense* Ancient.

He moved differently, like a shadow around the curve of the hill, gliding over the boulder a yard away from her feet. And instead of attacking, he stood still on top of the boulder and regarded her in silence. Only his long hair stirred in the breeze.

Slowly, Elizabeth lowered her stake. "Saloman."

Chapter Four

Saloman stepped down from the boulder and walked the distance between them. She tried to speak, questions and information tangling in her head and on her lips. In the end, she never made more than an inarticulate gurgle, because the words vanished as his sheer presence overwhelmed her. There was only his name in her head, his profound black eyes to drown in, his body pressing her flat into the rock. The hilt of his sword, a turning gift from Luk, brushed against her hip.

Wordlessly, she lifted her face to his. But he didn't kiss her mouth. His silken lips took her neck in a strong, urgent pull. The hard shaft of his erection pressed between her thighs, and inappropriate lust galloped through her. Well, it had been a long time, several weeks. . . .

It seemed he felt the same. His tongue lapped at her vein and without warning his teeth pierced her skin. Her mouth opened in a silent cry of pain that vanished into the surge of fierce, familiar pleasure. She gripped his arms hard, letting herself glory just for a moment in the blissful weakness of her blood rushing into his mouth in answer to the tug of his lips.

So lost was she in the blood kiss that it was a moment before she realized he'd unzipped her jeans and pushed them and her panties down over her hips.

"Saloman, the hunters are here," she managed. "They're coming now."

His cool, stroking hands left her hips, perversely disappointing her, until he seized the Ancient detector from her frozen hand and hurled it into the night. Before she could object to this vandalism, he lifted her and entered her body in one swift, gliding movement that shattered the remnants of her resistance.

Blood and sex and Elizabeth, he said inside her head.

Bastard. Can't you even say hello?

He detached his teeth from her neck and flicked his tongue over the wound to heal it. His burning gaze lifted to hers.

"Hello," he said huskily, and took her mouth.

Her gasp was at least part sob as she threw both arms around his neck and met his thrusts with desperate urgency. It was insane, the danger of discovery far too great, and yet the very knowledge of that drove her excitement beyond what she could resist. She was Saloman's. The world knew she was Saloman's. His hands spanned her chest, running down over her breasts, tugging them free of her clothing for more intimate caresses.

In the distance, Elizabeth could hear the voices of the hunters, anxious and questioning, but she couldn't stop, didn't want to stop. There was only Saloman and the wicked pleasure she reached for without inhibition. He ground her into the rock, hammering pleasure into her while he sipped again from her neck, dividing the attentions of his lips between the wound and her mouth. She could taste her own blood among the intensity that was Saloman, and it all became part of the same massive, necessary joy that tore her apart in his arms.

He came with her, shuddering in rare silence, even while he sealed her wound once more and held her upright against the hill's slope. His climax was different from those of the human males she'd known, though quite how, she'd never properly analyzed. Sometimes it felt as if her body absorbed everything he gave it.

She reached up and took back his mouth.

"Hello," she whispered against his lips. They smiled on hers.

"Go find your hunters. Tell them I'm here and I'll call later to talk." He kissed her again, hard, and slid out of her before fastening his trousers. He readjusted the sword, which she saw through his enchantment only because she knew it was there.

"You're leaving again?" she said, bewildered by the speed of this new change.

"I'll be back." He pulled her jeans up over her hips, as if now, *now*, he was in a hurry. With sudden pique at being so casually treated, she brushed his fingers aside to refasten them herself. When she glanced up again, he'd gone.

"Elizabeth!" Mihaela gripped her shoulders so hard they hurt. "Are you all right? We found your detector—"

Elizabeth hugged her back, too briefly because of her own guilt, and yet she couldn't help being touched by the show of friendship. "He threw it away," Elizabeth blurted, and perhaps fortunately was misunderstood.

"My God, he got that close?" Mihaela gasped. "Did you stake him?"

Elizabeth drew a little away from Mihaela. The other hunters, Turks as well as her Hungarian friends, used flashlights now that seemed blinding after the all-but-impenetrable darkness. Everyone gazed at her with round, avid eyes.

"He moved too fast. I knew in theory they could do that—I've seen Saloman run across cities." And been with him while he did. "But I guess he never troubled in any fights with humans. . . . He was alone," she added abruptly. "And he ran off back the way he'd come, far too fast to catch." She drew in her breath. "I don't think he's got any idea what's going on. He called me Tsigana, although I'm told I look nothing like her, and then he ran away as if genuinely distraught when I said Tsigana was dead."

"And when he came back?" Mihaela urged.

"Ah. He didn't come back. That was Saloman." She forced herself to meet each gaze in turn. She just wished she didn't feel so childishly defiant about it.

"So he *is* here," Konrad said flatly.

"Apparently. I think he's pursuing Luk, but he said he'd call later to discuss things."

"What things?" Mihaela demanded.

"How the hell should I know?" Elizabeth snapped. "Ask him when he turns up. Trust me, I am *not* his bloody keeper!"

She marched off in the direction of the car without looking back. After about five minutes of striding that probably looked more like stomping, István fell into silent step beside her.

"Sorry," she muttered at last. "I've had a trying day. Seems I can't take the constant suspicion when I'm tired. I'll get over it."

"She isn't suspicious. She's worried about you. We all are."

Elizabeth sighed. "Look, I don't blame any of you for the suspicion, but I do know it's there, whether you want it or not. It doesn't matter. I'm sorry. I'm not walking out on you over a disagreement about Saloman."

"I know that. We all know that." He pointed his key into the darkness and something chirped in response. He shone his flashlight on the car with a grunt of satisfaction and they made their way toward it.

"Where are we going now?" Elizabeth asked.

"To the house. To sleep. The Turkish hunters are going over to the commune. We'll go tomorrow."

"What house?" Elizabeth asked, latching onto the first point.

"It's a holiday villa in one of the hill villages. Very nice. Modern. Fantastic views."

She regarded him with half-amused fascination. "Does nothing faze you, István?"

"What do you mean?"

"I mean you go from vampires to villas with as much effort as breathing."

István shrugged. "All part of life."

You sound like Saloman. She bit her lips before the words tumbled out, but the thought remained.

The villa was substantial and built in a traditional Turkish style, although it was too opulent to blend in with most of the other village houses. Guarded by a pair of tall wrought-iron gates, the surrounding garden boasted an olive tree and some nice rosebushes, as well as some dry, scrubby-looking plants and a kidney-shaped swimming pool.

"The owners are British," István explained as he unlocked the front door. "They rent it for most of the summer. Fortunately for us, they had a cancellation."

"Best of both worlds," Elizabeth observed, looking around her at the curving marble staircase before wandering into the open-plan living area, where rugs were scattered across the ceramic-tiled floor and red plush sofas faced the bay window and a large television. Beyond was a dining area and a well-appointed kitchen with a washing machine and dishwasher. "Turkish style and British convenience."

István took her upstairs, where there were three bedrooms. "Share with Mihaela if you like—there are two beds in there—or there is a large attic room upstairs. The ceiling beams are too low for me. I got bruises just looking at it."

"It'll be fine for me," Elizabeth said quickly, and went on up the staircase. Right now she suspected Mihaela needed some space between them. And besides, there was Saloman.... Her desire for him was like a pain, mocking her anger.

"Hungry?" István asked, laying her bag on the double bed while Elizabeth took in her spacious surroundings. There was even an en suite bathroom. "There isn't much in, but the village shops are open late. Or we can go out when the others come back—there are a couple of decent restaurants."

"Whatever you guys want to do," Elizabeth said, and he left her to shower. She wasn't hungry. She felt too churned up with Luk and Tsigana, with Saloman and sex. Standing under the shower, her body still tingled with remembered pleasure, with excitement, because at last they were in the same country again. And yet it had been too quick, too much taken for granted by Saloman, and too easily welcomed by herself. It wasn't the steam that made her body flush when she remembered what they'd done almost within spitting distance of the hunters who were searching so anxiously for her. "What the hell is the matter with me?" she whispered, letting the water into her mouth and blowing it out again.

The same thing that had always been the matter, ever since she'd first wakened Saloman from his three-hundred-year sleep. Lust.

And he knew it, as he'd always known it. He didn't need even to crook his finger, it seemed. He just had to approach her and she opened her legs like a bitch in heat. He'd taken his pleasure without any lead-in, and left immediately about his own business, as if she were no more than a convenience. Which was what she'd made herself, when in fact she wanted to be so much more, to be to him what he was to her. Everything.

She turned off the shower and reached for the towel. She'd never been ashamed of sex before. Not with him.

Emptying her bag, she found some clean underwear,

an old skirt, and a loose top, and dressed. Then, while she combed out her hair, she examined the views from the two large windows in her room. Both opened onto balconies. One looked onto the village and some holiday apartments beyond, the other onto the swimming pool and the majestic hills. It was beautiful at night. She stepped out onto the second balcony to appreciate the sights and sounds of a new country and breathed in the fresh, calming air.

When she walked back inside, Mihaela stood by the bedroom door in white cotton trousers and a red top. Elizabeth paused, hating that she no longer knew what to say to her once-close friend. Saloman stood between them now, a beloved barrier she couldn't remove if she wanted to. And yet it was through him, and the hunters' determination to exterminate him, that she and Mihaela had met in the first place. At that initial encounter, Elizabeth had thought them either pranksters or nutters. There was no way she could have known then how much the hunters—or Saloman—would come to mean to her.

"You okay?" Mihaela asked at last.

Elizabeth nodded. "Are you?"

"Of course. Want to eat?"

In a small, basic restaurant five minutes' walk from the villa, over a delicious meal and unexpectedly fine wine delivered in an old Coca-Cola bottle, things were more normal.

"I thought Muslims didn't drink wine," Elizabeth said, after the waiter had left their bottle.

"They don't, for the most part," said Konrad, lifting his glass to her. "Doesn't mean they can't make it or sell it. Cheers."

"It's good," Elizabeth exclaimed, after a very tentative taste.

"Local," István said. "Made by a man who understands what he's doing. But don't touch the stuff at the back of the corner shop. You'll go blind."

The restaurant had a convivial atmosphere with a friendly, attentive staff, and Elizabeth found herself relaxing back into the old ease of banter. The hunters called her "Dr. Silk" and asked her about jobs and career moves. Elizabeth thought of the envelope still lying on her sofa in St. Andrews and mentally, ruefully, kissed the post in Budapest good-bye.

As she always did, she warmed to the hunters all over again, and found herself wishing it could be as it was before. But nothing ever stayed the same. Everything moved on.

They walked back to the villa in companionable silence. Only when Konrad pushed open the gate did unpleasantness intrude. István seized his wrist. "Wait," he breathed. "My detector's just gone off."

Elizabeth's, in her handbag, was silent. She took out the sharpened stake.

"Which one?" Konrad whispered. "Where?"

"Ancient." He pointed his thumb toward the swimming pool end of the garden, invisible from the gate.

Konrad jerked his head, and, stakes in hand, he and Mihaela crept around the back of the house. Elizabeth and István advanced toward the swimming pool.

The pool lights were on, and in their glow, a dark figure sprawled on a sun lounger. Supremely elegant and at ease in light trousers and white shirt, one foot crossed over the opposite knee, the sword that she doubted the hunters could see dangling over one side of the lounger, he looked impossibly handsome. His long black hair was tied behind his head, although a stray lock had escaped to fall fetchingly across his sculpted cheek.

Elizabeth's heart beat harder, yet for the first time since those very early days, her pleasure in seeing him was mixed with dread. She wasn't ready for this meeting, because she hadn't yet managed to deal with the last. *Tough.*

She caught István's wrist to show there was no danger and said loudly, "Don't you ever phone first?"

"Modern man is too dependent on those things. Besides, I told you I'd call."

Anxiously, Elizabeth watched Konrad and Mihaela advance on him from behind, their stakes still raised. Saloman didn't betray by so much as a twitch that he knew they were there, but surely Konrad would not be stupid enough to risk attacking him? He'd be dead in an instant.

"What for?" Konrad demanded. "What do you want?"

Still, Saloman didn't turn. "You have a problem, do you not?"

"One we are capable of dealing with," Konrad said stiffly.

Saloman's lip curved. "Really? You couldn't deal with me. What on earth makes you imagine you can deal with my cousin in thrall to your old friend Senator Dante?"

For the first time, he turned his head and looked directly at Konrad and Mihaela. Mihaela, as if embarrassed at being caught out in an impoliteness, hastily lowered her stake. Konrad kept his where it was.

"Is he?" Elizabeth blurted, as much to distract their attention as because she wanted to know.

"In thrall to Dante?" Saloman rose fluidly to his feet. "It would appear so. Certainly, when Dante calls, Luk runs."

"Why?" István demanded, moving closer. A concentrated frown marred his brow. "How is that possible? If Dante's a vampire at all—"

"He is," Saloman interpolated.

"—he can only be a fledgling. Luk is an Ancient, as powerful as—"

Again, he broke off with a quick glance at Saloman, as if suddenly remembering to whom he spoke.

"At least as powerful as I," Saloman said mildly. "But power is pointless if you can't use it."

Elizabeth walked over and sat down on a garden

chair on the other side of the white plastic table from Saloman. "Why can't he use it?"

Saloman met her gaze. His eyes were opaque, and yet she was that sure behind the glassy screen, emotion was boiling. "Because he doesn't yet remember how. Or even, probably, what power is."

"It didn't take *you* long to remember those things," Mihaela pointed out, moving around so that she could see Saloman's face. For all the world like the host of his own party, Saloman graciously indicated the nearby chairs.

"I never forgot them," he said, and Mihaela sank onto the nearest lounger, perching precariously on its edge.

"Then why did Luk?"

Gracefully, Saloman resumed his seat. "Our cases are very different. I was conscious the whole time. Luk slept as the dead are supposed to."

Konrad let out a crack of sardonic laughter at that. Saloman acknowledged it with a faint curve of his lip but said nothing. Elizabeth wanted to ask, *Why didn't you?* But István was before her, saying briefly, "How?"

"I gave him the enchantment of peace."

"That was big of you, after killing him," Mihaela observed.

Saloman didn't bat an eyelid. "I thought so. It wasn't a courtesy later granted to me, but then, I was the last Ancient, and there was no one left to perform it. The point is, at this moment, I very much doubt Luk remembers as much as his own name."

"He remembers something," Elizabeth said with odd reluctance. "He called me Tsigana."

Saloman nodded. "He smelled her blood in your veins. That's what drew him away from Dante and the others. But I imagine it was instinct rather than true memory. When he found you, he didn't recognize that you *weren't* Tsigana, and his distress at learning of her death makes it clear he has no understanding of the time that's passed."

"Will he start to remember?" István asked curiously, dropping onto one of the chairs and sprawling across the table to lean his head on his hand.

"In your opinion," Konrad added with contempt.

"In my opinion, yes. And that is when the true danger will begin."

"When he starts to hunt you down?" Mihaela inquired.

Elizabeth stared from her to Saloman, who merely smiled. "Will he?" she asked.

Saloman's eyebrow lifted. "I am his killer and my blood awakened him. Assuredly, he must hunt me down."

"In hatred? Will he be . . . as he was before?"

"Insane?" Saloman supplied blandly. "Probably. Unless his rest soothed his mind. If it did, I imagine being dragged without warning from something resembling your Christian idea of heaven into the hell of life with Dante will have pushed him back over the edge."

For the first time, Elizabeth caught the tinge of anger in his beautifully modulated voice. This time, it seemed, Dante had done something truly unforgivable. Like Zoltán summoning zombies, Dante had committed some sacrilege in waking Luk from his peace. Saloman, she realized, felt his cousin's pain as if it were his own. And this time, there would be no saving Dante from him.

"What about Dante?" István asked, as if he read her mind. "I've never heard of a fledgling maintaining any control over himself, let alone over another vampire. Isn't he more likely to try to kill Luk?"

Saloman seemed to hesitate. Then it was to Elizabeth he looked, as if directing his answer to her.

"Among my people, over the centuries, Luk revived many souls—made many vampires, if you like. Including me. Modern vampires have forgotten that there is more to the ritual than exchanging blood at the moment of death. There are ways of preserving the soul of the creature you revive, and once that is achieved there are ways of teaching the new existence. Luk became Guardian of the Ancient rituals as well as of the prophecies. They are part of him. So while he may have forgotten the teachings, at least for now, to create correctly would come to him as instinctively as drinking blood. I'm afraid what you have now is Dante himself, with all his human failings and all of a modern vampire's power."

István lifted his head. "Then your own creations, Maximilian and Dmitriu, missed the bestial fledgling phase?"

"Of course," said Saloman with a touch of hauteur. "If your records state otherwise, they lie."

"Will Dante have an Ancient's strength?" Elizabeth asked hastily.

"No. But he will be stronger than the average fledgling."

"Why are you telling us all this?" Mihaela asked.

A smile half formed and died on Saloman's lips. "Perhaps because you need to know."

"Why?" Konrad demanded. "You want us to take your cousin out for you?"

"You are trivial," Saloman remarked. "Like your ancestor."

Konrad flushed in the dim light. He was proud of his ancestor Ferenc's part in Saloman's murder and clearly didn't care to have him insulted. "And you aren't welcome in our house," he snapped. Turning on his heel, he stalked away. More reluctantly, no doubt because they sensed there was more to learn from Saloman, Mihaela and István rose to display solidarity with their leader.

Elizabeth stood also, and Mihaela glanced at her with a relief she couldn't hide before hurrying toward the French window with István.

Loud enough for them to hear, Saloman said, "The eastern commune is moving to meet Luk and Dante. Their strength is growing."

Mihaela and István turned back briefly, made almost identical nods, and walked on.

As Elizabeth hesitated, Saloman said, "I'm not Dracula. A lack of invitation cannot keep me out. Unless it comes from you."

Elizabeth looked up at the stunningly clear stars. "Tonight, Saloman, maybe it does."

She couldn't look at him, couldn't bear to see that it made no real difference to him. But she felt, rather than saw, the inclination of his head.

He said, "I see. You've had enough sexual fulfillment for one day."

Her head snapped around without permission. "Fulfillment? You used me and discarded me like a toy you'd finished playing with!"

He didn't move, just held her angry gaze. "I wanted to give you pleasure. And I thought you needed the comfort." *As I did.*

He didn't say the last words aloud; she didn't know if he'd thought them or if the idea simply entered her own head for the first time.

She said, "You're going to have to kill him again, aren't you?"

He didn't answer, and her pain intensified, fed by his own silent hurt. Her fingers clenched and released as the confusion of shame and rage dissolved into something far simpler that should have overridden all the rest. Love.

She reached out her hand to him. "Come to bed," she said softly.

He rose and clasped her hand, but he didn't smile or take her in his arms. "We were never about pity fucks, Elizabeth. I'd rather remember the way you melted into my arms on the hillside. Instinctive passion, instant gratification. Blood and sex and Elizabeth. I want them all."

He released her hand, and only when she realized he was walking away did she understand how much she needed him to stay. Not just for the sudden lust inspired by his words and by memory, but because he was hurting, and whatever the cause, she couldn't bear it.

"Saloman, they're all yours," she whispered. "They always were." Although she was sure he heard, he didn't turn back.

Chapter Five

Elizabeth woke at dawn to the Muslim call to prayer. Since it sounded as if it were right outside her window, she'd shot out of bed in alarm before she realized what it was. Investigation from the window revealed a loudspeaker attached to the streetlight at the villa gate.

Calmed by the explanation, she went back to bed. But it was too late. The birds were singing. The sun was up, and so were the village animals. Cockerels were screeching at one another as if in some ridiculous deejay contest, a dog somewhere close to the villa was barking erratically, and any spare silence was filled with the braying of an unhappy donkey.

Elizabeth rose and dressed and went to hunt down some coffee. Somewhat to her surprise, the others were already up, sitting around a table on the shaded porch, eating fresh bread and drinking orange juice and Turkish coffee.

Elizabeth's mouth watered. "That bread smells good."

István pulled out a chair. "We let you sleep after your long journey yesterday."

Konrad cut her some bread; Mihaela poured her coffee.

"We heard from Mustafa, one of the Turkish hunters," Konrad said. "The commune he mentioned yesterday has gone. We think they might have joined Luk and Dante."

"Saloman said they would."

Konrad shifted irritably. He didn't want to be reminded of that. "The Turks are looking for them, using both forms of detector, but so far, there's no trail to follow."

"Not even bodies?" Elizabeth said.

"Mercifully, no. Not yet," Konrad amended.

Elizabeth dipped her bread in some olive oil and ate. It tasted divine.

Abruptly, Konrad said, "What does Saloman plan to do?"

"I'm afraid I don't know." In fact, she rather thought Saloman didn't either.

"If he finds them first," Mihaela said carefully, "do you think he'll kill them? Or convert them to his cause?"

Elizabeth set down her coffee cup. "I don't think 'conversion' is an option here, do you?"

"So we sit back and wait for Saloman to kill them for us?" Konrad said disgustedly. He was addressing István and Mihaela, who had clearly already mooted this possibility.

"I think we have to find them before there are any more deaths," Elizabeth said quietly. "And before they get so much stronger that they become a threat to Saloman."

Konrad scowled at her. "Is that your priority now, Elizabeth?"

"Konrad!" Mihaela said sharply.

But this morning, it seemed, she could shrug it off. It would hurt later. "No one wants the chaos of a succession war. You've told me that since I first woke Saloman."

Mihaela drew in her breath, giving Elizabeth warning that she was about to say something difficult. "Do you know why he's here, Elizabeth? When he arrived?"

"I don't know for certain. I suspect not much before me, or he'd have found Luk sooner. As to why . . ." She shrugged. "He'll have sensed Luk's awakening."

She looked from Mihaela to meet the gaze of each in turn. "I know you don't like this, but I think we need his help. He can sense farther than your detectors. He probably knows where Luk is right now."

The hunters exchanged glances. Konrad said reluctantly, "Do you know where Saloman is?"

Saloman. Where are you?

Who wants to know? came the flippant response.

I do. So do the hunters, she added in the interest of honesty. *Have you found Luk and Dante?*

I've been following their trail, he admitted. *They're holed up with the commune vampires in some hill caves. This is the nearest village.*

A road sign flashed into Elizabeth's mind, as clear as a photograph. *Thanks. Can we drive there by sunset?*

Probably. There was a pause, then: *I won't let them kill Luk. That's for me to do.*

I know. Her throat closed up. She wanted to say, *I miss you*, but the connection was already broken.

Slowly, she opened her eyes. Disoriented as she always was after initiating telepathy, it took a moment to register that she sat in the villa's living room with the three Hungarian hunters. She dashed the back of her hand across her forehead and said briskly, "They're in a cave near this village. I can't pronounce it." Reaching for a pen and paper from the table in front of her, she scribbled down the name Saloman had shown her. "And they're with the commune vampires already."

Dante, still relishing every nuance of his new energy, poked Luk with the toe of his shoe. "Wake up. The sun's setting." He wanted to go out into the beautiful night, drink blood, grow stronger, collect followers. . . .

Luk, who seemed to sleep with his eyes open, if he slept at all, sat up wearily. He'd been increasingly morose since yesterday evening, when he'd run off on his own. Whatever he'd done hadn't made him happy. In fact, it appeared to have made him furious, for after feeding, he'd thrown the body of his victim at Dante. Even with his new strength to help withstand the force, Dante had fallen in an undignified heap with the bloodless corpse on top of him. He'd punished Luk with a tongue-lashing and a cold shoulder, neither of which the Ancient appeared to notice, so this time, he thought he'd try a little kindness.

"Now that your wound has finally healed, are you happier this evening?" he inquired jovially.

"No," said Luk. "I'm hungry."

"Me too. We'll wake the others and go out. What makes you unhappy, Luk?"

Luk threw back his head and laughed. "This." He stared at Dante, the laughter dying to fury and pain on his still lips until Dante's new blood ran cold. Then he uttered, "Tsigana."

Dante blinked, taking a moment to place the name. "Tsigana? She's been dead three hundred years." He grinned with vicious satisfaction. "Took Saloman out before she went, though."

"Saloman." Luk shook his head violently. It might have been rage or hurt. Or simple madness.

"What made you think of Tsigana?" Dante asked. "Did you go looking for her last night?"

"I found her. She told me she's dead. But she isn't undead."

Dante turned away. Sometimes talking to Luk was just plain pointless. Except . . . He looked back over his shoulder. "You found someone you thought was Tsigana? Perhaps Tsigana's blood ran in her veins?"

Luk nodded.

Dante laughed. "Elizabeth Silk. I'll bet you anything! Did you kill her?"

Luk shook his head impatiently. It could have meant anything.

"I hope you did," Dante murmured. "Especially if she had her tame hunters in tow." Another possibility struck him, wiping the smile right off his face. In his admittedly limited experience, where Elizabeth Silk turned up, Saloman was rarely far away. He seemed to regard his Awakener as some kind of pet. Dog-in-the-manger-like, though he hadn't yet killed her, he was damned if he'd let anyone else enjoy the privilege.

Dante glanced at Luk with frustration. So far, the Ancient had defended him from other vampires' instinctive aggression, but he shouldn't rely on such protection lasting forever. And looking at him now, hunched, unreachable, twitching with hunger and God knew what else, Dante couldn't see him troubling the might of Saloman. What self-respecting rebel would choose to follow this miserable creature?

"Come on, let's get out of here," he snarled.

The color of the sunlight had begun to change, darkening the shifting shadow patterns on the forest floor. Saloman could move now in safety; in another few minutes, he could even leave the shelter of the forest. Before the vampires left their cave, he could be there, waiting for them.

Except, trailing up the hill from the village, Elizabeth and the hunters were approaching. By the time they found him, he could have killed Dante and the others, returned Luk to sleep, and shown their followers the error of their ways. And everyone could go home. But Saloman refused to give up his long game, the wooing of the hunters that he'd begun with the rescue of Josh Alexander from Dante in Budapest. Their working together had to be more than a one-off, more than a vague idea. It had to be visible and real. And so, while the vampires stirred in their cave, he waited for the hunters. And for Elizabeth.

She moved through the trees with all the poise her new physical confidence had given her—part of the protective group of hunters who surrounded her, watching out for themselves and one another. It caused a pang of pain in Saloman that came dangerously close to jealousy, for the hunters would always be a part of who she was now.

Elizabeth had changed and grown over the last year as she recognized her strengths and dealt with the realities of her new life. Saloman was proud of her—proud too of his role in her growth. He'd shown her the way to develop her telepathic and sensory powers, through which she would reach whatever full potential awaited her. And he'd broken through her shyness, her inhibitions where love was concerned, taught her the giving and receiving of joy. And yet she remained the same person who'd intrigued and touched him when she'd accidentally awakened him—compassionate, intelligent, vulnerable, funny, unexpectedly sweet, brave, thoughtful, loving. . . .

Loving. Saloman's loins tightened as he watched her approach. Her red-blond hair was tied carelessly behind her head, revealing all the delicate beauty of her face; the skimpy top that he'd once called a whore's bodice emphasized the contours of her breasts and waist. Yesterday evening's hot, irresistible fuck hadn't been enough, not nearly enough. But then she'd overanalyzed, as she was prone to—it was an intellectual's failing—and wanted to punish him for a perceived lack of respect. Although her frail humanity was a large part of what drew him to her, sometimes it was totally incomprehensible.

But at least she smiled when she saw him, the quick, spontaneous smile that warmed his heart and drove his borrowed blood straight to his cock. Despite the presence of the grave-faced hunters, she came right up to him, and although she didn't kiss him, she threaded her fingers through his and squeezed.

"Are they still there?" she asked, just a little self-consciously.

"They've left the cave."

"Got them!" the Hungarian, István, exclaimed with satisfaction. He was examining one of his bizarre instruments on which the hunters relied to a ridiculous degree. Their detectors were clever, Saloman allowed, and he applauded their ingenuity, but the hunters seemed blind to the fact that by the time the instrument gave out any warning, a vampire could already be biting the owner's throat. A decent vampire moved a lot faster than their technology.

And so it proved. They scurried up the hill, past the cave where Luk and Dante had sheltered with their followers, and their instruments went dead.

"Follow in the same direction," Konrad ordered. "There's a decent-sized town on the other side of these hills. I'll get Mustafa to meet us with a car."

Saloman spoke to Elizabeth. *Go with them.*

She glanced at him, her expression uncertain. A frown creased her brow, as if she were annoyed by his instruction, and yet the softness of her eyes showed only that she'd miss his company, that she regretted her exclusion from whatever he was about to do. Sorry for it, he caressed her mind with his and slipped out of it as he lifted the sheltering branch that protected the cave, and stepped inside.

Saloman had to close his eyes as the echo of Luk's presence surrounded him. The strength of it was overwhelming, so much so that it almost entirely eclipsed the signature of the other, lesser vampires, including Dante. Crouching down, Saloman ran his fingers across the stone and earth that was the cave floor. He found the place where Luk had lain to rest, placed his palm flat, and let it all in, all the lingering essence that was Luk.

This was why Elizabeth could not be here. Because

Saloman could not bear the pain of Luk's hopeless ignorance. This was worse than the insanity that had clouded and tormented his cousin's once-great mind; this was as if the mind had been completely wiped, just leaving enough for Luk to know that it happened. And yet the soul was the same; it was still Luk.

Blood pounded behind Saloman's aching eyes. He wished he could weep to release the excruciating pressure, to honor the Luk he'd loved. But tears were the one thing beyond him now, as if some vital organ had been damaged on the night of his betrayal by those he'd loved the most: Maximilian, his first "child," and Tsigana, his lover. Tsigana, whom he'd forgiven so often because her human flaws had fascinated him. And yet he'd never imagined she would ever commit the ultimate betrayal and assist in his murder.

Tsigana. The whole cave was redolent with her echo. She'd filled Luk's mind as he lay here, as if he imagined he'd lost her to death. What would it do to him to know that she'd been back in Saloman's bed the day of Luk's burial? To Saloman, that had been a necessary if slightly perverse honoring of his cousin; to Tsigana it had been an imagined triumph. To Luk . . . Well, Luk didn't even know who Saloman was anymore.

Or did he? Saloman ground his fingers into the stone until they bled. He couldn't follow the lingering memory of Tsigana back to its source, Luk's mind, for fear of harming or even alerting Luk before he was ready. But the image left from Luk's thoughts was accurate, as was the scent, the feel of Tsigana, except, surely, it altered occasionally to fit the more vital, open face of Elizabeth, in whose veins ran Tsigana's blood.

Something was returning to Luk. He was holding on to Tsigana, using her memory to try to reach others, to work out how the other woman's blood smelled of Tsigana.

Saloman released the earth and stone between his fingers and rose to his feet. The dirt fell away from his skin, which began to heal over the abrasions he barely noticed. If Luk was remembering already, then Saloman, Elizabeth, and the whole world had better look out.

Outside the cave, Saloman lifted his face into the wind. He could smell Elizabeth and the hunters, hear their grumbles because they still could not pick up the trail of the vampires. There was a reason for that, of course. The hunters were heading in the wrong direction. Either Luk or Dante had worked out that they were being pursued. Perhaps Luk had mentioned seeing a woman who smelled of Tsigana, and Dante had put two and two together. Either way, the vampires had swung around in a large arc and were heading back south by a more western route.

Elizabeth. You're going the wrong way. Follow my signal.

If they timed it right, he could kill Luk and keep the fight going long enough for the hunters to arrive and take part. Another cooperative venture would then be won at very little loss. And Saloman could turn his attention to the rebellion rising among the vampires of Istanbul. Without Luk, it would be simple to quell.

Saloman began to run, lengthening his stride to massive leaps so that he covered the uneven ground faster than the human eye could see. The vampires were using some erratic, haphazard masking to disguise their presence. Saloman applauded their caution, which, however, was useless against him. If Luk ever troubled to mask, things would be different, but at the moment, Saloman was invisible to them while able to track their every move.

When they were finally visible to his naked eye, hundreds of feet below his vantage point, he acknowledged that he had to look into his cousin's eyes when he killed him. He owed him that. Again. And for that, he needed surprise on his side.

He jumped once, landing on a lower ledge, darting forward and downward before any of them could glance up. Dante led the pack at a moderate, resting pace now, with Luk trailing along in the rear, occasionally shaking his head as if plagued by some massive twitch.

Oh, yes, Dante would die.

A moment longer, Saloman listened to the beat of his own heart. Then he grasped the sword at his hip for strength and jumped again.

He landed lightly behind Luk, who must have felt the rush of displaced air, for he turned his head without interest to glance over his shoulder.

Saloman spoke softly, in the Ancient language of their people. "Greetings, Luk."

Luk froze, his mouth open, his eyes wide. Ahead, the others didn't appear to notice that Luk was dawdling again.

Luk turned slowly, as if he couldn't help it, and stared at Saloman. Oh, yes, they were Luk's eyes, hazel and luminous, the eyes of a seer and prophet. But curiously blank as Saloman had never seen them before—half-dead because only half-awakened. Without the memories that had formed him, he wasn't yet Luk. His lips moved silently; some huge, internal struggle crossed his face and ended in his eyes with a flash like lightning.

"Saloman."

It came out as a whisper, and yet the stupid joy of his recognition crashed around Saloman's ears like an earthquake. *Look out, world.*

Luk took two steps forward. "Saloman," he said again, loudly enough to catch the attention of the vampires in front. Saloman ignored them. Luk's lips twisted with effort or pain or both. Blood gathered at the corners of his eyes and he smiled.

Saloman's heart seemed to break. And then, with the sort of speed he'd almost forgotten, Luk launched himself at him.

Saloman fell back under the force. His arms, already lifted from instinct to defend and kill, lowered slowly around his cousin's heaving body.

He wasn't under attack; he was being embraced.

I can save him, Saloman thought, stunned. Luk was collapsing under the force of returning identity. Saloman sank to his knees with him, holding him in compassion and happiness and sheer relief from a horror he had never wanted to acknowledge. Luk the Guardian of his people, the prophet, was back.

Over his bowed head, Saloman watched the vampires' wary approach. Since his mask was already dropped for Luk, there was no need of any warning. They all knew they beheld Saloman, the Ancient, the overlord of the undead. And then there was Dante, looking exactly the same, although unable to resist smiling to show off his new vampire incisors.

Saloman wasn't fooled. It hadn't been part of Dante's plan to have Luk return to the arms of his cousin and killer. Dante was worried.

"Luk!" the senator said sharply, and with rising fury Saloman understood that this was how he always addressed the being whose boots he wasn't fit to lick.

Luk ignored him. The heaving of his shoulders had become almost convulsive, like a human battered by emotion. He needed peace for this, which he'd never get here.

"Luk, come with me," Saloman whispered into his cousin's hair.

"Saloman," Luk said in wonder. His fingers grasped at Saloman's back and slowly relaxed. His head lifted. "Saloman!"

There was no love, no happiness, left in those hazel eyes, just boiling fury and profound, gut-rotting hatred. It gave Saloman an instant's warning—not enough to get his blow in first, but enough to let him fall without breaking his neck when Luk hurled him into the side of the hill.

Luk flew after him, baring his teeth for the bite. But Saloman forced himself to his feet and simply leapt over his cousin's head, drawing sword and stake as he went, to face the lesser vampires. None of them was armed, except Dante, whom Saloman singled out.

"No mercy," he hissed. "No quarter."

"Saloman!" yelled Luk. "Don't hurt your 'brother'!"

Saloman adjusted his position to defend from either side. Luk lunged, but before he got close enough, Dante called in panic, "Stop! You're not strong enough yet! He'll kill us all! Back off!"

Then Luk stood between him and Dante as they backed away from him. Saloman strode forward, and they rushed backward to get away from him, tripping over each other. Saloman lashed out, killing two of the lesser vampires on Dante's left with as many lightning strokes of his stake. Their bursting particles shimmered and blew away on the breeze.

Dante's panic appeared to spread to Luk, who, with one last glare of hatred, grabbed Dante by the arm and ran, protecting his creation with his own body. Saloman contented himself with throwing his stake at one of the fleeing vampires trying to keep up, and felt a certain satisfaction when he turned to dust.

He stared after the running vampires until he could no longer see them, then slumped against the nearest rock. He had a plan for everything. For every possible contingency in the human and vampire worlds. Except killing the beloved cousin it might just be possible to save.

Luk was in Dante's control, recovering his memory and his power; he threatened Saloman's life and Saloman's rule; he threatened the world.

And yet there had been a moment. . . .

Saloman closed his eyes, floundering for the first time in centuries. *What do I do? Elizabeth, what do I do now?*

Chapter Six

Elizabeth opened her eyes with no clear sense of what had awakened her. It might have been the dog in the yard next door, emitting a kind of whimpering half bark, as if unsure whether it felt threatened.

She and the hunters, having lost the trail early and left Saloman to pick it up again—against Konrad's better judgment—had driven home and fallen into bed. Like the others, Elizabeth felt a sense of frustration, having traveled so far and come so close to the enemy, and yet failing to engage. And Saloman worried her. After sending his signal to guide her, he'd broken it off, only to communicate telepathically a little later that he'd killed a couple of the vampires but was still on the trail. And then, only a little after that, had come the advice to go home, because the vampires had separated, with Luk and Dante heading suddenly northeast, and the others south, closer to the hunters' base. Saloman was following Luk, but advised Elizabeth to look for signs of vampire attack in the villages inland from Fethiye. It was possible Dante, or even Luk, had instructed them to create a fledgling army to distract the hunters.

Konrad especially had bridled at being "advised" by a vampire, but in fact, as István pointed out, it was the only sensible thing to do. Although there were hours of darkness left, pursuing vampires who moved much faster than humans was a thankless task at the best of times. They had to be tracked and ambushed, and that night the hunters had simply gone too far off the right path. At Elizabeth's urging, Konrad had finally phoned Mustafa to let the Turkish hunters know Saloman's warning about Fethiye. After which, exhausted and irritable, they'd all retired, aware that they might have to spend the next night executing violent yet more or less defenseless fledgling vampires.

But Elizabeth could have been asleep for only a couple of hours. It was still dark outside; no call to prayer sounded; even the cockerels were silent. She lay still for a moment, straining her ears. Her heart began to beat faster as she wondered if Saloman had returned. She slipped out from under the sheet and padded across the cool floor to the window. No familiar dark shadow lurked on the balcony or in the garden below. Moving quickly across to the other side of the room, she felt ridiculously disappointed to see no sign of him on the swimming pool side of the house either.

She should go back to bed and sleep. Only . . . Only, something felt wrong. Straining for Saloman's presence, she was sure she sensed something else. Something she didn't like. She moved silently to the bedside table and picked up the stake she'd kept close ever since her early encounters with Saloman. Holding it made her feel better. But not for long.

A clash of broken glass rent the air, followed closely by a male yell.

Konrad.

Before the thought had passed through her brain, she was out of the bedroom door and leaping down the spiral stairs so fast she should have broken her neck. Konrad's was the first door at the foot, and she hurled herself at it without warning or apology in time to see Konrad standing up on the bed, thrusting his stake into a shadowy figure that promptly vanished into darkness. But two more faced him, while a third advanced toward Elizabeth.

Elizabeth didn't hesitate. She flung herself at one of Konrad's assailants and felt her stake slide in. But the vampire was strong, and twisted so fast that the wood jammed hard against a rib. Snarling with pain, the vampire struck her, knocking her off him. Elizabeth hung on grimly to the stake as she fell to the unforgiving tiled floor. Since the stake came with her, she ignored the pain, hooked her ankle around the vampire's leg, and yanked.

Taken by surprise, he fell awkwardly, and, knowing he would rectify that all too quickly, Elizabeth leapt onto him almost before he hit the floor. One powerful hand seized her throat, instantly squeezing, while the other grabbed for her stake. Evading his questing fingers for long enough to swap the stake to her left hand, she plunged down hard. Almost simultaneously, the constriction on her throat relaxed and the vampire exploded into dust. The familiar rush of the dead vampire's energy into her own body made her gasp. He *was* strong and she'd been lucky to get so easy a kill, but there was no time for smugness. She had to use his strength, which was now added to her own.

On the bed, Konrad wrestled with the two remaining assailants. However, as Elizabeth ran to help, István and Mihaela skidded in together and shared the kill, just as Konrad's last assailant paid the price of his distraction and turned to dust.

Slowly, Elizabeth reached up and switched on the light. Of their attackers no sign remained, except broken glass scattered under the window and a splash of blood on Konrad's rumpled sheets.

"Bastard bit me," Konrad muttered, holding his hand over his shoulder as he let himself flop into a sitting position on the bed.

"Let me see," Mihaela said efficiently. She'd been here before, patching people up after vampire attacks, and she sounded as she always did, cool and capable. And yet her hand shook as she lifted it to Konrad's wound.

Elizabeth swayed on her feet. To cover it, she strode to the window, trying to ignore the unspecific but very physical pain that started to consume her. The dizziness combined with a powerful, alien dread that made her grasp the window frame hard to dispel it. *Not now! Please, not now . . .*

Perhaps it was just the result of the vampire's blow. It must be. To her relief, the pain and the awful feeling she had no words for began to recede, at least enough to let her focus once more. There was no sign of anyone else outside, but although that oppressive sense of *wrongness* had dissipated, she was well aware she hadn't seen the attacking vampires from her own windows either.

"The detector's still registering," István said urgently. "We've got another one."

"Where?" Elizabeth demanded, spinning back to face him.

"Outside, I think," István said, running out of the door.

As Elizabeth crossed the room after him, Mihaela stood up. "Hold that over it," she advised Konrad, placing his left hand on the cloth she'd held to his wound, and his right on the wooden stake he'd used to such good effect. "It's healing already, so you'll be fine," she added over her shoulder, as she left the room side by side with Elizabeth.

They found István in the hall by the front door. Wordlessly, he showed them the detector, holding the blunt end of the stake over his lips to call for continued silence. From the direction and distance indicator, the vampire waited on the other side of the front door, no doubt ready to grab any fleeing humans. If he were strong enough, he'd already know his comrades were dead, so either he was stupid and relatively weak, or he was powerful enough to be confident of taking at least one of them out by surprise before escaping.

István pointed toward the living room, and Mihaela tugged Elizabeth's arm. Elizabeth nodded and crept through the living room to the French doors. The key was in the lock. Elizabeth touched it, remembering that it turned smoothly. She just hoped it was smooth enough to prevent the vampire's superhearing from picking it up.

She glanced back at Mihaela, who stood in the middle of the room, from where she could see both Elizabeth and István. Watching István, Mihaela held up one hand and began a countdown with her fingers. As soon as the last finger closed, Elizabeth spun the key, yanked open the door, and leapt outside, stake drawn.

Although she barely heard her move, Mihaela stood beside her. The night was silent. István should have been through the front door, but there was no sound of fighting or commotion. Elizabeth's spine felt cold. Exchanging glances with Mihaela, she began to move forward around the outside of the house as Mihaela set off around the other way.

Each step seemed to bring an increase of tension. The vampire had waited this long; Elizabeth couldn't believe he'd fled now without a kill. Surely he couldn't have taken István so easily that there had been no noise?

No. The long, lean figure of István stood on the edge of the porch, still and poised. Although there was no sign of the vampire, she could still *feel* him.

Oh, God, Mihaela!

But no, István still had the detector; if it had registered movement, he'd have followed it. Elizabeth's breath caught. *Up. He's gone up!*

Desperately, she scanned the roof of the little porch. Surely there was a blacker patch in the shadows . . . ? István must know. He was waiting for her and Mihaela to approach before he stepped off the porch, just in case the vampire was faster than he was.

In which case, distraction was everything. And she just prayed the others would understand her game.

She began to run, crying, "István!"

And István understood. He leapt off the porch on Mihaela's side, just as the vampire jumped from the roof on Elizabeth's. István spun at exactly the same time as the vampire, and Elizabeth had to shake her head to clear it. For one tiny, vital instant, she thought she was seeing double, before she realized it wasn't her head that was splitting the dark shadow into two vampires. There really were two, one grabbing for István, the other leaping for her like some impossibly fast darkness monster from her childish nightmares.

They'd hidden together to disguise their numbers from the detectors. Forcing her legs to pump faster, rather than skid to a halt and run back the other way, Elizabeth lashed out with her stake, drawing blood from some part of the vampire as he flew at her. He landed on his feet with a hiss and made a grab for her. Elizabeth dodged, but already his other hand snaked out and she had to stab it with the stake. His hiss became a snarl that was curiously like laughter. The vampire thought he could win.

Grimly, despite the sudden chill in her blood, Elizabeth begged to differ. It felt like some weird challenge, turned the lethal battle into a desperate game of tag—or "tig," as she'd called it growing up in Scotland. The vampire's limbs moved fast enough to blur, feinting and lunging, pulling back and grabbing. And yet it wasn't impossible speed like Luk's; it was nothing she couldn't deal with. She found she could counter his every move, dodging each grab, reading each feint, and blocking every blow.

She couldn't help the sudden, soaring triumph, but neither could she afford to draw this out. A glimpse of István, driving his vampire back into Mihaela's waiting stake, warned her to finish it. Ducking beneath the vampire's sweeping arms, she sprang up within them and stabbed him through the heart. His ludicrous expression of surprise before he turned to dust made her almost sorry the game was over.

Spinning to face the other fight, she saw that the vampire had managed to turn on Mihaela. István, picking himself off the ground, leapt on the vampire's back and plunged his stake.

With a yell of fury, cut off like a switch, the vampire exploded into silvery dust. Elizabeth skidded to a halt beside István, who gasped, presumably as he absorbed the rush of the vampire's strength, and grinned through it at Elizabeth and Mihaela. "Thanks."

"My pleasure," Elizabeth said faintly. "Any more of them?"

István glanced at the detector fastened to his wrist. "Not that I can see."

"We need to check the rest of the house, though," Mihaela said prosaically.

Together, they went back inside, relocking both doors. Then they went through each room in the house, including Elizabeth's and finally Konrad's once more. The injured hunter appeared to be quite recovered, standing guard over his broken window with characteristic impatience.

To be on the safe side, Elizabeth accompanied István out to the garden again, while Mihaela guarded the front door. All was quiet, save for a cockerel farther down the street. István collected some wood intended for the barbecue, and took it inside to board up Konrad's window.

That done, they all wandered into the dining area and sat down around the table. Elizabeth got up and switched the kettle on, just as the dawn call to prayer began.

She smiled. "Why is that sound so comforting?"

"Because you're still alive to hear it?" Mihaela suggested.

"It's an affirmation of all the goodness and beauty in the world," István said surprisingly.

Konrad smiled faintly. "Is that official Islamic doctrine, Professor?"

"No. It's my personal interpretation."

Only as Elizabeth set the coffee and cups on the table did she realize that none of them was dressed. She herself wore the sexy nightdress that had inspired Saloman to frequent passion in the past—now slightly torn from the fight. The men had only boxers on, displaying their pleasingly muscled if slightly scarred torsos to the world, while Mihaela wore a skimpy pair of shorts and a top.

Mihaela met her gaze with slightly embarrassed humor. "Maybe we should put clothes on to have coffee," she suggested.

"Stuff clothes," said Elizabeth, flopping down beside her. "They're overrated."

Mihaela raised her cup in a silent toast.

Konrad sighed. "Well, it looks as if Saloman's guess as to location was right. We are only ten miles from Fethiye. He just got the mission wrong."

Elizabeth looked at him. "You think that's who it was? Dante's minions?"

Konrad shrugged. "A gathering of five vampires in a place this size is rare. As is an attack targeted specifically at hunters. Also, from what you said, they knew how to fool the detectors. That has to have come from Dante."

"But how could they possibly have found us so fast?" Mihaela objected.

"A concentration of human readings?" Elizabeth suggested. "To a vampire, Konrad and I in one place is quite forceful. Only . . . you're right. I don't think they'd have found us so fast without help."

"Whose help?" Konrad demanded.

He thinks it's Saloman betraying us. "Luk's," she said

evenly. "He's seen me, smelled me; he could have passed that reading on to the others, used it to guide them remotely, if you like, to our house. Three hunters, one of whom is also the descendant of an Ancient-killer, plus an Awakener, is quite a haul."

"And yet doomed to bring trouble," Konrad snapped. "Vampires are rarely stupid enough to attack hunters unprovoked."

"We're dealing with rogue vampires here," Elizabeth pointed out. "Dante *wants* trouble. He wants *massive* trouble to boost the rebellion in order, ultimately, to use Luk to remove Saloman. I don't think he's got any idea how effective hunters are against vampires—he saw Dmitriu beat up a whole team, and he's only seen you fight in Saloman's company, which probably gave a false impression. He probably thought you were easy meat, easy propaganda. In the short term, he may even have hoped to distract Saloman by this attack on us."

"On *you*," said Mihaela thoughtfully. She gazed at Elizabeth. "Will it?"

"No, because I haven't told him about it," Elizabeth said calmly.

Mihaela said nothing more on the subject, but her gaze was uncomfortably penetrating.

After they'd chased ideas about the vampire attack around for a bit, the men went off to shower, and Mihaela leaned back in her seat, putting her rather elegant feet up on the dining table.

Elizabeth said, "Are you all right?"

Mihaela blinked. "Of course. It was the rest of you who bore the brunt. I did little more than turn up for the postshow party. Konrad owes you."

Elizabeth brushed that aside. "I was awake. We all did what we had to. I just thought you looked . . . shaken. I've never seen you like that before."

Mihaela's gaze fell. "It threw me," she confessed. She reached for her coffee cup and drained it before she said abruptly, "It's not something we deal with often as hunters—vampires breaking in. It reminded me of . . . the past."

Of the childhood attack that had killed her family. Elizabeth could only imagine the horror of that night, guess at the impact of a reminder such as tonight's. There was nothing she could say. So she sat by Mihaela's side in silent support until the other girl set down her cup and deliberately changed the subject.

"Heard from Josh lately?" Mihaela asked.

Josh Alexander, the American film star, was Elizabeth's distant cousin and fellow descendant of Tsigana whom they'd been forced to rescue from Dante and his vampire allies back in May.

Elizabeth smiled. "He invited me to the premiere of *Psychics 2*, knowing I couldn't go. But I appreciated being asked."

"Me too."

Elizabeth did a double take to make sure she hadn't mistaken the added smugness in Mihaela's expression, and then she began, slowly, to smile. "*You* and Josh? Now, that I like. When did this happen?"

"When he stayed with me after we got him out of the castle."

"Why didn't you tell me?"

Mihaela shrugged. "There wasn't much opportunity. Things were a bit rushed before you went back to Scotland. And we were celebrating your PhD. Josh and me was no big deal. I always knew that. We're from different worlds, with no intention of changing things. We were just both . . . needy. And he's very sweet as well as amazingly attractive!"

Elizabeth nodded agreement. "He's also," she observed, "looking for something deeper than a publicity relationship. He and his wife were very close until she died."

Mihaela's smile was a little twisted. "Well, I can't have a relationship at all, can I? Public or otherwise. But it was a good week. Made up for all the shit before."

Elizabeth knew she meant more than the vampire shit; she was referring to past encounters with unworthy men. Running one finger around the rim of her empty cup, Elizabeth said casually, "Do you miss him?"

Mihaela rested her head against the back of the chair. "I like to hear from him. I miss the idea, the illusion of someone being there. Maybe I'm getting too old to be a hunter."

"Take a holiday. A sabbatical. Hell, you've done more than your duty a hundred times over—retire."

"That's the weird thing. I don't want that either." She turned her head to look at Elizabeth with a hint of humor. "At the risk of sounding clichéd, a hunter isn't what I am; it's who I am."

Elizabeth stared at her. "Do you never think you might be more?"

Mihaela's gaze held, then fell, as her lips twisted into a smile. "No."

Elizabeth rose and hugged her hard. "You're a very wonderful person," she said, and before Mihaela could recover from her surprise, she released her and left the kitchen. But Mihaela got the last word.

"You're just saying that because I make better coffee than you."

Elizabeth laughed and went on up to her bedroom, both warmed and worried by the tête-à-tête with Mihaela.

Only when she stood under the shower, constantly peering through the spray at the bathroom door, did it come to her that the house no longer felt safe.

"They're dead," said Luk.

In contrast to his previous behavior, characterized by stillness and long periods of blank moroseness, he was striding back and forth without pause across the cottage's one downstairs room. They'd killed the cottage's occupants, Luk feeding with distracted efficiency. And now, with the sun fully up, he still wouldn't rest.

With triumphant excitement, not unmixed with wariness, Dante recognized that Luk's memory was returning to him, bringing with it knowledge of his old talents and powers, his old grudges and enmities. This would be an important turning point for Dante, when he could easily lose his dominance, even his influence over his maker. And yet he had to feed the hatred of Saloman.

Shit, that encounter in the hills had been close. Dante had seen it all slipping away from him as Luk wept blood in his cousin's arms. Fortunately, that had been a passing phase. Luk's emotions toward his killer now were satisfyingly murderous.

"Dead?" Dante said eagerly. "*All* the hunters? And Elizabeth Silk? The Awakener?"

Luk waved one impatient hand. "No. The vampires you sent against them."

"Damn," Dante said, annoyed. "We needed those vampires. So Saloman went back to the hunters after all?"

"No. He stayed close to us for most of the night. The hunters and Tsigana's descendant killed the vampires."

Dante shut his mouth.

"Hunters are powerful enemies. They have experience killing vampires, and each kill makes them stronger. Did you not know that?"

"No," said Dante, increasingly annoyed.

"And yet I thought you were once a hunter Grand Master."

"Did I tell you that? I was. But to be honest, it was a largely honorary position, and I was more interested in the vampires than the hunters. Can you really tell that the vampires are dead, and who killed them?"

"Of course," Luk said, not even sparing a pause in his pacing.

"Will I be able to do that kind of thing too?"

"In time. You have a lot to learn. You want to run before you can stand." Now Luk did vary his stride, veering toward his creation, his expression thoughtful. "But maybe that is good. Even necessary." He came to a standstill, gazing into Dante's eyes with an intensity that hurt. "We need support," he said abruptly. "Much more support."

"Agreed. A rebellion against Saloman's rule is rumbling just below the surface all over this country. In Istanbul, it's well under way. You'd make an excellent leader."

Luk appeared to accept that as his due rather than as the dubious flattery Dante had employed. "Good," he said with a decisive nod. "Then we'll gather support there, and then make our way to Budapest."

"Budapest?" Dante repeated, startled. "But the rebellion's base is here! It needs to spread all over the world! Besides, Budapest is Saloman's more than any other city in the world! We'll need to be *much* stronger before we can attack him there!"

Luk smiled unpleasantly. "Before it was Saloman's, it was mine." With sudden violence, he swept all the used crockery off the table in an almighty crash that caused the other vampires slumped in the corners to leap to their feet in alarm. "There are many ways to fight," Luk snarled. "My cousin will suffer and die, and the twin towns of Buda and Pest will see the dawn of the new age. That was always written."

"Was it?" Dante said doubtfully. Luk's memories and gifts may have been returning to him, but he didn't appear to be any saner.

"Oh, yes. We need a vehicle," Luk added abruptly. "Like the ones in the village. We used to have one, before the others found us. Can you get us another?"

Dante nodded eagerly. "Sure. And with a few adjustments—paint out the windows, that sort of thing—we can even travel by day too."

Luk slapped him on the back. "I'm beginning to like this new age. You must instruct me as we go, and I will instruct *you* in the ways of the undead."

"Deal," said Dante fervently. He began to hope again.

* * *

Unease stayed with Elizabeth as she walked out of the bathroom into the bedroom. She couldn't help the quick, anxious glances she cast toward each window and the bedroom door in turn. With the curtains still closed, the streaming sunlight was dimmed and the whole room seemed full of shadows she hadn't noticed before. Her spine prickled. Despite the heat of the early morning, she wished she hadn't put the air-conditioning on. It drowned out the tiny sounds that might give her warning.

Warning of what? she derided herself. It was daylight, the sun bright and intense enough to burn a human, never mind a vampire. But reason had little to do with this fear; it was heightened by the sense of invasion, because this house, however temporarily, was *theirs*. And she recognized what Mihaela had been dealing with on a far larger scale for most of her life.

As she approached the bed, holding her towel under chin like a shield from the threat that couldn't be there, a shadow moved in the corner by the window. Reason snapped. She jumped, grabbing up the already used stake from the night table, and stood poised, staring at the still-moving shadow that seemed to detach itself from the curtain. A big, tall shadow that would always be threatening, because it reflected the lethal body of Saloman.

Relief washed over her fear, leaving her weak and pointlessly irritated. "What the hell are you doing skulking there?"

"I do not skulk," Saloman said. For once, Elizabeth didn't know whether he was joking. "I was merely admiring your view while avoiding the sun."

Elizabeth dropped onto the bed, hurling the stake down beside her so hard that it bounced. "I still don't see how you got up here in this." She waved her hand at the window, indicating the strong sunlight.

Saloman's gaze lifted from her towel to her face. "I came in at dawn, singed but undamaged. Thank you for asking." He stood very still at the foot of the bed. "I perceive the conquest of your night visitors has not sweetened your temper."

Elizabeth grasped a handful of her damp hair and tugged. This wasn't how she'd meant it to be. She'd planned to welcome Saloman with open arms to make up for sending him away the last time. She wanted him; she wanted his arms hard around her, wanted him buried deep inside her, loving her, rocking her to the blind, addictive ecstasy only he had ever brought her. More than that, she craved his presence, as necessary to her now as breathing. And she knew that in denying him when he needed her, she'd let him down. If he'd wished to lose himself in sex with her, she should have taken that as a compliment rather than an insult. What was her incomprehensible, even childish, need for outward "respect" beside the facts of need and love?

And yet here she was bitching at him again like a nagging wife berating her husband for staying out all night even though she'd changed the locks.

She found herself staring at her hand in her lap, longing to make things right and yet somehow incapable of finding the way, or even the words.

"Elizabeth." She hadn't felt him move, but he was crouched at her feet, his strong, cool hand covering hers in her lap. Every nerve leapt at his touch. As if he'd pressed a button, her lips tugged upward in instant response.

"You know about our visitors?" she managed.

"I can feel them," he said with a hint of impatience. "I confess I didn't expect them to attack this place, but I knew you and the hunters could defeat them. Was it difficult?"

"It might have been. They broke into Konrad's room and could have killed him. I was awake—maybe I heard something, sensed them; I don't know. I just felt something was wrong, so I was prepared." She turned her hand in his to grasp his fingers. "It shook all of us, me included. I'd grown too confident, too . . . *smug*." She gave a quick smile. "Maybe I'm just angry because I liked this house and now it isn't safe. And I'm afraid I'll never feel safe again." *When you aren't here.*

She didn't like that either. She wanted to be independent of his power, and she wanted him to know it. Even though she couldn't help but benefit from the umbrella of his protection now that most vampires in the world knew she was Saloman's companion. Well, apparently there were vampires to whom that made her not out-of-bounds but a desirable target.

She realized she was agitatedly rubbing his fingers between her own and forced herself to stop. Saloman gazed at her consideringly. There was no anger in his dark, opaque eyes. Somewhere close to the surface lurked the flames of lust that sparked an inevitable response in the pit of her stomach.

But his words had nothing to do with sex. "You woke early. Like a mother who wakens before her baby cries. You sensed my presence, although not my identity, as you came into the room, even though I was masking."

Elizabeth frowned. "You mean I can use that instinct? Develop it to protect myself and my friends?"

"Of course. We are all vulnerable at times, even I."

Her heart melted, because she knew that. "How do you deal with it?" she whispered. She wasn't sure if she meant the physical vulnerability or the emotional one. Saloman took it as the former.

"I enchant my homes, my resting places, so that no one can enter without my permission. I believe you have that aptitude because of your ancestry." He rose fluidly to his feet, drawing her with him.

For an instant they stood close together, and Elizabeth heard the drumming of her own heart. She wanted to feel his too, slow and strong, vibrating through her aching, peaking breasts. Moisture that had nothing to do with her recent shower pooled between her thighs. The texture of his lips fascinated her as they moved in the half smile that never quite formed before it faded. She knew that gesture, in conjunction with the amber glint flaming in his black eyes. He desired her. Flushed with yearning, she tilted her face in open invitation. Saloman's kiss . . .

"Come," he said gently.

Her eyes flew open as she realized he wasn't leading her to bed, but to the window.

"Make yourself safe," he said. "Enchant your castle."

Chapter Seven

Saloman was proud. Hesitant, doubting as always of her own abilities, she had stumbled at first, but then, sensing the power of his own enchantments as he made and broke them to demonstrate, she began to concentrate, to give her considerable strength and intellect to learning. And when she finally "locked" the window with the spell and won his praise, she gave a crow of triumph that made him smile.

"So *anyone* can learn to do this?"

"Not anyone. Vampires, if they trouble to learn. A few rare humans."

She glanced at him with a hint of doubt. "Dante and I are part of the same exclusive club?" She knew Dante had used rudimentary enchantments in the past, not least to reinforce the underground hideout in the Buda labyrinth where the senator had imprisoned Dmitriu and Josh Alexander.

"Something like that," Saloman admitted.

"I don't think I want to join."

"You have no say in the matter. Your bloodline has determined it."

Her eyelids drooped, hiding her open, expressive eyes. "Tsigana again," she said, carefully expressionless.

He was glad to disabuse her. "In this case, not Tsigana. This gift—this gene, if you will—comes through another ancestor; precisely which now is impossible to tell. It wasn't even latent in Tsigana. But I believe her descendant Josh has it in a very latent form. In you, it's strong already and growing."

"Really? Can I enchant this other window on my own?"

"Probably." He leaned his shoulder against the wall and watched her as she tried. In nothing but a large towel precariously tied over her breasts, and with a frown of concentration between her delicate brows, she looked adorable—openly delighted to have discovered a new talent and throwing herself wholeheartedly into learning the details.

She stumbled over the unfamiliar words in the Ancient tongue, and had to be reminded of one of the more necessary gestures, but her focus was perfect, and Saloman was able to tell her in all honesty that very few vampires would be able to break through her new lock.

"Dante?" she asked.

He shook his head. "Nor anyone with him, except Luk. But then, Luk is a master of such enchantments."

"And you?"

"I learned from Luk."

"So how come random humans, like Dante and Josh and me, have this gene?"

"Inherited from my people."

Her eyes widened, staring into his. He wanted to take her in his arms and kiss her stunned lips, because this was one human he was happy to share his ancestry with. He'd suspected before, as her telepathy grew, had tried not to hope too much, because of the warmth that crept into his jaded heart at the thought that Elizabeth was part of his past as well as his present. He couldn't help the yearning for that extra closeness, even while he pushed it away. Just for a moment, exultant, he gave in to the happiness.

"How is that possible?" she managed.

"My people weren't all undead, as you know. A few of my living race coupled with humans and produced offspring in whom the gift was mostly latent. Few among those ever discover their gifts, let alone understand where they come from."

"You mean psychics, telepaths, those who claim other paranormal powers, are actually descended from live Ancients?"

"Probably, yes—the few among the fakes who are genuine."

"Cyn in New York," she murmured. "She senses vampires, knows where they've been. And John Ramsay heard the telepathic conversations of vampires. They must have your gene." The growing excitement lighting her face faded. "And Dante, who, like me, has the aptitude to enchant."

Saloman stirred. "Dante doesn't realize the rarity of his aptitude. He believes it to be a merely neglected art. But the gift makes him doubly dangerous, adding it to the fact that he isn't merely a vampire but Luk's creation."

Something like bleakness entered her eyes. "And me? Am I dangerous?"

"The gift does not make you dangerous. What you do with it does. In the short term, I suggest what you do with it is secure this house for yourself and your friends."

To his relief, she brightened again and whirled away, gathering underwear and a dress from the cupboard before she shrugged off her towel and dressed while bombarding him with questions about the details of the enchantments, who of her acquaintances could perform them, how, on what, and for how long they worked.

Saloman answered to the best of his ability while devouring her nakedness with hungry eyes. Although he hadn't fed last night and he needed blood, he wanted sex more. She wanted it too; he'd smelled her arousal since she'd first seen him, and he didn't doubt his ability to distract her from her enchanting mission. Seducing her would be deliciously easy. There was nothing he desired more than passing the hours of daylight buried deep in her delectable body, sweeping her from climax to climax, each more shattering than the last, until she was as lost as he. The ferocity of her passion would feed his own, and his appetite was voracious.

But he'd already offended her with his urgency. However much she'd enjoyed the experience in the hills, it had still hurt her, and although he didn't understand why, he refused to risk that hurt again, even for the rampant urge to take her and dominate her, to pleasure her and lose himself in her beauty. To have Elizabeth.

His loins ached. He had to move, to walk around the room, uncomfortably, in order to stop himself from seizing her and hurling her onto the bed. But he did so without for an instant removing his gaze from her. He longed to feel her surrender, hear her gasp with the pleasure of his caresses and scream his name at the moment of orgasm. It felt like pain.

Savoring the experience, like most in his very long life, he watched her pull the dress over her body and grab the comb. "Let me," he said, and walked toward her.

Taking the comb from her limp fingers, he met her surprised gaze and smiled as he began to run it through her long red-gold hair. Yes, there was new pleasure in this restraint, in being so close to her that he felt the heat of her aroused body and saw the tiniest hairs fluttering on her heated skin, and yet doing nothing to satisfy either of them. Only when her hair was smooth and untangled did he return the comb to her, and then, as their fingers met, he bent his head and kissed her trembling mouth.

Her lips parted instantly, hot and welcoming, as if almost relieved to enjoy his kiss. He savored her response, her taste, took her tongue into his mouth and caressed it with his. Her free hand crept around his neck, holding him closer. She pressed her soft body into him, fitting over the painful hardness of his erection, grinding herself into it, and he had to hold ever tighter to that fading restraint.

He let her feel his vampire teeth, because it always made her breath quicken, and he loved that he could bite her so easily and draw her strong, delicious blood into himself. He could, but on this occasion he didn't. He took nothing but her kiss, for as long as she could still breathe. And when that became harder for her, he released her mouth and drew back.

"Enchant," he commanded once more.

Conflict waged across her expressive face. Her reddened lips were alluringly wanton, her eyes cloudy with desire. They seemed to darken as she contemplated seducing him, and then her eyelids drooped, veiling them as, inevitably, she contemplated rejection. And the necessity of making the house safe. He made it easy for her.

"Display your gift to your friends."

Her lips parted again. "Is that what this is about?"

"No. But it's a fringe benefit I don't object to. All who practice inhuman magic are not evil."

Rueful amusement chased frustration from her eyes. "Do you ever stop planning and calculating?" she demanded, giving in and turning toward the door.

"Yes."

She glanced back over her shoulder, uncertain, but he only smiled and ushered her downstairs.

There was a small window halfway down the spiral staircase—not of a huge amount of use to an attacker, but a weakness nevertheless. Elizabeth was doing very well with it when the female hunter, Mihaela, suddenly came out of the middle bedroom and stood staring up at them. Distracted, Elizabeth broke off to look down at her friend and the enchantment unraveled.

"What the hell are you doing?" Mihaela said. She stared not at Elizabeth but at Saloman.

"Enchanting," Elizabeth said excitedly. "Saloman's teaching me. It'll keep the house safe from attacks like last night's."

Konrad, the descendant of Ferenc, appeared from the nearest room. The Hungarian, István, came running upstairs to see what was going on. Saloman sighed and sat down on the stairs.

"Is that what *he* says?" Konrad demanded.

"Yes," Elizabeth answered, with just a hint of defiance. "That's what he says."

"And by the time we discover it's no more than mumbo jumbo it's too late to realize you've just been lulled into a false sense of security!"

"Oh, Konrad, for—" Elizabeth began.

"What would be the point?" Saloman interrupted. Although he didn't trouble to raise his voice, it cut through the rising irritation in Elizabeth's without trouble, and she bit her lip to prevent the words she'd regret from tumbling out.

The hunters all stared at him.

He said mildly, "I am in your house. If I choose to consume a banquet of hunters, I am already in the perfect position."

Konrad's eyes flickered. "Yes, thanks for that, Elizabeth."

Elizabeth's eyes flashed with anger, making her look rather splendid as well as incredibly beautiful. But she had herself under control now. She simply said, "You're welcome. Well, Konrad, I want to make the house safe for us. If you don't believe in the mumbo jumbo, despite Budapest in May, when you saw the vampire Travis's enchanting in practice—and Dante's—you'll have no objection to my performing it in your room. Though with any luck you can take the boards down and even the mosquitoes won't get in."

With which she took a deep breath and turned back to Saloman. "Do I need to start again?"

He inclined his head, and she began again to enchant

the window on the stairs. As she did so, he listened, correcting the odd word or sign when necessary while keeping his gaze on the silently watching hunters.

After exchanging a quick glance with her colleagues, Mihaela simply watched Elizabeth, a sharp frown of anxiety marring a brow that carried too much care already. István and Konrad stood behind her, exchanging low-voiced plans that they seemed to imagine Saloman couldn't hear. Fortunately, they didn't act on any of them.

When Saloman, from his seat on the step, pronounced himself satisfied, Elizabeth gave a triumphant grin, as if she'd passed a particularly difficult school examination, and ran downstairs to the ground floor.

Saloman rose to his feet. As he descended the stairs, the hunters fell back to let him pass. It might have been progress.

There were many entrances to secure on the ground floor: not only the front door and windows, but French doors opening onto the garden too. Although Elizabeth went to work with enthusiasm and growing skill, she refused to recognize her tiredness.

Rest, he commanded inside her head.

When I've finished, she insisted.

She was enjoying herself, getting some kind of exultation out of the spells themselves. Saloman thought back over the centuries and with difficulty remembered something very similar. He'd been a child, barely twelve years old in his first existence. His father, eternally critical, had been dismissive of his early attempts, insisting he had no aptitude, that there was no strength in his mind to support even the weakest enchantment. But Luk, already undead, a powerful and respected seer, had shown him otherwise.

For an instant Saloman lost himself in the memory of running in huge excitement from dwelling to dwelling and on into the forest, enchanting whatever caught his attention. He'd laughed between spells, feeling his energy soar, and with it new happiness and triumph. Luk had watched him with indulgent pride, smiling. Afterward, Saloman had slept for two days. His parents had received several complaints because the villagers couldn't get into their houses; the other children had found that certain favored trees in the forest had become inexplicably impossible to climb.

And so Saloman smiled at Elizabeth's pleasure mirroring his own, and secretly patched up the mistakes her tiredness began to cause her to make. Later, he'd hammer home the importance of thoroughness; for now, she should enjoy her triumph, as he had done.

The hunters stood or sat watching in the background. When Elizabeth asked permission to secure their bedrooms, they merely shrugged. But only Mihaela accompanied her upstairs.

Konrad shouted after them, "I don't want *him* in my room!"

Saloman sighed. "It's as well I've become inured over the centuries to human ingratitude."

"What have humans got to be grateful to you for?" Mihaela snapped over her shoulder. "Apart from a race of bloodsucking killers stalking their streets."

Elizabeth, her hand lifting to Konrad's broken window, paused. Her slightly glazed eyes focused on Mihaela, then flickered to Saloman and back. She frowned, parting her lips to speak. But this was not the time, not for Elizabeth.

"Enchant," he said. "Talk later."

She no longer ran from window to window. Her feet dragged. By the time they stood in the third bedroom, Mihaela's, her words were slurring and Saloman had to hold her hand to the window.

Mihaela, who'd been watching stony-faced in the doorway, moved forward in clear alarm, but with gritty determination, Elizabeth forced herself through the ritual, although when she finished and turned away with relief, she stumbled and Saloman had to catch her in his arms.

Clever girl. I knew you could do it. Your gift is strong.

She smiled sleepily into his shoulder, warm with gratitude and pride in herself.

"What's wrong?" Mihaela asked, fright making her voice too high and loud. "What's happening to her?"

"She's exhausted. It uses considerable energy, and this is all new to her. She'll sleep now."

He brushed past the hunter, carrying Elizabeth into the hallway and on up to her bedroom. Concentrating on Elizabeth, he soothed her overexcited, weary mind to make it possible for her to sleep. Somewhere, she fought him, determined to enjoy her new skill as sometimes she resisted sleep to enjoy more loving with him; but behind that was recognition of his care, and gratitude shown in the faint fluttering caress of her mind against his. He'd never felt that before, and it moved him unbearably.

The hunter's sharp, determined footsteps dogging his irritated him. Ignoring her, he laid Elizabeth on the bed and smoothed the hair from her face. She smiled, turning into his hand so that it lay under her cheek. If the hunter had not been there, he would have kissed her. As it was, he contented himself with a faint caress of his fingers on her face before sliding them free as she drifted into the sleep of recovery.

Mihaela stood at the foot of the bed, white-faced and thin-lipped. Hostility radiated from her, and yet, recognizing that it came more from love of Elizabeth than hatred of him, he found himself warming toward her.

"She needs to sleep," he said as he straightened. "After that, she will be fine."

Mihaela's gaze flew up to him, then back to her friend. "Isn't it enough for you to have her in thrall?" she said intensely. "Does she have to be like you too?"

Saloman regarded her. "She doesn't have to be or do anything. She makes choices."

"Some choices she shouldn't *have* to make!" Mihaela swung away from him, her steps quick and angry.

"She should, perhaps, be kept in ignorance, hearing only one side of a story? Like you?"

Mihaela spun back, her large, dark eyes spitting with rage. "Oh, trust me, I've had all the information I need to choose sides since I was eight years old!"

Saloman could have looked, read it from her mind faster than she could consciously think it. But there was no need. He could guess most of it. "I'm sorry for your pain."

The anger that had flushed her pale face drained away, leaving only the pain itself—and something like bafflement. She let out a brief, humorless laugh. "Shit, you're good. I almost believe you. What is it you want, Saloman?"

Saloman raised one eyebrow. "From her or from you?"

Her eyes narrowed. "Is that what this is about? Are you using her to get to us? Why?"

"No," said Saloman, with perfect truth. Although, as he'd already told Elizabeth, he never objected to side benefits. "From the moment I took her from the Angel in Budapest, there has been no compulsion. She chooses to be with me from love."

Mihaela's lip curled. "Yes? Then why doesn't she choose it more often?"

Her words were like the twist of a wooden stake already buried in his flesh and so familiar that most of the time it went almost unnoticed. Although Elizabeth had promised to make her second home wherever he was, she came to him all too rarely. He didn't care to be reminded of the fact. For the first time in many years, he found it difficult to hold a human's gaze.

"She has her own life," he said evenly. "As you do."

"She certainly deserves her own life," Mihaela countered. "A husband and children. Mutual trust and respect."

Trust. "Shit, you're good," he mocked. "I almost believe you. But I think you're projecting your own desires rather than Elizabeth's."

Her breath caught; the hectic flush came back. But although her voice shook, she spoke still with furious intensity. "Why can't you just leave her alone?"

"As you are?" Saloman inquired, strolling past her to open the bedroom door. "Does being alone make you happy, Mihaela?"

He held the door open for her, and the struggle over whether to obey his clear command was waged visibly across her face. At last, with a quick glance back at Elizabeth, she snapped, "Happier than I would be enslaved to a bloodsucking killer."

She brushed past him out of the room, and Saloman, prepared now to follow where the discussion led, stepped over the threshold and closed the door behind him.

Mihaela halted on the first step and turned to face him with conscious bravery. Saloman liked her. Loneliness was something he recognized all too easily, and he wished better for the troubled hunter.

"Elizabeth is my friend," she said carefully, as if this were something he might not understand. "I care for her."

"I know that," he said gravely.

Her tongue flickered out, licking her dry lips. Behind the repression, he suspected, lurked a passionate woman capable of great happiness. "Sometimes," she muttered, "it has crossed my mind that in your own way, you also care for her."

"How very perceptive of you."

Under his mockery, her indignation rallied. "Yes," she agreed, "it is. Because your way isn't hers; you must see that. You don't, you *can't*, understand each other."

"Difference does not preclude understanding."

"No, but it makes it bloody difficult," Mihaela retorted. "If you weren't so damned smug, you'd *know* that you don't understand her. You haven't the faintest inkling that you make her unhappy. You've no idea that it hurts her not to travel with you, that you don't trust her enough to tell her where you are. You treat her like a pet! 'Come, Elizabeth, here's your petting ration for the month. Now go and play with your trivial friends while I'm busy with grown-up things like bloodsucking, murder, and world domination.' And trust me, Saloman, she wouldn't tolerate even that if she thought you knew what it did to her. So she hides it from you. She pretends she doesn't care about the hurt because *she* doesn't trust *you* enough to show it!"

Mihaela pressed herself back into the wall, probably with terror, reminding Saloman to resume control of his facial features.

What a pity I promised Elizabeth not to kill her friends.

Mihaela's brown eyes were huge in her pale face. Under his haughty stare, the flash of defiance died into something closer to a plea.

"You must see that's no way for her to live," she whispered. "She's losing everything she is, everything that makes her Elizabeth, just to spend a few days a year with you. Her whole life could disappear like that if you don't free her. Don't make her grow old and die like this. While you live on and on, if—"

She broke off to catch her breath.

"If someone doesn't manage to stake me?" Saloman supplied. The hunter's words shook him, angered him, mixing truth with possibility, untruth with a disturbing perception that owed nothing to telepathy and everything to intelligent humanity. He managed, not without difficulty, to hold on to his own intelligence, his own plans.

Leaning his head to one side, he regarded Mihaela. "You are a good and decent being," he observed. "I can see why Elizabeth loves you. But your sharp perception is somewhat blinkered. Is a glass half-empty or half-full? Do we concentrate on the differences or on the similarities?"

Mihaela frowned, but didn't interrupt. Saloman let his lips curve. "I don't hate you because some other human chained up my friend, tortured him, and starved him. Why should you hate me for what some other vampire did to you or yours?"

"I've fought vampires all my life. I've met, observed, and killed rather more than a few!"

"But you're always fighting the same one, aren't you, Mihaela?" he said softly, and at last she tore her gaze free.

"What has this got to do with you and Elizabeth?" she all but snarled.

"Everything," said Saloman. "You misjudge me as you misjudge my people. There is good even in modern vampires, although they need to be taught and disciplined."

"They need to be eradicated!"

Saloman smiled. "Once a hunter, always a hunter; once a vampire, always a vicious, thoughtless killer. That is no way to move forward. Would it surprise you to know that my people walked the earth before yours could stand upright? Yet I would not take the world from you. I merely deny your right to take it from me. We lived together before; we can do so again."

"As human slaves?" Mihaela said with contempt. "I don't think so."

"I do not want slaves. Neither Elizabeth nor anyone else."

Saloman smiled and waited until he was sure she could think of nothing to say, and then he inclined his head with civility and, opening the bedroom door, stepped back inside.

Mihaela went slowly downstairs and into the kitchen, where she grabbed the coffeepot and sloshed the remaining coffee into a cup. It looked like mud, but she stirred in two spoonfuls of sugar and gulped it down.

From the French window, Konrad turned and watched her.

István, his laptop open in front of him at the dining room table, swiveled in his chair. "Everything okay?"

Mihaela's hands shook as she laid the cup noisily back on its saucer. "That guy scares the shit out of me."

Konrad strode toward her. István stood up.

"Did he—" Konrad began.

Mihaela flapped one hand. "No, no. He's under some sort of promise to Elizabeth that he seems prepared to keep. He never touched me or her in that way. It's just . . ." She sighed and flopped into the chair beside István. "He's *big*. Everything about him is big, overwhelming. But the really scary bit is when he starts to make sense."

But I won't give in. And I won't let him have Elizabeth.

Chapter Eight

Elizabeth's dream was intense and sexy, and when she awoke, the first person she saw was Saloman. Although she'd been reluctant to leave the dream, it faded quickly as she realized reality was at least as good.

He sat on the bed, so close to her that the sleeve of his snowy white shirt stirred to the rhythm of her breath. His dark gaze held hers, and butterflies swooped in her stomach. She smiled. "Hello."

"Hello. You have visitors."

Bugger. The flicker of his eyes warned her they were in this room, not waiting for her elsewhere. She sat up as she turned on the bed and saw all three hunters lined up between her and the bedroom door.

"What's happening?" she said weakly.

"We have a lead on the vampires. Mustafa and the others found two bodies in an isolated cottage."

Elizabeth's false, cozy happiness slid away, leaving her cold. She glanced at Saloman. "Does it tie in with your observations? Do we know if it's where you left them?"

"It *is* where I left them."

The hunters glared at him. "Why the hell didn't you say?" Konrad demanded.

"You didn't ask me. It doesn't matter. They're not there now."

"We know that, but they must be close by. Judging by when the owners were killed, it was almost dawn."

"They're a hundred miles east of the cottage. And traveling."

"How?"

"Internal combustion engine," Saloman said dryly.

István was frowning. "How could they go out and steal a car in daylight?"

"Someone must have been unfortunate enough to visit the cottage," Elizabeth said. She turned again to Saloman. "Do you know where they're going?"

"Right now? No."

"Can we catch up with them?"

"Probably not; your detectors don't have enough range."

"If you were with us . . ." Elizabeth urged.

"I have to go to Istanbul, and then Budapest."

He could, she thought, deprive her of breath in so many different ways. "Now? Why?"

"Because there is unrest in Istanbul that I cannot rely on my friends to deal with, and Budapest is where Luk will go. Ultimately."

"To fight you?"

Saloman shrugged.

"But he doesn't remember who you are! Or even who *he* is."

"He does now."

The thin patience of his answers warned her not to press, but this was too important to leave. "You saw him," she breathed.

"I spoke to him. And now he's remembering."

Elizabeth searched his veiled eyes, looking, as always, for the things he didn't say. She thought she found some of them, and the ache in her heart intensified. "People are dying, Saloman," she whispered. "We have to try to stop him."

"We can't," Saloman said flatly. "Chasing him will not stop him; he'll always be one step ahead. All I can do is limit the damage in Istanbul. When he's ready, he'll come to Budapest for me."

"*We* have to try to stop him before he gets to Istanbul," Mihaela said grimly, with emphasis on the "we." "If that's where he's going. He's killing all along the way."

"We do," Elizabeth confirmed, reaching for his hand and pressing his fingers between her own. His eyes searched her face, looking, she hoped, for what she wanted him to understand: that here was another chance to work with the hunters as well as deal with his own problem.

Saloman drew his hand free and rose to his feet. "Twenty-four hours," he said. "And then I leave for Istanbul."

He walked out of the room with perfect grace, and without turning back. Mihaela lifted her brows in Elizabeth's direction. "Hey, at least he tells you where he's going."

"This is stupid," Konrad muttered, pausing just outside the front door. Saloman's hired car, a Mercedes with tinted windows, waited right in front of him with its engine running. Saloman himself sat in the driver's seat, wearing sunglasses, his long, slender hands resting so comfortably on the lower part of the steering wheel that he looked as if he'd been used to driving for decades. "I still think we should take both the cars."

"He'll be easier to keep track of this way," Mihaela said.

"He could kill us all like this and just walk away from the crash."

"He could," István said judiciously, "kill us all at any time. There isn't really much any of us could do to stop him. Besides, he wouldn't kill Elizabeth."

"Not deliberately, perhaps," Konrad muttered. "Can he even drive? Who the hell taught him?"

"Some joyriding hooligans on a Budapest housing estate," Elizabeth said with relish, brushing past him to open the front passenger door.

"What a comfort you are to us all," Mihaela marveled as she reached for the one behind.

By late afternoon, when they halted in a small town to pick up some bottles of water and some *pide*—rather tasty Turkish pizza bread—familiarity had at least reached the point where István was prepared to take the front seat beside Saloman in order to stretch out his long legs.

For a moment, after they all piled back into the car, Saloman didn't move. They'd parked in the village square, under the shade of a large almond tree, and he appeared to be watching a group of men climbing the stairs into the mosque at the far end of the square.

He said, "Luk is masking. I can no longer follow them."

The hunters exchanged glances. István said, "Are you out of range, perhaps?"

Saloman turned his head. "Range is unimportant. Luk has remembered his skills, and they far surpass Dante's feeble efforts. Luk will not be found until he chooses to be."

"But he must leave some kind of trail," Mihaela interjected.

"Of bodies? Perhaps. But he isn't a fool."

"What the hell is he doing?" Konrad demanded, dragging his hand through his hair in frustration. Elizabeth leaned closer to Mihaela to avoid his threatening elbow. "Where is he going?"

Saloman shrugged. "Gathering support so that he can enter Istanbul with a strong bodyguard. He knows you're looking for him, knows you've already killed some of his followers. He wants peace to recruit—to gather strength as well as vampires."

"Can't we stop him?" Elizabeth asked.

"Not until he comes to us."

"But then he'll be too strong!"

Saloman turned his shades in her direction. "I've defeated him before."

Elizabeth drew in her breath, glancing around the uneasy hunters. "What do you want to do?" she asked them.

"We can't take his word," Konrad snapped. "We have to look."

"Where?" Saloman asked mildly.

"Where you lost the trail would be a good start."

"In what way," Saloman asked with interest, "would it be a good start?"

Konrad scowled. "You promised us twenty-four hours."

Saloman straightened and started the car. "The scenery is very pretty. You'll enjoy it."

For the next two hours, Saloman appeared to turn himself into their tour guide. Elizabeth, convinced he began the game to make the point that they were wasting their time, suspected he soon started to enjoy it. His stark pointing out of beauty spots and famous views grew richer with stories and names from the past and histories that she was sure never made it into books.

At first stunned, even suspicious, the hunters didn't seem able to stop themselves from asking questions, and as they fell under his spell, Elizabeth felt an emotion akin to pride in all of them. Even when the light faded and darkness fell, and they could no longer make out with any clarity the mountain peaks or dry riverbeds that inspired him, still they listened and questioned.

And then Saloman stopped the car. There appeared to be no reason for it, on a winding road between villages, with no view to speak of, no houses to be suspicious of. Saloman gazed out of his side window, and some distance from the road, across scrubby ground,

Elizabeth could just make out a few uneven shapes, perhaps a camp of caravans and tents.

"Gypsies?" Elizabeth hazarded.

"Or itinerant workers. Once."

"Once?"

Saloman opened his door. "The only life there is the animals."

Peering into the gloom, Elizabeth caught the faint movement of a goat and some horses standing tethered in the shade of a large bush. She had a bad feeling. "Maybe they're away working," she tried, as she got out of the car.

"In the dark?" Mihaela said, following Saloman across the road.

"Eating, then."

Saloman said, "It smells of death. If you prefer, I will look."

"We don't prefer," Konrad said tightly.

There was no one left alive. The vampires had been on a spree, draining and dropping the bodies where they found them. A caravan had been turned on its side, perhaps to empty out its terrified occupants, who now lay sprawled and grotesquely bloodless around it. A tent had half fallen in someone's struggle to escape. A couple had been dropped contemptuously one on top of the other.

It wasn't gory, because very little blood had been wasted, and yet somehow that seemed to add to the horror of the scene. The whole camp stank of rotting corpses. Flies buzzed around them, and the air, redolent with death, seemed to hang still and heavy and eerie.

Quelling her rebellious stomach, Elizabeth watched Saloman picking his way through the carnage, looking inside caravans and tents, lifting wrecked doors, discarded clothing, and even other bodies in order to gaze on the faces of the dead. Their pale skin seemed almost to glow in the darkness. For an instant, she saw him through the hunters' eyes, a tall, beautiful angel of death moving gracefully, callously, among the victims of his kind.

Her throat constricted with the fear that always came with recognition of his sheer alienness. She couldn't help but share the hunters' horror, the outrage that held them tense and ready to lash out.

"And you tried to tell me there is good in these creatures." Mihaela's husky voice almost choked. "For God's sake, where is the good in this?"

Saloman, having pulled a body free of the fallen caravan, rose to his feet. He didn't look at Mihaela or Elizabeth, just at the white, rotting corpse. He said, "It is hard to envisage any circumstances in which this could be construed as good."

"Like a certain farmhouse near Bistrița?" Mihaela said harshly.

That wasn't fair. Zoltán and his followers had committed those crimes in the farmhouse. The only life Saloman had taken was that of a woman already damaged beyond recovery by Zoltán's vampires. But Elizabeth's defense of him died in her throat unspoken, repressed by the current horror, or perhaps by the knowledge that whatever she said now would sound like an excuse.

"Yes," said Saloman briefly.

Konrad spun away. "Tell Mustafa," he ordered, marching back toward the car. István already had his phone in his hand.

Elizabeth said low, "The hunter network will arrange the burial."

Saloman nodded once.

"Why?" Elizabeth said helplessly. "If, as you say, Luk's memory is returning, and he's hiding from you, why leave this open carnage behind him? Is he really that insane?"

Saloman gazed upward at the sky, almost as if he hoped to find an answer there. "Sanity is relative. I think he's warning the hunters. And greeting me."

"Like Leith?" Mihaela blurted. Leith, Scotland, where,

last October, the corpses of four young men had been discovered with their throats torn and their blood drained.

"Yes," Saloman said again, indifferently. "Like Leith."

"Was Zoltán insane too?" Mihaela snapped.

"No. It was I who killed the men in Leith, and they were not innocent."

Speechless, Mihaela stared from him to Elizabeth. "Jesus Christ," she whispered at last, and, turning, she all but ran across the ground toward the car.

"Somehow," said Saloman, "I think you're back in the front seat."

She stepped nearer to him and slid her hand into his. "If they don't drive off without us."

"Oh, they won't do that. They still think I can find Luk. I can't."

Something in his voice alerted her, causing her to stare at him through the darkness. "And if you could," she whispered, "would you?"

He said nothing, just began to walk after the others.

"Saloman." She tightened her grip on his hand. "Saloman, why did you leave them at the cottage? Why did you come back to the villa?"

"Blood and sex. I wanted to make love to you."

The smell, the horror behind them, all made this the wrong place. "You didn't," she managed.

"I'm still here. Unfortunately, so are the hunters, and I believe the sight of me fucking their friend among this carnage would ruin my chances of détente forever. I can't imagine it would do me much good with you either."

"Saloman—"

"I really don't know where they are," he interrupted. "They're probably headed for Istanbul, but they won't hang around long enough to be caught."

Elizabeth released his hand. She felt cold.

As Saloman had predicted, all three hunters were huddled symbolically in the backseat. Elizabeth climbed in and fastened her belt. Saloman sat beside her, close enough to touch, yet distant enough to be on the other side of the world. He looked in his rearview mirror at the hunters. "Where to?"

"Do you know which road they took out of here?"

"This one."

"Then follow it; see if you can pick up any more trails."

Please, God, no more like this one.

Saloman started the car and drove on up the hill. Without any instruction from the hunters he avoided the fork in the road that led into the next village, and turned east. No one asked, but inexplicably the mood began to alter to one of hope, as if they imagined Saloman had picked up a trail after all.

But Saloman, it seemed, was still finding places of interest. As they passed a road sign, István said, "This is where they had the earthquake last winter."

Earthquake. Impulsively, Elizabeth turned to Saloman. The huge fact of Peru had gotten lost. She'd never even mentioned it to him. And now she didn't know what to say, how to tell him she'd been going to run to him because she was so proud of him, that what he had done there had been so wonderful and she missed him so badly it was like not breathing. . . .

His gaze never left the road. But his lips quirked slightly, almost forming a smile, as if he knew.

"I don't remember that," Mihaela said. The hunters tended to be single-minded, almost blinkered. Very often, major news passed them by, because they lived in a different twilight world. "Was it a bad one?"

"Bad enough. Wrecked a few villages, I think."

"Bad," Mihaela agreed. "This must be one of them."

The village looked like a large building site. Many houses at various stages of completion had risen out of the rubble that still scattered the entire area. They surrounded a mosque that was still under construction. The minaret was built, though, and the inevitable loudspeakers clung to lampposts and new buildings, ready to pipe the call to prayer all around the village and nearby countryside. Although it was late, a few people still sat on their front steps, enjoying the cool of the night, watching their children play in the street or in their yards among the hens and goats.

A woman sitting outside her shop waved to them, beckoning, ever ready to seek out business, however meager.

"Ice cream?" Elizabeth suggested, with more levity than generosity.

But unexpectedly, Mihaela laughed in the backseat—a breathless, slightly sardonic sound. "Hell, yes. Ice cream is always good."

Without comment, Saloman stopped the car. Although his face expressed no more than patience, Elizabeth sensed a certain tension in him that she associated with excitement. Before she could ask him if he knew the place, he opened his door and got out.

"Merhaba," the woman at the shop greeted them, smiling.

"Merhaba." Elizabeth indicated the freezer that stood under the awning outside her shop. Although she'd picked up very few words of Turkish, she managed to make the transaction without resorting to Mihaela, who spoke the language fluently. By the time they began to eat the ices, Saloman was strolling back along the road toward the crossroads, where the half-built mosque was disgorging the faithful.

"Where's he going?" Mihaela asked uneasily. "Shit, he's not—" She broke off, but the unspoken words still hung in the air: *He's not going to bite someone, is he?*

A young boy, maybe ten years old, came out of the mosque with his father, looking bored while the adults stopped and talked. He began to move toward Saloman, who was wandering around apparently admiring the building work.

Without a word, Mihaela strode down the road, instantly in hunter mode. As the men followed, Elizabeth swore under her breath and went too, if only to try to prevent a scene. She could have told them, if only they'd waited to hear, that Saloman did not feed from children. The adults he certainly regarded as fair game, but he wouldn't kill them.

Once, this fact, that he wouldn't kill them, hadn't mattered much to Elizabeth. The biting, the drinking, the invasion of another body, had appalled her regardless of whether it led ultimately to death. Somewhere along the line, that view had gotten lost. Possibly when biting and blood drinking had become associated for her with sex, with love.

Perhaps Mihaela was right: She was losing herself and her principles, slowly but surely condoning everything he did because, whatever that was, she couldn't stop loving him. Was that slavery?

The boy and Saloman stood in the shadow of the mosque as they approached. The boy's smile was so wide it threatened to split his face, and he was chattering away as if Saloman were his oldest friend. She heard Saloman ask a question in Turkish, which the boy answered in another fast-firing stream before taking Saloman's hand and giving it a tug. Using his other hand, the boy waved it around the entire village, still talking and grinning.

Mihaela stopped suddenly, and Konrad walked into her heels. She looked so mesmerized that Elizabeth said, "What? What is it?"

Before Mihaela could answer, the man who seemed to be the boy's father came hurrying over, and Elizabeth tensed, expecting an argument of some kind. But the man went straight up to Saloman and embraced him, kissing him on both cheeks. His voice was loud in obvious welcome, and Saloman seemed to be hushing him, excusing himself almost.

The man stood back, arms wide, still smiling, but understanding. He spoke to his son, who objected vociferously and then sighed. Turning back to Saloman, he carried the vampire's hand to his lips and then his forehead.

"Jesus Christ," Konrad breathed in clear disgust. "They've just finished praying! Can't they sense what he is?"

"Oh, they know what he is," Mihaela said unsteadily. "He's their savior. He's been here before—last winter before the earthquake came."

Elizabeth stared at her, mirroring, no doubt, the gawping of the other hunters.

Mihaela said, "That's what they're remembering and talking about, the boy and his father. Saloman persuaded them to leave before it happened, hired vans and cars to ferry the villagers down to the town, which was barely touched by the shock. Their homes were destroyed, but he seems to have done something about helping them rebuild. Supplied men and materials, I think. I didn't quite catch that bit. But there's no doubt he's their hero. They'd be organizing a feast for him right now, with the entire village present, except he's refusing. He says he just came to make sure things were going well for them."

Of course he did. It made perfect sense. Had he come that winter because he'd sensed the earthquake? Or had he come to pay his respects at the tomb of the cousin he'd killed? It didn't matter. He'd saved them, without any of the publicity surrounding his Peruvian rescue, which made her think it had been spur-of-the-moment.

"I don't believe that," Konrad protested. "The woman at the shop didn't bat an eyelid when he passed her."

"He was masking," Elizabeth said. "Incognito."

"Then how come the boy and his father can see him?"

"He let them."

"Why?" István asked.

It was a good question, and one she probably knew the answer to. He meant the hunters to witness this, a perfect contrast to the carnage in the Gypsy camp committed by his enemies. Perhaps he really had come to check on the village's recovery, to speak to a couple of special friends while he was in the area, but certainly he would use the "fringe benefits," as he always did.

"The boy loves him," Mihaela said slowly. "They both do. It's not just gratitude, is it?"

Oddly enough, she seemed to be asking Elizabeth. Elizabeth cleared her throat. "No," she said. "Not just gratitude."

Mihaela turned to face her. "How do you do it?" she said. "How do you keep your head straight while he turns from the death monster of the camp to this?"

Elizabeth closed her eyes. "He isn't a death monster. He'd never do what Luk and Dante did. Although he could, if he felt it was right. His morality isn't ours, but it *is* there, and he isn't evil."

When the bombardment of angry protest didn't hit her, she opened her eyes again. Saloman, having said good-bye to the father and son, was now the center of the little group outside the mosque, like a prince gracious enough to greet his overfamiliar subjects. The hunters were gazing at the scene as if they couldn't look away.

Elizabeth said, "It's not the only time he's done this. Didn't you hear about Peru?"

They looked at her. István frowned. "The Peruvian earthquake last week? It was a big one, far bigger than this."

"But nobody died. Admittedly the population of the region wasn't huge either, but he got them to safety too."

"Did he tell you that?" Konrad asked cynically.

"No. There's video footage. It's probably on YouTube by now. I'll show you when we go back. But—"

"How?" István interrupted. "How can he do that? How can he possibly know what seismographers can't even predict?"

"I'm not entirely sure," Elizabeth admitted. "I haven't had the chance to talk to him about it. Everything's been about Luk and Dante. But he said to me once that his people, the Ancients, had 'an affinity with the earth.' I think he can feel the tension, knows when and where the crust will crack."

"Shit, Elizabeth," Mihaela said.

"Eat your ice cream," Elizabeth advised, becoming aware for the first time that her own was melting and trickling down her fingers. It felt surreal, dementedly eating ice cream in the dark, in total silence, while the villagers feted the vampire. When they finished their ices, they moved over to the tap outside the mosque, placed conveniently so that worshipers could wash their feet before entering, and rinsed the stickiness from their fingers.

Saloman used their movement to expedite his departure, first introducing them by name to the villagers, who all greeted them politely, and then waving good-bye. As they walked back toward the car, a woman in a dark pashmina ran after them and pressed some warm, paper-wrapped home baking into Elizabeth's hands. Everyone waved at the tinted windows as they left the village. And when Saloman followed the homeward sign for Fethiye, no one protested.

Chapter Nine

"Where's he going?" Mihaela asked. As they entered the villa, Saloman strolled away into the village without a word of explanation.

Loath as she was to spoil the somewhat stunned softening of the hunters toward Saloman, Elizabeth said, "I don't know. And I don't think you want to."

Konrad swore, and Mihaela groaned, smacking her head back against the door. "We can't just sit here and let him feed on these people!"

It wasn't even worth pointing out that they couldn't stop him. Elizabeth took the door from her friend's white-knuckled grip and closed it firmly. "He has to feed or he dies. He won't kill anyone. He won't even hurt anyone. They won't know it's happened."

Mihaela glanced at her. "Is that how you live with it, Elizabeth?" Oddly, it wasn't said with aggression, but with curiosity.

"It's the truth. That's why you've noticed vampire-related deaths so drastically reduced. Saloman has forbidden it, except in certain circumstances of defense or justice that admittedly might mean little to you or me.

Vampires can feed perfectly adequately without killing or torturing." She walked through the living room toward the kitchen. "Coffee?"

"Coffee."

It had been a strange journey back. Saloman had driven far too fast, so that the hunters had held on to their seats. In fact, even Elizabeth, who was well aware of Saloman's lightning reactions, had closed her eyes at several points. Passing police cars had remained curiously unaware of their reckless speed.

There hadn't even been much conversation beyond the occasional expletive, apart from the time István, apparently unable to restrain himself any longer, had leaned forward to put his head between the two front seats and uttered, "Why? Why did you save these people?"

Saloman had appeared to consider. "Because I could."

"That's no answer."

"Would you prefer 'earthquakes interrupt my food supply'?"

"If it's the truth," István said.

Saloman smiled faintly. "You like black-and-white truths, don't you?"

"Right now, I'd settle for any kind."

Saloman pressed harder on the gas, whizzing past an oncoming, hooting lorry. "They have a right to live," he said at last.

István sat back thoughtfully. An instant later, he was back. Elizabeth had rarely heard him so talkative. "How?" he asked.

"That too is difficult to explain to a human. Let's just say I can hear the earth moving." He flashed one raised eyebrow at Elizabeth, which she devoutly hoped István missed. And István sat back to think about that one too.

It was Konrad who, while the kettle boiled, lifted the lid on the laptop. "Show me," he invited, and no one doubted what he meant.

The Peruvian footage of "Adam Simon" leading the

exodus down the mountain was indeed on YouTube, along with the date it was taken. The hunters would know now for certain that Saloman could not have been responsible for awakening Luk. But no one spoke of it. It seemed a trivial matter beside the hugeness of the earthquake.

Elizabeth sat back and let them watch. She longed to discuss it with them, tell them everything, all the conflict and doubt, the new belief and hope that had come to her. And she yearned to be with Saloman himself, in his arms while they talked about the same thing, about the possibilities inherent in his amazing gift.

They watched it in silence, several times, on several different sites, including the BBC's. Elizabeth fetched the coffee, and they watched it again.

"It changes a lot of things, doesn't it?" she said.

"Oh, yes," Mihaela agreed fervently. "I just can't quite make out how. Or why. Or why he's here, helping us, showing us. It's not all to do with you, is it?"

"No," Elizabeth replied, a little too ruefully. "He believes that humans and vampires can, and should, live together. For this to happen, humans must be aware of vampire existence and realize they're no threat. A tall order, particularly given the current circumstances. As a first step, he wants you, who know about vampires already, to understand the good he can do for the whole world."

"It would be incredible," István burst out. "Predicting earthquakes, tsunamis, volcano eruptions . . . Christ, he can probably do hurricanes and tornadoes better than the meteorological experts."

"I don't know," Elizabeth said cautiously, "but I wouldn't be surprised."

"Can other vampires do this stuff too?" Mihaela asked eagerly.

"Whoa." Konrad sprang to his feet. "Slow down, here. Don't get so carried away. So we've seen a demonstration of a very useful gift—if it can be scientifically proven. But you're forgetting one vital factor." He glared around at them all, ending with Elizabeth. "We can't trust him," he said deliberately. "He's a vampire."

It was a killer blow. Elizabeth watched their hopes deflate like beach balls. "I trust him," she said boldly.

Mihaela's lips twisted. "No, you don't," she said, and Elizabeth stared at her, stricken.

"The other thing you seem to forget in this cozy scenario of togetherness that Elizabeth is relating—who manages this coexistence?" Konrad sat down again, sure now of their attention. "Who rules?" he asked, spreading his hands. "Saloman, of course. Which, if you recall, is what he aimed at from the moment Elizabeth awakened him. He's had his revenge, he's had his fun, and he's building power like there's no tomorrow. At this rate, you guys are next in his sights. But I for one am not falling for it."

Elizabeth, leaving them to their arguments and discussion, climbed the stairs to bed. Weariness seemed to have caught up with her, for her bedroom seemed a long way up. With a sense of relief, she pushed open the door and switched on the light.

Saloman sat on her bed, reading. He could, apparently, read in the dark. His black hair fell loose around his shoulders; his long legs stretched out on the bed, elegantly crossed at the ankles. He looked casual and comfortable and sexy as sin.

He glanced up at her and smiled, and butterflies swooped in her stomach. Carefully, she closed the door and stood leaning back against it while her heart drummed like a rabbit's.

"I see my 'locks' weren't that good after all," she managed.

"They're fine, but you left me with the key."

"Because the spell was yours in the first place?"

"Something like that."

"I told them about Peru," she blurted. "I meant to tell

you, talk to you first. . . . I was on my way to Peru to find you when Mihaela called about Luk. I nearly didn't come." With an effort, she forced herself to stop talking, because Saloman, tossing the book to one side, rose from the bed and walked purposefully toward her.

"You're agitated," he said, halting in front of her. Reaching up, he smoothed a lock of hair from her cheek, and her breath caught. "Don't be. Come."

He didn't take her in his arms, just led her by the hand in a familiar gesture that was both courtly and, because of its association for her, incredibly arousing. He held her gaze while they walked toward the bed. But she was being distracted again by her body's responses to his nearness.

"I had so many things to say to you," she got out. "Things I was *desperate* to say, because what you did in Peru was so wonderful, and I didn't understand before what—"

"Sh-sh." His hand slipped upward to her shoulder, turning her to face him. Amber flames seemed to leap in his dark, opaque eyes and then vanish, and she knew that this time there would be no interruption. This time he would make love to her. Her insides melted; her nipples, as if trying to reach out to him, began to ache.

"It's not so wonderful," he said. "I was in Mexico with Travis when I sensed the quake building. It was an easy thing to do; it barely even put me out."

"But you *can* do it, and you did do it."

Both hands lay heavy on her shoulders now. A faint, almost rueful smile played on his lips. "I wanted to please you."

She felt her lips part in surprise. "*Me?* Is that why you did it?"

"No." He shrugged. "Partly, yes. I did it because I could, but in doing it, I imagined your pleasure." His fingers stretched out, caressing her chin. "I imagine your pleasure a lot when we're apart."

She flushed hotter under his obvious double meaning. "Not when we're together?" she managed.

"Reality beats imagination," he murmured, bending his head and causing the butterflies in her stomach to take flight. "At least with you."

His lips were cool on hers, and yet at their first touch she seemed to combust. Desire surged through her, hurling her body against his as her mouth opened, gasping, to receive his kiss and to give her own. Reaching up, she tangled her hands in his hair, trying to draw him closer as the feel, the taste of Saloman consumed her. His powerful arms closed around her, holding her head steady in one palm as he devoured her mouth. She writhed against his body, irritated by the clothing that prevented her from getting any closer, yet loving the hardness, the contours of the steely bulge that pressed into her abdomen.

You are weary, he said inside her head. *We can do this tomorrow.*

Tomorrow, oh, yes. Tomorrow as well . . .

His lips stretched, smiling on hers as he broke the kiss. "You need to sleep."

"I need you," she whispered, and, reaching up, she took back his mouth. Eyes closed, she seduced it with her own while her hands swept over the hard muscle of his shoulders and arms. She found a way between their almost-fused bodies and began to undo the buttons of his shirt.

He didn't push her onto the bed. He lifted her in his arms and laid her there, finishing her job on his shirt by shrugging it off so that she could run her hands over his smooth, powerful chest. And then he undressed her with slow care, caressing and kissing each area of skin as he uncovered it. When he came to her breasts, stroking one tight, aching nipple into a peak between his fingers while he kissed and teased all around the other, she arched up into him, pleading, almost demanding his presence inside her.

He gave her his hand, sliding it between her thighs.

His eyes above her face darkened impossibly as he felt how wet she was for him. "I want to kiss you there," he whispered. "And yet I need to see your face as you come."

She swallowed. "Don't we have time for both?"

He smiled, moving his fingers among her folds until he found the swollen bud of her pleasure. Her mouth opened in silent bliss and he covered it with his, slipping one finger inside her, then two, while he slowly, tenderly caressed her toward the ultimate ecstasy. Unable to be still, she undulated, squirming on his hand as the waves gathered. Her delight was reflected in his open, blazing eyes, and in his mind, where he let her feel his joy in her pleasure. With his free hand he stroked her breast, cupping, kneading, and pinching until, with a growing, desperate cry of joy that she muffled in his mouth, she fell over the edge.

Somewhere, in the part of her brain that could still think, she had vaguely planned that as soon as she'd orgasmed, she would roll him over, impale herself on him, and ride him triumphantly to his own climax. But somehow it didn't work out quite like that.

Perhaps the orgasm was too long, too shattering, intensified as it was by the union of their minds, because before she could even move, he lay over her body, sliding inside her. But not for the quick, frantic fuck that would bring the fastest release. Instead, he moved slowly, almost soothingly, taking time and pleasure in every part of her as he rocked and coaxed her back to ecstasy. At the last moment, he completed her happiness with his own, collapsing on her in that rare, awesome loss of control that moved her so profoundly.

Damp with sweat, sated, exhausted, she turned with him as he eased his body off her, so that he remained inside her. She smiled sleepily into his shoulder, licking a bead of her own salty moisture from his pristine skin. She felt his lips in her hair and snuggled against him to savor the moment. She had no intention of sleeping just yet, but somehow it came to her, soothing, healing, and deep.

She woke to daylight, the brightness of the sun filtered by the room's curtains. She knew he was there before she even opened her eyes and saw him at the window that looked over the village. Wearing nothing except his dark trousers, which he hadn't troubled to fasten, he appeared to be observing through a small gap in the curtain.

"Saloman?" She sat up as reality in the shape of the current crisis broke into her happiness. "What's going on?"

"A market has set up in the street. They're using your gatepost to support an awning."

Elizabeth closed her mouth. She narrowed the question. "Where are the hunters?"

"Downstairs." Saloman released the curtain and turned to face her. "Discussing me. And you. They've just decided not to wake you."

"Why? Where are they going?" she demanded, electing to leave the discussion about the propriety of eavesdropping until later.

Saloman shrugged, walking toward her. "Nowhere yet. They've been debating the comparative merits of Istanbul and Budapest. And of just staying here for a few days to see what happens."

She eyed him doubtfully. "Can you really hear all that?"

"If I stick my ear to the floor."

Laughter caught her unaware, and the flickering smile of response in his eyes warmed her as he sat on the bed beside her.

"Are they . . . all right?" she asked with difficulty.

"They are excited, frightened, confused. But whatever you said to them last night has made an impression."

"I think it was you who made the impression." She hesitated, then added, "To some, whatever impression you make will never be enough. Mihaela's family was killed in front of her by a vampire when she was a child. Konrad . . . Well, Konrad will always have difficulty accepting you."

"Another excellent reason for killing him."

She peered at him. "You *are* joking, aren't you?"

He made a small sound that in a being that breathed would have been a sigh. "Not entirely. Are you hungry?"

She leaned forward and wrapped her arms around his neck. "Maybe," she said, smiling into his eyes.

"Ah. That sort of hunger I can more easily assuage." With the pressure of his body, he pushed her back into the pillows and tore the sheet from between them. He drew back, and, under his avid gaze, Elizabeth squirmed. Heat surged through her. On the verge of losing herself once more in sensuality, she realized with a hint of desperation that their time together would pass and she still would not have said what she needed to.

"I missed you," she whispered, as the smile died on her lips.

"I know." He laid his palm flat over her heart, and as if he acted as a conduit, she heard its rapid increase in beat. "I thought of you when the mountain shook. I wanted you in my arms to complete the experience."

The wonder of that joined the sweetness induced by his hand turning on her breast. He held his palm flat, only just touching her nipple as he brushed it back and forth. The pleasure was exquisite. She wanted to thrust her breast fully into his hand, yet she couldn't bear to change what she felt now.

With an effort, she said, "I sensed something. Round about the time of the earthquake. It felt like you. I was frightened for you." Reluctantly, it seemed, his gaze lifted from her flushed, elongated nipple to her face. "Were you still there? In danger?"

"A little, perhaps. It's a foolishness I can't resist. I love to feel the power of the earth. I like to feel one with it when it shakes." His hand closed suddenly on her breast, and she moaned, pushing into his palm at last. "I wanted you when it did. I wanted to be loving you and share two climaxes at once. Perhaps that is what you felt. Or perhaps it was Luk's awakening immediately afterward. Because that's what truly scared me."

"Why?" She gasped as he lowered his lips to her other breast and began to tease the nipple with his clever, sensual tongue.

"Because he should have remained at peace. Wakening him was a cruelty that amounts to sacrilege. Sometimes the dead have to stay dead."

His mouth closed beguilingly on her breast and began to suck. With an almost superhuman effort, she caught his head in her hands and tugged until he released her nipple with a reluctance that fed her desire almost more than the act itself.

"Why didn't you kill him the other night? Why did you let him go?"

Almost angrily, he said, "Because there was a moment—" His eyes closed. "Just one moment when he looked at me with Luk's eyes. With friendship and love."

Her fists closed involuntarily, tangling in his hair. His eyes opened. "And then he kicked me into the dirt, and the moment passed. He hates me and is protecting Dante."

She touched her forehead to his. "Saloman. *Can* you kill him now?" She didn't mean his physical strength, and they both knew it.

He moved, covering her body, and she felt his hardness slide against her inner leg. "Yes, I can kill him now. You are very wet between your thighs. Perhaps there's something else I can do for you."

She pushed at his chest, and he let her dislodge him and roll over until she lay on top of him. "And I for you," she said, laying her hands flat on his chest to lift herself. She found his shaft without difficulty, captured it between her thighs, and adjusted her position. Then, her gaze never leaving his, she lowered herself onto him and moaned as he filled her. He thrust upward, grasping her hips, and in the frantic, sensual fight for control of their loving, all else disappeared. There was only Saloman, and love, and fierce, hot, unstoppable pleasure.

Saloman bit into Elizabeth's throat, loving the way her body jerked beneath him in mingled pain and delight. He would climax again very soon, and wanted to do so with her blood rushing into his body in an endless cycle of pleasure. No one tasted like Elizabeth: power and sweetness, passion and . . . her. Simply her. He drew harder on her wound, feeling her buck under him with helpless ecstasy. She loved the blood drink, and he let her see in his mind how much sensual joy it gave him, doubling her enjoyment.

Hammering into her in strong, forceful thrusts, he took her, body and blood and mind, until a climax roared through him. One more twist and she was with him. He wanted to drink from her forever, feel that hectic, drumming heartbeat slow to match his own, feel her teeth in his veins, drawing his blood into her as he drank and made love. It was the one most exquisite of pleasures that he had never enjoyed with Elizabeth and never would.

He was taking too much. He had to force his mouth to loosen, to heal her wound before the pain intruded. As her convulsions eased, he rolled onto his back so that she lay sprawled across his body while he savored the last waves of physical ecstasy.

"I must trust you," she whispered, so quietly and muffled into the skin of his chest that he barely heard her. "I wouldn't let you drink from me if I didn't."

Saloman listened to the sound of his own heart, forcing it to slow down. "To be fair," he said calmly, "there is nothing you could do to stop me."

For an instant she lay still, as if surprised to have gotten an answer, as if she hadn't realized she'd spoken out loud. Then she raised her head and propped her chin on her hand to look at him. "But there is. I could say no, and you wouldn't. *That* is trust." She gave a quick, wry smile. "Of course, I couldn't trust you not to bite anybody else who says no—"

"Be easy. They hardly ever do."

"Only because they don't know it's happening."

"You know it's happening."

"I love you. That's different."

Saloman twitched lazily inside her. "To each his own. Have you been talking to Mihaela?"

"She said something last night that bothered me. She said I didn't trust you. And I do."

Clever Mihaela. Perceiving the seeds of dissension and watering them. He said, "There are levels of trust. We can't reach them all at once."

She slid one of her hands up his chest to touch his lips. "We walk a bit of a tightrope, you and I," she whispered. "I overbalance and overcompensate. . . ."

"But you don't fall." *Never fall . . .*

She smiled. "Not yet." Her lips parted again, as if she'd say more; then, as if changing her mind, she kissed him instead. Saloman had no objection to that. He held her buttocks, caressing and kneading until she slid out of his hands, tracing kisses down his chest and belly, and reached, inevitably, the rigid obstacle of his cock. Apparently it was no obstacle, for it received more than its share of kisses. Closing his eyes, he tangled his fingers in her hair and let her have her way. It was sweet and intense and left him momentarily helpless.

Afterward, he drew her up the length of his body to lie with him in the afterglow.

Greetings, Saloman.

He froze. Although the waves of orgasm still clouded his mind and his self-control, he was certainly not imagining the clear, mocking voice in his head. He shouldn't have been so surprised; he'd left the door open to communication that hadn't, until now, been initiated.

Luk, he managed, with an effort at urbanity. *How are you?*

Angry. Vengeful. Gathering strengths, old and new. All the things you expect. And fear.

I don't fear you, Luk.

Luk's laughter was mocking, too loud and too much for whatever amusement had caused it. It echoed around Saloman's head, chilling his warm, sated blood.

You should, Saloman. You should. You know I'll come for you.

I know.

Another burst of manic laughter. *Look forward to it, Saloman.*

Luk's huge, disturbing presence slipped away. Saloman didn't try to prevent it or to follow. Curiously, what he chiefly felt wasn't anger or even the fear Luk was trying so hard to instill. It was loneliness. The massive presence of another Ancient in his mind was something he had never thought to feel again, and even threatening and full of hate, it had made him yearn for more.

"Saloman. Saloman!" It was Elizabeth, lying across his chest, her large hazel eyes dark with anxiety as they stared into his. "What is it? What's happening?"

"Nothing. I was talking to Luk."

Her eyes searched his. "What did he say?"

"Nothing. He just wants me to know he's strong. Which might mean he isn't yet as powerful as he would like to be. Support from Turkish vampires doesn't come as fast as he expected."

"You know that?"

He moved, rolling her under him. "I know there will always be a few vampires tempted by the return of chaos. I know who is still loyal to me. And outside of Istanbul that is the vast majority, at least while I'm known to be in Turkey."

"Maybe you should stay until *he* leaves."

You should stay. Always "you," never "we." Why did he

want that? Why did he always want more when she was already everything he needed? When he could feel with every glance, every touch, that she would die for him?

He veered away from that thought, banishing it ruthlessly. He said, "Perhaps. But I have too many other things to do in too many other places. I can't afford to let this rebellion spread beyond Turkey. And we both know he'll come to Budapest eventually."

"You can't really know that," she objected.

"I know it as well as I know Luk. He'll remember the prophecy he made centuries ago. That in Buda and Pest would begin the new age, when I am supplanted and the new dawn of the vampire breaks."

Her eyes changed, fear whipping through them, swiftly chased by skepticism. "That's bollocks," she said roundly, and he smiled with genuine amusement, kissing her mouth.

"It's not bollocks," he said judiciously. "But I'd say it's open to interpretation."

"Wasn't he ever wrong?"

"Not that I can recall. But then, he doesn't see everything, and doesn't tell everything he does see. And many things haven't yet happened that perhaps never will." He released her, and she sat up.

"I'm hungry," she said, reaching for her clothes. "I'll just get some coffee and breakfast."

"And then come back to bed," he said, rising on one elbow to watch her dress. It was an experience he always found peculiarly erotic.

"Why?" she teased, pulling on a short, provocative top. "Do I need more sleep?"

"You need more fucking," he said, and before her blush had properly begun, he reached out too fast for her to see and dragged her back onto the bed.

At which inconvenient moment, a brief rap sounded on the bedroom door, swiftly followed by Mihaela, walking in with all the ease of friendship.

"Elizabeth, are you awake? We want to— Oh."

* * *

It could have been worse. She could have been naked in his arms, lost in the throes of simultaneous orgasm. At least she was fully dressed, and although Saloman loomed over her with intent, he wasn't actually groping her. Nevertheless, she couldn't help her agitated shove on Saloman's restraining arm.

He released her without comment or obvious embarrassment.

Mihaela said, "I see you are. Awake."

Elizabeth mumbled something as she scrambled off the bed.

"I'm sorry; I didn't expect you to have company. Stupidly enough." Mihaela's gaze flickered to Saloman and away. Her golden skin began to flush as he swung his naked legs off the bed and reached down for his pants, which had been flung carelessly on the floor, but she kept looking determinedly at Elizabeth.

"What's happening?" Elizabeth said, as calmly as she could. She understood this was difficult for Mihaela. It was one thing accepting that her friend had a vampire lover; it was quite another to have the reality flung in her face, especially when that reality was a large, naked Saloman, all smooth skin and rippling muscle. It wasn't just his male, alien beauty that was overwhelming; it was his very presence.

"We've spoken to Mustafa and we think we should stay here for a few days." Again Mihaela's eyes flickered in quick alarm as Saloman rose from the bed and walked across the room to find his shirt. She dragged her gaze back to Elizabeth. "Mustafa and his people will come here as secret backup. We hope you and Konrad—and Saloman, if he hangs around—will prove bait enough to bring Luk and Dante this time."

Saloman picked up his discarded shirt and looked thoughtfully at Mihaela, who struggled, but managed to meet his gaze as he crossed the room, donning his shirt as he came. "I suspect I am the only bait that will count for Luk. And he won't come for me until he's ready. I need to be in Istanbul, but I can make my, er, signature? . . . linger a little longer. It might fool Dante, at least."

Elizabeth said, "Without you, are we strong enough to kill Luk?"

Saloman looked at her. "*You* are."

Her breath caught. "Because I'm the Awakener?"

"Most probably."

"Then I *could* have—" She broke off. *I could have killed you in St. Andrews.* Physically. Emotionally, she'd been completely incapable, because already her unacknowledged and unwanted love had been too strong. She couldn't do it; she could never do it.

"Yes," he said, understanding at once. "You could."

For an instant, she wondered what her life would have been like if she'd done it: if she'd actually plunged the stake all the way down into his flesh and pierced his ancient, incomprehensible heart. Just as she'd planned then, her internal conflict would have been over. She'd have avoided all the subsequent soul-searching and divided loyalties. And always, through whatever excesses of grief and guilt she suffered, she'd have wondered. . . .

She blinked away the fantasy. It was unthinkable now. She stood by her choice and regretted nothing.

Mihaela said to Saloman, "When are you going?"

"Today."

Elizabeth's gaze flew to his impassive face. There was a short, curiously pregnant pause. She had the odd impression that it was not she, but Saloman, who waited for the suggestion neither would make. And then his lips quirked and he moved toward the window. "The market has good carpets. I shall buy one for Dmitriu."

Chapter Ten

One day, Saloman thought, hacking his way through rebel vampires like a vandal in a moonlit wheatfield, he would bring Elizabeth to this amazing city. He'd show her where the market had been before the Christian army sacked the city during the fourth crusade. He'd show her where he'd lived when the Ottomans had finally taken Constantinople and Byzantium fell. It was a cosmopolitan city of many cultures, and Saloman still loved it. He'd enjoy showing it to Elizabeth one night when the streets weren't strewn with the blood of friends as well as enemies. Not that Saloman minded the blood. It was the clouds of undead dust floating in the air that sickened him.

Without looking, he knew that Volkan, the rebels' chief leader, still watched proceedings from his vantage point on the Galata Tower balcony, surrounded by his bodyguards. As if he imagined he were safe up there, while his foolish followers did the work of dying. It was a pointless fight, used by both sides as a mere demonstration of strength. And yet, now that Luk's presence in the city was inspiring the rebels, it had to be done.

Saloman laid about him with his sword, carving a path through the street toward the great fourteenth-century stone tower that overshadowed it. From habit, the vampires fought in grim silence, but there was little hope of keeping a major street fight from the humans who lived in the many apartments lining the vampires' battlefield. Twitching curtains, agitated voices, darting shadows at windows and balconies all told Saloman the police would soon be on the way.

One brave man stood in a doorway near him, as if protecting his family from the mob. Or perhaps he was just insatiably curious. Either way, he paid the price as a rebel snatched him up in passing and bit into his throat. A piercing scream rent the air, as someone, perhaps the victim's wife, witnessed the attack. Matters were about to escalate. Humans would intervene, even before the police got here.

Saloman had had enough. Sweeping his sword around in a wide arc that cut the flesh of several vampires at once, he leapt, jumping over the heads of friends and foes alike to reach the human-killer, who, with a snarl at Saloman, let his victim drop to the ground.

Too stupid to live. And too greedy to tolerate. As quick as thought, Saloman used the stake he'd been saving for Volkan and leapt through the fool's remaining dust to land facing the rebels' back line defending the tower. It was an unexpected move that placed his enemies between himself and his allies, and he could feel Volkan's alarm filtering down from above. The rebel leader even stepped backward on his balcony, out of Saloman's vision.

Unworthy, Saloman mocked, and knew he heard.

The rebels began to surround Saloman, deserting their individual fights to close in for the big kill. And Volkan moved forward again, urging his followers on with excited telepathic commands. He imagined he was safe, because now, so close to the tower, Saloman's angle was wrong for a massive jump. Nor could Saloman move back because of the rebels closing on him. Or so Volkan must have thought.

Saloman jumped anyway. He reached the smooth stone wall only a few feet above the vampires' heads, and heard more than one laugh of ridicule. Those didn't last either. Even as an enterprising rebel jumped after him, no doubt with the intention of knocking him off his precarious hold, Saloman swarmed up the tower. It was a mixture of running and jumping, with barely any hand- or footholds, like some huge insect, fast enough to stun both sets of fighters below him.

Above, from the observation balcony, Volkan's bodyguards reached down with their stakes and swords, hacking so wildly that the sound of steel clashing on stone echoed around the street. Saloman simply shoved through them, jumping over the railing at last and hurling the first bodyguard he encountered over the side.

The others rushed him in panic. Even Volkan went into action, but there was no time to drag this out. Vampire deaths were already high enough, and if the hunters and the police arrived, then the human death toll would climb.

Saloman brushed aside the thrusting stakes with his sword, and with one of his lightning movements, faster than any modern vampire could clearly see, he simply grabbed Volkan by his collar and swung him around so that he acted as a shield against the remaining bodyguards.

Below, he knew the fight had tailed off as everyone gazed up at the tower to see what would happen next.

Saloman gazed at the spitting rebel vampire leader with more despair than anger. *Unworthy,* he observed. *In every way. Why on earth did they choose you?*

Volkan knew he was going to die. Fear as well as resignation stood out in his defiant eyes. "Because I'm not you," he said aloud. "You can't rule us. You'll never rule us."

"I can," Saloman said so that everyone could hear, telepathically and physically. "And I will. It's over."

From the watchers, as Saloman drew the pointlessly resisting body to him for ritual execution, came a wave of terror or exaltation, depending on the allegiance of the individual. Only Volkan continued to spit out his rage. He'd nothing left to lose.

"It's not over! Don't you understand? We don't need you, Saloman. *They* don't even need *me*. They always have another leader, strong enough to protect them, wise enough to let them do what they choose."

It gave him pause, but only for an instant. "Wise? My insane cousin, Luk? He can't even protect himself. There is no feasible choice but me. Make it." His words were aimed at the whole rebel community and they knew it. But he had little time to analyze their effect. Police sirens were drawing closer. The hum of agitated human speech was increasing. He could sense hunters.

Saloman bit into Volkan's throat and cut ruthlessly through the dying vampire's mental babble of fury, fear, and resistance. *Where is Luk? Where did you meet him?*

Here in Istanbul. You've done all this for nothing. It will only begin again.

Saloman finished the conversation by ending Volkan's existence. And when he lifted his head, glaring through the scattered dust at his unruly people below, they began to disperse with swift, silent efficiency. A few scattered sticks lay on the ground. One of Saloman's allies dispatched an injured rebel currently incapable of moving. When the police arrived, they would find nothing.

The door into the tower opened and Saloman's ally Mettener came through. For an instant, he stood in silence beside Saloman, watching as three humans strode down the street.

"Hunters," Mettener observed. "They'll give out it was a human riot that dispersed at the sound of police sirens."

"Many people live here," Saloman said, glancing up the length of the street, then turning to walk around the balcony that circled the whole tower. The stunning views of the city and the sea, which hadn't changed so very much in nearly seven hundred years, were incomparable. The Genoese had known what they were about when they'd built this tower to protect their colony.

"The truth can't be completely suppressed," Saloman said. *Every cloud has a silver lining. . . .*

"Had he seen Luk?" Mettener asked.

"Oh, yes. He's here." An unseen and unfindable focus for discontent. Volkan was right: It *would* all begin again. That was bad enough, but what truly concerned Saloman was that it could spread across the whole world. That everything he'd built so far would come crashing down and all his great plans would amount to nothing.

"Amyntas," Mihaela said, when she and Elizabeth had recovered their breath after climbing what felt like hundreds of steps. "I wonder who he was?"

"Rich dude from the fourth-century B.C.," Elizabeth answered vaguely, gazing at the fascinating tomb in front of her. Like several others, it had been carved into the hillside above the town of Fethiye. From a distance they looked like temples; close up, they were more like little houses.

Mihaela glanced into the empty tomb chamber. "Always worth taking a historian with you when you visit historic sites," she said sarcastically.

Elizabeth laughed. "Seriously, I don't think anyone knows much more than that! I wonder if he'd be surprised we were still talking about him two and a half thousand years after his death?"

"I think he'd be gratified. You wouldn't have a tomb like this if you were happy to sink into historical obscurity. It's like living forever."

"Hmm," Elizabeth said doubtfully, taking her water

bottle out of her backpack and unscrewing the lid. "'Who wants to live forever?'" she quoted.

"Vampires," said Mihaela, taking a swig from her own bottle. She lowered it suddenly. "Hey, do you suppose Saloman was—" She broke off with a quick, almost embarrassed shrug, as if she'd inadvertently brought up a taboo subject.

"Around when this guy was?" Elizabeth finished for her, determined to keep the conversation natural. "Yes, probably. He might even have known him if he was that important. I'll ask him."

Mihaela took another drink and put the top back on her bottle before she glanced again at Elizabeth. "Doesn't that freak you out?"

Elizabeth shrugged. "No. Not that part of it. To be honest, it always fascinated me how much I could learn from him. He was a friend of Vlad the Impaler, King Stephen, emperors and princes, soldiers and scholars throughout known—and unknown—history."

Mihaela reached out and ran her hand over the rough stone pillar. "He could have built this. Hundreds of years before Christ was born." She shivered. "Who wants to live forever?" she repeated. "Saloman does." She turned abruptly back to face Elizabeth. "Do you?"

Elizabeth smiled ruefully. "No." She moved to lean against the ancient pillar and gaze down over the picturesque town and the sparkling blue sea dotted with boats. The sun shone on her face, hot and relentless. It felt good. "But sometimes I think it would be nice to have a little longer."

Mihaela turned her back on the sun, frowning. "What do you mean by that?"

"Oh, I don't know. I'm thirty-one years old and sometimes I feel ninety."

"Don't we all? A vampire hunter's work is never done—and that gets depressing after a decade or two."

"Yes, but I mean physically." They were being normal tourists, normal friends, and she hadn't meant to spoil that, not today, not on this strange, peaceful hill. But the words seemed to tumble out without permission, as if someone had opened a locked door. "What does vampire killing actually *do* to you, Mihaela? Does anyone understand how their power makes you stronger when you kill them? What if all it does is speed everything up, so that you move faster but so does your whole life? Do vampire hunters ever live to be old?"

"Yes," Mihaela said staunchly, but she sounded frightened all of a sudden, and she moved closer to Elizabeth. "Of course they do. What is this about?"

Elizabeth gave a quick, embarrassed laugh. "Nothing. You asked if I wanted to live forever, and the answer is no. I don't want to be immortal, and I won't be turned to 'the dark side.' But I would like to live beyond thirty-five."

"Is there any doubt of it? They way you fought those vampires at the villa, nothing and no one can hurt you." Her breath caught. "Elizabeth . . . are you . . . ill?"

"Oh, Lord, no." Wishing she'd never spoken, Elizabeth tried to shrug it off. She'd wanted someone to hear and laugh at her stupid fears; she hadn't wanted Mihaela to look like *that*, as if she were already dead. "I thought it might be something to do with the vampire killing, that's all."

"*What* might be to do with the vampire killing?"

"I get spells where I feel ill," Elizabeth blurted. "Sick and dizzy and so tired I can barely stand. Something hurts, physically, so much that my whole body trembles, yet I can't always locate the pain."

"When you kill vampires?"

"No . . . I don't think so. I feel strong then."

"Then is it reaction afterward?"

"No, I don't think it's that either. It seems to happen at all sorts of odd times, when I'm nowhere near vampires or any of this stuff."

"How often has it happened?"

Elizabeth shrugged. "Maybe six or seven times in the last couple of months."

"Have you seen a doctor?"

"Oh, yes. I went for a checkup after the third episode or so. They couldn't find anything wrong with me. I suspect I've developed hypochondria, worrying about nothing. It's not as if it ever lasts more than a few minutes."

"When did it happen last?"

"The other night, when the vampires attacked. After we'd killed the ones in Konrad's room and I was looking out the window to check for any more." Elizabeth eased her shoulder off the pillar. "It was very brief. I seemed to be able to throw it off by willpower that time—which is another reason I think it can't be serious."

"And yet it happens."

Elizabeth took another drink of water and knelt to replace the bottle in her bag. "It happens," she agreed. "I don't suppose anything similar ever happens to you? Or the others?"

Mihaela shook her head. "Not to me. And no one else has ever mentioned such symptoms. I don't think it's anything to do with vampire hunting. I think you should see another doctor. I'll ask Mustafa about—"

"No, no," Elizabeth said hastily, already feeling she'd made far too much fuss. "I'll see my own doctor again when I go home. Look." She pointed down the umpteen stone steps and the steep slope of the hill. "I just climbed all the way up there in ninety-degree heat. I don't think I'm actually ill!"

Mihaela slung her bag over her shoulder and took two steps before spinning back to face Elizabeth. "Shit, you're not pregnant?"

"*Pregnant?*" Elizabeth stared at her, the instinctive scoff dying unspoken on her lips. Pregnant? By Saloman? Was it possible for a vampire to make a child? Without meaning to, she touched her stomach, wondering. Wondering what it would be like to bear Saloman's child. A rush of regret hit her like a steam train and she had to close her eyes.

Opening them, she said flatly, "It isn't possible with Saloman, is it? You're winding me up."

"Vampires don't breed," Mihaela agreed, "but I wasn't winding you up. You're an attractive woman subject to the same temptations as the rest of us."

"I'm also a relatively intelligent woman who knows how to use proper protection!" Since she'd met him, there had never been anyone else in her heart or in her bed. And no protection had ever been necessary with Saloman, who harbored neither disease nor seed in his beautiful, sensual, ancient, undead body.

And yet there is something. . . .

Mihaela touched her hand. "You want that, don't you? A child one day."

Elizabeth smiled, able to bear the pain and the regret. "Maybe. Maybe you and I both do." She took Mihaela's hand and gave it a quick squeeze. "As Saloman says, we choose our path. But that doesn't mean we can't change it."

Mihaela's dark eyes refused to acknowledge her own regrets. "Change yours, Elizabeth," she pleaded. "Please. Before it's too late."

Elizabeth dropped her hand and gazed up at the cloudless azure sky. The sun was blinding, even from the corner of her eye. "Everything's changing. Can't you feel that?"

Mihaela shivered in the heat and took the first step back down the hill. "I feel we've been deep enough for one day. Let's go and drink wine by the harbor."

"Sounds good to me."

They had lunch with a bottle of local wine at one of the restaurants along the seafront, sitting at an outside table and watching the people and the ships go by. Relaxed by the morning's exercise and the beauty of their sun-drenched surroundings, they talked of trivia, of Josh Alexander, the problem of Luk, and the internal politics of the hunter organization.

Elizabeth told Mihaela about John Ramsay, the young Scottish soldier who'd survived a Taliban ambush only to be attacked by vampires.

Mihaela topped off their glasses. "Bastards," she observed. "That's the sort of carnage that happens when someone rocks the boat and there's a leadership dispute. It's happening in Istanbul too. There was a major fight there the other night. A man died. Is he recovering, your soldier?"

"Yes, I think so. He e-mailed me yesterday that he's out of hospital, convalescing at home. He's an interesting bloke, though. He could hear them talking, telepathically, while the attack was happening."

"Really?" Mihaela lifted her glass, frowning over the rim. "Are you sure his mind wasn't just playing tricks in a highly traumatic situation?"

"I don't think so. I was talking to Saloman about it, and he says certain humans have a gene inherited from his people—the ones who never became undead, obviously—who interbred with humans. Apparently the gene gives them latent paranormal abilities, like telepathy and enchantment."

Mihaela frowned. "You mean *you* have this gene?"

"Apparently. So does Josh, although it's not inherited from Tsigana. And on the flip side, so does Dante. I think John Ramsay might have it too. And Cyn, one of the rogue vampire hunters I met in New York."

"And Konrad?"

Elizabeth sipped her wine thoughtfully. Konrad had occasionally heard the voices of vampires at the moment he killed them. "I'm not sure. Maybe. It just struck me that these people must have odd, inexplicable experiences in their lives that might make it easier for them to believe in other paranormal oddities."

"Like vampires walking among them?"

"Exactly."

"Let's hope not!"

"Why?" Elizabeth argued. "I've been thinking about it a lot, and I'm not really sure this secrecy achieves anything. The more people who know or suspect in a gradual sort of a way, the less shock it will be to the masses when the secret is finally out."

"Elizabeth, the secret will never be out. It mustn't be!"

"But I think it *is*, Mihaela," Elizabeth said, setting down her glass with emphasis. "I think it's out already and growing. I was following John's story on the Internet and found lots of references and rumors flung up during the Afghan revolt and spreading ever since. What if that happens here too as the revolt spreads? Admittedly the more bizarre stories are going to be dismissed by most people, like the so-called gang fights in New York this spring, but don't you think it's all adding up to more and more people *knowing*?"

"I hope not," Mihaela said heavily.

"Why?" Elizabeth asked again. "You were happy enough to tell *me* what was going on when you'd never even met me before. And to warn Josh and the other descendants that—"

"*Warn*, Elizabeth," Mihaela interrupted. "It's sometimes necessary to warn to save lives. And saving human lives is our guiding principle. But all the people we've ever told doesn't amount to a spit in the ocean. It needs to remain that way."

"I'm not sure you're right." Elizabeth sat back to let the waiter remove her cleared plate while Mihaela asked him for two Turkish coffees. When he'd gone, she leaned forward again. "But either way, my point is, if people do become more aware, does the organization have any kind of plans for dealing with it?"

Mihaela shuddered. "For a human-versus-vampire war? Just prayer."

Elizabeth smiled lopsidedly. "That's a bit fatalistic, isn't it? I imagined you'd be much more interventionist."

"Oh, we'll be in there, but I doubt many of us will live

to tell the tale, let alone get a fine tomb like your friend Amyntas up there." She jerked her head at the hill behind them, but despite the sardonic humor, Elizabeth knew the idea seriously appalled her beyond all other possible catastrophes.

"I don't think it needs to be like that," Elizabeth said. She hesitated, then added, "Saloman wouldn't want a war either. If you had some lines of communication open with him and the other leaders, you might be able to prevent it. And gradual education of humans might prevent the panic you're so afraid of."

Mihaela's gaze grew bleak. She raised her glass and drank rather more than a sip before setting it back down. "Do you know what I hate, Elizabeth? I hate not knowing whether you're speaking your own thoughts or his."

Elizabeth sat back, deflecting the hurt. After all, she hadn't expected anything else. "I haven't been possessed, Mihaela. I still think for myself. I still collect and analyze evidence, and I still don't want people to die before their time. If you think I'm such a monster, why are you sitting here eating with me?"

Mihaela had the grace to drop her gaze to her glass, but a moment later, she glanced up again with a twisted smile. "I don't think you're a monster, idiot. I think you're in love with one."

"Waiting for vampires?"

Mihaela twisted around in her sun lounger to see István approaching through the darkness. Though she'd switched off the outside lights, her night vision was good enough to make out his distinctive, almost lanky shape.

She straightened. "They're not coming, are they? All the action's in Istanbul. Just like Saloman said."

"Mustafa's gone there. He asked Konrad if they could call on us for extra help if they need it."

"That bad?"

"Bad enough." He sat down on the lounger beside

her, leaning his elbows on his knees. "Is that why you're out here alone? Worrying that we did the wrong thing?"

Mihaela smiled faintly. "If we did, we can still rectify it. I doubt our presence in Istanbul would have made any difference to what's happening now."

István didn't say anything else, simply sat and waited. All around the grasshoppers chirped away, supplying constant background music. Something that might have been a mosquito whined past her ear. Mihaela ignored it.

Elizabeth had spoken to her in confidence today; she understood that. But she needed another perspective, and there was no one in the world she trusted more than István.

"Do you remember the prophecy we found in Szilágyi's memoirs?" she said abruptly. The memoir of the sixteenth-century hunter had been a chance find among the hordes of historical texts lovingly preserved in the hunters' library in Budapest. Once again, its significance was nagging at Mihaela.

"The one we thought might relate to Elizabeth?" István said. "Of course."

"'To see the new age, she must give up the world,'" Mihaela quoted.

"Doesn't make any sense," István observed.

"Maybe it does. If you take it as 'see the new age *in*,' as in *usher* it in. Then it could mean she dies to bring in the new age."

One of the things she liked most about István was that he never dismissed anything without consideration. She could see him considering now, staring down at his hands in the darkness.

"It's a bit of a leap, isn't it?" he said at last.

"Not so much, when you have all the information."

His head turned toward her, waiting.

"She's ill," Mihaela blurted. "The doctor she saw couldn't find anything wrong, but Elizabeth thinks it might be something to do with *this*. With vampires and hunting. What if it's something serious? Something terminal? Or worse, what if it's some curse? What if *he*—" She broke off, waving one hand dismissively, because she couldn't bring herself to say the words. They sounded stupid spoken aloud.

István, however, couldn't leave it there. "Saloman? Why would Saloman curse her?"

"Oh, I don't know. Maybe it's a curse of Luk's or something. He made the damned prophecy in the first place."

"If you believe Szilágyi or his memory of the event."

"Well, the first bit came true. She *did* smite Saloman's friends—the vampire Severin in New York—just as the prophecy foretold."

István considered that too. At last, he stirred. "In many ways," he observed, "Miklós, our revered librarian, is a fussy old woman. But one of the things he's right about is that you can't make decisions based on ancient prophecies. They're vague, contradictory, and subject to the failings of whoever made them, whoever wrote them down, and whoever's reading them. Szilágyi's words needn't mean it's Elizabeth's destiny to die in Saloman's fights. Feeling ill doesn't mean she's dying or cursed. I know Elizabeth's in a scary place right now—scary for us, that is. I don't think she's frightened in the least."

"But she *is*, István," Mihaela burst out. "Oh, I don't mean she's scared of Saloman or his influence, because she clearly isn't! But I think this illness thing scares her. What it is, what it might lead her to do. And *that*'s what scares *me*."

István nodded thoughtfully.

Mihaela drew in her breath and pressed her back into the lounger. "She's not the same girl we tried to warn about Saloman a year ago, is she?" A girl István himself had never been indifferent to.

Rather to her surprise, István smiled. "She's sort of . . . grown up," he said. "But in any way that matters, I think she *is* the same. If she wasn't, you wouldn't be out here worrying about her."

Thoughtfully, Mihaela watched him stand up and walk back in the direction of the house. He had a point.

But she still needed to get Elizabeth away from Saloman.

•

Sauchiehall Street in Glasgow on a Friday night was an unexpectedly lonely place. John Ramsay had come out mainly to get away from the fussing of his mother and the snoring of his father, whose traditional start to the weekend was two hours in the pub, followed by ten on the sofa and a Saturday-morning hangover. John had already offended him by refusing to join him for the two hours.

It wasn't that he didn't want to get drunk. Part of him longed for the release of alcohol-induced forgetfulness. It was just that he couldn't bear the helplessness that went with it. Lying under clear Afghan skies, unable to move while monsters killed his comrades, was more than enough helplessness to last him a lifetime. And so here he was, feeling like the only sober person in the city, while all around him couples and crowds of friends milled in and out of the clubs, bars, and restaurants, laughing and talking and shoving one another, oblivious to anything except the next drink, the next dance, the next fun, or just the next fuck. Just as if the world were still the same.

Isn't it?

The voice froze his blood. Stopping dead, he swung around to see where it came from. Two lads swerved to avoid him. One said, "Forgot your warning lights, mate!"

John ignored him. Peering among a crowd of young girls in short black skirts and dramatic makeup, he saw a woman watching him. Although she wasn't close enough to have spoken the words he'd heard, neither was anyone else.

He turned his steps toward her, dodging through the crowd. She wore an open trench-style raincoat over a red dress that seemed to be glued to her tall, slender form. But it wasn't her figure that drew John. It was her poise, the complete lack of embarrassment with which she met his stare. She didn't flirt; she didn't beckon. She was merely curious.

As soon as the space between them was empty, John said, "Who are you?"

The woman gave a half smile, as if he'd disappointed her, and turned on her high heels, walking with swift, incomparable grace toward St. George's Cross.

"Wait," John called, running after her.

She moved too fast, dodging among the crowds of young people who littered the street outside a nightclub. When he got past them, there was no sign of his quarry. John glanced at the nightclub with irritation, and strode grimly toward the bouncers who guarded the doorway.

What's wrong with the club? the same woman's voice asked, half-amused, half-curious. *Don't go in if you don't want to.*

John stopped dead, tugging instinctively at one ear. One of the bouncers folded his arms and gave him a repelling stare. John wasn't going to get in very easily.

Damn it, where the hell are you? The thought had no sooner filled his mind before it was answered by a musical laugh and he knew his worst nightmare had come true: Another vampire was speaking inside his head. He was the only one who could hear her.

I'm in the doorway ten yards down the road. You'd never make a vampire hunter.

The word chilled him, and yet he was conscious of a thrill at the same time, the same thrill that had lifted him talking to Elizabeth Silk in the hospital.

John winked at the scowling bouncer and strolled away, hand in pocket. The fingers of his right hand curled around the sharpened wooden stick he'd put there yesterday. He'd felt like an idiot at the time, but Elizabeth's e-mail had urged him to do it. She'd said he'd feel safer;

she'd said he'd *be* safer. He halted at the next doorway, a student hall of residence.

The woman—the vampire—in the red dress stood there as she'd promised, lighting a cigarette.

So what's your story, soldier? You think very loudly for a mortal.

John took a step closer. "You heard me."

She took the cigarette from her lips and regarded him. "Anyone can hear you, if they choose. You need to get control of that for a comfortable life. For a life at all."

John narrowed his eyes. "Are you threatening me?"

"Nah," said the beautiful vampire carelessly. "I've had my tea."

The reminder of childhood conversations over whether someone had already eaten "tea"—dinner to most of the world—and was therefore available to play made John grin without meaning to, and the vampire accorded him a wink by way of reward.

"Are there many of you in Glasgow?" John asked.

She shrugged and took a draw on the cigarette. "Enough."

"Enough for what?"

"For you to run into if you keep your eyes open. What's on your mind, soldier?"

"You," John said with a half laugh, waving his hand from her to the street in general. "Vampires. It's all new to me, and I've no idea what to do about it."

"Nothing you can do," said the vampire. "It just is."

"It shouldn't be, though, should it?"

The vampire's lips twisted. "You're talking to the wrong person, son." She considered him, head leaning to one side. "I'd tell you to talk to the hunters, but they're a bunch of bastards, and you look as if you've been in the wars already. Literally."

John didn't let his gaze drop for a moment, or allow his facial expression to alter. Without warning, the vampire gave a smile that took his breath away.

"Cheer up," she said. "If I was a hundred years younger—and hadn't had my tea—I'd invite you home for a bite. You take care, soldier. You've got rare gifts for a mortal, and some of my kind won't like that."

She moved forward and John grasped his stake harder, but she only stepped out of the doorway and resumed her walk toward St. George's Cross. With a last draw on her cigarette, she dropped the butt on the ground and stood on it.

Experimenting, John sent his thought after her. *That's a filthy habit. You should give those things up.*

What for? I'm not going to die of lung cancer, am I?

John gave a twisted smile and turned back toward home. He didn't even know her name, but without meaning to, she'd filled his floundering life with powerful new purpose. He hoped Elizabeth Silk was online, because he had a thousand questions for her.

Saloman stepped over the twitching, injured vampire bodies that lay on Adile Aslan's luxurious carpets, until he found Adile herself, huddled on a cushion in the corner. Once, possibly only a few days ago, she'd been beautiful, wealthy, ambitious, and, probably, bored. She'd run a successful business with her handsome husband and lived in a big, opulent house with two sweet children. And then Luk had come.

The children had been taken away by grandparents, to whom they clung. Her husband was dead, and Adile herself was thin and pale and exhausted, with two betraying puncture wounds in her neck that Luk hadn't troubled to heal.

"Was it worth it, Adile?" Saloman asked sadly.

"He promised me everything," she said dully. "Not just moderate success, but everything. I'd have been his queen."

It was like talking to Tsigana. Only Tsigana had never been this gullible. Adile raised her eyes from the carpet and would have glared at Saloman if only she'd been able to summon the energy. Luk had sucked it all out of her while he lived in her house and recruited his followers and his expendable fighters to throw in Saloman's path.

"You took it from me," she told Saloman.

"No, I didn't. He never gave it to you because he never had it."

"And now, because of you, he's gone."

Another burst of rebellion cleared up, a few more vampires to forgive and persuade. He might have been making progress, but looking around the carnage that was Adile's house, Saloman doubted it. He needed to find Luk, and soon. He'd almost gotten to him this time. Almost.

"Where did he go?" Saloman asked, watching as a vampire whose back had been broken began to sit up very slowly and gingerly. Halfway there, he met Saloman's gaze and gave a rueful smile and a shrug that said, *Sorry. You were right; I was wrong.*

"Away," Adile said, and started to cry huge, silent tears. They weren't for her husband. Or at least, not yet. Saloman whirled around and sat beside her. His heart beat fast with sudden relief and, beyond it, excitement.

"Far away?" he asked.

Adile nodded. "He won't come back, will he?" she whispered.

He was right: Luk was leaving Turkey. He'd gathered the support he needed, and now, at last, Saloman could stop fighting the same battle over and over and return the city to peace. Before he went home to face Luk.

"No," he said. "He won't come back." He licked one finger and touched the woman's bruised, abused throat. She didn't flinch, but her eyes lifted to his, startled and wondering. "May your pain make you strong and not bitter. We've all been used by Luk."

Standing up, he walked back across the room toward the door. He glanced back once, and the recovering vampires who'd fought him an hour ago jumped to their feet with alacrity to follow him.

I won't let this happen in Budapest, he promised.

How will you stop me? came the immediate response.

Saloman smiled. He'd meant Luk to hear, and he did. Because he was too afraid still not to listen. That was another relief. *Budapest is mine.*

Count the days, Saloman, and make the most of them.

Chapter Eleven

The vampire Dante was thrilled. Budapest was in the grip of a massive electrical storm, and the crashing thunder vibrated through his new, ultrasensitive self like an entirely new experience. The pelting of the rain on his upturned face made his skin positively sore, like hailstones. He felt as if he were drawing the forked lightning from the sky into his own body, boosting his already massively greater strength and energy. The angry thunderclaps seemed only to echo his own power.

Besides which, the storm matched the atmosphere he desired for the occasion. Black skies, filthy clouds obscuring moon and stars, thunder and lightning—every good horror film should begin with these things. And Dante was determined to make an impression.

Luk, interestingly, was not immune to the storm either. The Ancient had paid only erratic attention to his surroundings on the journey into Hungary, as if his mind were on higher things, like power and revenge. Dante had no quarrel with that, but it was good to see Luk smile at the thunder; it meant he was paying attention.

They had eight Turkish vampires with them. Not a great haul, much to Luk's fury, for although the presence of an Ancient had impressed every vampire they encountered, Saloman's was the name and reputation they knew. The discontented would cling to Luk for a while, using him in their quest for freedom from Saloman's restrictions on matters like killing, but with each defeat they'd trickled back to Saloman. All Luk could do was latch onto other rebels and annoy Saloman. And at least Saloman *was* annoyed.

Should Luk defeat him, it would be a different story, of course.

Another fork of lightning flashed across the ominous sky, briefly illuminating the narrow street and the carved stone angel above the doorway on the left. Dante had nearly walked past it. Again. As the thunder tore through his head, Luk stopped dead, gazing up at the angel, frowning.

"Maximilian," he said slowly. "That is Maximilian's work."

Impatiently, Dante began, "Who the hell is—" He broke off. "Oh. Saloman's other creation? Did he enchant it?"

"You spotted that? Good for you. Yes, he enchanted it, and through it the whole building. Subtly, and not badly done." He reached up, as if trying to touch the angel, then dropped his hand back to his side. "He carved it too. Most talented sculptor I ever saw. He could have been better than Michelangelo. . . . One of the strongest of the new vampires too, ambitious. We could use him, although I suppose he will side with Saloman."

"Not necessarily," Dante said thoughtfully. "As I recall, it was Maximilian who led the conspiracy against Saloman and killed him back in the seventeenth century. No one knows where he is now."

Luk dragged his eyes down from the angel and laughed. "Saloman taught him well! They both killed their creators. Is this your 'club'? The building is full of vampires and humans." His eyes glittered. Although he didn't talk about it so much, Luk was still eternally hungry.

"We need Angyalka on our side," Dante said uneasily. "I've done my research on her. Once, she was Zoltán's lover—Zoltán, who deposed your friend Maximilian—until Saloman appeared on the scene. Clearly, she follows whoever is the strongest, with one important caveat. She doesn't tolerate anyone breaking her rules. No violence or feeding on the premises. It keeps her safe from the hunters. I've made sure the others understand the rules."

Luk curled his lip. "I do not follow rules. I make them," he said, and pushed open the door beneath the stone angel. Impatiently, Dante beckoned the others to follow. In a fresh bolt of lightning, he caught sight of the angel again, and instead of the exquisite carving, he saw now just a dull, all but featureless decoration. Surely that was a bad omen? As if his powers lessened when Luk left his side, as if he weren't quite as in control as he wanted to be.

He bolted upstairs after Luk, taking the steps two and three at a time, which at least helped restore his confidence. Dante, before he'd been turned, had been a fit man for sixty years old, but he would never have contemplated bounding up a steep staircase at such a pace. As a vampire, it seemed, all things were possible.

And once Luk had killed Saloman, Dante couldn't wait to go home to America, oust the current vampire leader, Travis—once Dante's partner in crime and now, against all the odds, Saloman's ally—and take over the reins of human and vampire government. As yet he hadn't quite decided on his methods, but he rather thought a bit of terror, carnage, and war might be best. Humans could be shown the murderous power of their unsuspectedly undead neighbors and allowed to go on their inevitable rampage against them. There would be mass slaughter, mainly of humans, and out of the chaos could step wise old Senator Dante, adviser to several successive United States presidents and the most influential politician of his age, the only man who could restore calm and order. They'd never guess he was a vampire himself until he just didn't die, and by then it wouldn't matter. He would be too firmly in control.

But this was no time to daydream. He had to keep Luk in order while letting him impress the local vampires enough to follow him. Just like Turkey, really.

When the vampire bouncers welcomed them inside without so much as a glance of suspicion, Dante's elation rose higher. With his new, immortal eyes, he was even more appreciative of the Angel Club's interior decor, its contrast to the outer dinginess of the entrance sharper than ever. He could even appreciate the loudness of the music, the relentless sensuality of its vibrating beat. It was a young band of human males who'd clearly grabbed and held the audience's attention—although whether for their musical talent or the sheer handsomeness of their singer was debatable.

Dante's visits here as a human had been a trifle frightening, since he hadn't been able to tell people from vampires. Now he knew at a glance, and he'd never guessed just how high the proportion of vampires was. Decidedly this was a fine recruiting ground. None of them even troubled to mask—apart from Luk, who allowed only his undead status to be read.

Dante, who was learning all the time, knew he had to keep the secret of his own identity for a little longer. They didn't want Saloman or his loyal cohorts turning up before they were finished here. To this end, he was sure Luk was helping to cloak him, for several of the vampires here were strong, strong enough to see through the best mask Dante could muster. And among those strong vampires was the Angel's beautiful owner herself—Angyalka.

He recognized her at once. Her luscious hips seemed to shimmer as she sashayed across the room toward the bar in her simple yet sexy black dress and boots. Dante remembered being surprisingly aroused by her beauty on his previous visits here; now, with his heightened vampire sensuality, he seemed to sizzle. He wanted to bite Angyalka. He wanted to screw her across the bar.

As if she felt his surge of lust—which, on reflection, she probably did—she looked directly at him. He almost exploded.

Angyalka changed direction and came to meet him, her gaze flickering watchfully but quite without anxiety to Luk and their followers.

"Grayson," she said in English, her exotic accent doing quite unexpected things to his nether regions. "How nice of you to come back. I see you no longer need Dmitriu."

Now her eyes did widen slightly as they flashed around his companions as if searching for something.

Luk spoke telepathically to him alone. *She's trying to reach Saloman,* he said in some delight. *I'm blocking her, and though she feels that, she has no idea how or who's doing it. You never told me you'd already annoyed Saloman to that extent.*

You read all that from her?

Of course. I suppose I should have read it from you. What other secrets do you keep?

A pain, sharp and agonizing, shot through his head. Dante couldn't help clutching it in both hands, but Luk's interest was apparently brief, for he was released almost immediately. It felt like someone had loosened some huge steel clamp around his skull, and withdrawn the massive iron bolt that had bored its way through his brain.

Angyalka hadn't moved. "What can I get you, gentlemen?" she asked mildly.

Relieved of pain, Dante let his libido rush back to the fore. He smiled. "A little wine," he said, slipping his arm around her waist and jerking that soft, luscious body against him. "And a lot of sex," he whispered in her ear. "Take me upstairs."

He could feel that was where she lived. A room upstairs, behind the club, redolent with her scent, her presence.

She didn't shove him; he didn't land winded against the bar. And yet he felt as if he had. Somehow, she'd extricated herself from his arm and stood now a foot away from him.

"I do not have sex with fledglings," she said contemptuously. She said it loudly enough for all who cared to hear, and in the sudden silence of the room—the band had just stopped playing and were coming down from their stage for a break—he guessed many did. However, before embarrassment could strike, if it was going to, Luk provided a most unwelcome distraction.

He let out one of his wilder laughs. "Is that another of your pathetic rules?" he asked. "Like no feeding?"

Without any further warning, he reached out one arm and seized a passing human male, who happened to be the band's handsome singer on his way to the bar.

"I'm hungry," Luk said to the surprised youth, and sank his fangs into his jugular.

Dante groaned. His plan was aborted, as it were, at takeoff.

As once before, Elizabeth found the door of Saloman's huge house in Budapest simply opened when she pushed it. And as always at the prospect of seeing him again, her heart hammered in her breast so hard it seemed to curtail her breathing. *Ridiculous. He might not even be here.*

He could still be in Istanbul, where, she knew, a major vampire battle had been waged. In fact, she and the Hungarian hunters had been preparing to go to help their beleaguered Turkish colleagues when word had come from Mustafa that things were quiet in the city once more. One of Luk's living victims, a wealthy and respected businesswoman, had come forward to tell the hunters all she knew: that Luk had left the city and wasn't coming back.

Inside Saloman's front door, Elizabeth closed it and

dropped her suitcase to tug her hand through her soaking hair and wring out the rainwater. Shaking herself like a wet dog, she dragged her bag along the spacious hall before abandoning it at the foot of the stairs. As she began to climb, a flash of lightning seemed to spring from several points in the house before the crash of thunder filled her ears.

Saloman's head appeared over the banister from two floors up and she paused, overwhelmed by the whole setting.

Her heart lurched with pleasure and with hope. But he was too far away for her to make out the expression on his face, to read his difficult but not impossible body language.

"Hello," she called, feeling slightly foolish. "Can I come in?"

"Always. I left the door open for you."

He'd probably sensed her arrival in Budapest, felt her drawing nearer to him across the city.

"Come up," he said. "I want to show you something."

She'd never been in this portion of the house before. Most of her time had been spent in his bedroom. Intrigued, she climbed up past the landing where both drawing room and bedroom were located and found him waiting for her at the top of the next flight. Taking her hands, he kissed each of them in turn and then, briefly, her lips. But when she would have returned for a longer kiss, he was already leading her away. "Come."

Smothering her disappointment, she asked, "What is it?"

"I've had some more rooms made livable. What do you think?"

Reaching past her, he flung open the door on her left. Elizabeth walked past him into a large, bare room with three sets of shuttered windows. At the far end another door opened into another empty room beyond. They were gracious, well proportioned, with the high, decorative ceilings of the nineteenth century. If you really looked, you could see where some of the ornamental plaster had been repaired in a couple of places. The floors were polished wood; walls and ceilings were painted white. A large, elegantly carved fireplace occupied the center of one wall.

Elizabeth walked through the empty space, gazing around her, and peered into the next room. They were mirrors, really, of the rooms he largely lived in below, except without the character of opulence and comfort he'd achieved there.

"They're lovely rooms," she acknowledged. "What will you use them for?"

He came and stood beside her in the doorway. "I thought I would give them to you."

She blinked. "To me?"

"For when you are here. You can decorate them, furnish them as you see fit. Have a sitting room and a study if you like. Or a bedroom, a gymnasium, a library, whatever. They are yours to do with as you wish."

Stunned, she took a moment to take in his meaning, to recognize the gladness that seemed to surge upward from her toes until it constricted her throat. And yet she still had to ask: "You're not even doing this to keep me out of your hair, are you?"

He shook his head. "The opposite, in fact. I thought you might feel more at home if you had a space that was entirely yours."

She smiled, letting her doubts fall away. "In this house, it would never be that. I like to share with you." Leaning forward she touched her forehead to his hard, cool shoulder and closed her eyes in pure happiness. "Thank you, Saloman."

He touched her at last, his fingers stroking through her hair. "Then you like this? You have ideas?"

She smiled again and lifted her head. "I have a thousand. Saloman . . . ?"

"Yes?"

"There's a job," she blurted at last. "At Budapest University. For a year, with the possibility of extension. Or at least, there was a job. I never sent the acceptance because this stuff with Luk came up before I had a chance to post it." *The chance or the courage.*

His eyes searched hers. "Well, you are in Budapest," he observed. "It is easy enough to give your acceptance in person."

She swallowed. "You'd be happy for me to do that? To live here for a year?"

His hand slid down under her chin. He was smiling. "I would like nothing better. Unless it was two." He bent and kissed her mouth, and she wound her arms around his neck. "You think too much, agonize too much over things that are basically simple. Is this what's been eating you up?"

"Partly," she admitted. "And I suppose I worry that there's nothing in me to keep the attention of a being who's lived for millennia. I'd rather die than trail around after someone who simply tolerated me, or didn't notice me." As his expression changed, she bit down on her lip to shut herself up. "I'm sorry. I—"

"No more self-deprecation," he interrupted. "You more than anyone should know that we do not choose whom to love; we do not need reasons. Thirty years old or three thousand makes no difference to that. I would always have been drawn simply to who you are, the beauty that is you."

"Truly?" she whispered.

"Truly." His gaze shifted to her neck. "But you . . . you grow day by day, and that fascinates me beyond love." He bent, drawing her up against him so that she could feel his growing hardness in her abdomen, his silken lips on her throat.

Her eyes closed.

"Let me taste you," he whispered, and she gasped soundlessly as his sharp, wicked teeth grazed the skin over her vein. The familiar rush of helpless desire caused her to fall back against the wall. She twisted her head in blatant invitation. Somehow, there was almost as much sensual pleasure in offering herself to him like this as in the strange, tugging ecstasy she felt when he sucked her blood into his own body.

Moving against her, he pierced the skin of her neck and she moaned aloud. Saloman held her in his arms and began to suck.

It wasn't a long drink, more of a hello. Withdrawing his fangs, he licked the puncture wounds with tenderness and lifted his head. "Now come to bed," he whispered. "And be loved."

Elizabeth, melting at his words, resisted from instinct when he released her. She clung to him with all her strength, grinding her body against him in blatant, demanding lust. "Let's christen this room instead."

Flames danced in his black eyes. "You want me to take you on the floor? Hard and rough?"

"Oh, yes." She pressed her mouth to his, drawing him through the doorway, already burrowing under his shirt to feel the smooth skin and hard muscle beneath. He tugged once at her top, and as the buttons rolled to the floor, his hand found its way to her naked breast. And then he paused. Maddeningly, his eyes lost their exciting focus.

"What?" she whispered against his lips.

He closed his eyes tight with a sound like a groan. And when he opened them, they blazed like burning coals. "Anticipation will have to sustain us for now. I must go."

"Go? Go where?" Inclined to outrage, she tried to draw back and found herself pulled hard against him once more in a quick, enveloping hug.

"To the Angel." Releasing her, he stepped away. "Luk and Dante have broken cover at last."

Dante doubted it would make any important difference to the outcome, but at least Luk chose not to kill the boy.

His weak human heart still beat when Luk dropped him, and he slumped dizzily to the floor.

"And now that I've got your attention," Luk said, "let me introduce myself."

Dante actually felt the mask slipping away as Luk revealed himself, and knew he'd been right: that the Ancient *had* been propping up his own clumsy mask. The vampires in the club all stared. Several stood up and came forward for a better view. Humans glanced in their direction, uneasy, bewildered at what had happened to the singer sitting on the floor absently rubbing his neck, and wary of being involved in any violence.

Angyalka herself lifted one hand to prevent the advance of her vampire muscle, who either didn't register or didn't care about Luk's identity.

"I am Luk," said the Ancient with a flourishing bow. "Guardian of the Undead Prophecies. And I come to offer you the greatest gift of all: freedom."

"How kind," Angyalka said politely. Her eyes were wary but unafraid. If Luk had unmasked, Saloman would know he was here. The only trouble was, they didn't know where Saloman himself was. He could be in Budapest or still in Turkey. Or anywhere else in the five continents. "Er . . . freedom from what?"

Luk smiled. "Silly rules. Vampires should live as vampires, not as slaves to the oppressive controls of my cousin Saloman. Behold your savior. Follow me and win back your freedom."

He may have been mad, but he'd just replaced Dante's cautious plan with a much bolder move of his own, and he was an impressive bastard. In the same sort of way Saloman was impressive. And, of course, he was saying what the rebellious vampires' spirits wanted to hear. Dante could swear there wasn't one of them not touched by the prospect of doing what the hell they liked. Like life-sentence prisoners suddenly released en masse into the community. How the hell could he and Luk control that?

Quashing his sudden panic, he realized they didn't need to. All Luk needed was the overlordship, the acknowledgment, the backup to fight his powerful cousin. Dante saw several pairs of eyes flicker between Luk and Angyalka, known to be Saloman's friend. At least in this place, they would take their lead from her.

She smiled. "I regard the Angel as a microcosm of the world," she said conversationally. "And here we enjoy the freedoms we do only because of the rules I insist on. Rules you gentlemen have just broken."

There was a backward movement as the club vampires aligned themselves physically away from Luk. It didn't matter. The invitation was made and would spread. Away from the Angel, support would rush in.

"I must, therefore, ask you to leave." Angyalka was perfectly safe saying that. She knew just as well as Dante did that Saloman could be on his way, and that they were not ready to face him, certainly not with all the vampires of the Angel on Saloman's side.

"You are too beautiful to disregard," Luk said gallantly. He wrinkled his nose. "Besides, the place stinks of my cousin. Until we meet again." He gave another of his flourishing bows and swept from the room with effortless speed. The humans wouldn't even have seen him go. Dante, emphasizing the pecking order, spared Angyalka a wink before he swept past the Turkish bodyguard and followed Luk downstairs.

The Ancient had masked again, so it took Dante by surprise to see him standing very still in the doorway to the street.

"Dmitriu," Luk said abruptly.

"What?"

"Dmitriu is coming. Saloman's younger creation."

"I'm only too well acquainted with that bastard," Dante said with feeling. "You can kill him, can't you? If there's a way, I'd like to help."

"But I cannot feel Saloman. Saloman could be with him."

"Or he could be a thousand miles away."

"I'm not ready to take the chance," Luk said grimly. "Not on an empty stomach. Run."

Without further warning, Luk seized him by the hand and leapt through the air.

Dante had never run like this. It was terrifying being pulled at such speed and at such heights over buildings and roads, trees and cars, wherever Luk could gain the briefest foothold from which to spring next. After the initial paralyzing shock, Dante began to make his own stumbling efforts to cooperate, to move when Luk did, and discovered he learned fast. It would take years, maybe centuries, to find the speed and height of Luk's leaps, but the new power exhilarated him, and he took as much pride in his ability to learn as in Luk's obvious return to strength.

You are so *dead, Saloman.*

"He went that way," the vampire Dmitriu said with a negligent nod into the downpour as Saloman settled on the Angel's roof beside him. Even in the relentless rain, he smelled of the Awakener. "Looked suspiciously like fleeing to me, and he had Dante with him. Can you sense him?"

Saloman shook his head. "Luk's masking them both."

"Their bodyguards are still lurking on the stairs inside. They seem a little bewildered as to where their masters have gone."

"Their masters are a little careless with the lives of their followers," Saloman observed.

Dmitriu glanced at him. "You want them dead?" They varied in strength; one was strong enough to give a little trouble, but Dmitriu didn't doubt that between them he and Saloman could easily kill all eight.

"We kill a few; the rest flee," Saloman said, gazing around the dark streets on either side of the building. His mask was in perfect place, even for Dmitriu—which was unusual enough to alert Dmitriu to the tension thrumming through his powerful friend. A tension that he suspected had little to do with the coming fight and everything, surely, to do with the vampires who had fled. Saloman brought his gaze back to Dmitriu. "Damage limitation. Word gets around that Luk abandoned his followers and therefore is a poor choice of leader. And it's a visible punishment for breaking Angyalka's rules. She'll be so pleased, she'll give me free wine."

"She always gives you free wine. They're coming out."

They jumped in perfect time, and Saloman unmasked. Dmitriu caught a hint of fury, a trace of sadness, and knew that neither would make any difference to the inevitable outcome.

"Merhaba," Saloman said, seizing the stunned lead vampire and biting into his throat. Draining him was the work of an instant, but it was long enough for the remaining vampires to overcome their shock.

The fight was brief and brutal, and as the third Turkish vampire shattered to dust under Dmitriu's stake, the door of the Angel opened to reveal several vampire spectators. As one, Luk's remaining followers fled into the night, their feet casting up puddle splashes that glittered in the streetlight.

Angyalka, hands on hips, observed, "They weren't the ones who bit my guest."

"Picky, picky," said Saloman.

"They'll spread the word," Dmitriu assured her. The other vampires, denied the entertainment of a fight, began to drift back inside or off into the night in search of prey.

Angyalka glanced at Saloman. "Was that really Luk?"

The pause was slight. "To all intents and purposes."

"You have a powerful enemy," she said with a hint of malice. "I'll be interested to see how you deal with him."

"I'll win him to my side by sheer personal charm and give him your bar as a reward," Saloman said flippantly.

Dmitriu laughed. Saloman inclined his head to Angyalka in a mocking sort of way, and strolled up the street in the opposite direction from the fleeing vampires. It might have been an illusion caused by the streetlights, but there seemed to be a sort of halo around him where no rain fell.

"I wish I knew when he was joking," Angyalka said.

"You do better than most."

Angyalka glanced at him. "He doesn't like this, does he?"

Dmitriu steered clear of the personal baggage. "He's already had to kill Luk once. But Luk's a formidable opponent. Especially in some sort of thrall to Grayson Dante."

"He's made Dante too strong for a fledgling." Angyalka cast an anxious glance over her shoulder at her beloved club. "There's going to be a huge battle, isn't there?"

"I hope it isn't huge, but yes, there will have to be a fight."

"Saloman *will* win." It wasn't quite a question.

"Oh, yes," Dmitriu agreed. *But at what cost?*

Chapter Twelve

Rudy Meyer shut his front door after the last American vampire hunter, with obvious relief, and turned to face Cyn, who leaned against the living room wall.

Cyn scanned his face with some anxiety. The hunters were a revelation: fascinating, organized, knowledgeable, strong, and—

"Assholes," Rudy commented.

Cyn let out a laugh of relief. "No, they're not; they're just stuck in their ways and convinced they're superior."

Rudy ran his hand through his graying hair with uncharacteristic agitation. "Maybe they're right. I'm getting old, Cyn. Maybe we do go about things all wrong. Maybe we need the organization."

"They'd put you in an office and make you do research and write reports."

"I'm sixty years old."

"You're fifty-four, and fit as a fiddle, with more kills under your belt than that damned annoying kid in the green vest." Cyn walked back to the lumpy old sofa and sat down, waiting for Rudy to join her.

"You're young and quick," Rudy said. "You've got the skills they need and psychic abilities to top it off. You'd do well there. And get paid for it."

"I'd be suspended in a week." She twisted her hands in her lap and lifted her gaze to his familiar, rugged face. "They make me uncomfortable, Rudy. They're too . . . inflexible. I mean, what the hell is this? 'Normal people aren't capable of dealing with the fact that vampires exist'? Really? That's people like you and me! If you'd known about vampires before you were attacked, you wouldn't have needed me to save your ass. How many other people could be saved if they just *knew*?"

"We're just as guilty, Cyn. We never tell either."

"Because we think we'll be laughed at. I don't know how we get around that one. And I don't know what's the deal about our redheaded vampire not killing Pete. They never explained that either. Guess we're too *normal* to understand." She straightened her back. "But you're right about one thing, Rudy. We do need an organization. Just not this one."

"What, then?" Rudy demanded, wandering through to his tiny kitchen to make coffee.

"Our own," said Cyn.

Rudy stuck his head around the door. "You mean expand? Take on Pete Carlile?"

"Maybe Pete. And a few others. I've been looking on the Internet, and there are people out there, people in this city, who've had encounters with vampires. And what's more, there seem to be increasing numbers of them."

"Maybe they're just coming out of the woodwork with the growth of the Internet."

"Maybe. And maybe it's because of the other things the hunters were telling us about. This power struggle over whether to accept Saloman. Humans will get caught in the cross fire, increasingly so. I've been e-mailing Elizabeth—"

"How is Mrs. Sherlock?"

"She's fine. Apparently there's a vampire war in Turkey too. Bad things are happening, and I think she's worried."

Rudy brought two mugs of coffee into the room and sat down beside her. "So what is it exactly that you want to do?"

Cyn drew a deep breath and gave voice to the bold idea growing inside her. "I want to form an army. A small mobile unit of hunters who can protect themselves while finding out what the hell's going on. Who can go anywhere as fast as they're needed and blast the bad guys, whoever and whatever they are."

"You want to join the SEALs?"

"No, but I wouldn't object to a bit of military training." She grinned triumphantly. "*And* I think I've found just the guy to do it. He's ex-army, an Afghanistan veteran, British. His name's John Ramsay, he's telepathic, and he wants to save the world from vampires."

Elizabeth, summoned to the hunters' headquarters by no less a person than the executive operations manager, was both relieved and puzzled to discover Mihaela, Konrad, and István already in the large, impressive office. She gave them a swift, interrogative glance on entry, and received minimal shrugs in response.

Like much of the headquarters building—which was situated in a quiet yet central Budapest street, protected from the curious as well as the ill-intentioned by an array of alarms and vampire detectors, and probably by some kind of masking spell too—the operations manager's office gave an impression of faded grandeur. A Renaissance painting of the Madonna and child hung on the wall behind his large, antique mahogany desk. The high ceiling was divided into panels by ornately carved beams that showed traces of recent woodworm treatment.

Beside the stranger at the desk sat Miklós, the chief

librarian and number two to the Grand Master of the Hungarian hunters. Elizabeth, whose dealings with Miklós in the past had been somewhat mixed, wasn't sure how she felt about that. A small, intellectual man of middle years, wearing his usual suit and tie, he stood as soon as Elizabeth was shown in.

"Elizabeth. How nice to see you again. Let me introduce our operations manager, Lazar. Lazar, Dr. Elizabeth Silk."

Surnames were never used among the network staff, presumably to lend the hunters some protective anonymity. Lazar, a large, bearlike man in his late thirties with a rather alarming scar running down one side of his face and neck and disappearing into his collar, rose from behind his desk to shake hands. He too wore a tie, perhaps to distinguish himself from the field hunters, who wore more casual dress, but it was loose, the knot pulled down below the open top two buttons of his shirt.

"Dr. Silk." His handshake was brief and firm, his pleasant voice businesslike. "I can't quite understand how we haven't met before. Your name has cropped up so often in the last year that I've begun to think of you as a member of my staff."

Elizabeth, who'd been wondering whether this meeting was about recruiting her to the network, smiled a little warily, and took the seat he indicated beside Mihaela.

Lazar resumed his own seat. "In case you don't know, my job in the organization is to coordinate the various field teams. I assign the tasks and receive the reports, decide if further action is needed and, if so, what. Our lead team here"—he paused to indicate the three hunters—"is pretty independent, self-finishers as well as self-starters, so occasionally reports appear on my desk of missions not assigned by me. I'm happy with this—important work is done faster, and obviously it makes my job easier."

He spared a glance and a nod of recognition for the hunters. In the short pause that followed, he picked up a pen from his desk and began to tap it rapidly and lightly on the paper in front of him, while his gaze slid from face to face and ended up fixed on Elizabeth.

"However . . ." he said ruefully. "I know you've all been waiting for the 'however.' And this is it. I'm worried the operation concerning the Ancient vampire Luk is getting away from all of us. Basic principles are being broken, threats ignored, lives endangered."

Mihaela opened her mouth as if to speak, then with an impatient shrug closed it again.

Lazar threw down his pen with a small clatter. "And, Dr. Silk, I'm afraid this is down to you. I know the network's gratitude has already been expressed to you for your cooperation in the initial mission against Saloman, for your help in trying to keep the Sword of Saloman out of the wrong hands, and for aiding in the rescue of an American national from a nest of foreign vampires here in Budapest. I join my thanks to that. But I have to tell you all, I have some serious concerns now."

His gaze moved to take in the hunters. "Dr. Silk is not a member of your team, or even of the hunter network. And yet lately it seems you have recruited not only Dr. Silk but Saloman, the most lethal vampire of all time and your natural, number one enemy."

Miklós cleared his throat. "You used Saloman to locate Josh Alexander in May, and in the subsequent rescue of Mr. Alexander from the labyrinth. During which you allowed not only Saloman but two other vampires to escape. And now we understand that in Turkey you've been working with him to locate Luk, *and* had him living in your house—your *safe* house!"

"*Not* safe," Lazar said severely. His gaze, no longer amiable, scoured the hunters and came to rest once more on Elizabeth. "My understanding is that this aberration occurred through you and some telepathic connection you have with Saloman, possibly stemming from the fact that you awakened him."

Elizabeth, unable to dispute this or to think of anything to add, took a leaf out of Saloman's book and simply inclined her head.

He turned back to the hunters. "This won't do. Look, I've been a field hunter. We all have occasional informants, vampires or their human minders whom we can bribe or threaten into revealing important information. We're human. Bonds form without our permission, but we have to be aware of their danger. And this isn't just threatening to become a danger—it *is* one."

He picked up the pen again, in both hands this time, as if he were about to snap it in two, while he positively glared. "You cannot, you simply cannot, regard a vampire of Saloman's stature as some kind of pet."

Elizabeth laughed. She didn't mean to, but the idea of anyone regarding Saloman in this light was just so ridiculous that she couldn't help it. Beside her, Mihaela's breath caught in a slight choke.

Both Miklós and Lazar stared at Elizabeth with stony disapproval.

She tried to sober. "I'm sorry," she said unsteadily. "I can assure you that none of us regards Saloman in that way." She paused to let the hysteria die back and to haul her thoughts into some kind of order. Her heart beat too fast, but she had to take the opportunity. "Saloman isn't like the other vampires any of us have encountered." She cast a glance at the hunters. "I think we all agree on that, at least. He can impose order among his own kind, and on many issues he's actually in agreement with us. On these issues, he's prepared to ally with us. And in fact, without him we wouldn't have retrieved Josh or prevented Dante from turning."

"And yet Dante has been turned," Miklós snapped.

"True," Elizabeth returned. "But that wasn't Saloman's fault. It was mine. I wouldn't let Saloman kill Dante when we rescued Josh."

Lazar blinked. "Wouldn't *let* him? How the hell—"

"It's true," István interrupted. "She talked him out of it. Although we agreed with her, we thought she was wrong at the time—for safety reasons—to insist. Time has shown Saloman's instinct to be more right than ours."

Lazar scowled at Konrad. "That wasn't in your report."

Konrad flicked imaginary fluff from his neatly pressed jeans. "It didn't seem important at the time."

Lazar's gaze switched back to Elizabeth. It was one of those piercing stares that used to unnerve her. Not anymore. "Exactly how did you 'talk him out of it'?"

Elizabeth frowned, trying to remember. It was Mihaela who said, "She stood in front of Dante when Saloman threatened him with his sword."

"Yes, it wasn't undiluted success, was it?" Miklós said waspishly. "You were meant to retrieve the sword."

"How?" István said.

Miklós closed his mouth, his lips pursed with displeasure. He didn't have an answer. Lazar returned to the main subject. "He could very easily have killed both of you."

Elizabeth shrugged. "I knew he wouldn't." *I will never kill you,* he'd said the night she'd confessed her love, the same night they'd each tried to kill the other and failed.

"You can't have known that! You awakened him; you're descended from one of his killers. By rights he should have killed you a year ago."

Elizabeth said, "We have an . . . understanding."

Lazar leaned forward over the desk. "What kind of an understanding? Dr. Silk, did you make a deal with Saloman?"

Reluctantly, Elizabeth glanced down the line of her friends, all watching her. She drew in her breath. "Only an unofficial one. That we won't kill each other. And he won't kill *them* either," she added, with a nod toward the hunters, "even though Konrad is descended from another of his killers." She looked away. "Except, I suppose, in self-defense."

"And you believed him?" Konrad burst out.

"We're still alive, aren't we?" Elizabeth retorted.

With a violent gesture, Lazar threw himself back in his seat and chucked the pen on the desk so hard that it rolled off onto the floor. "Have you considered, Dr. Silk, that Saloman's using you? *All* of you?"

"He isn't," Elizabeth said quickly. "Or not in the way you mean. He wants them—and you—to understand the good he can and will do. Do you know what he did before the Peruvian earthquake? And the Turkish one last year? Do you really not see possibilities in that for humanity?"

Lazar waved it aside. "Again, we simply don't know why he's doing it. There must be a payoff. He wants us to turn a blind eye to his own vampires, perhaps, while he defeats the rest."

"Or he wants our help to remove them!" Konrad exclaimed.

"No. He's offering his," Elizabeth insisted.

"You're playing with words," Miklós objected with a dismissive wave of one hand. "They mean the same thing: alliance with a powerful and extraordinarily dangerous vampire."

"Unsafe," said Lazar grimly. "Unwise and unacceptable."

"Also unprecedented," Elizabeth said. "Or so I understand."

"There is a reason for that. A vampire has never been discovered who is not treacherous, murderous, and totally untrustworthy."

"I don't think that's true," Elizabeth said at once. "I've met at least two in the last year who are not treacherous or untrustworthy once you understand something of the way they think. As for murderous . . . I can't deny there have been murders committed by those same vampires—including Saloman—but they were never random violence, or acts committed without justification, at least in their own eyes. I feel if you—"

"And how many vampires of any description did you meet prior to this last year?" Lazar inquired.

"None," Elizabeth admitted.

"Then I really don't think your experience qualifies you to lecture the rest of us on vampire behavior."

Elizabeth flushed. She lifted her chin. "On the contrary, my experience is fresh and untainted by personal tragedy. Most of you became hunters through some vampire attack, either suffered or witnessed. Your experience dictates that you regard all vampires alike—bestial killers who must be exterminated. I can't deny—and don't want to!—that there are many like that. But all?" She swung around to Mihaela, and beyond her István and Konrad. "You've met Saloman. Is he like other vampires?"

"No," said Mihaela, definitely enough, even though it wasn't necessarily a compliment.

Elizabeth pursued her point. "What about Dmitriu? The first time you mentioned him to me, you said he wasn't a bad fellow, despite being a vampire."

"Yes, but you can't say he didn't turn out to be treacherous!" said Konrad.

"Yes, I can," Elizabeth disputed at once. "He displayed loyalty to his friend and creator, whom he never has deserted. Your only issue with him is that he didn't put loyalty to us first. Why should he? He knew Saloman for five centuries, you for what? Two or three years?"

She found she was talking more to her friends than their superiors, but instead of switching her attention, she just carried on, after a quick glance at the latter to make sure they were listening. "The trouble with hunters is they're too focused to be impartial, too much on the front line to see things from the so-called enemy's point of view. Look again at Saloman's creations, Dmitriu and Maximilian. Look at his closest associates across the world and I think you'll find more than the mindless killers you expect. As for Saloman himself, he could be humanity's greatest asset."

"Oh, too far, Elizabeth," Konrad said, actually bouncing to his feet in his agitation to glower at her. "You're *obsessed*—"

He broke off abruptly, most probably because Mihaela had aimed a kick at his ankle. Elizabeth bit back her retort, and the words seemed to dissolve in her dry mouth, leaving her witless. Stupidly, this had never entered her head—that the hunters would cover for her. It wasn't just herself she was embroiling in this conflict of interest; it was her friends too.

Fuck, fuck, fuck, fuck, fuck . . .

Lazar said, "What exactly *is* your relationship with Saloman?"

I love him. The words stuck in her throat, because it wasn't any of Lazar's business. She refused to allow her relationship to be analyzed and picked over by strangers. Fortunately, it appeared to be a rhetorical question. Or perhaps Lazar too was scared by the possibilities of her answer.

"Because it seems to me," he said sternly, "that it lacks any sort of common sense or discipline. And I think that's the problem. Circumstances have flung you into the vampire world without proper training or basic defenses. I know you did a little emergency physical training with us last year, but that really isn't enough to deal with what you're facing now. Relaxing your guard, relaxing the rules, is dangerous. That's when people die, and it seems to me this whole team is being contaminated by your laxness."

Lazar lifted his hand when all three hunters began to talk at once, and shushed them. "I know. I know this has all stemmed from the best of intentions, and a devotion to duty none of us here could deny. But you're putting yourselves in acute danger now, and that we can't allow.

So," he said, gazing from face to face, "here's what I propose."

Running me out of town? Forbidding me the premises? Denying me any rights to friendship or information?

"Join us," said Lazar.

Elizabeth blinked. "I beg your pardon?"

"Join the network in an official capacity. Train as a hunter. As you go through the process and discover your strengths and weaknesses, we can decide among us where you would best fit in, as a special adviser to various teams or a permanent part of one team. Your undoubted value would then be properly harnessed and protected by our code of conduct; you'd stand a better chance of survival. To say nothing of the survival of your friends, who are also at risk through this laxness. I don't think you'll have any quarrel with our pay, conditions, or pensions."

Elizabeth felt as if she were picking her jaw up off the floor. It seemed to take an awful lot of time and effort. After everything that had just been said in the way of criticism, disapproval, and distrust, he really was recruiting her. "Are you serious?" she managed.

"Deadly serious."

"How did you get here?" Saloman asked in tones of vague amusement as Dmitriu bolted into the house and slammed the door on the sun.

"By means of a taxi and a thick tarpaulin," Dmitriu replied, throwing the latter carelessly on the floor of Saloman's uncluttered hall. Saloman stood at the top of the first flight of stairs, wearing only a pair of dark linen trousers that he hadn't troubled to fasten.

"How very enterprising of you," he murmured as Dmitriu strode the length of the hall and began to climb the stairs. "Er . . . did you want something?"

"Just news," Dmitriu replied. Pausing, he sniffed the air. "Is *she* here? The Awakener?"

"Her name is Elizabeth," Saloman said mildly, "and no, she isn't. She's communing with the hunters."

Dmitriu glanced at him as he passed into the drawing room. "Isn't that rather an unholy alliance for Saloman's mistress?"

"That rather depends on what she does with it. News of what?"

Dmitriu felt the steady gaze on the back of his neck as he looked around the drawing room. Saloman's computer was open on one of the tables, surrounded by a clutter of papers. Dealing in the human world, Dmitriu thought, with a familiar mingling of bafflement, admiration, and distaste.

"Luk," he said, turning to face Saloman. "Have you found him?"

"No. I doubt I'll be able to before he breaks cover again. I couldn't in Istanbul."

Dmitriu frowned, dropping into the nearest chair, which was almost ridiculously comfortable. "That leaves us no time to prepare for the fight. I don't like these odds."

Saloman shrugged. "I might be able to get to him through Dante, but so far Luk has him covered as well."

Dmitriu studied his face, looking in vain for traces of anxiety. "Are you worried?" he asked at last.

Saloman strolled over to the polished grand piano. "About what?"

"Luk! Can you kill him?"

Saloman sat on the stool and sounded a random note with one finger. "I killed him before."

"This time he has allies, and he'll use them. When he strikes, if you're alone, Saloman—"

"I'm assuming I can call quickly for support."

"Here, in Budapest, you'll get it," Dmitriu acknowledged. "But perhaps not quickly enough. Will the Awakener fight for you?"

Something almost like a smile crossed Saloman's face and disappeared. "Elizabeth. Yes, she would fight for me.

But I'd rather she didn't. Not against Luk at full strength."

"Is he?" Dmitriu pounced. "At full strength? Aside from the fact that he hasn't yet taken the life of his Awakener."

"No. He ran from us too fast last night. He isn't ready yet, and he's sane enough to know it."

"Then when he *is* ready, he'll strike quickly, hoping to catch you alone and unprepared. You should consider gathering bodyguards."

Saloman spread both hands on the piano keys and began to play. "Luk would simply blow them through the wall. Besides, I will not move about the city like a despot frightened of assassination."

The music was familiar to Dmitriu, and beautifully played. Chopin. He'd almost forgotten this talent of Saloman's.

Dmitriu stood up. "I will come and live here. Bring in another few vampires—strong ones who are your friends. No one will suspect you of fear if you're simply with friends."

"I do not want other vampires here. I'm not afraid of Luk." He spoke tranquilly; his face was serene as he continued to play. But it was too late. His fingers had stumbled on one of the notes, telling Dmitriu all he needed to know.

Saloman wasn't afraid of Luk. Not physically. He'd face anything the world threw at him, with joy in the fight. But he did fear all the emotional baggage that came with Luk.

Without a word, Dmitriu got up and left the room.

"Good-bye, Dmitriu." Saloman's voice followed him down the staircase.

"I'm not leaving," Dmitriu said grimly.

Instead, he walked through the kitchen to the basement staircase and jumped down into the cool, damp darkness of the cellar. Here there were no distractions and he could think.

He tried quite hard to talk himself out of it. He remembered his own anger and Saloman's pain and suffering in every detail. And yet what lingered with most strength was the vision of a solitary vampire stepping out of the misty darkness that surrounded the ruins of a Scottish church, sword raised in defense of the maker he'd betrayed.

Dmitriu sighed. "Please, no," he begged of no one in particular. But it was a question of Saloman's tolerance. Saloman's survival. It was time.

Maximilian. Maximilian, you bastard, speak to me.

The message went through clearly, and yet there was no immediate response. Unless you counted the stunned astonishment that seemed to bounce back to him.

Dmitriu?

Get over it.

There was another pause. Then: *What do you want?*

Shift your despicable arse to Budapest.

I don't leave Scotland, Maximilian said distantly, as if that settled the matter.

Yes, you fucking do.

Silence greeted him. For a moment, rare rage swamped Dmitriu, before he realized Maximilian hadn't actually gone. He had nothing to say, but his path was open.

Max, he needs you.

Even when they'd escaped the building and found a table outside their favorite café, it seemed that no one wanted to be the first to speak. Elizabeth glanced up from her coffee and watched the hunters gaze thoughtfully into their own steaming cups.

Konrad, continuously and rhythmically stirring, suddenly dropped his teaspoon. "All right. What do you think, Elizabeth?"

Elizabeth sighed. "I don't know. To be honest, I turned up half expecting him to make this suggestion. I'd nearly decided to refuse, and then when he started bringing up everything I've done wrong, I thought I was mistaken and he was going to ban me from the premises instead. You could have knocked me down with a feather when he offered me a place."

"Then you'll still refuse?"

Still. Elizabeth smiled faintly. "You asked me before."

"You turned us down," Konrad recalled.

"That was before the battle with Saloman. I just wanted it to be over. I wanted nothing more than to be free of all of that." She waved her cup around the table. "Not you guys, obviously, but everything else. Vampires, killing, emotional turmoil. I wanted it all to go away so that I could crawl back into academia and be safe."

"But you don't really want that," Mihaela said shrewdly. "You grab each crisis with us as if it's a lifeline."

Elizabeth's smile turned lopsided. "Do I? Probably. Things changed after the battle in St. Andrews."

"Because you realized you were good at it?" Konrad hazarded.

"No . . . not really." She set down her cup and met his gaze. "I discovered I couldn't kill Saloman."

"Not on your own," Konrad agreed.

"No, I *could*, in theory, kill him on my own. Because I'm the Awakener. My body could do it. The rest of me just wouldn't." She'd never told them this before. Yet despite the discomfort that wouldn't allow her to be still in her seat, she knew it was time. "I held the stake; I could feel the power in me and *knew* I could do it. But I dropped the stake. Deliberately."

She turned to face Mihaela. "It was like a veil falling away from my mind. I knew it didn't matter what he'd done or what he would do; it didn't matter how much I hated myself or tried to fight it. I couldn't run away and I couldn't change it."

Mihaela's dark eyes were wide, almost frightened. "Change what?" she asked huskily.

"That I loved him. I had since the night he kidnapped me from the Angel. Or maybe before. I don't know, and it doesn't really matter. Because I still can't change it. And now I don't want to."

It couldn't have been much of a surprise to any of them, and yet the sudden wave of almost physical pain that emanated from Mihaela nearly knocked her off her chair. She felt it like a blow, yet the pain was undoubtedly the other woman's.

"Mihaela," she whispered, seizing her friend's hand and squeezing it. "I'm not *dead*."

Mihaela let out a sound that might have been a sob or a laugh. "No. Sometimes I think I am," she said incomprehensibly. Her hand turned in Elizabeth's, squeezing back, and the pain seemed to recede. Glad as she was, Elizabeth felt curiously shaken, not just by Mihaela's obvious unhappiness, which turned out to be far more profound than Elizabeth had ever guessed, but by the strength of her own empathy. She'd always been good at reading people's emotions, but recently, with the development of her telepathy, she seemed to be picking up far more than facial expressions and body language.

Forcing her mind back to the discussion, she glanced at Konrad and István. "You see my predicament here. I'm pretty sure Lazar would withdraw his offer if he knew what I've told you. As a hunter, in many eyes, I'm too badly compromised."

István shifted his chair to give his long legs more room. "And in your own?"

Elizabeth lifted her cup and drank before she answered. "In my own . . . I can see the advantages. I want to help protect humans from vampire attacks, from unspeakable fear and violent death. I have no conflict there with the aim of the organization. But—and training me won't change this—vampires are worthy beings too. I believe that under Saloman that will become more and more obvious. There will always be rogue vampires, as there are violent and criminal humans. Society needs to be protected from both."

"You know you're speaking heresy," Mihaela said, withdrawing her hand in order to pick up her coffee cup.

"I know. I couldn't join without voicing it. And in voicing it I *would* be ejected from the premises forever. Perhaps I should just remain an unofficial friend of the network."

"The network won't change," Konrad warned. "It must remain true to the principles of its foundation. Eliminating vampires."

"Everything changes," Elizabeth insisted. "The world is changing now—Luk himself prophesied some major change of power stemming from what happens here in Budapest. It could be change for good if we just play it right. . . ."

"Under Saloman?" Mihaela said. "You do realize you're now advocating his domination of the world? The thing to which, more than anything else, you were once steadfastly opposed."

"I still am. I'm not keen on tyranny of any description, however benevolent. And, in fact, Luk's prophecy seems to imply that Saloman *loses* power. Look, I've sown the seeds of the idea of mutual cooperation in Saloman; I'd like you to think about it too."

István smiled slightly. "Tiny cogs like us don't influence matters like that."

"Yes, we do," Elizabeth argued. She hesitated, then: "Saloman doesn't believe that revealing the existence of vampires will lead to the war and slaughter that you envisage."

"But it would," Konrad retorted. "And rightly so. Elizabeth, however good your intentions—and I believe they are good—your thinking is seriously flawed. There can be no peaceful coexistence with vampires. Not now, not tomorrow, not ever."

Elizabeth transferred her rueful gaze to István and Mihaela. "You see? I'd make a rotten hunter. Besides which," she added, making a clean breast of everything, "I've been offered another job in Budapest. At the university."

"You can do both," Mihaela said earnestly. "Many do."

It seemed nothing Elizabeth said could rid them of the idea that her rightful place in life was as a hunter. It baffled her, in a pleased sort of way—until she saw Mihaela's gaze flicker to István, and realized they hoped that being a hunter would finally part her from Saloman.

Chapter Thirteen

Rudy murmured, "Nice one, Cyn."

Apart from that, there was no sound in the basement of the building he and Cyn had worked hard to turn into a gymnasium and training area. They'd done it all with material found in dumps and junk shops, mainly because they had very little money between them. Cyn was proud of what they'd achieved, and her confidence had been further boosted by the praise of Pete Carlile and the two other survivors of vampire attacks who'd joined their little troop and come to the basement tonight to help welcome the soldier John Ramsay.

At the Brit's entrance, all conversation and clowning cut off as if someone had thrown a switch. John Ramsay stood just inside the door facing them. A backpack was slung over his right shoulder. Apart from one important point, he looked exactly as he had in the photo Cyn had seen on the Internet.

Although his steady eyes didn't flicker as they moved around the room, there could be no doubt that he heard Rudy's remark.

At last his gaze found Cyn, whom he must have recognized from her own photo. “Don’t sweat it. I shoot with my right.” He sounded very Scottish, and aggression clearly boiled beneath the deceptive calm of his mocking voice.

“Shooting doesn’t touch the bastards we’re fighting,” Rudy snapped.

Ramsay moved. It looked as if he simply flexed his fingers, and yet an instant later, something flew from his one hand with enough force to whiz as it passed her ear.

Cyn jerked around in fear. *Typical! Only I could find the Internet knife psycho from hell. . . .* But it wasn’t a knife that had buried itself at the center of the dartboard target hanging on the wall. It was a wooden stick. She dared to breathe again.

Rudy turned his gaze from the board to Ramsay. Although his lip curled, Cyn could tell from the gleam in his eyes that he was secretly impressed.

“You learn that in the British army, son?” Rudy asked.

“Nah. Glasgow pubs on a Friday night. You get all sorts of bams in there.”

Rudy grinned openly.

Cyn said, “What’s a bam?”

“Nutter.” Ramsay stuck out his hand. “John Ramsay. Pleased to meet you, Cyn.”

Cyn, inclined to think she might just have made the right choice after all, let her face relax into a smile as she took his hand. His grip was firm, but naturally so, without anything to prove. She liked his eyes too. They were what had drawn her to invite him here. Blue and piercingly intelligent, they seemed to have layers of character: a certain attractive calm, even wisdom beneath the turbulent defiance of youth.

“And you, John. This old fart is Rudy Meyer. He likes you.”

As Rudy and John solemnly shook hands, the others ambled forward to be introduced too.

"And you're all survivors of vampire attacks?" John said, examining each of them with open curiosity.

"Except Cyn," Rudy replied. "They steer clear of her unless she attacks them first."

The blue gaze came back to her. "Why's that?"

She shrugged. "I can feel them. I know what they are. They seem to get that and it freaks them."

John frowned. "Me too. Only, I met one once who didn't mind. She seemed more curious than dangerous."

"They're all dangerous," Cyn warned.

"I know." He dropped his backpack on the floor. "So what do you want me for? You all seem able to take care of yourselves."

"We want to take care of other people," Cyn said, just a little self-consciously. "We've been killing vamps for years, Rudy and me, but we want to understand the bigger picture. We want to be more effective. Fight as a team, protecting one another as we go."

He knew this, of course. They'd discussed it by e-mail.

"We want to be able to go to wherever there's a crisis, like Turkey, and make a difference. A real difference." She lifted her chin. "We want the world to hear about vampires and not laugh. We want people to *know*."

When Elizabeth finally fell asleep, and he'd had his fill of gazing down at her peaceful face, Saloman gently unwound his limbs from her warm, soft body and rose from her bed. At least, it was the bed she had chosen for her rooms from the several stored in the attic.

He was aware she'd elected to make one of her rooms a bedroom so that neither of them ever felt obligated to sleep in the same bed as the other. It would remain a choice. Saloman, who had lived through many ages and many customs, found this arrangement as acceptable as any other, and when she'd made the bed up to her satisfaction and brought him to see it in situ, he'd admired it, laid her upon it, and made love to her for most of the night. In between lovemaking—and sometimes during—

they'd talked about things that didn't matter to the world, only to him and to Elizabeth.

He could lose years of his existence this way, he thought without displeasure as he pulled on his shirt and trousers. Elizabeth was a distraction, however he looked at her, and for a vampire with the world to rule perhaps that wasn't a good thing. Saloman didn't care. Right now, the distraction was especially welcome. He could locate neither Luk nor Dante, nor even their remaining Turkish followers.

Perhaps it would be a good time to make his presence felt at the Angel and gauge how many vampires were defecting to Luk. Recent telepathic sweeps had encountered a worrying number of vampire minds closed to him. This could be because the vampires were simply nervous, because they hadn't yet made a decision, or because they'd already changed allegiance.

It wasn't beyond Saloman to find out which by force-reading their thoughts, but aside from his personal distaste, that wouldn't bring them back to him. He needed to impress. He needed to be seen by his people, particularly by those who hid. But Dmitriu was still out hunting, and Saloman would not leave Elizabeth here with no protection. Not when Luk could break just about every enchantment he'd ever set. Mostly because Luk had taught him and understood the workings of his mind too well.

Even insanity hadn't prevented Luk from seeing into Saloman's soul. He'd known exactly how to inflict the most exquisite pain, fully appreciated the effect of the doubtle betrayal on Saloman when he'd enticed Tsigana away. And the final, devastating blow of his attempted assassination.

When Luk had leapt on him, hurtling through the black, wet sky with murderous intent, the Guardian had been well aware that the identity of his killer would weigh far more with Saloman than death itself. Luk had known it would shrivel Saloman's heart, had probably expected it to crush his spirit entirely. What Luk clearly hadn't counted on was the black rage that had drowned Saloman's despair, imbuing his lethal hands with a will of their own. Since the clouds of insanity had diminished Luk's powers as a fighter, Saloman could have disarmed him and spared him. But fury had kicked the weapons from Luk's hands, and rage had plunged the stake that killed him.

And so Saloman had been left standing over the still body of his dead cousin, whom he would have died to save, rain streaming down his face like human tears, as if water could wash away the blood. He was the last of his kind, alone for eternity.

Saloman shied away from the unbearable memory and returned to Dmitriu. He'd reluctantly let him stay, because of the added protection it afforded Elizabeth, and yet now that he was here, Saloman had to quash the eternal desire of the parent to know where his child was, and stop himself from seeking him across the city.

Mocking himself, Saloman glided downstairs, barely touching any of the steps with his bare feet, and entered his drawing room. Pulling back one heavy red velvet curtain, he looked down onto the quiet street, half hoping for a glimpse of Dmitriu. He wanted to feed on his way to the Angel. He'd already drunk from Elizabeth—increasingly this diet seemed to be all he wanted—but if he took all he needed from her, he would very quickly sap her strength. Right now, she needed all of that, physical and mental.

Leaving the curtain open, Saloman turned back into the room. Although he would never influence her to take the step, he hoped she would become a hunter. While they obviously planned to turn her against him in this way, he hoped for the opposite: that through her, they would learn his true value, gain an insight into the gentler side of his nature and the good that was to be found in vampires.

Unlike the rest of the world, the hunters' organization had stagnated. You had only to look at Konrad to see that. Of course, during the three hundred years of Saloman's sleep, vampires had done themselves no favors there—indiscriminate killing, chaos, and occasional mass slaughter did tend, in modern parlance, to piss the hunters off. But Saloman had made a start toward reversing the trend. He doubted Konrad would ever convert—and frankly, he was no loss—but the other two were more thoughtful and receptive. It would take time, naturally, but at least they weren't shutting their ears or their hearts. And from them, the new tolerance and cooperation could spread.

Saloman sat down at the computer, read the news on various sites, flicked through his e-mail and fired off a couple of replies to the offices of two world leaders. Then he sprawled back in the wooden chair and thought about returning to Elizabeth's bed. Except she needed sleep, and he needed blood. There was only an hour left until dawn, and if Dmitriu didn't come home soon, Saloman would be reduced to biting the postman.

Worse, these days Elizabeth seemed to sense his hunger. And when she offered her smooth, tender throat to him, she was too damned alluring to resist. Blood and sex and Elizabeth . . .

Hard once more, he ran his hand over his crotch as if that could calm it, and rose to his feet. Something prickled the back of his neck. He spun fast enough to be invisible to the human eye, just as Luk swung through the glass of the middle window.

He landed a few feet away from Saloman, haloed in a sparkling cloud of falling glass shards. More from instinct than thought, Saloman threw up another barrier over the window to prevent any further invasion. Not that Luk couldn't pull that one down too when he felt like it. But Saloman could sense no other vampires. For whatever reason, Luk had come alone.

Fastidiously, Luk shook glass off the sleeves of his dark velvet jacket.

"What an unnecessarily spectacular entrance," Saloman said by way of greeting. "You could just have knocked."

"I was in too much of a hurry to see you, *cousin*."

"I'm flattered," Saloman said, strolling toward the cabinet on which stood a decanter and two glasses. He began to pour without taking his gaze from Luk. "You must have worked quite hard to find me."

Luk appeared to consider. "No. I worked quite hard to find your Awakener. Imagine my elation when I tracked her here and discovered not only her presence but your signature enchantments all over the street. You have improved, Saloman. I might never even have noticed them, had I not been so focused on your Awakener."

"Thank you," Saloman said politely. He picked up the two glasses and proffered one to Luk. "What do you want with Elizabeth?"

Luk walked toward him without hurry. Every one of Saloman's senses strained to catch the faintest chink in his cousin's armor, the tiniest potential threat in every move he made. It was a risk, being so close, and they were both aware of it. But at this stage it was important to display no discomfort, to acknowledge no danger. To remember the past, the best and the worst of it, with no more than detachment.

Luk's gaze was deliberately neutral as it met Saloman's. Neutral, yet hard as agate. Under Saloman's stare, the corner of Luk's right eye twitched, almost as if he were trying to keep the madness in, hold back something that raged out of control inside him.

Luk raised his right hand and closed his fingers around the glass. Saloman released it, and Luk smiled brilliantly. "What do I want with Elizabeth? I want to kill her."

Saloman lifted one eyebrow. "You are aware she is my Awakener, not yours?"

"If *you* kill her, you might just be strong enough to threaten me," Luk said thoughtfully.

"I have no need to kill her," Saloman returned.

Luk sneered. "Arrogance was ever your downfall, Saloman."

Saloman raised his glass in a mocking toast. "And yet here I am."

"And here am I."

"Indeed. Too late for sanity, too early for strength. You know I have to kill you again, Luk."

Luk laughed, a wild, almost unnatural sound. "I know you won't. Guilt won't let you. The past has weakened you, as it has strengthened me. You could have killed me easily in Turkey, before Istanbul, and you didn't. Here I am again, alone, weaponless, vulnerable to the attack you'll never make, drinking your wine, killing your whore."

Saloman moved before he meant to, hurling his glass so close to Luk's head that it made a whizzing noise on its way to the wall, where it smashed.

"You will not touch Eliz—"

"Pardon, Saloman?" Luk lashed out, grabbing Saloman by the hair. Saloman broke the hold with the force of his fist and his mind, but it was too late. One touch was enough. Pain seized his head like a jagged claw, squeezing with galloping intensity, paralyzing him. He could barely see Luk crashing against the wall beside the bloodred wine still trickling there from the broken glass. Saloman couldn't reach Elizabeth to warn her; he couldn't move to go after Luk.

I should have killed him quickly when I had the chance, he thought in blind despair. *If he harms Elizabeth . . .*

His cousin's laughter echoed inside his head. Then his mind filled with Luk's voice, so achingly familiar, so terrifyingly unfamiliar, adding to the excruciating pain and to the blinding fear and revulsion that now tore him into pieces.

I will *touch Elizabeth. I will kill her, and you will watch. Elizabeth . . . come to Saloman. Come and see the pathetic power of your lover now.*

* * *

Elizabeth woke to pain, terrible, gut-wrenching pain that she couldn't even locate. Disoriented, she pushed herself up from the pillows, crying out, "Saloman!" Because the pain was his. Or at least some of it was—a physical one she could do nothing about and an emotional agony that seemed to tear her apart.

But more than that, something tugged at her, drawing her toward another frighteningly intense source of trouble: jumbled, dreadful, black with rage, jealousy, and weird, insubstantial longing. It appalled her, terrified her, and yet called to her. It even spoke her name.

Elizabeth . . . come to Saloman. Come and see the pathetic power of your lover now.

She threw herself out of bed, grabbing up the ivory silk robe that had been Saloman's gift, and wrapping herself in it as she stumbled toward the door.

Hurry, Elizabeth, said the voice, tugging harder. From instinctive fear she pulled back, realizing at last that whatever Saloman's pain, the one inflicting it was compelling her in his direction. The last veils of sleep dropped away, removing the dreamlike torpor that had surrounded her, and with it the pain seemed to vanish.

Straining, she yanked herself back several steps, fighting the growing compulsion. The stake she always carried lay on the bedside table. "What's this?" Saloman had said, apparently amused. "In case I get too rough?"

"In case you stop," she'd said huskily.

Her legs began to shake with the effort of moving against the opposite pull. With a jerk, she flung her foot back one more pace, reached out and grabbed the stake, and then, with a sense of relief that was almost more terrifying than all the rest, gave in to the ever-increasing coercion, all but running to the bedroom door.

Good girl. Speed it up now.

She hid the stake inside her robe, drawing the tie belt tight to keep it in place, and ran along the hallway, rushing down the flight of stairs to the drawing room. It wasn't *just* the irresistible force that drew her; she needed to be with Saloman, to ease his pain if she could. Fear couldn't stop either compulsion.

She saw them from the doorway. Saloman stood with his back to her, rigid but upright. Luk—of course it was Luk—lay sprawled against the wall between the windows, incongruously smiling. His gaze was fixed on Saloman with vicious satisfaction. Something red stained the wall beside him. Blood? She hoped it was Luk's blood.

"Elizabeth Silk, the Awakener," Luk said aloud, his voice strong and mocking. "Saloman's latest whore." He laughed. "I see you don't like that term either. I had hoped you wouldn't make the same mistake as Tsigana—imagining you were any more to him. Don't just stand there, girl. Come in; join the party."

Elizabeth's feet moved forward without her permission. Her heart thundered; she hung on desperately to her train of sensible thought and observation, tried to shut out the wild speculation that would reduce her to helplessness.

"So," Luk said without moving, "you let him fuck you in the hope of eternal life?"

"I let him fuck me because I love him," Elizabeth said clearly. Closer now, she could look at Saloman. His eyes closed as if at fresh pain rather than comfort at her words. What the hell was going on?

"Oh, you *love* him," Luk mocked. "Tsigana did too, for a time. Such a waste," he mourned. "He doesn't love *you*, you know. He can't."

"I know," Elizabeth whispered. "It doesn't matter." *Eat that, you supercilious bastard.*

The expression on Luk's face never changed; his gaze never flickered as it continued to hold Saloman's like some bizarre staring contest. He didn't appear to be picking up Elizabeth's thoughts, although he still compelled her feet, drawing her slowly across the room toward him. Because, she realized suddenly, the bulk of his mind was preoccupied with Saloman. Inflicting the pain she'd felt when she first awoke?

"You don't believe me, do you? Well, let's have a rummage, see what we can find."

A tortured groan was torn from Saloman's lips.

"Stop it!" Elizabeth burst out. "What are you doing to him?"

"He hates this," Luk confided. "Other beings fishing around in his mind. Frightened of it ever since childhood. His father, my revered and rather nasty uncle, was particularly good at it. Could tear secrets from a boy's heart as easily as blinking, and destroy him with one good sneer. Saloman could never bear to be found wanting, but he always was. So by the age of eighteen he'd grown an almost unbreachable mind shield, hadn't you, Saloman?"

Luk smiled and raised one hand toward the approaching Elizabeth. "No one gets in there now. Hasn't for more than two thousand years. Except me. Help me up, Elizabeth Silk." Elizabeth found herself bending from the waist and taking Luk's cold proffered hand.

Luk's smile broadened, perhaps at what he was reading in Saloman's mind. "Oh, I see he gives you the odd tidbit—a little telepathic fillip to intensify sexual pleasure. Nothing of himself, though, nothing that makes him Saloman. He keeps his distance perfectly to avoid all that. It's what drove Tsigana to seek other lovers, you know, that distance. It destroyed her as it would have destroyed you, Elizabeth, in the end. If I hadn't been here to kill you first."

Elizabeth's body straightened, taking Luk's almost crippling weight as he let her draw him to his feet. The bastard was actually using her to save his energy.

"You like the blood drink," Luk observed, apparently pleased. "That's good. It will pain Saloman more to see you die in pleasure given by me."

Saloman jerked. "I won't let you kill her." It didn't sound like him. It barely sounded at all. With an almighty effort that almost broke her heart, he took a staggering, trembling step forward.

It surprised Luk. The sudden convulsive squeeze on her wrist told her that. Although this might well prove a useful distraction, it had the unfortunate effect of forcing Luk to speed things up. Throwing one arm around Elizabeth, he jerked her against the side of his body so fast that she barely had time to withdraw the stake from her robe. At the same time his head seemed to jerk forward, almost as if he were throwing something at his cousin.

"So many pathetic fears, Saloman," he said viciously. "No wonder you hide them." As his head bent, the compulsion drained out of her. He controlled her physically now, or thought he did. Certainly, if Luk hadn't been holding her, her trembling limbs would have collapsed. Gritting her teeth, she fought her own body's weakness, refusing to give in to the fear.

She held her breath through her internal struggle, cringed at the first graze of his teeth. His incisors pierced her skin, and with the violation, rage finally came to her rescue. She could speak to Saloman.

Don't worry. I've got him.

She laid the stake carefully against Luk's back and pressed. At the same time, she summoned it all, every strength she'd ever acquired or been granted, every confidence in her own ever-increasing power. And every particle of hatred.

"I'm one of the very few beings on this earth who can kill you," she said distinctly. "And I will."

Luk paused on his first suck. Elizabeth ignored the throbbing pain. "Release Saloman. Release me."

It hung on a knife edge. Elizabeth could almost feel him wondering whether he could drain her before she could drive the stake far enough into his heart. She wondered the same thing. But she was banking on Luk having used up a lot of energy in holding Saloman's mind in torment, and in forcing her cooperation. He needed this over quickly now. There would be another day for Luk. He could only get stronger.

She drew in her breath to push. Luk detached his teeth from her skin and raised his head.

"Lively," he observed.

Saloman rocked on his feet and righted himself. Now was the moment to kill, and she desired it with a strength that frightened her. But a wave of someone else's pain hit her. Saloman's. A tiny distraction, yet enough for Luk to throw her off. She stumbled backward, still holding the stake, and found herself in Saloman's powerful arms.

Luk's lip curled as if starting to sneer, and then without warning his mouth relaxed, and the intensity of his stare increased. Terrified he was attacking again, Elizabeth reached up one desperate hand to Saloman's face, her stake poised in the other. Saloman only caught her hand in his, gazing at Luk.

"She," Luk muttered. "The missing piece. *She* and he . . ."

Uncomprehending, Elizabeth frowned, lifting her gaze back to Saloman for enlightenment. He said nothing. But his arm dropped. With the speed of lightning, he leapt at Luk. A blur of movement tangled before her, and an instant later Saloman stood alone by the window. The only sound was her own rattled breathing and a burst of insane laughter fading in the street below.

Saloman lifted his hand to the broken window and began to intone. Elizabeth used the moment to try to analyze what she'd seen.

Saloman let his hand drop to his side. "That should hold him up for a minute or two should he or his followers return."

Elizabeth said slowly, "What the hell just happened?"

Saloman walked toward her. "We appear to have chased off the invading dog, and I have just re-marked my territory. Are you all right?"

"Am *I*?" She stared up at him as he came to a halt in

front of her. He grasped her arms and bent to her wounded neck, licking it once before raising his head and releasing her. "Saloman, what did he *do* to you?"

His gaze fell, then returned to her face. "It's a mind trick, a sophisticated variation on the one my father used to read children's thoughts without permission. It was outlawed by my people. . . . I never thought Luk would stoop so low. He never did before, even insane."

"I sensed *pain*," Elizabeth whispered.

"Oh, yes. He found the pressure point unerringly and hung on there. It is painful, but more than that, it renders the victim immobile, both mentally and physically, while the perpetrator can root around and do more or less as he likes. In the mind and out."

"Did he *damage* you?"

"No," said Saloman, moving past her toward the cabinet and the wine decanter. "Although I did lose my temper and break a perfectly serviceable glass."

Elizabeth's throat closed up. "You're doing it again, aren't you?" she said huskily.

He paused. "What?"

"What he said. Pushing me even farther away. Because of what I heard him say, I'm unbearable. Is that it, Saloman? Is that it for me?"

She stuffed her hand into her mouth and bit down as if that would stop the words from flowing, as if it would haul back the ones she'd already uttered so unwisely. He didn't need this now. Trauma had shaken the words out of her; his own trauma made him incapable of dealing with them. She was just speeding up the inevitable parting.

She tore her gaze free, knowing he would turn away from her and continue pouring the wine for both of them. But he didn't move, and when she lifted her gaze to his face, it wasn't distant at all, but racked with some turbulent emotion so intense it hurt to see. As if forcing himself, he began to move, not away from her after all, but back to her, until he stood close enough to bend and touch his forehead to hers.

"Elizabeth," he whispered. "Elizabeth, I am raw.... Don't kick, not yet."

She reached up blindly to touch his face, his lips, with trembling fingers. "I won't. It doesn't matter. I love you."

"Don't be hurt by what he said. It was nothing you didn't already know; nothing *he* didn't already know without invading my mind. I am so old, Elizabeth, and you are so new. You shine so brightly, so briefly, while I go on and on. It is hard to give and give and lose...."

"I know," she whispered, unable to stop a tear from escaping from one eye. "I know."

His thumb slid over the tear. "All I have, I give to you. All that you want."

"All that you can give is all that I want."

He kissed her mouth once, slowly, tenderly. "And he lied. I do love you."

She smiled a little tremulously. "'For this moment, this night,'" she quoted. "I know." *And I so wanted it to be more. I so ached for you to love me as I love you....* The thought escaped without permission, and inevitably he heard it.

No two people love the same. You can't limit feeling with time or quantity. You are precious, Elizabeth, and I will not lose you.

This time, his mouth came down on hers hard, demanding, almost desperate. Emotion swamped her, her own and his, vital, consuming, overwhelming. Blood and sex and Elizabeth. Of the three, for this time if for no other, it was Elizabeth he needed, and she could only give herself with gladness.

When the storm of urgent loving was past, Elizabeth slipped into a doze. She didn't mean to. There was so much to discuss—things to do with Luk rather than with herself and Saloman—that she was determined to stay awake. Especially when, despite his hunger and her offer, he didn't bite her. He stroked her throat, staring at it with fierce yearning as she came, but he didn't drink, merely distracted himself with his own climax. And then, moved by his abstinence and secure in his strong arms, she had fallen asleep.

She woke with a start when the front door slammed, and stared up at Saloman's averted face. He still lay with her on the floor, on the soft rug by the empty fireplace. They were both naked.

"What . . . ?" she began in sudden fear.

"Dmitriu." His voice was too carefully calm. "And someone I've been forgetting to watch for." Abruptly he reached over her body for her robe and wrapped it around her.

"Will they come in here?" Elizabeth asked, alarmed.

"Oh, yes," Saloman said serenely, and rose to pull on his trousers. By the time the drawing room door flew open, Elizabeth knelt by the fireplace, modestly covered in her silk robe, and Saloman was pulling on his shirt by the sofa.

Dmitriu came first, stake in hand, eyes darting.

"He's gone," Saloman said.

Dmitriu relaxed, throwing the door completely open. "We could smell him. Everything all right?"

"Certainly. You've brought me a visitor."

Dmitriu stepped aside and a tall, dark vampire with a shock of unruly hair came in. Elizabeth had seen him before, though only briefly. It took a moment to place him.

"Maximilian," Saloman said.

Maximilian, the first vampire he'd created, who'd betrayed and killed him for the sake of a power he'd failed to hold on to. Maximilian, who'd isolated himself for centuries, hidden in the mists of some Scottish island, emerging only once, so far as Elizabeth knew, to stand by Saloman's side against the alliance of Zoltán, the hunters, and Elizabeth herself.

"I told him he was pushing his luck," Dmitriu said, strolling across the room. "Just because you didn't kill him in Scotland doesn't mean you'll never do it. 'Max,' I said, 'you're a treacherous bastard. You deserve to die.' "

In the tense silence, Max met his creator's gaze. "The last bit is true," he murmured at last. "He did say that." He had a pleasant enough voice, deep and strong, but with a slightly husky intonation and careful pronunciation, as if he were unused to speaking.

"Well, if he drove you from the airport, I'm surprised you *didn't* die," Saloman said. "To what do I owe the honor?"

"Luk," said Maximilian briefly.

Saloman's gaze flickered between him and Dmitriu. He turned away from them as if irritated, but with relief, Elizabeth caught the smile curving his lips. "I see," he said, sinking onto a sofa. "You consider yourselves my bodyguards, despite the fact that I've never had any and never needed any. I have another proposition for you. Consider yourself *her* bodyguards."

He nodded toward Elizabeth, who sat up straight in alarm. "Forgive my remissness," Saloman said politely. "I realize you haven't been formally introduced. In case you haven't already guessed, this is Maximilian. Max, my friend and companion, Elizabeth Silk."

Maximilian inclined his head, according her a brief if penetrating stare. "I have heard of you."

"I've heard of you too."

A flicker of something that might have been a rueful smile sparked in Maximilian's gray eyes and faded.

"What happened with Luk?" Dmitriu demanded. "How did he get in? Where did he go?"

"He tried and failed to kill Elizabeth. He got in by unraveling my supposedly unravelable enchantments, and I don't know where he went. He masked as he hit the street. For once, I didn't feel like following him."

Dmitriu threw himself down beside Saloman. "Then nothing was achieved for him or us. We're exactly where we were before," he said in frustration.

"Not exactly," Saloman said. Elizabeth looked at him.

So did the vampires. He crossed his legs. "There was an instant, when I spoke to him, that he forgot to guard everything."

Elizabeth's lips parted. "You saw into his mind? *Then?*" So full of excruciating pain that he couldn't move, could only speak by some massive act of will that had taken even Luk by surprise?

"No," Saloman said regretfully. "Not Luk's. Dante's."

Chapter Fourteen

After carrying Elizabeth to his bed and covering her, Saloman paused a moment to gaze down on her sleeping face. She'd always moved him; now the thought of being without her was almost unthinkable. She'd come to mean so much so quickly, and he mustn't, he really mustn't, make the mistake of assuming that the speed of the emotion precluded its importance. If he lost Elizabeth now through aloofness—and Luk had been right about that; there were depths he simply didn't reveal to anyone—how tragic would that be?

Afraid to touch her in case she woke from the sleep she needed so badly, he turned the focus of his mind inward instead. He wasn't a rebellious teenager anymore; his father's painfully spiteful assessments had been proven wrong many centuries before. There was little need for his obsessive isolation. Elizabeth knew what he was, roughly, and still loved him far beyond the sexual infatuation that he'd once set out to exploit for the pleasure of them both. And if she *felt* shut out, was that not just as bad as *being* shut out?

She sighed in her sleep and stirred, altering the position of her head on the pillow. Saloman let the emotion rise up. He refused to lose this woman either to Luk's poison or to his own pointless secrecy. In keeping her, he risked himself, of course. Insanity, the scourge of the Ancient undead, could be triggered by profound grief, and as Elizabeth grew old and sickened and died, that was what he would have to face. But was not his own philosophy and his people's to enjoy every moment to the extreme? It was a crime not to seize experience with this amazing woman to the full and treasure it.

Perhaps his real crime was that it had taken Luk to show him what he was doing. Or not doing.

Saloman turned away. There was everything to give, everything to share. And as time went on, maybe, just maybe, she would decide that eternity with him wasn't so bad.

That was a long-term goal. First, he had to deal with Luk. And with Maximilian, who appeared to have come to help.

The drawing room was empty. Dmitriu had retired to his own temporary quarters, but Saloman could feel Maximilian closer by. Opening the door into the hall, he saw the top of Maximilian's untidy head, unmoving, halfway down the stairs.

Their conversations had been brief and few since Saloman's awakening. And the only meaningful one had been largely to ensure that Maximilian did not join Saloman's enemies. On a cold, misty island off the coast of Scotland, Saloman had found the shell of his once-vital, brilliant creation, in hiding from the world and himself. Yet Max had come to St. Andrews and fought at his side in the now legendary battle—before melting back into the mist once more.

Saloman walked down the stairs until he came to Maximilian's step, and sat beside him. He waited, but Maximilian had never been exactly verbose, and his isolation seemed only to have cast him further into the way of silence.

Saloman said, "Why did you come, Max?"

Maximilian shrugged. "Dmitriu said I should."

"And you have always been so slavishly influenced by what Dmitriu says you should do."

Maximilian's lips stretched. It might have been a smile. "It depends what he says."

"I'm trying to work out," Saloman explained, "whether I should be flattered or frightened that you've turned up to support me against Luk."

"Neither. I just . . . chose it." Maximilian turned his head, his gray eyes as direct and turbulent as they'd been in the old days, and yet overlaid now with something that looked very much like desperation. This, then, was to be the conversation they should have had a year ago on the island. "Some debts are too great to pay. For what I did there can never be recompense, and I won't even try. But you gave Luk peace, and I'll help you give it back to him."

"Because you failed to give it to me?"

Maximilian's eyes closed. The last time Saloman had brought the subject up, even obliquely, he'd done the same thing. "Don't," he'd said, in a clear anguish that had given Saloman hope that Maximilian, his Maximilian, was still present in the vampire who'd let overriding ambition rule his heart and his head.

This time, Saloman said nothing to turn the subject. He said nothing at all.

Maximilian said low, "I meant to. When the others had gone. I wasn't sure I knew how, but I thought if I dragged Dmitriu with me, between us we could remember or work out how to give you peace. But the human battle outside drove us into the open. The vampires revolted, and while I was away, Tsigana and János moved your body."

That much Saloman had always known.

Maximilian swallowed. "No excuses, Saloman. I tried. I killed János for not telling. Tsigana tried to barter the information for eternal life, which was when I first began to understand what I'd done. I couldn't make any of it right."

"Dmitriu worked out where to find me. But he never knew I wasn't at peace."

"Dmitriu and I did not speak. It doesn't matter. As time passed, I didn't want to be reminded of what I'd done. It was hard enough just to hold on to the reins of power. You know all this. I can't explain or exonerate myself for any of it. 'It was all a mistake. Sorry,' just doesn't seem to cover it."

He stopped talking. He swallowed again, convulsively. His gaze, which had had strayed to the artwork on the walls, to the sunlight filtering through cracks in the curtains, finally resettled on Saloman's face. "But I am," he whispered. "Sorry."

In the detached, aloof part of his mind, Saloman wondered why he needed to hear that so much. Perhaps because the betrayal of a born son could not have hurt him more than Maximilian's. He wanted Max to be sorry. And more than anything, he wanted him not to do it again.

"Halfway there," he murmured.

"What?"

"Nothing. There is a room here for you. Always."

Maximilian turned away, as if he couldn't bear the kindness. "I never understood why you didn't kill me."

"Some punishments are worse than death."

Maximilian closed his eyes again, and Saloman laughed. He put his hand on Maximilian's tense shoulder and rose to his feet, letting his grip linger there as he added, "I meant yours, not mine. I had three hundred years to think and plan, and this time, I intend to do it all properly."

Elizabeth found István, Konrad, and Mihaela all together in the hunters' library. She had meant to catch them early in the morning, somewhere neutral, like Mihaela's flat or the café, but unfortunately, after the many excitements of the night she'd slept in.

In fact, she'd fallen asleep in the drawing room while Saloman, Dmitriu, and Maximilian talked in low voices around her. She woke up in Saloman's bed late in the morning, rested but shocked at the time. Of Saloman himself there had been no sign. Only the silent Maximilian had been left in the house, and she discovered him by almost tripping over him on the shadowy staircase on her way out of the house.

After politely greeting the assistant librarian who was on duty, Elizabeth came upon the three hunters huddled around a table near the back of the cavernous room. At least they were quiet there, not too likely to disturb other researchers.

"Busy?" she asked lightly.

With more relief than respect, Mihaela let fall the ancient-looking tome she'd been reading. "Yes, sort of. Trying to find some clues as to Luk's whereabouts by finding out his old haunts. Not easy after several hundred years. Also, trying to get a lead on the Turkish vampires from Istanbul—see if any of them know Budapest."

"It could be a total waste of time," Konrad grumbled. "We don't even know if they're still *in* Budapest. Would it not make more sense for Luk to go somewhere else, somewhere safer, to recruit his strength and prepare to do battle with Saloman?"

"It might make more sense," Elizabeth allowed, "but he hasn't done it."

Three pairs of eyes regarded her expectantly.

"There's been a development," she said, low-voiced. "Luk broke into Saloman's place last night."

"Shit," said Mihaela. "Were you there?"

"Oh, yes. Apparently, it was me he was looking for."

"Was there a fight?"

"Sort of. Between us, Saloman and I saw him off. He's not strong enough yet to win a one-on-one battle with Saloman—which is good for us, I suppose—but he's gaining power very fast."

"He's an Ancient," Konrad said ruefully.

István frowned. "Was he testing the water? If he knew he wasn't strong enough to face Saloman, why did he risk the confrontation? Just to get at you?"

"And why?" Mihaela added. "Why go after you?"

Elizabeth sank into the chair István obligingly hooked over for her with his foot. "Because, as an Awakener, I'm capable of killing him single-handedly. Because it would piss Saloman off. Because it would boost his status in the vampire community. And add a significant amount to his strength, I suppose."

"Fair enough," Konrad said. "But what the hell gave him the idea he could do it under Saloman's nose?"

Elizabeth hesitated. She didn't want to reveal Saloman's earlier reluctance to kill Luk in Turkey, nor the vulnerability it implied. It seemed too personal. And yet, in the upcoming fight, the hunters needed to know everything.

At last, she said, "I think he knew he'd take Saloman by surprise. Luk can do this mind trick that temporarily paralyzes his victim, even Saloman. While doing it, he certainly doesn't have the strength to kill another Ancient, but he figured he'd have enough strength to kill me and bolt before Saloman got him."

Mihaela's face had whitened. "He paralyzed *Saloman*? How in God's name did you get out of that?"

Elizabeth gave a quick, self-deprecating smile. "I think he underestimated me. But he knew I *could* kill him, theoretically, and when I threatened him, he wasn't prepared to take the chance that I wouldn't."

Konrad's frown deepened. "The question is, did Luk gain anything by this incident? Did he drink your blood?"

"A tiny drop. I doubt it could make any real difference to him. I think he mainly gained the prestige of breaking into Saloman's stronghold and surviving. The vampires will all know that now."

"Will he be able to break in again?" István asked.

"In theory, yes. In practice, he'd be stupid to, because Saloman would kill him."

"Not if Luk pulled his paralyzing mind trick again," István argued. "And if he brings support next time, the others could kill Saloman while he's vulnerable."

Although the idea wasn't new to Elizabeth, it still made her blood run cold. "That's what Dmitriu and Maximilian are for. He has added protection now. Besides, he says the trick won't work next time, that he can avoid it."

"Then why didn't he?" Konrad demanded.

"I think because he didn't expect it," Elizabeth said, shifting uncomfortably. "It was regarded as illegal among the Ancients, and it wasn't something Luk would ever do. Not even when he grew to be insane. Saloman thinks his use of it now shows his fear as well as his determination."

"Maximilian?" said Mihaela unexpectedly, latching onto a previous point. "Saloman's Maximilian? He's in Budapest? Since when?"

"Since last night."

Mihaela frowned. "He came to protect Saloman? Whom he previously killed? Are you sure that's why he came?"

"Saloman and Dmitriu seem to trust him. It's hard to tell. He doesn't say much."

The librarian, rustling past their table to the bookshelves at the very back, cast them a quelling frown. Elizabeth lowered her voice. "There's more. While Luk was distracted, he let his guard down over Dante, and Saloman managed to glimpse something in the senator's mind. Not where he is, unfortunately," she added quickly, as hope sprang into the hunters' eyes. "But something."

Elizabeth nodded to the disapproving librarian as she passed back that way with her arms full of papers and books. "What ever happened to the lady who used to sleep on duty? I liked her."

"What?" Konrad demanded impatiently, dragging

her back to the point. "What did Saloman learn from Dante's mind?"

"That they're not waiting to defeat Saloman before they make their bid for the vampire leadership. They're planning something soon, some big attack that will bring the vampires flocking to their side. They're certain it'll leave Saloman deserted and the way clear for Luk. After which, Dante can return to America and, with the vampires behind him, make his move for ultimate power, as he always wanted."

Konrad's lips pursed. "Where? Where is that attack to be?"

"There was no time to ferret for details. Saloman's convinced it'll be somewhere in Budapest, but that's all he knows as yet."

Konrad shoved his pile of books into the middle of the table, knocking off two at the far end, which István caught in one hand. "Then he's given us nothing," Konrad said discontentedly. "He's stringing us along on his pretense of cooperation when God knows what he's really up to. Hasn't it struck anyone else that he could be in league with Luk? Why didn't he—the great, all-powerful Saloman!—kill the newly awakened Luk in Turkey? Surely that wasn't beyond his capabilities! All he achieved was preventing us from doing it."

"I don't believe that's true," Elizabeth said stiffly. *Wasn't it?*

"You're blinded by him," Konrad said dismissively. "The sooner you join the hunters formally and learn to understand what being a vampire truly means, the better and the safer you'll be."

Mihaela and István exchanged uneasy glances.

Elizabeth bit down on her angry retort. Into the silence, she said carefully, "You're wrong. But you *have* picked up on one important point. It *is* hard for Saloman to kill his cousin again. Before Luk's insanity, they were very close, and Saloman told me he let him live much longer than he should because of that affection. I think that came back to him in Turkey. There was a moment when he almost believed he could retrieve the old Luk from whatever it is he's become now."

She raised her gaze to Konrad, glanced around at the others, and came back to him. "That shows compassion, but not collusion. In any case, it doesn't matter now. What happened last night rid him of any lingering doubts. Luk *must* die again, and Saloman will do it. He wants, he really wants, your cooperation in this. But he will do it anyway."

Mihaela began to tap her finger restlessly on the open book in front of her. "Are you sure, Elizabeth?" she said abruptly. "Are you sure that's what *he* wants? Isn't it you who wants a way of living in good conscience with your relationship?"

Elizabeth closed her mouth, staring at her friend. "Yes," she said defiantly. "I do. And he does. And so should you."

Unexpectedly, Mihaela reached out and grabbed her hand. "Join us," she pleaded. "Please. Become a hunter."

Elizabeth's lips quirked. "So that *you* can live in good conscience with *our* relationship?"

"Yes! Something binds you to us, and us to you. Whatever our disagreements or misunderstandings, you're one of us in spirit. Make it reality. Come on, Elizabeth, you must have thought about it."

"I have. Part of me wants it, but I'm still not sure it would be the right thing." She rubbed her forehead with quick, impatient fingers. "Damn, I never used to be this indecisive."

"What about the university job? Have you formally accepted?"

"I'm going up there later this afternoon," Elizabeth said, and that at least won a few smiles of approval.

István pushed his chair back from the table and stretched out his long legs. "This telepathic connection with Dante. Can he take it any further?"

"Hopefully. Whenever Luk's guard is down."

"Won't Dante know? Or Luk?"

"Not necessarily. Saloman can be very subtle."

"Bloody subtle," Konrad muttered, rubbing his neck at the spot where once Saloman had bitten it.

After a quick coffee, the hunters left to pursue their leads, and Elizabeth returned to Saloman's house to change before visiting the university. As she ran upstairs, she heard odd bumping and clashing noises, loud enough to make her pause on the landing, wondering if there was another attack. It was unlikely in broad daylight, but still . . .

The sounds seemed to be coming from farther along the passage, where the rooms were largely empty—or had been the last time Elizabeth looked. Silently, she crept into the drawing room.

Saloman. Are you there?

End of the first-floor hall, the phlegmatic response came back. Elizabeth relaxed, but curiosity sped her steps back out of the drawing room and along the hall to the double doors facing her at the very end.

As she reached for the handle, she recognized the familiar clashing of steel on steel and knew before she opened the door that fencing was taking place.

Vampire fencing.

Elizabeth slid inside the room, closed the doors, and leaned against them, spellbound by the sight of Saloman and his two "sons" stripped to the waist, muscles rippling across backs and chests, shoulders and arms as they leapt around the huge room, their blurred swords thrusting and parrying faster than Elizabeth's eyes could easily see.

There was blood. She could see drops of it on the floor and on Dmitriu's light-colored trousers, but when you healed with vampire speed there was little point in practicing with blunted swords. In any case, they couldn't kill one another this way; they needed wooden stakes for that. Unless the head was cut off and kept separated from the body. This was their idea of training, perhaps, or lighthearted swordplay. Fast, violent, graceful, and strangely alluring.

It wasn't just the beauty of all three fit, seminaked male bodies whirling, spinning, stretching, almost flying through the air, that mesmerized her. Despite their exertions, not the faintest sheen of sweat clung to their pale skin. There was no panting, no yelling, no pauses to gather breath, which added to her sense of unreality, like a sanitized picture. Elizabeth couldn't look away.

Maximilian halted in front of her, the muscles across his broad shoulders rippling as he moved from side to side to see which of his opponents would attack first. It was Dmitriu, lean as whipcord and just as fast. There was a brief, hectic duel, and then suddenly both hurtled across the room in different directions, and Saloman stood there, his sword raised in front of his face.

In spite of herself Elizabeth's heart thundered. It didn't seem to matter how often she saw him. The lust only increased. She defied anyone not to desire this magnificent, seminaked body, his thick, dark hair flowing over his powerful shoulders, half obscuring his handsome, predatory face.

"That," Saloman said to the other two, "is how quick he will be. You can't afford to waste time on duels. No showing off. If you can't kill an opponent immediately, disengage. Always face Luk."

"There isn't always an option," Dmitriu protested. "Disengage, face Luk, and some fledgling could stick a stake in my back."

"A vampire of your caliber is more than capable of dealing with peripheral inconveniences. You bear my blood. Honor it and use it."

Saloman turned, lowering his sword, and bestowed a smile of welcome on Elizabeth. Taking her hand, he kissed it in a courtly fashion that made her blush. "How are the hunters?"

"Pursuing leads. So far without success." She lifted her eyes from his chest to his knowing dark eyes and wondered whether they could fit in a quick lovemaking before she changed.

As if he read her thought, Saloman's eyes darkened, and he smiled. "There is a time for everything. Today is a time for survival. Learn from them and from me."

"What?" she asked, confused. Her mind still lingered on the many delicious things she could do to his gorgeous body, and what he would do to hers in return. Dampness that was not due to the heat spread between her legs.

Saloman strode to the far wall and pulled down one of the last two swords that hung there. He threw it to her and she caught it by the hilt from pure instinct.

"Practice with us," Saloman commanded. "You need it."

Elizabeth couldn't deny it. Since this had all begun a year ago, she had fenced regularly, kept up with judo, trained with the hunters when opportunity offered. But even with the hunters, lately, she hadn't felt her abilities or potential had been stretched. No human, however strengthened by vampire kills, could move with the speed of an Ancient.

Slowly, Elizabeth stretched out the sword, flexed her arm, tried a few passes through the air.

"All right," she said. "But remember I bleed. And I die."

Under Saloman's harsh gaze, the vampires were too careful with her at first. It wasn't until she actually sliced into Dmitriu's shoulder and Saloman laughed that they began to take her seriously.

"Come on," Saloman mocked. "She doesn't bleed that easily! She's the Awakener, not the bimbette next door."

Dmitriu regarded his wound with disfavor. "Consider it revenge," Elizabeth said. "For the thorn."

The thorn he'd planted in her palm a year ago, so that it would later bleed over Saloman and awaken him.

Dmitriu grinned, unabashed, and bowed with a flourish. "En garde."

After that, it was more fun. In fact, it grew increasingly exhilarating as they all took more chances. They adjusted quickly to her speed and skill and tested her accordingly. After a while, Saloman joined in too, and they fought in rotating teams. The best was when she finally came up against Saloman himself, one-on-one. In him she had implicit trust, and held nothing back as she tried her damnedest to get through his guard while maintaining her own. She could almost feel her movements grow faster and faster, her reflexes sharpen and hone. This was the joy of the fight without any of the bad stuff, and it felt marvelous.

She barely noticed the other two dueling close by. There was only Saloman's sword and her own. Until without warning, a sharp pain sliced across her fingers, causing her to drop her weapon.

Abruptly, Saloman jerked up his sword. "What is it?" he demanded, seizing the hand she held dizzily under her face.

"Nothing. I thought . . ." *I thought you'd cut me.* She stared at her uninjured hand. There wasn't so much as a scratch on it.

Saloman dropped her hand and looked across at Dmitriu and Maximilian, who'd stopped fighting to see what the problem was. Maximilian's hand was bleeding sluggishly from a healing gash across his knuckles.

Elizabeth frowned, uncomprehending.

"Pain transfer," Saloman said, as though pleased. "Your telepathy is growing very strong. Again," he added, raising his sword.

Tired but willing, Elizabeth raised her own. As the duel resumed, she was vaguely aware of Dmitriu and Maximilian drifting away.

"You're weary," Saloman observed when he broke too easily through her guard.

"I can go on a little longer," she argued, unwilling to give up.

Saloman locked their swords, drawing her inexorably toward him. "No. That's enough for today. More tomorrow."

His naked chest came to rest against her damp T-shirt. The hilt of one sword pressed into her chest. She smiled. "All right."

Saloman, still holding both swords between them, bent around them and kissed her mouth. "You learn quickly."

"I wasn't always like that."

"Then you had the wrong teachers. You should eat."

"What did you have in mind?"

Amber flames leapt in his darkening eyes. "Lots of things. But first, food."

Since her stomach rumbled at that moment, she gave in, and, after another hot, delicious kiss, she left him to change and went down to the kitchen to rummage for food. By the time Saloman joined her there some ten minutes later, she was dishing pasta and cheese onto a plate with some salad.

"This could be a good kitchen," she observed with enthusiasm.

He shrugged, leaning his hip against the table as she sat down to eat. "Do what you like with it."

She nodded her head in the vague direction of the room next door. "What do you use these front rooms for?" she asked curiously. One was decorated in a bland sort of way as a dining room, the other as a not very comfortable sitting room.

"Entertaining," said Saloman grandly.

Elizabeth grinned around her pasta. "The neighbors?"

"On one occasion. Other people come to do inexplicable things, like reading meters and asking me to sign petitions or buy things I don't want." His eyes gleamed. "If I'm in the right mood, I invite them in for a drink."

Elizabeth choked and reached for a glass of water, which Saloman obligingly put into her hand. "The really worrying thing about all this," she said when she could speak, "is not that I believe you, but that I'm not even angry anymore. You've bitten your neighbors, salesmen, the man who reads the electricity meter . . . ?"

"And the postman."

She regarded him with fascination. "Aren't you at all worried that word will get around?"

"They don't remember. I don't hurt them, and they leave very happy. The woman two doors down even came back for more a week later."

"I'm sure you obliged!"

"Why look a gift horse in the mouth?"

She frowned, uncertain and not quite comfortable, however blasé she'd grown about his feeding proclivities. "It doesn't seem right not to ask," she said at last.

"In theory you're right, of course. And one day I hope there *will* be only willing providers. But the world has to be educated for that to happen."

"You really think that's possible?"

"Don't you?"

She smiled deprecatingly. "More than I once did. The hunters think I'm mesmerized, enslaved, blinded, brainwashed, whatever."

"Not you," he said with surprising warmth, and when she gazed up at him, he reached down and touched her cheek. "Come with me tonight. Meet my world, my people. Come to the Angel."

The Angel was not the easiest place for Elizabeth to return to. The last time she'd been there, she'd set out as bait to trap Saloman by seduction and had ended up being kidnapped and seduced herself. Memories of her behavior and his still made her body flush from head to toe. On top of which, arriving with Saloman and an escort of two other powerful vampires, she had no hope of not being recognized as the Awakener. The vampire world must already know of Saloman's bizarre choice of companion.

And so she paused at the door to gather her strength, gazing up at the blurred, undefined carved angel until it became the work of beauty it was in reality.

"That's what I like about you, Max," Saloman murmured. "You just throw these things out and then disguise them so that hardly anyone appreciates their true beauty."

Maximilian, some distance behind them, didn't say anything.

Elizabeth glanced over her shoulder at him. "*You* enchanted the angel?"

"I showed Angyalka how," Maximilian said briefly.

"He is also the sculptor," Saloman said dryly. "If he had chosen to, he could have been more famous than Donatello and Michelangelo."

Elizabeth blinked at this revelation. She wondered if anything would truly surprise her now, but at least it gave her something to think about while she followed Saloman up the bleak, dingy stairs to the club. The vampire bouncers on the landing welcomed Saloman with familiar deference, and herself with a curious but unthreatening stare. The glare they accorded Maximilian looked rather more aggressive, but if he noticed, he ignored it. By that time, the door had been opened for them and the wall of noise blasted out to meet them.

Maximilian swore under his breath. Over her shoulder Elizabeth saw Dmitriu laugh and push him inside when he hung back. Straightening, Elizabeth held her head high, as she'd done on her previous visit, and, side by side with Saloman, prepared to meet whatever hit her.

It was very nearly Angyalka herself. The club's owner, a beautiful, dark-haired, elfin vampiress in a sexy black dress and boots, glanced up from the bar, and on encountering Saloman, her eyes lit up. A smile, half-mocking, half-seductive, curved her lips, and jealousy curled in Elizabeth's stomach like a claw. Here was one of Saloman's lovers—past or present? Elizabeth didn't know even that much.

Angyalka slid off her stool and strolled toward them. But after a couple of steps, a frown creased her brow; her gaze glanced off Elizabeth without interest before she actually looked around Saloman to see who else was with him. Angyalka began to run, and Elizabeth stood still, braced to meet her attack.

It never came. Angyalka flew past her and Saloman without a word, and when Elizabeth turned, she saw the vampiress embracing Maximilian. A greeting of old, long-parted friends. Or lovers. It didn't matter. Vampire relationships were not so very different from human ones.

Saloman's arm was firm at her back, urging her on toward a vacant alcove table. Behind them, the live rock band reached a crescendo, carrying the audience with it in a blaze of stamping feet and rhythmic shouts.

Saloman's eyes gleamed. "Rock and roll," he said. "We must dance again."

The fading flush rose up her body once more. She hoped the friendly lighting would cover it as she slid onto the sofa.

"You brought me here for a bit of public flirtation?" she murmured.

He sat beside her, his thigh hard against hers. "I don't mind whether it's public or not. The flirtation itself was such fun the last time, I look forward to repeating it when you're not scared for your life."

A quick surge of something that wasn't quite laughter caught in her throat. "That's what gets me about you, Saloman. Just when I think we are alike after all, you say something like that. How could you enjoy it, knowing I was scared?"

His dark eyes didn't waver. "I enjoy everything about you."

It was part of the alien "experience everything, value everything" philosophy of his people. It was weird, but when the outrageous words came from him, she almost understood them. Maybe the hunters were right about her enslavement. At that moment, she didn't care. She wanted to kiss him, but made do with rubbing her cheek on his shoulder in a quick caress.

Dmitriu and Angyalka slid in beside them, one on either side.

Angyalka set down a tray of champagne and five glasses, and looked at Saloman. "He came here just to be your bodyguard?"

Saloman raised his eyebrows and reached across

Elizabeth for the bottle. "Maximilian? If that's what he said, it must be true."

"Of course it's not what he said. He doesn't say anything. It's what Dmitriu said."

"Then of course it must be a lie." Saloman began to pour champagne into the glasses.

Dmitriu hooted and stretched out his legs under the table, but Angyalka was not to be deflected. Leaning forward, she said, "This isn't some perverse revenge of yours, is it, Saloman? You wouldn't bring him here just to—"

"I didn't bring him here at all," Saloman said, putting down the bottle. "Apparently he came of his own volition."

"Saloman, Maximilian more or less gave me this place, helped me make it safe. I can't and won't forget that. If you kill him—"

"What makes you think I have any intention of killing him?" Saloman interrupted, presenting Elizabeth with a glass of champagne.

"Oh, just the fact that he killed you!" Angyalka exclaimed. "You can't expect me to believe you've forgiven him. *You* don't forgive." Although, distractedly, she curled her fingers around the glass Saloman gave her, she didn't seem to be aware of it.

Saloman smiled and pushed the third glass toward Dmitriu.

Dmitriu said, "He does forgive." Leaning forward, he picked up his glass and gave a slightly twisted smile. "I won't say he forgets."

Angyalka swung on him. "Do *you*?"

Dmitriu shrugged. "Neither. That isn't important. We need him against Luk."

"And because he came out for you in Scotland, you trust him." Angyalka sat back, her gaze flickering between Dmitriu and Saloman. She seemed to make a decision. "Cheers," she said, and drank.

Elizabeth looked around the room. "Where is he?" she asked curiously.

"Gone to block out the noise." Dmitriu grinned. "He'll be back when he's, er, psyched himself up."

"I love modern language," Saloman murmured.

Angyalka, her most pressing concern apparently dealt with, turned her disturbing gaze on Elizabeth, who might have found it harder to cope with had she not already grown used to Saloman's.

"Welcome to the Angel, Dr. Silk."

"Thank you." What else could she say?

"The last time you so honored us, there was a little . . . contretemps."

"I haven't invited the hunters this time."

"They seem to have decided to leave me alone," Angyalka observed.

Elizabeth searched her curious, unreadable eyes. Was she fishing for information? What was the correct response for the hunters' friend? For Saloman's companion? Elizabeth drew in her breath. "I believe they will, so long as your own current rules are followed."

Saloman set down his glass. "However, it may be that you're forced to, er, relax your rules, at least on a temporary basis. And even admit the hunters."

Angyalka's eyes narrowed. "Why?"

"Luk. He's planning some major attack that will strike more at my prestige than at my existence. I don't know where that will be, but the Angel, given my support of it and your loyalty, is one possibility."

Angyalka groaned. "I knew as soon as I saw you sit down in here a year ago that my peace was over, one way or another."

"But they've already been here," Elizabeth pointed out. "They've already proven they can walk in when they like."

"The same with your palace," Dmitriu added. "Which would be the obvious choice."

Angyalka's lips fell apart. "They broke into your house?"

Saloman shrugged. "Luk did. He was making a point. I'm surprised you didn't know already. He won't do it again."

"What about your offices?" Elizabeth suggested. "Adam Simon's businesses?"

"They would be easy targets," Saloman allowed. "But I can't see their destruction impressing vampires." He picked up his glass once more. "For now, I think our best hope is for me to reach Dante again and discover the rest." His gaze drifted beyond his companions, to the dance floor and the stage, where the band was now playing a slower and marginally softer ballad.

"Elizabeth." Amber flame sparked in his black eyes. "Would you care to dance?"

Since Angyalka promptly stood up to let her through, it would have been churlish to refuse. She didn't *want* to refuse, except for the opaque stares of the vampires boring into her back as she walked beside Saloman onto the dance floor. In fact, she suspected the stares pierced more than her back; they were coming from all over the club.

Saloman turned and drew her into his arms quite naturally. Despite her mental discomfort, her body reacted from pure instinct, fitting itself to his as they began to sway together to the music. Elizabeth gave up caring about the stares, disapproving or otherwise. There was only Saloman and the delicious excitement of his powerful arms around her, and his erection growing against her abdomen.

His lips nuzzled her ear. "So how does it feel without the fear?" he murmured.

She couldn't help smiling. "Weird. And strangely *right*. But then, it felt right the last time too—that's what scared me most."

"It was very exciting, each of us pretending, playing a game to trap the other. And yet . . . not. I wanted you so very badly, and I knew you would be worth waiting for."

She caught his hair in her fingers and tugged until she could see into his face. "And am I? Still?"

"Still," he agreed. The smile on his lips began to die. The half-amused, half-aroused glint in his eyes altered subtly, confusing her. "I will not lose you, Elizabeth Silk. Not to the suspicions sown by your friends and my enemy. If you can bear what's inside me, I will show you."

A frown tugged at her brow, even as her heart beat harder. "To keep me?" she whispered, unsure whether it was awe or disapproval that choked her voice. "Or because you want to?"

"Questions, questions." His fingers tangled in her hair, gently pulling. His lips parted to speak and then closed. His body pressed closer into hers with something akin to desperation. At last he said, "I couldn't bear to lose you through something I hadn't done. If knowing me kills your love, then that is different."

The music played on, raw, emotional. Elizabeth held his face in both hands. "Saloman . . . You don't believe my love is real. You think it's an illusion. You think I don't know you already."

"You know you don't."

"Learning the layers," she whispered, "is part of the love." Reaching up, she kissed his mouth, achingly, as if the kiss could convey what words could not: her fear that she had too few layers to hold so ancient a being, her realization of his, that he had too many.

I'm not afraid, she told him. *I want all you can give.*

His mouth hardened on hers, deepening the sensuality of the kiss. *You want everything. Except eternity. I know that; I've always known that.*

She gasped into his mouth. *You never asked.* Her mind spoke without permission, blurting more than she would have shown of accusation and hurt.

Rejection is never good for a relationship.

She broke the kiss, somewhere between a sob and laughter. "Why are we having this conversation here?"

"Because it came up," said Saloman, rubbing suggestively against her. She pressed her hips into him, glorying now in the lust as well as the awed exultation of her discovery. He wanted more. He wanted *her*, for eternity.

The music stopped. Around them, the dancers cheered and applauded as the band members took their final bows and left the stage. Her gaze still locked to his, she slowly laid her head on his chest. One arm dropped away from her; the other moved her forward off the dance floor and back toward their table.

Maximilian was glad to get away from the noise. On the roof of the Angel, he could at least hear himself think. He had been isolated too long to be comfortable in crowds, even when they contained old friends and those he'd once loved.

For many years, he'd had little to do but perfect his masking techniques and scan for danger. It was second nature to do it now, gazing over the city that might not have been his hometown but nevertheless brought back too many memories. Blotting out the vampire presences in the building below, he concentrated on the rest. It was still a city of vampires, their signatures dotted here and there on both sides of the river. And one close by.

Skirting the glass dome that formed the centerpiece of the club, he gazed across the roofs until he found what he'd sought. Another lone vampire, masked as strongly as he. Had he not been so close, he'd never have seen him at all. And there was something odd about this mask; it didn't seem to come from the vampire himself.

And considering he was watching the Angel, there seemed to be only one explanation for that. He was one of Luk's followers.

To speak to him telepathically would be to lower his mask, and he wasn't yet ready to do that. So he did it the old-fashioned way.

In seconds, he startled the watcher by appearing at his shoulder.

"Hello. I hear your master is looking for recruits to defeat Saloman. Do you think he'd find me of any use?"

Angyalka and Dmitriu had vanished from the table. Neither was there any sign of Maximilian. Perhaps he'd simply gone home.

Saloman looked thoughtful as he raised his half-drunk champagne. "Your friend Mihaela spoke a lot about trust—to both of us. Not surprisingly. We have not always had the same aims. Do we now?"

A trifle bewildered by his sudden turn from the profoundly emotional to the practical, Elizabeth dragged her thoughts into some kind of order.

"Mutual cooperation," she said at last. "Yes. Revelation of the vampire world to humans . . . Yes, if it were done in such a way that would avoid panic and chaos. There has to be honesty if we live together. But it isn't something that could happen overnight, probably not even in my lifetime. I'm prepared to help make a start, if we do it in agreement with the hunters."

Watching her, Saloman drank.

Elizabeth said, "I realize this wasn't your original agenda."

"Revenge and world domination. I've had my fill of one—for the moment—and I haven't given up the latter. You've just convinced me to do it in a different way."

Elizabeth frowned. "That wasn't quite what I meant by 'cooperation.' "

"I know. But it would never be a partnership of equals, would it? I have both the power and the experience."

"And we have the numbers."

Saloman sat back, a smile shimmering in his dark eyes. "I think I said once that I needed you to make me happy. But your role was always meant to be more, wasn't it? You can make me palatable to humanity."

Elizabeth picked up her glass and sipped, regarding him over the rim. "And I can make you behave." *Please, God . . .*

"I think I might enjoy that," Saloman said softly. "I wonder if that's what Luk saw in his vision?"

"What vision?"

"The one that distracted him and gave me the chance to throw him back out the window. He saw something then involving you and me. He called you the missing piece."

"Missing from what?" Elizabeth demanded.

"Who knows? *He* probably doesn't anymore. The visions were largely what disturbed his sanity in the first place, and it was one involving me that turned him against me."

"Did he ever tell you what it was?"

Saloman shook his head. "No. As far as I know, he never told anyone. Which normally meant he hadn't worked out exactly what a vision signified, if anything. In this case, I suspect he'd deduced that I was some kind of threat, either to him or to the world. But his mind was failing by then, and since he no longer trusted me, I couldn't help him interpret whatever it was he saw. I've had to guess from his behavior, which was jealousy of every tiny power I gained, and of Tsigana, of course."

"Perhaps he foresaw *this*," Elizabeth said lightly. "That you and I—*I*, not Tsigana, being 'the missing piece'—would defeat him here in Budapest."

Saloman smiled faintly. "Maybe." He regarded her with unexpected seriousness. "Actually, that isn't so far-fetched. But I suspect there are conflicting visions—one that made him jealous of me and one that curtailed my power."

Elizabeth curled her fingers around the stem of her glass. "That doesn't make sense."

Saloman sipped his wine elegantly. "Prophecies don't, as a rule. The art of the seer, the Guardian, was more in interpreting the visions than in simply receiving them.

The future isn't written in stone. Events, people, choices, change all the time. A vision, at best, is only ever one possible future."

Elizabeth raised her glass and took an almost angry gulp. "Then what the hell use are they? Why did Luk get so wound up against you?"

Saloman shrugged. "Because his vision confirmed some deep-seated fear in him. Because he could no longer analyze clearly. Because he was insane and he didn't want me to have Tsigana."

"Tsigana . . . She keeps cropping up." Elizabeth set down her glass and forced herself to think rationally. "What was it about her? Not one but two Ancient vampires running after her. To say nothing of Maximilian. For a young human, however beautiful, she must have had one hell of a personality. Or did Luk just want her because he thought she was yours?"

Saloman regarded her thoughtfully. "I've always assumed that to be the case. And yet his grief for her on awakening implies the feeling went deeper. The truth is, I lost Luk a long time before I killed him. I have no idea what goes on in his mind anymore."

Luk disengaged his teeth from the woman's throat with a grunt of satisfaction, and reached for her friend. "You know, I think my cousin might be onto something. Keeping his meals on the premises. There's nothing like coming home to a favorite dinner. Except coming home to two," he added, sinking his teeth into the second woman's throat.

The first, a brunette with blond roots, scooted away from him and huddled in the corner. She was pale from blood loss. Her eyes were huge, both anxious and fervent as they watched him feed from her friend. He'd picked them both up in his fit of euphoria after breaching Saloman's defenses, and brought them here to this attic, where, on a whim, he'd kept them and fed them between his own feedings.

The second girl wrapped her legs around his hips, pressing herself into him, and Luk was briefly tempted to fuck her while he fed.

"Oh, for God's sake, do you have to do that here?" Grayson complained from the doorway. Returning from his hunt with the Turkish vampires, he appeared to be offended by the sight of Luk sprawling on the old mattress and cushions while being caressed by his luscious prey. Grayson had a very peculiar puritanical streak.

Luk healed the second girl's wound with a flick of his tongue and turned to face Grayson. Just to annoy him, he put his hand over the woman's eager breast.

"Do what here?" he inquired provokingly, and gazed up out of the open skylight to the stars, inhaling the scents of the night.

"Screw your . . . dinner," Dante said in disgust.

"Modern language is so picturesque. I have not, er, screwed my dinner. Too much pleasure would disturb—and indeed drain—the energy I need to mask all of you all of the time. To say nothing of this place. All it takes is one second for Saloman to be onto us."

One of the Turks knelt down by the brunette, tugging her toward him with clear intent. Luk swatted him away without so much as a glance, more irritated by the discourtesy than the territorial invasion. He didn't like living this close to uncivilized vampires. In fact, even Grayson's whining was becoming annoying. He couldn't remember any of his other creations ever telling him off or commanding him as Grayson seemed inclined to, even after Luk had been forced to show him physically who was in charge.

Unbidden, a memory of Saloman flashed into his mind, a mere couple of weeks after being turned. A young, eager, awed Saloman, desperate to learn, to fly before he could walk, answering him back with a fearless impudence he had always forgiven because it had never descended to insolence. Besides, there had always been a certain wit about Saloman, a charm that had shone as brilliantly as the sun....

Luk shook his head like a dog trying to dislodge a troublesome insect. It had been fun rooting about in an Ancient mind again. In Saloman's mind in particular. So many layers and locks and depths. And such desperation to resist him. Euphoria rose once more, fierce and consuming. The being who'd outstripped him, eclipsed him, defeated him at every turn had been easy to trick after all, to best in his own palace. It didn't matter that between them, Saloman and his Awakener had managed to push him out. They all knew who'd won that round, and who would therefore win the next. Luk had learned what he'd gone for: Saloman's strengths and weaknesses.

"Then why do you keep them here?" Grayson carped. "All it takes is for one of them to escape and our cover is blown."

Luk spared each of the women a dispassionate glance. "Look at them. They can't exactly run fast. They've lost too much blood."

"Then you're going to need stronger blood soon. Why don't you just kill them, or let the boys kill them," he added with a wave of his hand toward the Turkish vampires who were now settling down to play backgammon.

Something twinged in Luk. He couldn't recognize it. He just knew he didn't like the feeling, the impression that something wasn't right. Confusion, never far away, began to churn his mind up, reminding him how little he knew about this new world and the creatures who inhabited it. The unfamiliarity scared him, until he focused on the well-remembered hatred of Saloman to bring everything back into place.

Somewhere he longed for the peace of the sleep Grayson had wakened him from. But that was impossible now. He had an older, more important mission to fulfill. Even the new world was changing. She, the Awakener, was the missing piece who would cause Saloman's power to wane. And he, Luk, would win at last. Over whatever was left. But he wouldn't think of that.

He reached for the first woman again. She couldn't lose much more and not die, but he wanted another mouthful to calm himself. When her eyes closed, he pushed her aside angrily and turned on the other vampires.

"I need fresh blood! I hate being cooped up in this stupid box! Did any more vampires approach you tonight? How many can we count on now?"

"*Count* on? Maybe five, but how can people even join us when all we do is hide? Five in the whole of Budapest!" Dante said disgustedly. "They're the ones who contacted me during your little battle in Saloman's palace and liked your style. And someone spoke to Timucin tonight—he seemed stronger, at least. I'll meet with him tomorrow. But the rest are still on the fence. Waiting."

"Of course they are. Hybrid vampires have very little honor." Luk leapt up through the skylight and onto the roof, from where he surveyed his motley group of followers and slaves in the room below. "It doesn't matter. When we strike, they'll flood to us so fast that Saloman will simply get washed away."

Meeting with Saloman's world that night turned out to be a not undiluted pleasure. The civilized vampire haunt of the Angel Club gave way to glimpses of the darker side of human nature, the side Elizabeth had always avoided.

Teetering with him on a rotting roof, his arm steadying her, she gazed in horror at the room lit up like a goldfish bowl in the building opposite. Small children huddled in a corner like puppies while an angry man punched a woman full in the face, then picked her up by the hair while the children seemed to scream silently.

"Stop it," Elizabeth whispered, though to whom wasn't clear.

"What should I do? Jump through the window and kill him in front of his children?" Without warning he dived off the roof onto the road, sweeping her along with him, cushioning her landing as he always did, before running along to the next street. He pointed out two youths breaking into a house, a woman beating a whining dog with a stick, kids setting fire to an abandoned car, two men beating up a third in an alleyway.

At the last, unsure whether she was angrier with the thugs or with Saloman, Elizabeth broke away from him, shouting, "Enough, Saloman! I get it, all right?"

The men in the alley paused, and with a quick glance in Elizabeth's directions, the two attackers ran. In fury and pity, Elizabeth made a move to the bleeding man left behind. But another figure detached itself from the shadows and knelt, phone already clamped to his ear—presumably the victim's friend, who'd been too late, or too afraid, to help against the attack.

With a swallowed sob, she swung away again and hit the wall of Saloman's chest. "Why are you doing this?" she whispered as he swept her around the corner in the circle of his arm. "I know what humans are! I've always known."

"I want you to *feel* it too. Like you feel the brutality of vampires. And I want you to feel safe with me."

She stared at him in outrage. "*Safe?* For God's sake, how is forcing me up against *that* going to make me feel safe?"

His long eyelashes swept down like a veil and lifted to reveal only blackness. He said steadily, "I want you to be aware that if you leave me, you won't have left violence and darkness. It's present in all beings."

It took a few moments to sink in. Something cold and furious squeezed around her heart as she backed away from him. "That's how you do it, isn't it? Teach your flock to toe the line with little demonstrations of cruelty or benevolence or whatever the problem calls for. Well, I'm *not* one of your bloody flock, Saloman, and I *won't* toe your line."

Spinning on her heel, she marched away from him. She didn't care where she was going; sheer anger propelled her, to the extent that if he'd dared to follow her she'd have snarled at him like a bitch dismissing her annoying suitor. And yet the fact that he didn't follow only fed her rage.

Safe, my arse!

Finally, as she hit the busier part of town, she calmed down enough to laugh at herself. She didn't, since it would probably make her cry instead.

A few yards in front of her, a nightclub was emptying, and the cobbled street became suddenly full of people. Elizabeth moved forward into the brightly dressed, happy crowd, weaving between them until, by the next junction, their numbers had thinned. Elizabeth paused, glancing up the narrower, badly lit street, which looked more like a delivery alley, looking for a street sign to give her a clue where she was. She'd been walking so furiously, paying so little attention, that she'd lost her sense of direction.

There were no street names to guide her. A few yards down the alley, shadows moved in a shallow doorway, and Elizabeth's spine prickled. *Vampire*.

Instinctively, she moved down the alley, her hand inside her shoulder bag, finding and gripping the sharpened stake as her heartbeat increased to welcome the sudden danger. A burst of loud laughter from the crowd of young people outside the club reached her ears, and then she heard nothing except the rustling of clothing in front of her, a tiny moan that could have betokened anything from terror or pain to sexual pleasure.

As her eyes adjusted to the deeper darkness, Elizabeth could see two people clinched in the doorway. The shape was unmistakable as the male figure's head bent over the female's neck. She could have stumbled on lovers groping in the dark, perhaps about to enjoy a quickie, as she'd done with Saloman up against the rocky hillside in Turkey. The unmistakable slurping sound told her the rest.

Elizabeth leapt forward before they could register

her presence and thrust the stake up against the vampire's back, just over where his heart should be.

"Stop," she said harshly. "Right now. Let her go."

The hunters would expect her to kill the vampire instantly. It was the only safe course. But she'd just spent a civilized evening drinking wine with several vampires whom she'd have needed a damned good reason to kill. *Compromised? Me?*

The vampire released his victim. Bizarrely, the girl said, "What is it? What's the matter?"

"A hunter has a stake held to my heart," the vampire explained.

Am I? Am I a hunter?

Perhaps the vampire sensed her distraction, for without any warning, he grabbed his chance, knocking her backward with one elbow in the chest. The pain was sharp, winding her, but as he leapt after her, she acted from instinct, kicking out at his legs and throwing him to the ground. She landed on him with deliberate force, her stake raised for the kill.

The girl, his victim, let out a low, moaning scream. "Oh, don't hurt him; don't kill him, oh, please!"

Elizabeth paused. With the vampire immobilized, she spared the girl a frowning glance. There was softhearted and there was stupid. "He was biting you," she pointed out.

The girl trembled from head to toe, her eyes wide with fear and panic, her young face almost contorted with ridiculously intense pleading. "Of course he was. He's my boyfriend."

There was no sound but the beating of her own heart. In the grip of her legs and hand, the vampire lay very still. Staring at the girl, Elizabeth couldn't even see his face, but with a mental push she found quite suddenly that she could speak to his mind.

She knows what you are?

She knows, the vampire answered. Hope mingled with smugness in his mind. *She likes it.*

Elizabeth couldn't breathe. She stumbled backward, to her feet, away from the vampire and his human lover. As the vampire slowly rose and the girl collapsed into his arms, Elizabeth turned on her heels and ran.

Words rang in her ears, silent and mocking, the words she'd said so often to Saloman, flung back at her now with a vengeance.

Who are you to choose? It isn't up to you.

She'd nearly killed someone else's Saloman.

Chapter Sixteen

Despite the fact that it was almost three in the morning, Mihaela opened the door only seconds after Elizabeth rang. She wore the shorts and top she often slept in, and her dark eyes were huge with concern.

"Elizabeth! What is it?" she demanded, opening the door wide in clear invitation.

Elizabeth stepped in. "I'm sorry. It's ridiculously late. I just thought you should know. I thought *somebody* should know."

"Oh, shit. What has he done? Elizabeth, has he hurt you?" Mihaela closed the door, leaning her back on it as she stared at Elizabeth, fearful expressions chasing across her face almost as clearly as words.

Elizabeth gave a shaky smile. "No." *Yes, he has. He has hurt me, and he didn't even mean to. Was Mihaela right all along, that this can never work?* "This has nothing to do with Saloman. I just came across something really weird. It scared the hell out of me."

Mihaela pushed herself off the door and padded across the hall to her kitchen. "I'll get coffee."

Elizabeth followed on suddenly weary legs, and while

Mihaela worked, she told her what she'd seen near the nightclub, the vampire and his girlfriend.

"Is this important, Mihaela?" she finished. "Have you ever come across this sort of thing before? Vampires having relationships with humans?"

"Vampires have always had relationships with humans," Mihaela said, pushing a mug of milky coffee toward her. "Usually master-slave relationships." She frowned, picking up her cup and walking toward the living room. "What is different here is the openness and public acknowledgment of both parties." Both she and Elizabeth seemed to be ignoring the similarities to her own case. Elizabeth was fine with that.

"So this girl begged you to spare her boyfriend's life," Mihaela mused, curling herself onto one side of the sofa. She cast a penetrating glance at Elizabeth. "Did you?"

"Spare him? Of course I did!" Elizabeth kicked off her shoes and sat on the other side of the sofa, drawing one knee up under her chin.

Mihaela's frown deepened. "No 'of course' about it. You should have killed him at the outset. The sob stories of slaves should never distract you from your duty."

Elizabeth said, "That's just it; I don't think she *was* a slave. She was too obviously terrified of what I could do to him. I don't believe he hurt her or had any plan to kill her. I think they were in a genuine relationship."

Mihaela looked at her. "Could you be mistaken?" she asked. Elizabeth heard the unspoken addition. *Are you projecting your own case onto the unknown girl's and simply getting it wrong?*

Elizabeth sipped her coffee. "I don't believe I am," she said evenly. "I wouldn't have brought this to you tonight if I thought that was possible. I would have killed the vampire and told you tomorrow."

Mihaela watched her for a few moments before she looked away, absently drinking. "Is it important?" she repeated. "I don't know. It depends whether it's a one-off or not."

It was never a one-off. At the very least there was herself and Saloman. *Is there?*

Abruptly, Mihaela was speaking again, distracting her from the despair threatening to rise up and consume her. "I'll tell you another weird thing. We've been looking for new patterns in vampire attacks, trying to locate Luk—there's a whole commune of them out there, after all, and they all have to be feeding. We couldn't trace them, of course. But we *did* find two recent reports from victims of vampire bites who remember it happening."

Mihaela shifted position. "In fact, in the last six months there've been *several* reports of nonlethal bitings. Statistically, there shouldn't be any at all in that time. Vampires who don't kill—that is, the ones that are avoiding trouble in the shape of us—mesmerize their victims so they don't tell and start up a hue and cry. Some of them have stopped bothering. It's almost as if . . ."

"As if what?" Elizabeth prompted.

Mihaela met her gaze. "As if the vampires had stopped hiding."

Elizabeth drew in her breath. She reached out and set her mug down on the coffee table. Mihaela had put her own growing realization into words. "I think you're right, and I think it's happening all over. Before I left the UK, there was a case of a vampire openly feeding in some village down in Cornwall. And remember John, my injured soldier? I got an e-mail from him saying he'd encountered another vampire, this time in Glasgow's city center. She spoke to him because she was intrigued by his telepathic powers, but she made no attempt to kill him, or even to feed from him. And now he wants to know more. He *needs* to know more. And he's precisely the sort of determined young man who'll manage it."

Mihaela's free hand tugged at her hair. "It's Saloman. He's changing their behavior, and they're revealing themselves. Put that together with all the stuff we couldn't cover up in Turkey, and this could be disastrous for all of us. I really don't want to have to clear up the carnage once this secret is out in the open." She gulped her coffee. "If it *can* be cleared up."

Thoughtfully, Elizabeth reached for her mug once more and took a few sips before she said, "Like I said before, I think we need a strategy for dealing with this revelation."

"I spoke to the others. And to Lazar."

"What did they say?"

Mihaela gave a lopsided smile. "Konrad thinks Luk's behind the changes, because Luk rather than Saloman would benefit from the upheaval of a vampire war. Lazar grunted. Which may mean he's thinking about it or that he believes we're insane. I'll take this stuff to him in the morning."

"Thanks."

Mihaela glanced at the clock on her bookcase. "Want the spare room?"

Elizabeth's free hand flew to her throat and pinched. Stupidly, although staying with Mihaela was a natural and sensible thing to do, it seemed a monumental decision. Because she'd quarreled with Saloman, and she was too confused even to work out whether she wanted to make up. She'd gotten over far larger hurdles in this relationship, and yet . . .

"Elizabeth." Leaning over the space between them, Mihaela squeezed her shoulder. "What's the matter? You think he'll mind if you're not there?"

"I'm not even sure he'll notice." He was probably teaching some other recalcitrant underling to follow his rules. She closed her eyes, appalled by the meanness of her own thoughts. "He'll know I'm safe," she added in the interest of honesty.

Mihaela shrugged. "I doubt he's paying much attention to that either," she said dryly. "He's obviously happy enough for you to be wandering about the city on your own at this time of night, even after Luk tried to kill you."

"That's not fair." It came out as a whisper. "I left him, stomped off. He knew I didn't want him to follow me."

"Why?"

Elizabeth smiled unhappily. "Why? Why any of this? He's manipulative, Mihaela; I've always known that. I just don't want my strings pulled by his cruelty or benevolence—"

"Cruelty?" Mihaela interrupted, her fingers digging suddenly harder into Elizabeth's shoulder. "What has he done to you?"

"Oh, nothing. Nothing like that. He just showed me things, unnecessary things, to remind me of *human* cruelty. I'm not an idiot. I don't *need* reminding."

Mihaela's hand fell away. "No," she agreed. "You're right. That was unnecessary. I'm not surprised you don't want to go back to him."

"Oh, Mihaela, it's not as simple as that. I know why he did it. He's afraid—" She bit the words back. Not just because of the skeptical curl to Mihaela's lip, but because baring her heart would bare Saloman's confidences too.

"And yet you can't forgive him."

Elizabeth closed her eyes. "Not yet," she whispered.

Mihaela set down her mug carefully. "You don't have to," she pointed out. "Not if it isn't right."

Elizabeth opened her eyes. "I know."

Mihaela stood up, her eyes shrewd even through the concern. "It isn't so much the cruelty, or even the implied manipulation that hurts, is it? It's the fact that he's treating you like everyone else."

Elizabeth looked away. "You know what I hate about you, Mihaela? You're too bloody perceptive. Can I call a taxi?"

There was a pause, then: "Sure."

While Elizabeth made the call, Mihaela took the empty mugs back into the kitchen. The taxi summoned, Elizabeth followed her. "Sorry for waking you up and hitting you with all this. I know it could have waited till morning."

"Sometimes you have to talk. What you need is a good dose of normality."

Elizabeth smiled. "If only to remind me why I need to be taken away from it?"

"Exactly. Come for dinner tomorrow night. By yourself," she added, presumably just in case Elizabeth got the wrong idea and brought Saloman. "And whatever happens today, we won't talk about any of this stuff."

"Bet we will," Elizabeth said, and Mihaela smiled, clearly taking that as she was meant to: as an acceptance.

In the morning, after a bare three hours' sleep, Elizabeth found another e-mail from John Ramsay. He'd hooked up with Rudy and Cyn, thanks to her reference, and seemed to have joined the little private army they were forming in New York. Though it was all part of his necessary quest for learning, which Elizabeth thoroughly approved of, she wasn't sure about this latest venture of the unofficial hunters. Paramilitary organizations made her uneasy, and Cyn didn't talk to her enough for her to get the gist of what she was up to. The American, she thought, was the opposite of herself; Cyn needed to think more and do less.

Rushing as she was, Elizabeth merely dashed off a quick reply. "Hope you find out what you need to. Take care—there's still a bit of a leadership dispute in America. Avoid confrontation with the vampire Travis, who's strong and wily but won't kill you without provocation." Her fingers paused on the keys. Telling John, Rudy, or Cyn to use her name to save their lives from Travis stank suddenly and unbearably of playing God again, of choosing who was to live and who was allowed to die. Saloman might be comfortable in that role, but she sure as hell wasn't. She'd told John the score. She'd have to trust in his common sense and Travis's semireformation.

She typed hastily, "Things a bit wild here in Budapest.

Expecting a major attack, so may not be online for a bit. Best to Rudy and Cyn. Elizabeth." Then she shut the computer lid with a snap, threw on the rest of her clothes, grabbed her bag and her phone, and made her way downstairs.

She'd come straight up to her own rooms last night. Pausing only for an instant outside Saloman's drawing room door, she'd reached for the handle with trembling fingers, but she'd felt no trace of him. She'd let her hand fall back to her side and walked on to the staircase. One of the others had been in the house—Dmitriu or Maximilian; she couldn't tell which. But it was interesting that she could sense the presence and know it was unthreatening.

And yet, after that night's discovery, could she trust her instincts?

Storming away from Saloman had not been a mature way to deal with his behavior. If anything she'd just reinforced his view that she was some kind of ignorant child to be shown the error of her ways. Now, as she crossed the landing in front of his rooms, the longing to see him clawed at her. She needed to be with him, to tell him what she'd seen after she left him, what she'd so nearly done. She needed to carry on quarreling with him, or make up, or *something*.

She paused, staring at the doors to the drawing room. He was in there now. She couldn't hear him moving, but she sensed him, as he would sense her. He could come out at any time and discover her, and she realized suddenly that she didn't want the matter taken out of her hands. She wanted to be in control.

Decisively, she took a step toward the door, just as the phone in her hand beeped. She glanced down at it and saw a text message from Mihaela. There was a meeting with Lazar at eight thirty sharp and she should be there.

A rushed two-minute conversation with Saloman was not enough. Elizabeth dropped the phone in her bag and ran downstairs before she changed her mind.

* * *

"I want you to set up a meeting with Saloman."

Lazar's words cut through the brooding silence in his office, startling Mihaela out of her distracted thoughts. She glanced at Elizabeth in some alarm, but it was Konrad who demanded, "With what purpose?"

"With the purpose of finding out what the hell's going on," Lazar snapped. "And if vampire behavior *is* changing in the way Elizabeth and Mihaela both fear, then we can at least ask him to make them more discreet!"

"Why would he do that?"

Lazar stood up, indicating that the meeting was at an end. "Because, according to Elizabeth, he wants our cooperation. Let's see his goodwill. Can you do this, Elizabeth?"

Elizabeth nodded. "When? Where?"

"As soon as possible, and wherever he agrees to that doesn't endanger the rest of us. Use your common sense. I want the team there. And you."

Wily old Lazar. He'd already worked out that Elizabeth's presence protected the rest of them. It made Mihaela slightly uneasy as she filed out of Lazar's office with the others. She knew just from looking at Elizabeth that all was still not well between her and Saloman, and Mihaela didn't want any inconveniently quick reconciliation interfering with her plans for the evening. But then, placing Elizabeth firmly on the hunters' side at this civilized meeting of Lazar's might be just the thing to shove the wedge further between them.

Elizabeth sat down in the foyer, texting. *Good,* thought Mihaela, reaching for her own phone. *Keeps things more impersonal.* She was glad to see she'd received a text of her own from Tarcal. "Love to. What time?"

She called him, suggested that he and his brother Rikard arrive around seven that evening. As she broke the connection, still smiling, she found István at her elbow.

"Got a hot date tonight?"

It wasn't like him to ask such personal questions. He knew she was up to something. Mihaela took his arm and turned away from Elizabeth, who was still staring at her phone as if she expected it to do tricks.

"Not for me," Mihaela said, low. "For Elizabeth. I've invited this friend of mine, along with his gorgeous, divorced, highly intelligent brother."

István raised one eyebrow. "Sounds like *you* should snap him up."

"Elizabeth's need is greater," Mihaela said dryly.

"You really think some ordinary bloke, however attractive, is going to displace Saloman for her?"

At his disbelieving tone, Mihaela glared at him. "Trust me, ordinary's attractive to her right now. She needs to remind herself what she could have along with ordinary." Mihaela cast a quick glance at Elizabeth, who'd just stood up and was listening to Konrad's urgent speech.

Mihaela pinched István's arm. "Look, I'm not saying she's going to *marry* Rikard. She just needs to doubt. And so does Saloman. That would be enough to end this thing."

István drew in his breath. "You're playing with fire, Mihaela. You can't tell people what to feel."

"I'm not telling her," Mihaela insisted. "I'm reminding her of options."

"And have you considered the fallout for the rest of us if Elizabeth pisses Saloman off? Konrad, at least, is alive only because of her protection. To say nothing of the bigger picture."

"What bigger picture would that be, István?" she said intensely. "The one where she dies through proximity to him? Or turns to please him? Or the one where he tells us all what to do?"

István stared at her. "You sound like Konrad."

Mihaela opened her mouth to protest, but before she could, Elizabeth's voice interrupted.

"The Angel Club this afternoon," she said, referring

presumably to the meeting she'd just arranged with Saloman. "And I've had an idea. Saloman told me once that in Turkey, Luk actually took over the house of a wealthy couple, living off their blood and mesmerizing them to do his bidding. I don't think he'd pick on anyone so prominent in Budapest; Saloman knows it too well. But what if he's taken someone with a lower profile to supply him with blood whenever he's short? Have you looked into missing persons?"

"Good idea," Mihaela said, relieved to have something positive to do. István had made her uncomfortable with her own perfectly sensible plan for tonight; at least searching out vampires was something she had no doubts about.

As Saloman took a step backward, the better to examine the rather fine oil painting on the wall of the vampire Elek's home, Elek woke up.

He sensed Saloman's presence immediately, as he was supposed to, and sat bolt upright on the sofa. "Saloman!"

Saloman turned without hurry. The vampire sat tensely poised between flight and attack. But he must have known either response was useless. In the daylight, he had nowhere to go. He knew why Saloman was here.

"Have you come to kill me?" he asked. He sounded more resigned than angry. He didn't even ask how Saloman had gotten there under the sun.

"It's not yet a crime to talk to the execrable Dante, although it might be regarded as a lamentable lapse in taste and good manners."

Elek sprang across the room, in the direction of the door. For a modern vampire, he was fast, might even have succeeded if Saloman hadn't been ready for such an attempt. The odds were against Elek surviving anywhere, but here in this room, he obviously imagined he had no chance whatsoever.

Saloman moved faster than was strictly necessary. He

had a point to make. But it gave him no joy to see the despair settle over Elek's face when Saloman reached out from in front of the door and grabbed him by the collar.

After the first instinctive, useless jerk to free himself, Elek stood passive in Saloman's hold. Fear surged out of him, helpless, despairing.

"How did you know?" he whispered. "Because I closed myself off?"

"Many have done that since my cousin Luk arrived in Budapest. They're hiding from him at least as much as from me."

Elek's eyes narrowed. "But you wouldn't be here if you thought I was hiding from Luk."

"No." Saloman released him and waved him to the nearest chair. Elek blinked in surprise, then slowly backed off to sit. Suspicion lit his watchful eyes. Saloman let his lips form a faint half smile. "I saw in Dante's mind that you'd met him, made him some promises to come out for Luk."

Elek wanted to avoid Saloman's insistent gaze; that much was obvious. But Saloman gave him credit for forcing himself to look the leader he'd betrayed in the face.

"I did," Elek said with a brave attempt at defiance.

"May I know why?"

Elek waved one impatient hand. "You know why. I miss the old ways, the old freedom to do what the hell I like without fear of being picked up for it by anyone more important than the bloody vampire hunters."

"You miss the old ways," Saloman repeated, gazing around the small but comfortable apartment, tastefully decorated and hung with good-quality lined curtains and carefully chosen pictures. A century-old globe and a sepia photograph of a Victorian lady stood on a shelf above a large television set. On the sofa beside Elek lay a handheld video game console.

Saloman returned his gaze to Elek. "What is it that

you miss most? Creeping around a dank cellar from which you're obliged to scare off interlopers every couple of weeks? Or being chased out by the hunters when they track too many bodies to your home?"

Elek's gaze fell. "I didn't say it was perfect. I just don't see why we can't have comfort *with* the old ways."

Saloman curled his lip. "Because without law, you'll have to protect yourself and everything you own from interlopers, and even if you can cope with that, the hunters will track all those dead people to your door and pursue you, and before you know it, if you still exist to know anything at all, you're back in that dank cellar, scaring off interlopers every couple of weeks. You get the vicious-circle thing."

Saloman strolled forward and rested his hip on the mahogany dining table. "It seems a waste of existence to me, but if that's what you want, by all means follow my cousin Luk until I kill him. I could still arrange for you to live in the cellar, if that's what you crave."

Elek squeezed his eyes shut and opened them again. "What is it you want of me?" he asked, low. "Why have you not killed me?"

Saloman considered. At least, he let Elek see him considering, just as if all his decisions had not been taken before he set foot in the apartment. "I do not wish to kill more vampires than I have to. Our success depends on a thriving population. And so, having pointed out the choices to you as I see them, I'm prepared to let you choose. And to pass on my reasoning to your comrades. If you don't take too long about it. No one will die for returning to my fold."

Saloman eased his hip off the table. "So, you may abandon everything we've achieved here and follow my cousin if you so desire. Although you should know that I *will* kill him, and after that I will *not* be feeling merciful to traitors. Or you can think about what we have gained here and the excitement of moving forward into a new future, not an old, miserable past. And return to me."

He glided swiftly across to Elek, who pushed himself into the chair back as if trying to escape through the wood and fabric. The vampire's stunned hope of survival drowned in a new surge of fear for his life. "You have until tomorrow," Saloman told him softly. Through Elek's unguarded eyes, he saw how he appeared to the other vampire: big, implacable, overwhelmingly powerful, his moment of mercy balanced on a knife edge.

"For now," Saloman continued, "you may just tell me when and where Luk means to make his move."

"I don't know," Elek whispered. He was like a dog groveling, except that among the abject fear was the hint of confused shame that was preserving his existence. For now. His mind fell open for Saloman, showing him all he knew. The meeting with Dante, which Saloman had already extracted subtly from Dante's own mind in an instant of Luk's distraction. The promises of freedom and protection that had sounded both beguiling and too good to be true. And Elek's doubts, already there before Saloman's visit. The knowledge of a devastating strike that would deprive Saloman of power and open the way for Luk's new age of vampire dominance.

But no details. Dante had given none and Elek had read none. Luk was telling no one.

Saloman swung away from the defector. "You know how to reach me," he said distantly. "When you've made your decision."

He left by the front door and simply jumped through the stairwell to the ground floor. From the basement ran a disused drainage pipe that led to a nearby dump, where Saloman had parked his car. In the modern world, it was really quite easy to get about in daylight.

Which was fortunate, since he had a date at the Angel this afternoon. His pulse leapt as he thought ahead to that—perhaps because of what the discussions with the hunters might entail, perhaps because Elizabeth would be there. She'd avoided him since his stupid demonstration last night. His own fear of losing her had made him insensitive, led to bad judgments he couldn't afford. Even last night, as he'd dragged her from human crime to cruelty, he'd been ashamed of distressing her; he knew she had enough to bear right now. And yet he couldn't make himself stop until it was too late. Even understanding, she'd run from him.

Saloman dragged himself along the old pipe, ignoring the overpowering stench that would stick to his clothes, if not to his skin. Whatever his reasons, he'd pushed Elizabeth away, just as Luk had said he would.

As Saloman approached the circle of sunlight, he speeded up. The car waited for him, its door open, and he sprang inside with minimum pain, slamming the door. In the dump, a couple of boys, playing truant from school, were kicking a ball about among the rubbish heaps. They didn't notice him, as they hadn't noticed the open car, which he'd enchanted to near invisibility before leaving it.

He started the car and drove around the boys to the road. Saloman thought of everything. He'd even worked out what he would do if the world he was building collapsed under his failure—as it looked capable of doing now, as his support in Budapest trickled away. Ominously, there were vampires converging on the city, not just from the Hungarian provinces but from Romania and Croatia as well. Their purpose wasn't clear, and Saloman wouldn't lose face by interrogating them over so many miles. Nor was he any nearer to discovering either Luk or his attack plan. So he had an exit strategy. But although he pitied the suffering of the world if Luk won, he wouldn't give up. He'd begin again. Even without Elizabeth.

A dense, black chill settled over his heart. He knew she was still unhappy, but he didn't know if he could make it right. Ironically, he'd helped teach her her own worth, which could well be what would keep her from him now. They both understood that she deserved more of him than last night's clumsy lesson. She was Elizabeth, and she was his. Without her, the next centuries, regardless of whether he failed, would be unbearably dismal.

"I'm not convinced meeting here is a good idea," Lazar said as Konrad pushed open the door of the Angel Club to let him pass inside.

"It's quiet during the day," Konrad reassured him, "and the staff is largely human."

István, studying the detectors lined up in his backpack as they trudged upstairs, said, "One Ancient, one ordinary vampire. Some distance apart."

Elizabeth saw him at once, seated by the bar. Her heart leapt into her throat. Pure longing drowned her lingering resentment, and she had to force herself not to run to him. But although he must have been aware of their entrance, he didn't turn. Was he angry with her? How could she tell if he chose to hide it? Would it impact his dealings with the hunters?

No. Whatever else he is, he's not trivial.

He appeared to be in conversation with the girl behind the bar, who gazed into his eyes with undisguised worship. At the very least, another blood source, Elizabeth thought savagely, before she remembered that Angyalka allowed no feeding on the premises. She sniffed.

Saloman wore black. He resembled a panther as he slid off his stool and walked to greet them, all sleek, lethal grace and rippling muscle beneath his silk shirt. Although his veiled gaze scanned them all equally, Elizabeth's breath caught as his glance glided over her. A frisson of electricity twisted around her spine, distracting her from the point of this meeting. Since Konrad stepped back in distaste, Elizabeth performed the briefest of introductions.

"Lazar, Saloman," she muttered.

Saloman inclined his head. "Please sit down," he invited with perfect courtesy, indicating the nearest booth. "Katalin will bring coffee."

Lazar, who'd never before had the pleasure of Saloman's overwhelming company, closed his mouth and did as he was told, although he didn't once take his gaze off Saloman. They sat in silence while the coffee was served and the waitress, Katalin, retreated back to the bar.

Then Saloman sat back and regarded Lazar once more. "How can I help you?"

Since he didn't have his usual, much-abused pen in hand, Lazar was reduced to drumming his fingers on the table. "I need to know what's going on," he said abruptly. "Do you know about this vampire Elizabeth saw openly feeding last night? Apparently in some kind of relationship with his victim? We have an increasing number of victims who're remembering attacks. It's as if vampires are no longer bothering to cover their tracks."

Saloman continued to regard him, as if waiting for more. Not by as much as a flicker of an eyelash did he reveal that he knew nothing of Elizabeth's story. At last, he observed, "You appear to know exactly what's going on."

"But why?" Lazar demanded, leaning forward with sudden aggression. He'd been a field hunter; he was surrounded by his colleagues; he didn't feel threatened by Saloman. "Have you told them they don't need to be afraid of us anymore? Are you trying to provoke a war with humanity by bringing vampires into the open?"

"No," Saloman said mildly when Lazar paused for breath.

Mihaela said, "And the two young women who disappeared after a night out on Wednesday? Have they taken up with vampires too? Do you know anything about them?"

They were the likeliest victims that had come out of Elizabeth's suggestion this morning, and she hadn't given up hope that they might lead to Luk.

"No," Saloman said. "I don't, but they might well be worth tracking to get to Luk. Wednesday was the night he attacked Elizabeth. He used a lot of energy and would have needed a lot of blood to recover."

Mihaela nodded once, perhaps by way of thanks, and absently picked up her coffee cup.

Lazar said, "Can we stick to the point, here? Why are the vampires changing their behavior?"

"The world is changing," Saloman said. "And rightly so. Stagnation is never good."

"Is it your doing?" Lazar persisted.

Saloman drank his coffee. Elizabeth watched his elegant fingers and the grip of his lips on the cup, remembering quite inappropriately how they felt on her body. A rush of tangled emotion tugged at her. She quashed it ruthlessly.

"Is it my doing?" Saloman repeated as Lazar shifted restively. "Yes." His gaze swept around them all and he set down his cup. "You want me to elaborate? Very well. I have, more or less, stopped the vampire killings. Most vampires have learned that they do not need to kill to survive, and that not killing brings them less trouble from you." He smiled faintly. "And from me. As a result, many have stopped regarding themselves as a threat to humanity, and if they are no threat, why should they hide? Why should they not have human friends? A human lover for sex and feeding? If the human is willing, it solves many problems."

"It's bringing them into the *open*," Lazar said intensely.

"Yes," Saloman agreed. "It is. It's begun in Romania and in Hungary, because that's where I first imposed my will, but it's already spreading. And on top of this, there are growing rumors from Turkey, where the depredations of the rebels could not be entirely covered up by hunters—one good to have been achieved from that mess."

"Oh, shit," said Konrad with feeling.

"You *want* this," Lazar accused.

"Yes, I do," Saloman said. "And so should you. It's a natural progression."

"There will be carnage!" Lazar exploded. "In their panic, humans will rampage through your population, and I really don't see you accepting *that* as progression. There will be war, apocalyptic war—"

"You paint a worst-case scenario," Saloman interrupted. "With the same arguments I heard in the seventeenth century. What you have just now is a tiny trickle of information, a tiny proportion of people who've been made aware one way or another of the existence of vampires. None of them, I believe, has set out on a killing spree or sought to convince the general population. It seems to me what you need here is a policy, a strategy for gradually educating humanity."

Lazar's eyes flickered to Elizabeth and Mihaela. Since it wasn't the first time he'd heard this point of view, he might be more amenable to Saloman's suggestions.

"There are several things it would help you to consider," Saloman continued. "First, what vampires can and should do for the world we all inhabit. My people have lived in chaos for too long to be properly aware of the gifts they may possess, but in time we can help you increasingly with predictions of natural disasters, with matters involving tracking—mountain rescue, apprehension of criminals, finding lost children, and maybe even with healing, although that is a rare gift that may have been lost altogether.

"Second, if we live in peace together, we can pool resources to eradicate crime in both our communities. It needn't be a matter of human versus vampire.

"Third, tolerance is only ever achieved through knowledge.

"And fourth, we have the means to begin this in a gradual way, introducing ourselves first to those who already have an inkling of the paranormal, those humans who share an Ancient gene. Like Elizabeth and Josh Alexander."

In spite of herself, Elizabeth's heart jolted at the sound of her name on his lips.

"And Grayson Dante," Mihaela said wryly.

"Grayson Dante will not be a problem for much longer," Saloman said with such quiet certainty that, beside her, Lazar shivered.

"Your justice isn't ours," he warned. "We will never condone a vampire killing a human, for whatever reason."

Saloman raised one eyebrow. "Then you must stop condoning the murder of vampires without reason."

"There is always a reason," Lazar snapped.

"No, there isn't," Elizabeth said quietly. They all turned to stare at her in surprise, but, leaving all personal matters aside, she'd already chosen the side she believed was right for the world. Avoiding Saloman's piercing gaze, she said more strongly, "You said I should have killed that vampire last night, when he was doing no harm."

"He was feeding from a human!"

"With consent," Elizabeth argued. "And consider this: If vampires are feeding with consent, then they're less likely to do it *without* consent." Before Lazar could explode, she gave him a quick, friendly nudge that seemed to take the wind out of his sails. "Look, all of this takes time. No one's advocating television announcements or teaching this stuff in schools, but I think Saloman's right. The world *is* changing, and it's up to all of us to make sure that's for the better. We need to adjust our thinking to reconsider what is actually wrong. Because I'd say this cat's climbing out of the bag anyway."

Lazar looked slightly baffled by her last words until Mihaela translated curtly, "Secret's getting out."

Saloman stood up. It was, Elizabeth thought, a measure of the hunters' unconscious acceptance of him that only Lazar shot to his feet in instinctive defense.

Saloman said, "All I ask at this time is that you discuss these matters with your colleagues. I have enjoyed our conversation and I hope we can talk again soon." He inclined his head to Lazar and to the hunters. His gaze lingered on Elizabeth an instant longer than was strictly necessary, and yet there was no invitation there, no telepathic message, not even a command she could defy. She felt like a mesmerized rabbit. Then he released her and simply turned away.

As Saloman strolled back toward the bar, Elizabeth said brightly to Lazar, "Well? Did that help?"

"No." Lazar groaned. "It's just given me another headache."

Konrad stood abruptly. "Come on; let's go and track down these missing girls. I would *so* love to find Luk before *he* does."

And without Saloman, what the hell are you going to do with him? she wondered.

Chapter Seventeen

Mihaela's front door was opened by a handsome stranger.

Startled, Elizabeth snatched at the stake in her pocket. "Where's Mihaela?" she demanded.

"Kitchen!" came Mihaela's amiable if distant voice.

"Oh." Feeling a trifle foolish, Elizabeth released the stake. At least she hadn't actually threatened Mihaela's guest with it.

The handsome stranger smiled, opening the door wider. "You must be Elizabeth. Sorry to startle you."

Elizabeth walked into the hall just as Mihaela stuck her head out of the kitchen to say, "Elizabeth, Rikard Varga. Oh, and this is Rikard's brother, Tarcal," she added as another man strolled out of the living room, wineglass in hand. The brothers were in their thirties, blond and good-looking. Hiding her surprise, Elizabeth took off her jacket and delivered her bottle of wine to Mihaela in the kitchen.

"You didn't tell me you were having other guests," she said.

"Hope you don't mind. I thought it would be the best way to avoid us talking shop."

Elizabeth sighed. Talking would get them nowhere anyway. They'd found someone who'd seen the missing women with a shadowy man she couldn't describe. It had to be Luk, masking, but the discovery had gotten them no farther forward. The women had disappeared as completely as Luk.

"Good plan," Elizabeth said ruefully. She lowered her voice. "Who are they? Are you seeing one of them?"

"Not in that way," Mihaela said, with a hint of regret. "I met Tarcal at the gym. He has a long-term girlfriend, but we go for drinks occasionally—which is how I met his brother. Who is unattached," she added with a quick grin. As Rikard chose that moment to wander into the tiny kitchen, she dropped the conspiratorial tone to say lightly, "Rikard is a doctor."

"You too, I understand," Rikard said to Elizabeth.

"Yes, but not of the medical variety."

"Rikard, will you pour Elizabeth some wine?" Mihaela asked, opening the oven door. "Go through to the living room. It's boiling in here."

Although Elizabeth couldn't help feeling a trifle annoyed that her comfortable night in with Mihaela had been hijacked by complete strangers, she quickly found the Varga brothers to be rather charming, intelligent, well-read, and amiable. And as the four of them sat around the table, chatting over Mihaela's delicious dinner, Elizabeth acknowledged that it was an unexpectedly fun way to spend the evening, well away from vampires, missing women, and the pain of a love that seemed impossible either to bear or to forsake.

Tarcal, she reckoned, was a born flirt, which was both flattering and fun, since he divided his attention pretty evenly between Elizabeth and Mihaela; but Rikard seemed a more serious character. He specialized in pediatrics.

"I imagine that can be distressing at times," Elizabeth remarked.

"It can be. Mostly it's rewarding, though. I love working with kids."

"You'll get sick of it when you have your own," Tarcal interpolated with a quick grin.

"Are you planning on it?" Elizabeth asked, a little amused.

"One day. I hope so, yes." Rikard hesitated, then confided, "To be honest, that's why my wife and I split up. She's a surgeon too, and didn't want to halt her career to have kids." He put down his fork and smiled in a self-deprecating sort of way. "But that's an oversimplification, isn't it? Let's say the problems in our relationship were highlighted by our disagreement over kids."

"Is your separation recent?" Elizabeth asked, wondering anxiously whether Mihaela was about to get herself into hot water with Rikard, in whom Mihaela seemed to have a greater interest than in Tarcal.

"We've been divorced for a year. What about you, Elizabeth? Do you want children?"

Elizabeth picked up her wineglass, as if it could protect her. Without warning, she imagined herself with Rikard, holding a baby over which they both smiled with loving pride. A happy, contented existence. A good life, with a good man and a child, maybe lots of children . . .

Fortunately, her own choke of self-mocking laughter interrupted her vision. She set down her glass. "It's not something I think about right now," she said, and changed the subject. "Mihaela, that was delicious! What herbs did you use?"

And yet, as she risked another glance at Rikard, she noted again how handsome he was, how kind and sensual his lips were. She wondered what it would be like to kiss him, to have babies with him, to live with him into old age.

Clearly, she'd had too much wine. Rikard was a much better match for Mihaela.

Later, after dessert and coffee, Elizabeth helped Mihaela clear the table, leaving the men to debate whether

Tarcal should drive home himself or get a lift with his brother, who'd drunk rather less wine.

"He likes you," Mihaela said, smiling, as she piled plates into the sink.

"Who does?"

"Rikard, of course."

"I think it's you he's aiming for," Elizabeth said dryly, but Mihaela, who avoided long-term relationships, frowned at her in an irritated kind of way.

"Do you like him?" she demanded.

"Of course I do," Elizabeth said warmly. "He's charming." And if Mihaela could just get over her view that being a hunter precluded her from any kind of normal love life, maybe he *was* just the man for her. A sudden longing to be with her own love rose up, and she said hastily, "I've got to go, Mihaela, but I've had a lovely time." She gave her friend a quick hug and whispered in her ear, "Go for it."

Mihaela looked startled, making Elizabeth laugh as she swung out of the kitchen to say good-bye to the men. Without warning, she bumped straight into Rikard in the hallway and jumped back with a word of apology.

Rikard's hands were on her arm and waist to steady her. "My fault," he said with a smile, but although she was quite stable on her feet, he didn't at once remove his hands. His blue eyes were warm, giving Elizabeth an instant's warning before he said, "Tarcal's making his own arrangements. May I take you home?"

Elizabeth stepped back out of his reach. "No, thanks."

He followed her, raising one hand to touch her cheek. "Elizabeth. You're very sweet. I'm asking for no more than to drive you home tonight, but I would like to see you again."

"Um . . . I don't think that's a good idea," she said. She looked him in the eye. "It's complicated, but I'm in a relationship with someone else."

"Mihaela told me," he said with a gentleness that amounted to sympathy. "If you like, we can go to my place. Or I can drop you off close to your home. Let me help."

Elizabeth's breath caught. She felt winded. "That won't be necessary," she said, forcing her teeth apart to speak with anything approaching normality. "Nice to have met you, Rikard. Good-bye."

She went to the bathroom to give the brothers time to leave. She couldn't trust herself to speak until they'd gone. Sitting on the edge of the bath, she had to summon all her self-control just to call her usual taxi firm and order a cab.

As she emerged from the bathroom, Mihaela faced her in the hallway, her expression unreadable.

"What did you tell them?" Elizabeth asked. "That Saloman beats me?"

Mihaela's chin lifted. "I left it to their imaginations."

"While implying I was unhappy and in need of a knight in shining armor?"

"Aren't you?"

She stared at Mihaela. "No. And no. Why do other people keep deciding what I need?"

"Because you don't seem to see it for yourself!"

"What if it's you who can't see, Mihaela?"

Mihaela brushed past her. "You're making an issue out of nothing. All I did was invite some friends to meet you, introduced you to a nice man who has the same interests and the same goals in life as you. I didn't sell you into sex slavery."

Elizabeth's temper snapped. "Damn it, Mihaela, how can I trust you when you're doing this stuff behind my back?"

Mihaela's whole body whipped around. *"Trust?"* Her face flushed a deep, intense red. "Don't you *dare* talk to me about trust! I've stood by you when you lied to us, betrayed us, slept with our greatest enemy! Even when you try to win us to his cause, I don't denounce you. I keep your secret in front of my employers, who *do* trust me. Why? Because you're my friend. And if I hope for your happiness, I believe *that's* a part of friendship. If I hope that you'll see sense and leave him, to give yourself a chance to live, is that such a fucking crime against trust?"

The truth in Mihaela's angry words lashed her. The blood drained from her head, leaving her weak and dizzy. *Not now, damn it, not now . . .* Closing her eyes, she tried to force the nausea back. To think through it.

"I don't deserve a friend like you," she whispered. "I know that. And whatever you think, I do value our friendship. I value you and the others more than you'll ever know. But this thing with Saloman . . . you mustn't touch it, Mihaela. It needs space to grow, even to survive. . . ." She trailed off, aware she was making no sense.

Mihaela said, "I don't want it to survive."

Elizabeth opened her eyes and smiled weakly. "Mihaela." It seemed her legs would move after all. They got her across the hall until she could put her arms around her friend. "It isn't up to you," she whispered on a weird, aching kind of a laugh.

Mihaela didn't get it—how could she?—but after a moment's rigidity, she gave in and hugged Elizabeth back before pushing her away. The sickness began to fade, allowing Elizabeth the strength to move, to pick up her jacket and bag off the chair in the corner of the hall.

At the front door, she paused and gave a lopsided smile over her shoulder. "I really did enjoy tonight. Thanks."

Mihaela let out a laugh and threw a snatched-up glove at her. "Get out of here."

Dante saw the vampire at once. Although the evening had grown cool, he wore a black tank with his jeans and sat unmoving between a statue and one of the stone pillars that framed it. He looked unexpectedly boyish, a shock of dark, curly hair falling forward over his face. From Timucin's description, Dante had imagined someone more imposing.

There were always people in Heroes' Square, even in

the dark of the evening. It was a good place to blend in, despite its huge size. However, the vampire's chosen position at almost twice the height of most men, lit up by the floodlight, was not exactly subtle. Crossing the square toward the semicircle of statues, Dante had plenty of time to examine Luk's would-be follower, and he felt both excited and intimidated.

Dante wasn't used to feeling intimidated. In his life he had regarded few men as his equal, absolutely none as his superior, not even presidents of the United States, most of whom he'd known since they were snotty-nosed kids. Now, technically at the bottom of the vampire hierarchy, he was nevertheless aware of his own advantages; this was why he had been so determined to be turned by the Sword of Saloman or, failing that, by a vampire who bore the blood of an Ancient. It made him intrinsically greater than ordinary fledglings and most other vampires he had yet encountered.

But this vampire was strong and subtle. He had layers of masking that hid his identity, and yet he allowed a glimpse of simple vampire, enough to draw Dante to him. The vampire didn't even look at him as he came to a halt before him. Dante examined the statue and the name on the plinth.

"'Bethlen Gabor,'" he read. "What did he do to deserve such honor?"

"The honor of the statue? Which is nothing like him, by the way. Or of my companionship?" His voice was unexpectedly quiet. Without vampire hearing, Dante doubted he would have heard him.

"Either," Dante said.

"He was a soldier. And a friend of mine." The vampire slid smoothly to the ground in front of him. "Where is Luk?"

"He sent me to speak for him."

"I'm bored speaking with dog's bodies. If Luk isn't interested in my support, it would be more polite to say so."

The vampire turned his back, already walking away.

"No, wait. Of course he's interested," Dante said hastily, forced to leap after him in a manner that did not improve his dignity.

"So he sends me a fledgling?"

"We don't know who you are," Dante blurted. Why the hell was he pleading with this creature?

The vampire glanced over his shoulder. "Maximilian."

In his attic, Luk howled with glee. "Maximilian? His own child? I couldn't have hoped for better! It will hurt him all the more because he hasn't yet managed to find and kill this most important of his slayers. Oh, I love this!"

"Is Maximilian as strong as he seems?" Dante asked.

"For a modern vampire, yes. He was good. Very good. And he can only be stronger now. He'll be very useful when we strike." Luk spoke impatiently, almost distractedly, for his mind was dwelling on all the hurts he would soon inflict upon Saloman. He'd leave him with nothing; he'd turn his mind inside out again, and then he'd kill him. It would indeed be the dawn of a new age, and Luk would have his revenge on the whole world.

He couldn't quite remember, and he didn't much care, what it was the world had done to him. He just knew everyone had to pay for his being here. Maybe then the peace would come back. No Saloman, no hate, no gut-wrenching anger. No fear.

As the last word hit his mind, he swung back to Dante. "You didn't tell him our plan, did you?"

"No. But why do you ask?" Dante frowned. "Don't you trust him?"

"Of course I don't trust him, fool. Word must not get out by any means. The shock will be all the greater, as will our success. And I'm almost ready. Almost."

Emerging from Mihaela's flat into darkness, Elizabeth could see no sign of the taxi she'd ordered.

"I sent it away," Saloman said, his dark, tall figure appearing to materialize beside her. "I thought we could walk."

A sudden rush of gladness rooted her to the spot. Could she deal with this now, so soon after the confrontation with Mihaela? She was too emotional. And where Saloman was concerned, so ridiculously unsure.

His lightest touch on her arm urged her forward. Behind and above, she knew Mihaela watched them from her window. She wondered whether the hunter found any comfort in Saloman's protection of her, or if she simply hated to see them together.

"To what do I owe the honor?" she asked lightly, still not looking at him. "Are you afraid Luk will try to kill me again?"

"It's a possibility," Saloman admitted. "And Dmitriu and Maximilian appear to be busy."

Earlier, it would have hurt, but it seemed quarreling with Mihaela had put things back in perspective. She knew he was joking. Hiding a smile, she finally turned her face up to him.

He was watching her intently, his eyes pools of darkness that occasionally glinted under the streetlight.

"I can mask you over a distance, hide you from him, as I did last night," he said, "but I prefer to be sure you're safe." Slowly, he threaded his fingers through hers, and she found herself clinging to them as if to her only lifeline.

He gazed up at the moon as they walked along the silent street, and she waited. The rhythm of her heart drowned out their footsteps, soothed the turbulence of the last day's hurt. She could leave it alone, simply bask in the current happiness of his presence—and wait for something similar to happen again. Or she could face up to it now.

"Safe," she repeated. "That's what you said last night. You want me to feel safe with you. Do you really think I need a demonstration to feel that? To understand?"

The pause went on so long, she thought he wouldn't answer, and the despair began to settle around her again. Then his fingers moved on hers, lightly caressing. "You may call me crass. But I suppose I wanted you to compare me fairly to humans as you learned more of me."

Elizabeth stared up at him. She didn't know whether to hit him or laugh. "That's what last night was about? You still think I'll leave you when I see into your heart. Is it so very black?"

A muscle clenched in his cheek. The silence stretched. Then: "I don't know. It's been so long since anyone's looked and told me."

Slowly, hesitantly, Elizabeth drew closer, until she could rest her head against his shoulder, letting the jumble of wonder and pity resolve into more than forgiveness, into the beginnings of new understanding.

"I'm sorry," he said, low. "I shouldn't force you to see such things when there's nothing you can do to help. I promised you the night, not the horror. Come." His stride lengthened, causing her to trot to keep up with him. "This is what I would have shown you next; *all* we should have seen last night."

Sweeping his arm around her waist, he leapt onto the roof of the tall building on their left, and while she still gasped at the dizzying height, he pointed out stars and constellations that meant something to him, together with amusing beliefs and superstitions from various cultures, and how these had helped or hindered him in Egypt, Greece, Byzantium, and India at various points in history.

Jumping from the roof with no word of warning, he kissed her as they plummeted, and she gasped with pleasure at the wild experience. Hand in hand, he led her among the older parts of the city, across the dark, rippling Danube to some of the smarter nightspots, describing the buildings and the people with a vampire's heightened perception. It sounded like a wonderful painting, like life enhanced with more vibrant colors and sharper contrasts.

"It's as if you see some inner beauty blended with the outer," she said once, gazing after the ordinary-seeming young man in glasses he'd just drawn her attention to. "Would I see that too?"

"If you were a vampire?" Saloman said. "Probably."

If I were a vampire. Forbidden ground. Unthinkable ground. She pushed it aside.

Saloman said, "Forty or fifty years together is not so very long."

Had she really wanted him to bring up this discussion once? She forced herself to smile, gazing above the crowd to the stars that never changed. Or not in one lifetime. "It wouldn't even be forty years, would it, Saloman? In thirty I'll be old." *If whatever it is that's making me ill lets me live that long.*

He paused, turning her face up to his, searching her face. "You think I won't love you as you age?"

"You *couldn't* look on me the same way. You'll never change, Saloman. I'll become a wrinkled old lady with hairy moles and arthritic joints." *If I'm lucky.*

"The inner beauty doesn't disappear," he said softly. "In you it will only grow stronger."

"Will you grieve when I die?" She hadn't meant to ask such a stupid question. There was no answer she would like, neither his pain nor his lack of it. From somewhere close by drifted the sound of a choir, singing in perfect, moving harmony. Elizabeth moved forward in its direction, drawing him with her by the hand.

"I always grieve," he said simply.

"Is that why you hold part of yourself so aloof? Like Luk said?"

His lips twisted. "It would be too simplistic to say yes. I welcome every experience to the full, including love and grief. It's never the feeling that's lacking."

She lifted her face to his, gazing at his strong profile. "Trust," she said in wonder.

"We're more similar than I gave us credit for," he said with a self-deprecating shrug. "It seems neither of us trusts completely in our own worth. I can rule the world; I have every confidence in that. But I can't rule you; I can't make you stay. And so I make mistakes."

As if he couldn't bear to have said the words, he flung his arm around her waist once more and leapt onto the nearest roof to begin the mad roller-coaster run to his palace. He took a circuitous and unfamiliar route, extending this spell of rare closeness in the open.

It came as a shock to realize they were standing on the high wall opposite the hunters' headquarters. Elizabeth opened her mouth to tell him, before the knowledge slammed into her that he shouldn't know. This was the hunters' secret, sacrosanct area, and to them, if not to her, Saloman was the enemy.

The only too familiar reality of her impossible situation crashed back, yanking her soaring spirit down to earth. She lifted her gaze to Saloman's face and found him staring across at the hunters' building.

"You know!" she blurted.

"I've always known." The crease in his brow deepened. "And yet never recognized . . ."

"What do you mean?"

His grip tightened at her waist almost painfully before he noticed and relaxed it. Excitement vibrated through his body into hers. "I mean, I've got him. I really think—I'm sure—I've got him."

"Got who?" she asked, bewildered.

His gaze came back to her, blazing with triumph. "Luk."

Chapter Eighteen

The worst thing about fighting with just one arm, John Ramsay thought as he staked a vampire with an unerring throw, and fell under the charging body weight of another, was remembering that he didn't have two. There was no use in his brain telling his left hand to punch.

But he refused to be defeated, to let this strong, stupid animal spoil the euphoria of the group's first battle. It was snarling for his throat, and if he let up the pressure of his right arm in order to snatch up another stake, it would undoubtedly bite and kill him.

John head-butted it with a yell of "Ouch!" and while it reared up in stunned surprise, the pale moonlight casting tree-branch patterns across its forehead, John grabbed the stake from his breast pocket and plunged it into the creature's heart. It exploded to dust, just as Rudy had promised, just as he'd seen the Afghan vampires do when the über-vamp had bitten them.

John stumbled to his feet, a little less gracefully than he'd have liked, but the pleasing situation in Central Park more than made up for that. They'd stuck to his plan, invaded in formation, attracted and faced the attack they sought with highly trained efficiency. John was proud and triumphant, especially when the last vampire fell to the once unathletic accountant Pete Carlile.

He grinned, slapping Pete on the back as he went forward to meet Rudy and Cyn. "Not bad, eh?"

Rudy nodded. "Satisfying."

"We all did well," John said warmly, and was pleased to see his little group of trainees preen under his praise. The army had been right: He'd have risen quickly in the ranks. And for the first time he didn't resent leaving. There were other wars to fight.

His gaze fell on the silent Cyn, efficiently gathering up the fallen stakes around the battle site while the men compared notes. After a moment, he followed her, and when she straightened beside him, he said, "What's wrong? Aren't you pleased?"

"Pleased? Yes," she said distractedly. "Of course. It shows we're trained better, at least."

"But . . . ?" John prompted.

Almost angrily, Cyn stuffed the retrieved stakes into his wide pocket. "Forget it. You did great with this, Johnny, and we're a team." She glanced up and met his steady gaze. "I'm not taking that away. It's just . . . Rudy and I were doing this stuff on our own, beating up the fledglings. It's like nothing's changed except we have more people doing it!"

"You want to be in the bigger picture, aye? Taking out the über-vamps."

"I guess."

He regarded her. He hadn't been going to say it, because he hadn't been sure they were ready, but surely if tonight showed anything, it was that they were a capable team. "I heard from Elizabeth Silk the other day."

"She okay?"

"She's in the middle of a war in Hungary. They're expecting some major attack. Any day now."

Cyn's eyes began to gleam.

* * *

The heavy red velvet curtains could not prevent filters of sunlight from creeping in through the cracks. Sprawled on cushions in his bedroom, Saloman was working on his computer to hold together the various strands of his plans for the world, while every available sense reached out to Luk, who was doing his best to thwart them. He still had space and time to love the tiny, breathy sounds of Elizabeth sleeping in his bed close by. The illusion of companionship, as he'd once called it, had become a reality, and one he valued more than anything else in the world.

When you lived for millennia, you learned not to think too far into the future. Life died and changed and was born around you all the time. Long ago, Saloman had accepted that he would love and lose, even before Tsigana. It had become part of the pain he was proud to live with. But Elizabeth . . . Elizabeth was different. So young and new, and yet her soul was old and wise. She'd grown so quickly since awakening him that it was clear she was meant to be with him. And this peace, this unique happiness her very presence brought him, was a sign he could not ignore. Elizabeth was more, far more, than a meaningful incident, more than a beloved tool to keep him sane and contented for a few more years.

Elizabeth should be his eternal companion, a joy he had never allowed himself even to hope for as his species waned and died to extinction. He'd certainly never expected to find it with a human, and whatever Luk did now, Saloman would be grateful to him for forcing him to see the truth, to face the torture of losing her through his aloofness.

And so, as they made love until dawn, he'd let her deep into his mind. Knowing him couldn't be achieved overnight. But her delight in him gave him hope that however deep she went, she would still love more than the outer shell. That shell, the part of him he chose to reveal to the world, had grown and deepened with time, until even the outer Saloman was more profound than most people could handle. And over the millennia, one grew so many layers that one could lose touch with several of them for centuries. Saloman had the peculiar, not unpleasant feeling that with Elizabeth, he was relearning himself.

He should be concentrating on finding Luk before the attack began. But as his fingers whizzed across the keyboard, e-mailing, shuffling money, making decisions, and deliberately expanding his influence as if Luk were no threat, the free part of his mind kept returning to the woman who slept and dreamed in his bed.

She'd texted the hunters last night to call a meeting for early the following morning. Like him, she understood the importance of the moment. Since Saloman felt no disturbance, no warning of an imminent strike among the vampire world, she was preparing to get her point across to them: that, short-term and long, they needed Saloman. And with luck, the very real threat of Luk, whose victory would destroy them all, would be instead the tool that brought them together.

Saloman hit "send" on his keyboard and flicked onto the Internet news pages. A gasp from the bed brought his gaze to Elizabeth, who lay half–pushed up on her elbow, breathing too fast.

He reached across to her. "What is it?"

She grabbed his hand, squeezing it tightly as she lay back down on the pillow. "Nothing. Stupid dream."

"About Luk?" he asked, pulling himself onto the bed beside her.

She shook her head. "No. Mostly my own demons. I dreamed I was about to die."

"You didn't."

She smiled. "Clearly." Her eyes searched his as the smile faded on her lips. She swallowed, then blurted, "I think about dying sometimes."

Watching the rise and fall of her breasts under the sheet, Saloman tried very hard not to jump the gun and imagine her dying and reviving undead in his arms. But the hope was there, sweet, seductive, and so temptingly achievable now. "In any particular context?" he asked steadily.

She grimaced. "In the context that I don't want to. Not yet."

"I won't let that happen. I'll protect you."

She reached her arms up around his neck, burrowing under the silk of his robe. "You can't protect me from everything." Her hands clung to his skin, making his nerves tingle and shiver. If he hadn't sensed the difficulty of the revelation she was forcing herself to make, he'd have pulled the sheet away and covered her luscious body with his own.

She drew in a deep breath, speaking into his neck. "It's struck me recently that there are more relentless enemies than big, bad vampires. It seems I can deal with those, and if I can't, you can. But things that *seem* much more trivial, like illness and accident, can just carry you off." She'd snapped her fingers against his back. "Poof! And it's all over."

Saloman rolled her under him, the better to see her face. "First of all, it's never over. What you are and what you've done live on in those who knew you. Little comfort, perhaps, when you'd rather do the living yourself. I can take care of that."

Searching her troubled face, he found confirmation that her anxiety was specific. Worryingly specific. He brushed against her mind, asking for permission. As if from instinct, she pushed him away, but then all at once she caved in and opened to him, and he saw it all.

Behind the fear, he felt the erratic, inexplicable pains and short-lived illnesses that had plagued her in recent weeks. Although her doctor had found nothing wrong, the symptoms continued, stronger and more frequent. She didn't let them hold her back, but she couldn't ignore them or her belief that they were important. She didn't know what caused them, had wondered about everything from cursing to cancer, and could rule nothing out. Torn as she was between worry and self-ridicule, she'd told no one apart from her doctor and Mihaela, who, according to Elizabeth's mind, had fed her fear by taking it seriously.

"I'm no healer," Saloman said steadily. "I couldn't make you well if you were sick or injured. But healing used to be a gift among my people, and if you let me look, I can at least tell you if everything is as it's supposed to be."

"Look?" she repeated doubtfully. "Look where?"

He smiled. "Telepathically. Like this." He laid his hand on her forehead, concentrating, and moved it slowly across her face and head. Focusing hard on the health and rhythm of individual organs, he worked his way around her whole body.

"I can find nothing wrong, no intrusions or interruptions," he said at last. "I believe your doctor was right."

She drank in his soothing words like water in a desert, her whole body relaxing under his now blatantly caressing hand.

"They could be caused by the stresses of coping with your increasing powers," Saloman said. "And they're probably something to do with telepathic pain transference—you felt Max's cut hand, and you say you felt something when you visited the injured soldier in Scotland, and when Konrad was bitten by the vampire in Turkey. You are developing fast, perhaps too fast. We should slow it down if we can."

Or turn you so that your body can cope without pain. He didn't say the words; he didn't need to. Along with his explanation, she was considering it at last, with an open if slightly fearful wonder, and Saloman's hopes grew.

"Bugger!" Elizabeth exclaimed.

Saloman's hands paused on her breasts as he regarded her in some amusement. "What?"

"I forgot to go the university the other day. I got sidetracked into fencing with you."

"Won't today do instead?"

"I missed the deadline yesterday. They could be offering it to someone else as I lie here."

"Then stop lying here and go," Saloman advised.

"But I have to be at hunter HQ. . . ." Her hands fell away from him. "Maybe I shouldn't do it. Maybe I should just be a hunter."

"A new breed of hunter," said Saloman with some satisfaction.

Elizabeth flung herself out of bed, padding naked across the room in search of her phone. Saloman watched her, enjoying his inevitable surge of arousal as much as the beauty of her body and the swift, unconscious grace of her movement.

"I need to talk to them," she muttered, grabbing up the phone from the floor where it had spilled out of her bag. At the sight of her bottom at such close quarters, Saloman felt a growl rising in his throat. Lust was now critical and would have to be assuaged. But as she straightened, the phone rang.

"Hello, Joanne," she said in some surprise. Saloman remembered Joanne, one of her friends in St. Andrews—funny, eccentric, fiercely intelligent, and comfortingly loyal. Apparently, Elizabeth had asked her to check on the flat while she was away, for she seemed to be inquiring where to send mail on to.

"Oh, just leave it," Elizabeth said vaguely. "I'll be back soon enough."

"One's from our agent," Joanne said dryly. "Your book, remember?"

"Really? Open it," Elizabeth commanded, and Saloman watched indulgently as she grinned at the good news. Another academic success was on the way. When the celebrations had calmed and her smile died, she said ruefully into the phone, "And, Joanne, I think there's a letter addressed to Budapest University on the arm of the sofa. You might as well tear it up."

"Can't," said Joanne with unexpected satisfaction. "I posted it already."

Elizabeth sat down too fast, fortunately landing on one of Saloman's spare cushions. "When?" she asked faintly.

"The day after you left."

"Joanne, you're amazing."

"I know," said Joanne comfortably.

When she finally broke the connection she looked at him and said, "Phew! I'm a lecturer for the next year."

"Good," said Saloman. "You mustn't lose who you are."

Her gaze clung. Her lips parted. "No," she agreed, her voice oddly husky. "I mustn't." She jumped to her feet and ran for the ivory silk robe he'd given her. "I'm going for a shower and then I have to see the hunters."

He could have distracted her, but he chose not to. She had many things to clear up in her head and in her life, and he wouldn't stand in her way. In any case, he needed her now to be close to the hunters if his ultimate plan was to succeed. And they needed to be warned of Luk's plans as quickly as possible.

He liked to listen to the mundane sounds of her washing and dressing while he worked. And when she flew back into the room and kissed him breathlessly before rushing on downstairs and out of the front door, he felt curiously content.

He rose and walked to the window to watch her as she hurried out into the sun. Her beauty caught at his breath all over again. In a simple, well-worn print dress, she looked cool and vital, so alive it made him ache. Her hair shone, seeming to glint all the colors of a sunrise as she turned her face upward to the warmth. She raised both arms, as if embracing the day, confident, alert, and happy; and then she spun around to glance up at his window. Seeing him, she grinned and waved and half ran along the road to do her duty and face the dangers. His Elizabeth.

Slowly, Saloman let his forehead fall forward onto the smooth, hard glass. Her figure was blurred, but he couldn't stop looking.

I can't do it. I can't take the sun from her. She belongs in the light and I in the shadows.

He'd always known it, and yet it had never hurt so much. Because he'd let himself hope. A drop of blood spilled on the sill, showing a deep, dark red against the stark white of the paint. He hadn't wept in three hundred years. *Elizabeth* . . .

Behind him, the door opened, and he wiped his shoulder against his eye like a boy caught crying by his father. Perhaps that had happened too; he could no longer remember it all, it had been so long ago.

Dmitriu said, "Where did Maximilian go last night?"

The pain went on and on.

The Grand Master of the Hungarian Order of Hunters was regarded largely as a mere figurehead. In any case, he wasn't in the country. In his absence, the early morning meeting took place in the office of his number two, Miklós, off the main library. At Elizabeth's request, Lazar was present too, along with Konrad, Mihaela, and István.

"I only have ten minutes," Miklós warned as everyone filed in. He flapped one impatient hand around what seats there were in the room, which, like the librarian himself, was small and austere and just a little grubby.

Elizabeth chose to stand. Lazar and Mihaela sat on the rickety seats across the bare, dusty desk from Miklós. Konrad propped up the wall by the door, and István leaned one casual hip on the corner of Miklós's desk. The librarian glared at him, which István appeared not to notice, and in the end Miklós apparently decided they wouldn't be cluttering up his office long enough for it to matter, for he turned his glare on Elizabeth instead.

"What is it? If you have an announcement about accepting the position of hunter, you should put it in writing. I offer you my congrat—"

"It isn't about that," Elizabeth interrupted. "It's about Luk. Only, the fight's gone beyond him and Saloman. He isn't just threatening the stability of the vampire world anymore—he's threatening everything, including our knowledge."

"How?" István asked at once. "Has Saloman discovered something more?"

Elizabeth nodded. "He knows where the attack will be."

"Where?" barked Miklós.

Elizabeth waved one hand around the room. "Here. Hunter headquarters. In particular, the library."

It didn't quite have the impact she'd imagined. Lazar actually grinned, while Miklós snapped, "Don't be ridiculous."

"What makes him think that?" Mihaela asked, and Elizabeth had the lowering feeling that her friend's unease was more for Elizabeth's dignity than anything else. "Has he seen into Dante's mind again?"

"No," Elizabeth admitted. "Apparently Luk's making sure no one gets in there. Saloman gets occasional glimpses of Dante and the Turkish vampires, but only for brief moments, and rarely enough to read them. It just came to him last night when we passed this building."

Now she had silence, and the full attention of everyone. Even her friends stared at her with accusation and a disappointment that was peculiarly hard to bear. But while words of denial stuck in her throat—after all, how long would it have been before she *did* tell Saloman?—it was Lazar who voiced what they were all thinking.

"You betrayed this place to *Saloman*?"

Elizabeth lifted her chin, feeling like a defiant schoolgirl. "I didn't need to. He already knew."

"He can't have—" Miklós began.

"Yes, he can," Elizabeth interrupted. "He's been around longer than this building, longer than the hunters, longer than any of your documents, which, like any historical text, don't always give the full facts."

"Why do you think no vampires have ever attacked

our headquarters at any time in history?" Miklós said with exaggerated patience. "This building is shielded, masked—"

"And who the hell do you think masked it?"

Perhaps it was the spurt of anger or bad language that finally pierced their too-comfortable, long-standing confidence, but all of them began, finally, to think about it.

"Saloman?" Mihaela said, her voice husky with dread.

"Worse," Elizabeth replied. "Luk."

"Oh, no," Lazar said, as if in relief that he could now safely discount her ravings. "I'm not buying that."

"Why not?"

"What reason could he possibly have had to mask this building from his own kind?"

Elizabeth gave a quick lopsided smile. "Your oldest documents only hint at that, and you have to read between the lines, but it *is* there. I found several texts last year when I was studying Saloman in your library."

She began to pace the confined space in front of Miklós's desk, because she couldn't be still as she told the story Saloman had explained to her last night.

"The Ancients never used to be regarded as the enemies of humanity; they worked openly or in secret with rulers, princes, churchmen, scholars, and whatever the local equivalent of the police was at the time. Back in the Dark Ages, when the Ancient race was being outnumbered by unruly human-hybrid vampires, humanity needed a means of protecting itself from the vampire threat. They created the hunter organization, with the full cooperation and help of the Ancients, who even enchanted the site of their safe building for them."

She stopped pacing and turned to gaze directly at Miklós. "The Ancient who performed the enchantments was Luk. He made them strong enough to last for centuries, millennia, probably forever, even through leveling and rebuilding. They'd have been hard for most Ancients to break through, and as they died out and only modern hybrid vampires remained, there's been damn-all chance of anyone ever discovering this place."

Miklós's spectacles seemed to glint at her. For once, the librarian was speechless. István eased his hip off the desk. "And now Luk is back as our enemy. And the one being who can destroy us."

Elizabeth inclined her head. "Who *wants* to destroy us, and Saloman, and whatever order there is left in the world."

"But why?" Mihaela burst out. "Why does he want those things? Insanity just doesn't cover it!"

"Saloman thinks it's hate. He hates the world, almost without realizing it, because he was dragged back into it."

"By his awakening?"

"Exactly."

István took a step nearer her, peering into her face. "Correct me if I'm wrong, but Saloman has never given me that impression. He relished his awakening."

Elizabeth couldn't help the quick smile flitting across her face, although she tried to hide it by pushing at an imaginary stray lock of hair. "Yes," she agreed. "But their positions were very different, remember? Saloman wasn't insane when he was staked. Luk was. Luk had had enough of the world, even if his mind wasn't capable of recognizing the fact. And Saloman gave him peace, performing some ritual enchantment that took away his pain and gave him the rest that we might think of as death."

"Heaven," Mihaela said. "To all intents and purposes, Luk was dragged out of heaven."

"Something like that."

"Then why doesn't he want to go back?"

"He does. He just doesn't know it yet. According to Saloman. That's why he's breaking all the old rules, killing without reason, invading minds, inciting chaos for the ill of the humanity he used to care for—"

"All very interesting," Konrad interrupted. "But what the hell do we do about it? Summon every hunter back to headquarters to defend it day and night? Have we any idea when this attack will happen?"

"Or even *if* it will happen?" Miklós said heavily. "All we have so far is the guess of the vampire Saloman, without any evidence."

Everyone gazed at Elizabeth once more. "Think about it," she urged. "Saloman knows Luk; he was educated, turned, initiated by him. They were friends and allies for centuries before Luk's mind clouded. When we came to this building yesterday, Saloman recognized Luk's enchantment signature, and it all fell into place. Luk doesn't just want to kill Saloman; he wants Saloman to fail, to lose his power and authority to *him*. And for that purpose, there's nowhere better to attack than hunter headquarters. In addition, he has a grudge against hunters: He was their ally, and now, as he sees it, they've turned against him, betrayed him."

She gave a slightly twisted smile. "Besides, as you say, no one has ever attacked it before, or even known where it was. If Luk succeeds in this, he's perceived immediately as more powerful than Saloman. The vampires flood to his cause; his prestige is enormous, far eclipsing Saloman's, and so Saloman's allies abroad change allegiance to Luk too. Because there's no one left to oppose him or vampire-kind. Destroying the library destroys the organization in the short term, and knowledge in the long term."

"We're only one part of the hunter network," Lazar pointed out.

"Yes, but you're the pivotal part. Other networks have access, computer links, but the oldest, rarest stuff is here, because this was always the epicenter of vampire activity."

"We're hunters," Konrad protested. "Not helpless civilians!"

"But there are only—what?—nine of you based in

Budapest?" Elizabeth said, with a quick gesture toward the window to indicate the country at large. "And the world acknowledges you as the best, so to lose all of you at once would be an undeniable blow to the whole organization. Luk has five Turkish followers left, plus Dante, and we don't know how many Hungarians have defected to him since the Angel and Saloman's home incidents. Saloman reckons on ten at the very least. And the biggest weapon of all is Luk himself. He's an Ancient close to his full power—strong enough now to have a chance of killing Saloman, and I think we can all imagine how powerful that would make him."

Somewhere, she wondered at the dispassion with which she was able to speak of the deaths of her friends, of Saloman himself. It wouldn't have been possible if she didn't still harbor hope of avoiding these tragedies.

"Saloman's convinced," István said slowly. "You're convinced." He lifted his gaze to Lazar and then Miklós. "I think we have to take it seriously."

Lazar stood up, throwing his pen on his chair. "Does Saloman know you came to us with this?" he demanded.

"Yes, of course." She drew in her breath. This was it. "He offers his help unconditionally. To defend this place with you."

Chapter Nineteen

"No," said Konrad flatly. "Under no circumstances!"

"He's right," Lazar said, although at least there was reluctance in his uncharacteristically slow speech. "We couldn't risk a vampire, let alone Saloman himself, in headquarters without proper guards. And offhand I can't think of any guards that would hold Saloman."

"There aren't any," Miklós agreed.

"You wouldn't need any," Elizabeth pointed out. "He's on your side."

"Why?" Konrad demanded. "Why would he be?"

"Because he needs to defeat Luk before there's any further discontent and all he's built slips away. He's holding on to Turkey by a thread, but if Hungary falls, it all collapses like a house of cards. And because knowledge in all its forms is important to Saloman. So is cooperation with you, as he explained in the Angel."

While they considered that and Lazar sat back down, dragging another pen from his jacket pocket to tap on his knee, Elizabeth pressed the case.

"Also, consider what strength you have. Even if Lazar fights and you have all the Hungarian hunters present, you'll still be outnumbered. Possibly badly. Together, without any other distractions, you could probably kill Luk. But there *will* be other distractions; he'll be surrounded by devoted protectors who'll lose everything if he dies. They'll keep you apart. I'm the only one who can kill Luk without help."

Her smile felt twisted. "But anyone can kill me. Anyone at all. And they'll all want to. Without Saloman, I don't really have much chance. None of us do."

That went home. It was almost tangible.

"For what it's worth, he has also offered the help of other powerful vampires whom he trusts: Dmitriu, Angyalka—"

"No." They all spoke at once, in such perfect time that Elizabeth threw up her hands in surrender.

"All right. We both thought you'd say that. They would bring us extra strength, but Saloman's presence isn't conditional on theirs. It's him we really need."

"That's debatable," Lazar said. "I don't deny his strength would be bloody useful, but once we let one vampire in here, we'd never be safe again."

"Lazar, we aren't safe now! Luk can come in here whenever he likes. Saloman can help us defeat him, and he can reenchant the place afterward."

Lazar looked at Miklós. Mihaela exchanged glances with István and Konrad. There was a long, drawn-out silence during which Elizabeth was chiefly conscious of the word "please" repeating in her head over and over like a prayer.

At last, Lazar swung around on his hunters. "Well? You've had more to do with him than I have. What do you think?"

Mihaela's intake of breath shuddered. "I think we have to take the chance. I've come to believe he doesn't mean us ill, whether or not I agree with him. We have to trust him or go under."

Elizabeth smiled. As an accolade, perhaps it was lacking, but nevertheless, knowing Mihaela's feelings about their relationship, it warmed her.

"I agree," István said quietly.

Konrad lifted his shoulder from the wall and walked into the center of the room. He was the leader of the team. His opinion counted; it counted a lot.

He said, "I don't agree."

Elizabeth closed her eyes.

"I don't care how plausible the bastard is," Konrad's voice went on, hard and implacable. "He's a vampire. I don't even care that he's on our side in this venture—and he probably is; I don't see any other alternative for him. But he's still a vampire and our fundamental enemy. If we let him in here, we lose more than we would if Luk simply took it from us. We have to rely on our own strength and pray it's enough. It always has been in the past."

"That's no guarantee of the future, Konrad," Mihaela said, low. Proud of her, Elizabeth opened her eyes again.

"We have to find a way that doesn't involve him," Konrad insisted. "For God's sake, we're *vampire hunters*! That's why Luk's after us in the first place!"

"And if we die," István said conversationally, "if the library and the whole network are destroyed because we refused to bend, will it still be worth it?"

"Or will you not care, because you'll be dead?" Mihaela added. The decision wasn't yet made, Elizabeth realized with hope. Mihaela and István frequently disagreed with Konrad, but when it came down to the wire, they backed him. She hadn't expected them to go this far to support her against him. Of course, it had as much to do with the impression Saloman had created on them in the last couple of weeks as with friendship.

"It's a belief I'm prepared to die for," Konrad said steadily.

"It's possible there will be more than you who die for

it," Lazar pointed out. He got to his feet again, pacing the room. He shot Elizabeth a penetrating stare on the way past, then spun around and fixed his stormy gaze on each of the hunters in turn before resting it finally on Miklós. "I don't like this," he said. "I don't like it at all. They may be right that we can trust Saloman; we have no precedent to base any decision on. But I think—at least until we know more, if we ever do—I have to side with Konrad on this."

Elizabeth sat down in Lazar's vacant chair. Miklós was nodding. "As do I. Lazar, you're in charge of defenses."

"What defenses?" Elizabeth raged. "What can you possibly do to defend against *this*? You've relied on enchantments you don't even understand for hundreds of years!"

"We have detectors," Miklós said with dignity.

"Which have never gone off in my lifetime," Mihaela muttered. "Do we even know they work?"

"Yes," Lazar said seriously. "Large and small, integrated and mobile, they're all tested and reset every afternoon at five o'clock, three in the winter."

Elizabeth frowned, distracted. "Why is resetting them so important?"

"Er . . ." Clearly baffled, Lazar glanced at István.

"Over time, they adapt to changes in the atmosphere—temperature, moisture, light, even the chemistry of passing people. It gets too jumbled for them to pick up any changes—such as vampire presence—accurately. So they're switched off every morning to recharge, and reset every night. As you know, the mobile units, especially the pocket ones, are switched off until we enter a place of possible danger, which is effectively resetting them. The new ones we developed to detect Ancients—"

"Yes, exactly, we get the point," Miklós interrupted. "Which is that we have them and they work and they will give us warning and locations of any attack." He turned back to Lazar, saying fussily, "We have to be ready for this by tonight, because it could come at any time—"

"Wait." Elizabeth sprang to her feet once more. "You're prepared to believe Saloman about the attack but not about anything else? Can't you see the inconsistency of that? If you trust him, you trust him!"

"We don't," Konrad said simply. "The defense is a precaution."

"Oh, no. You *know* it will happen, and you know the chances are you and all of us will die and leave the world unprotected. Or do you expect Saloman to do that for you? Supposing *he* survives Luk?"

Catching the flash of anger in Konrad's bright blue eyes, Elizabeth swallowed more hasty words and tried, deliberately, to rein in her temper. "Okay. I know you don't trust him. It's a huge leap of faith for someone who's been a hunter all his adult life. I get that. But you trust *me*, don't you?"

"I trust you," Mihaela said staunchly.

"And I trust you," István said.

Konrad didn't glance at them. "I do trust you, Elizabeth. Just not in this, not about . . . *him.* I know you wouldn't mislead us, not knowingly. I just believe you're mistaken."

Elizabeth's lips twisted. It wasn't quite a smile. "The feeling, as they say, is mutual. But I'm not mistaken, Konrad. In the last year, I've grown to respect my own beliefs and conclusions, my own instincts. I haven't always acted on them, and that's when I've been most miserable and things have gone wrong."

She looked around at them all, desperate to make them understand. "Everything changed for me when I awakened Saloman. I had to look beyond academia and trust my decisions in real life as well. And do you know what? They're *good* decisions. I chose to trust you. I chose to believe Saloman is not evil, that he can do good in the world. Over the last year, I've been tugged both ways, and done things I knew were wrong in order to please you. I tried to kill Saloman; I *did* kill the vampire Severin in America. I've hidden information both from you and from Saloman so as not to betray the other. These things ate me up because I *knew* in my heart I was wrong, even while I was doing them."

She grasped the back of her chair, holding on hard, as if the force of her grip would somehow compel her audience to believe. "When we rescued Josh, when we tried to stop Dante and find Luk in Turkey, I was at peace here in my heart." She thumped her chest for emphasis. "Because that's when you and he were pulling together. That cooperation is what my instinct tells me is the right way to go, not just in this crisis but in the whole future. Every instinct I possess screams this at me, including those I've acquired as the Awakener and a part-time, unofficial hunter. My intellect tells me the same thing. I learned to trust that before I even met you. I wish you would too. Please let Saloman help us. We need him."

For the first time that she could remember, István put his arm around her shoulders. It wasn't just a gesture of comfort, although now that her speech was finished, she had an overwhelming urge to lean into it for strength. It was proof of solidarity.

Mihaela gave her a slightly watery smile of stunned approval.

Miklós stood up. They'd had rather more than his ten minutes. "You are eloquent, Elizabeth, but I've made my decision."

Oh, Jesus Christ help us! After all that, she'd failed.

"As I think you've made yours," he added into the silence that could be cut with a knife.

"I have," she said, low, understanding him at once. "I can't become a hunter." She wiped her eyes on István's suddenly too-inviting shoulder and straightened. After their sheer, wasteful stupidity, she wanted to shout and stamp; she wanted to slam the door and ignore them forever.

Instead, she said, "But I'm still the Awakener and I'll do my best to kill Luk."

Saloman sat down and faced the only two vampires he had created throughout his long existence. He'd just informed them of Luk's chosen target.

"Fair enough," Dmitriu said. "I never liked the hunters anyway."

Saloman aimed a kick at his ankles, and he shifted his feet. "All right, all right, I'm joking. I'll go and fight for the unspeakable hunters. Although I can't see them being exactly delighted to have the Antichrist in their midst."

"Elizabeth is trying to persuade them to the contrary."

"Good luck to her," Dmitriu said fervently. "Can you get into Dante's mind to find out when it will be?"

"Not yet. The odd glimpses I've had, he's always thinking of something else, which makes me think the decision as to timing is not yet made. When it is, hopefully Luk's protection will relax through his inevitable excitement and I can get a closer look. I doubt that will be long. The vampires traveling from Romania and Croatia will make it to Budapest tonight."

"On your side or his?" Dmitriu asked.

"We have to hope for the former. And plan for the latter." Saloman sat back and crossed his bare ankles. "But it's time to look beyond the coming fight, which has already been far too distracting. We must prepare now to move forward."

Dmitriu looked nervous. "Where else is there to go?" he demanded. "Either Luk wins and we're all in the shit, which I refuse to think about. Or we win, Luk is dealt with, and you'll have a little punishment, a little more consolidation to take care of. That will leave you in complete control of the vampire world. No one else is strong enough, or stupid enough, to oppose you. America is loosely allied, thanks to my pal Travis; Turkey is quiet again. At least while Luk is. And you're wealthy in human terms. You have the power of influence and friendship among the strongest governments in the world. Your boat is sailing just fine, Saloman. Take my advice and don't rock it any more."

"Dmitriu," Saloman mocked. "When did you grow so timorous?"

"I'm not timorous," Dmitriu retorted. "I just appreciate what I have—and so should you."

"I do. And I have identified two steps that I would like your help with."

Dmitriu sighed and pushed himself back in his chair. But it was Maximilian this time whose head snapped up in alarm. "What steps?"

"To help humans with the movements of the earth that cause natural disasters. And to introduce humans, peacefully, to vampires and their benefits. I believe these steps rely on each other and will advance us significantly."

"Do you?" said Dmitriu dubiously. "And exactly what is it you expect *me* to do?"

"Research. Find those with the Ancient gene and introduce yourself. Recruit them to our cause. Make a team of vampires to help you."

"How the hell—"

He broke off under Saloman's steady gaze, and swore under his breath. "All right, all right. I'm on it." He stood up, already striding to the door as if in annoyance, but Saloman wasn't fooled. Dmitriu was intrigued by his new task and even anxious to make a start on it. Saloman couldn't help smiling. "You'll be good at it, Dmitriu. Human interaction was always your forte. I'm relying on you, and whoever you choose to help, to make the noblest impression."

Dmitriu didn't look back, but he did incline his head before he closed the door.

Maximilian said, "You play him like that instrument over there."

"Piano," Saloman said mildly. "And if I do, it's because I know him. It doesn't make what I say any less true."

"And how will you play me?"

"By asking. Your feeling for stone has been intensified in your vampire existence. You can hear the earth, as I do, help the humans avoid the tragedies from earthquakes, volcanoes, and tsunamis."

"Perhaps," Maximilian said, with a curl of his lip. "But I see no way of making them believe me."

Saloman shrugged. "I managed it. But those incidents were largely luck, and I take your point. I aim to set up new seismic study centers—in fact, I've already begun them. I see you in an official advisory role, traveling and listening and pointing scientists in which direction they should look. Find ways to make their instruments tell them what they need to know, until they trust us and we can be more open."

Maximilian met his gaze, frowning. He looked oddly helpless. "You place a lot of trust in me," he said, low. "I can't imagine why."

"I can."

Maximilian closed his eyes. "There are others you could train in this role."

"There are," he admitted. "But I would rather have you."

Maximilian's teeth pulled at his lower lip. Abruptly, he stood and strode to the velvet-covered window before he spun around to face him again.

"What do you say?" Saloman asked softly.

Maximilian opened his mouth. "Saloman, there's something you should know—"

The drawing room door burst open, and Maximilian closed his lips.

Elizabeth stormed into Saloman's drawing room. "They wouldn't listen! They won't let you in the damned building! I can't bel—" She broke off, finally realizing that

Saloman was not alone. Maximilian was with him, but staring at her so intently from his place by the curtained window that she wondered whether her words had some special interest for him.

"I have to go," he muttered, breaking eye contact and striding from the room. Distracted, Elizabeth watched him leave. Like Saloman's, his face was hardly an open book, and yet when their eyes had met just now, she'd imagined some profound, desperate grief in them that went way beyond her own anger and frustration. As he passed her, she had to grab hold of the sofa back to steady herself from the sudden dizziness.

As she forced the feeling back, she felt rather than saw Saloman rise from the piano stool and come toward her. "What is it?"

At least the incipient sickness attack didn't come to much—perhaps because she felt so much better about the episodes after talking to Saloman this morning. She straightened, dragging her gaze away from Maximilian's retreating back. "Is he all right?"

"Max? Oh, yes."

"I don't think he is," Elizabeth argued. "I felt some kind of pain when he passed me—emotional pain. It felt like . . . guilt."

"That's Maximilian. He has a lot to be guilty for. Why are you so upset? Because the hunters wouldn't play?" Taking her hand, he led her around the sofa and sat beside her.

"I *nearly* had them, Saloman," she said tiredly. "So damned nearly. I put everything into it, including some stuff I didn't even realize until I said it. But I couldn't persuade them."

"None of them?"

"Mihaela and István would have played. They agreed with me, even spoke up for our plan. I think Lazar might have gone for it too, but he was swayed by Konrad in the end. It's just too hard to get over their conditioning that all vampires are bad, that their very existence is evil and you certainly can't have one running loose around hunter HQ, even if he's all that can save the world. Better all just die in a blaze of useless glory!"

"It won't come to that," Saloman said quietly. He touched her cheek. "Well-done. I think there's great promise in Mihaela's and István's reactions."

"What use is that if we're dead? If the library's destroyed and Luk's rampaging across the world, the vampires back to their brutal, chaotic worst, and—"

"I won't let that happen," Saloman interrupted.

Elizabeth squeezed his hand hard. "Will you show me how to kill Luk?"

"I will kill Luk."

Elizabeth blinked. "Before he attacks the library? How?"

"If opportunity arises, then yes. I doubt it will. If it doesn't, I *will* kill him *in* the library."

"You can't!" Elizabeth had never found him remotely obtuse before. It crossed her mind that he was too obsessed, that she'd explained the situation badly. "They won't let you in."

"Elizabeth." He lifted her hands to his lips, one after the other, and kissed them. "They don't need to let me in."

"You'll attack Luk outside?" she guessed, brightening.

"He'll be expecting that. We'll wait for them in the library as I planned. Dmitriu, Maximilian, and I." He smiled and kissed her bewildered lips. "I learned enchanting from Luk. I can unravel his enchantments almost as easily as he can unravel mine. In effect, I have my own key."

Elizabeth's lips fell apart. "Then you could have entered the hunters' building whenever you chose?"

"I could. Until now, there has been no point. They had nothing that I wanted."

Elizabeth balled her hands into fists and thudded them into his chest. "Saloman, you . . . you . . . !"

"What?" he asked, pushing against her fists until she half lay under him against the arm of the sofa.

"Nothing," she said with a sigh, and slid her hands free to hold him instead. His mouth bore down on hers, and after that, sex was inevitable.

It began quick and fierce, with urgent pulling and throwing off of clothing, until Saloman found his way inside her. Once there he groaned and paused, unmoving, his eyes closed in obvious bliss. Elizabeth gazed up at him, feeling the mad surge of lust morph into a slower, deeper love that made her want to weep. She touched his face with her fingertips.

"Saloman. Saloman."

His eyes opened, like pools of darkness glinting in moonlight. He began to move inside her. "I could make love to you forever."

"I wish you could."

His eyes changed, darkening with grief before he buried his face between her breasts and dragged his mouth across to her peaked, begging nipple. "Elizabeth . . . my dawn, my light . . ."

She smiled, holding his head to her breast. "I like that."

"I watched you in the sun today," he murmured, giving her nipple one last brush between his lips before he lifted his head to gaze down into her face once more. "I've never seen you so beautiful." His movements grew deeper, harder inside her, mirroring a new wildness in his profound dark eyes, and yet as she writhed beneath him, his voice dropped to an unbearably tender whisper. "I want you to know that I wish I could walk there with you."

Her lips parted with shock, and she lost the rhythm of the loving. His words brought a rush of longing she could neither fight nor articulate. There was no point. She drowned in the tragic darkness of his eyes, in the sweet, relentless urgency of his thrusts, and clung to him.

"I wish you could too," she whispered. As she

wrapped her legs around him, massaging him toward climax, her mind flooded with visions of Saloman in the sunshine, walking with her on the beach in St. Andrews. Blurred visions, because they were so impossible. "Nothing's perfect, is it, Saloman?" she said with a gasp.

"No," he agreed. "If it were, there would be nothing left to fight for." His fingers caressed the wetness of her cheek. "I didn't mean to make you cry. I just wanted to tell you."

She smiled, kissing him deeply, because there was more, much more than regret in her heart; there was knowledge that he'd never said this to anyone before, and probably never felt it so strongly. It was more than enough; it was joy.

But Saloman could never walk in the sun, not without ending his existence.

His tongue teased and pleasured her nipple. She pushed farther onto his shaft and twisted as the tide began to rise.

He could die with her, ending his existence and all the good he could do for the world.

Or she could die for him, and go on forever.

Saloman's thrusts grew wilder, faster, out of control. His mouth left her breast, brushing greedily at the other nipple on its way to her throat. His teeth pierced her vein and she cried out, reaching for the pleasure of his suck even before her blood began to flow into his mouth.

It wasn't wrong to live like this. It wasn't wrong to be a vampire.

As the tension broke and ecstasy swamped her, convulsing her body under him, he released her throat and pounded into her harder. She smiled through her discovery and his exploding orgasm, and as their minds and pleasures became one, she basked in the moment of complete, utter joy.

Sated and helpless, she lay under him, stroking his soft hair with trembling fingers, loving the feel of his smooth, hard flesh against her sweat-slickened skin. If she were a vampire, that was one sensation she would lose.

Her fingers stilled. Another truth was fighting its way into her head and heart, one she didn't want to listen to, not now. Desperately, she roved her hands down his back, feeling his instant response, trying to drag back the moment of uncomplicated happiness.

It wouldn't come.

She'd finally learned to be at peace with herself. To like herself. To be a vampire was to lose the humanity, the compassion that made her who she was, the woman Saloman loved, who could temper his inhumanity and make his domination more like cooperation. Not just she but the world needed her humanity.

You mustn't lose who you are.

Tears mingled with the sweat of love as Saloman eased his body out of hers. Tears of grief as well as love, and, somewhere, joy too, because she'd broken through another barrier and made another good decision.

So long as she didn't die fighting Luk.

Saloman said, "I won't let you die fighting Luk."

Although Luk had hunted and fed last night, Dante found him with his face buried in the brunette's throat. Without ceremony, Dante threw the newspaper on the floor where he could see it.

"The hue and cry is up for them," Dante said grimly. "Their photos are all over the papers. We have to get rid of them."

Luk sealed the woman's puncture wounds with one flick of his tongue and dropped her to face Dante. "Nonsense," he said. His wild eyes had a new look of intensity that was increasingly scary. They seemed to burn in his pale face. "After tonight, they'll be able to live in a palace instead of this dump." He gave a shout of laughter. "Saloman's palace."

But Dante had latched onto another point. "Tonight?" he repeated. "After tonight? Why?"

Luk smiled and stood up to stretch. The roof beams got in his way. "I'll be so glad to get out of this place," he remarked. "No more hiding."

Dante said breathlessly, "We attack tonight?"

"Tonight," Luk confirmed. "I'm as strong as I'm going to get without killing Saloman. And I certainly don't want to give him any longer to figure out where I intend to strike."

"Shall I inform our contacts?"

"Not yet," Luk snapped. "Bring them here and I'll mask us all up until we attack. I can't have word leaking to Saloman in advance—he still has far more followers to call on than we do. After tonight that will be different. Then, when he knows it, I'll kill him."

Luk spun around and around, holding both arms out like a child playing airplanes. "This will be such fun! I shall kill his Awakener and watch him suffer. . . ."

"But we don't want him there tonight," Dante argued.

"Oh, yes, we do. And trust me, he'll come. Too late. We're not just destroying the library; we're taking the building, and Saloman and his very odd choice of whore will walk right into our trap."

It was all coming true. With tonight's kills, Dante would grow massively in strength, and soon he'd be able to return to America and take over his world. He grinned at Luk like a schoolboy with a special treat. "May I kill Dmitriu?"

Luk laughed. "Of course. But you'll need help—ask Maximilian."

"There," Elizabeth said, throwing her sleeping bag in an untidy bundle at the foot of the nearest bookcase. "Behold my fearsome weapon."

Mihaela smiled sourly and dropped her own bedroll

next to it. "In this fight, it's likely to be as much use as Miklós's cupboards full of stakes."

Elizabeth nudged her. "Don't despair," she said lightly. "Saloman won't desert us, whatever Miklós decrees."

Mihaela stared at her, then glanced around to make sure no one else was within earshot. In fact, there was no one else in the library, apart from Konrad on the other side of the entrance area, standing in the doorway of Miklós's office, presumably listening to instruction.

"Of course," Mihaela whispered. "Once Luk's in, Saloman will be able to join the fight without anyone's consent. Which might just save our hides. Only, what if we kill the wrong vampires?"

The wrong vampires. Oh, yes, there was hope.

Elizabeth smiled. "I think we'll recognize our friends."

Mihaela sat on her rolled-up sleeping bag, frowning up at Elizabeth with fresh anxiety. "But won't Luk be expecting something like that? Won't he have some precaution in place against it? Saloman could walk right into a trap."

She could tell Mihaela the truth, force her to lie to Konrad and her other superiors. Or not.

"Trust in Saloman," she said lightly, and looked directly into her friend's eyes. "I do."

Mihaela got it. Her smile was slightly twisted. "Maybe you do."

Satisfied, Elizabeth waved one expansive arm around the library. "So what's the deal here? Is the library officially closed for the duration?"

"No, they can't do that. But it'll close at five each evening, giving us time to prepare before the sun goes down. No researchers or admin staff will be allowed in after that, only hunters."

"How many do we have?"

"Tonight? Five hunters. The three of us and two of the second team—one of their members is in the hospital. The third team's in Croatia, and should be back by tomorrow night."

"Six, then, counting me. We're outnumbered, even if Luk has no other support in Budapest."

"Lazar will fight with us. He used to be very good, and he's still a strong hunter. And, of course, you're our secret weapon."

"Not so secret," Elizabeth pointed out as István wandered in. Lifting one casual hand in greeting, he threw his sleeping bag down against the bookcase opposite Elizabeth and Mihaela and jerked his head toward Konrad, who'd left the departing Miklós and was standing by the window in an expectant sort of way, with two vampire detectors in his hands. Lazar and two hunters whom Elizabeth recognized by sight sat at the table in front of him.

Sighing, Mihaela got to her feet, and, together with her and István, Elizabeth walked up to join the party.

"The plan is simple," Konrad explained. "We operate a watch system from five o'clock onward each night. The sun doesn't set until after seven, but we know that Ancients can walk openly in the dusk, and Luk may have some means of sheltering his less powerful followers. We've no idea how many vampires will attack, or even which part of the building they'll infiltrate first. But the library will be their ultimate target."

He raised the detectors. "We all have these, and there are larger, more sensitive ones scattered throughout the building. We'll know when the attack is imminent. So that the vampires won't be aware until the last moment that they're expected, the detectors will be silent. Those on watch must keep their eyes on the computer display." He waved his hand at the reception desk computer.

"There are seven of us tonight, hopefully ten from tomorrow night on. Watch teams will be: Mihaela and Elizabeth; Lazar, Karoly, and Seb; myself and István. As soon as the detectors go off, the watchers will wake everyone. I don't need to tell you how to fight. Some of the vampires may use swords against us, so use your own—or spares you'll find in Miklós's office—for protection and the longer reach. Remember that although a sword can't kill a vampire, it can slow him down. You should all be aware of the difficulty as well as the priority of killing Luk in particular. Elizabeth, as an Awakener, is the only one of us who can kill him without direct help. Let's try to make that happen."

He shrugged and glanced at Lazar to see whether there was anything else he should add. "Okay. Apart from Mihaela and Elizabeth, I suggest we all get our heads down. We're going to need all the energy we can muster for this fight."

"And then some," Mihaela muttered.

From the barstool beside Maximilian, Angyalka looked around her busy club. There was no live band tonight, but the music was loud and lively and appreciated, judging by the numbers on the dance floor.

"Quiet tonight," she observed.

Maximilian knew what she meant. Apart from himself, the guests were all human.

"Something's going on," she said. "Or is about to. Where is Saloman?"

Maximilian shrugged. He turned away from the crowd of human revelers and gazed instead at the beautiful, piquant face of his old friend. Subtle, clever, elusive, strong in self-preservation, she'd still been, to his knowledge, unswervingly loyal. For once, with difficulty, he said what was in his heart.

"I'm glad I met you again."

Her eyes widened. "Are you leaving?"

"Yes," said Maximilian, already turning his back and walking to the door. "I'm leaving."

Eleven Budapest vampires came in to Luk in the end. It would have been ten, but hearing that the hunters were the target, one persuaded a wavering friend at the last minute. It wasn't a huge haul, Luk acknowledged, but with Saloman present in the city, he couldn't have expected more. The icing on his cake was made up of the vampires who'd drifted in from Romania and Croatia: seven so far, and they were still coming. Together with himself, Grayson, and the five remaining Turkish vampires, Luk knew there would be enough. Even if Saloman followed—and he was bound to—it would only bring other vampires to the site. And what vampires would be able to resist beating up their old enemies the hunters? Even Saloman couldn't stand in their way. If he'd want to.

Euphoria had Luk literally hopping from one foot to the other in desperation to be off. In the dark, they stood together like a line of crows on the roof of the apartment building, above the attic that had sheltered him since his arrival here. But Luk hesitated to give the order to move.

"Now?" Grayson asked impatiently again. "Now?"

Luk ignored him. He felt the unmasking of the vampire he'd been waiting for. An instant later, a dark figure in jeans and a T-shirt leapt from the next roof and landed by his side, almost shoving Grayson off his perch.

"Maximilian," Luk said fondly. "So glad you could join us." Now they had *more* than enough. Maximilian's strength—to say nothing of his propaganda value as Saloman's "child" and onetime leader of the Hungarian vampires—more than made up for the poor Budapest turnout. He was the difference between victory and total, overwhelming success.

And this time I'll see him betray you. How will you like that, Saloman?

"Stop!" Cyn yelled. She threw herself forward as if she meant to yank up the handbrake herself, but fortunately, Rudy's steady hand was before her.

"What?" he demanded, sparing her a glance as he slowed down. "What the hell is it?"

They were all tired after their long flight to Budapest,

and John was looking forward to nothing more than a bath and bed. And yet at Cyn's cry, his weariness fell away from him like a blanket. It reminded him of sudden night alerts in Afghanistan.

"Look," Cyn commanded, pointing out of the window of the large car they'd hired at the airport. John followed her finger through the darkness to two men hurrying along the quiet road. They were quaintly dressed, a bit like untidy versions of the Gypsies in old-fashioned films, but Cyn was a New Yorker and unlikely to be so struck by the mere dress sense of passersby.

Rudy pulled to the side of the road just a little ahead of them, and Cyn inched open her passenger door. "Can't you feel it?" she whispered. "They're vampires!"

John glanced at her, impressed. "You could sense that from inside the car?"

"No; they just moved wrong, too fast. But I can feel it now."

"Want to say hi?" Rudy asked casually. All his passengers sat up. Excitement surged around the car at the prospect of a fight.

To see if he could, John flung out a mental feeler and brushed up against cold, angry purpose. "Wait," he said, grabbing Pete's arm as it stretched across him to the car door. "They're up to something."

Ignoring them, the vampires strode past the car.

"What?" Cyn demanded.

John opened the car door and got out. "I don't know. Why don't I ask?" Leaning his arm on the top of the car door, he called out with his mind.

Hey, where are you going?

One of the vampires paused and turned his head. Cyn and Rudy scrambled to get out of the car; there was a flurry of movement as everyone reached for the meager stakes they'd hidden through customs.

The vampire found John's gaze. His lip curled. *Fuck off,* he said distinctly, and he and his companion moved forward so fast that they seemed to glide.

"Follow them," John said grimly, diving back into the car. "They're too secretive, and they're ignoring us because they're focused on something else entirely."

"What?" Rudy asked, starting the car again.

"I don't know," John said, "but I'm afraid it's Elizabeth's big fight. I'm afraid she needs us."

"Elizabeth," Mihaela whispered. "Are you asleep?"

"No." Elizabeth turned her head to face Mihaela. Although they lay in sleeping bags side by side on the library floor, Elizabeth had never felt more wide-awake. Perhaps it was too difficult to fall asleep with the library lights on, even dimmed as they were. Perhaps she no longer needed the rest. Or perhaps it was just impossible to get any when her nerves hovered on a knife-edge, waiting for attack. "Why aren't you?" she whispered back.

"I don't know. I think I almost fell asleep. I keep imagining shadows down there." She jerked her head to the far end of the cavernous library, which was lit up only on the rare occasions anyone went that far.

Instinctively, Elizabeth raised her head to peer past Mihaela into the dark, almost eerie distance. The library was so silent that if she hadn't known better, she would have imagined that Konrad and István, on watch at the reception desk, must have nodded off. The others lay, if not slept, closer to the library entrance.

"Don't worry about it." Elizabeth reached out one hand and found Mihaela's, which grasped hers strongly.

"It's half past three," Mihaela murmured. "I don't think they'll come now, do you?"

"I suppose it's less likely so close to dawn." There were still two hours until dawn, and they both knew it.

Mihaela said, "We stand a better chance tomorrow, when the others come home."

Elizabeth nodded, and Mihaela lapsed back into silence. Elizabeth lay back down and gazed at the small, frosted-glass windows that were all the natural light the library had. Although they stood at pavement level outside, they were never, apparently, damaged by accident or design. More of Luk's protection?

"Elizabeth?" Mihaela whispered.

"Yes?"

"Are you afraid of dying?"

There was only one honest answer to that. "Yes," she whispered.

There was a pause, then: "Are you still getting those pains and sick spells?"

"Not so badly," Elizabeth said lightly. She hadn't been thinking so much about those as about losing Saloman, about death without sleep. Eternity. "Saloman thinks it's because my telepathy is growing. I'm picking up other people's feelings of pain and illness."

"Makes sense," Mihaela whispered eagerly. "Don't you think?"

"Sometimes it's certainly true," Elizabeth agreed.

"But you don't really believe it." The anxiety was back in Mihaela's whisper. Elizabeth could barely hear her.

"I do," she protested. "Mostly. I just can't shake the feeling that however true it is, there's more to it. That scares me too." *But if the illness kills me, I have time to decide. If I die tonight, would I let Saloman turn me?*

You mustn't lose who you are. . . .

She shifted restlessly. There was no point in thinking ahead, beyond the fight.

"Elizabeth," Mihaela said, low-voiced, "about last night—"

"Forget it, Mihaela. We go beyond quarrels."

Mihaela's hand came up, rubbing at her forehead. "Yes, but I accused you of dishonesty when *I* haven't been entirely honest with you."

Elizabeth smiled into her sleeping bag. "I got over that a long time ago."

"I'm not talking about the ancestry business," Mihaela said impatiently. "This is something else. We found a book, a prophecy, that we think relates to you. We didn't tell you because . . . well, because we thought you'd act differently if you knew, put yourself in greater danger. We've tried not to think about it ourselves, not to let it influence us, but I can't get it out of my head. And when you told me about your illness—"

She broke off, dropping her hand on the floor with a soft thump. The knot of unease that had been sitting at the bottom of Elizabeth's stomach, quiet and ignored, began to tighten.

"What prophecy?" she asked. "What did it say?"

"That you would cleave to Saloman's enemies—us—and smite his friends—vampires." Mihaela turned her head and met Elizabeth's gaze. "And something else about giving up the world to see the new age. It's stupid. It contradicts itself and is open to so many interpretations that it might not even apply to you! Only . . ."

Mihaela trailed off, so Elizabeth finished it for her. "You thought I might be about to give up the world. By death." *Or undeath*. She wouldn't bring that up here.

"Yes," Mihaela whispered.

"And if I'm not dying, then I can still be killed, especially in a battle against huge odds. Is that why you're telling me now?"

"Partly. I'm sorry. It's probably rubbish, but I wanted you to know the facts." She waved one self-deprecating hand. "If we can call it fact."

"Is it Luk's?" Elizabeth blurted.

"The prophecy? Yes, according to the medieval hunter who noted it down."

Elizabeth nodded. Luk had seen her in visions; she was sure of that. Although some of them might have been of her ancestress Tsigana. Hell, Mihaela's prophecy could equally apply to Tsigana, although she wasn't sure what that lady had ever done to smite Saloman's friends. But she couldn't dwell on that stuff here. Right now, she needed to calm Mihaela, and herself. And that meant talking, not thinking about things she couldn't change.

"What about you?" she asked. "Are you afraid of death?"

Mihaela shrugged. "No. I never have been. I think I've always believed I was on borrowed time anyway."

Elizabeth turned back to her. "Since your family died?" she asked with difficulty.

Mihaela nodded. "It doesn't matter, though," she said, still in the low, whispering tones they'd both used throughout the conversation. "I never wanted to die for nothing. I wanted to make a difference, root out evil to make the world safer."

"You have," Elizabeth said fervently.

"But this? If we die, Elizabeth, the world won't be safer at all. Not if the hunters' network and all our knowledge is destroyed. Not if Luk defeats Saloman."

"And if Saloman defeats Luk?"

"I'm beginning to think the world stands a chance," Mihaela said ruefully. "More of a chance, at any rate. We need at least to talk to Saloman." She kicked inside the sleeping bag, and Elizabeth could only guess who was at her imaginary receiving end. "Maybe the world *is* changing and we have to change with it. Or maybe we'll never have the opportunity."

"Don't say that, Mihaela. We *have* to win now."

"You really think we *can* win?" Elizabeth had never heard her sound so hopeless. "After what you said this morning?"

"Yes," Elizabeth whispered, just a little too loudly. She lowered her voice back to a whisper. "I do. And whatever happens, Mihaela, it won't be for nothing."

Mihaela's fingers gripped hers harder. "Because Saloman will still be here?"

"And us." Elizabeth squeezed her hand in return. "Believe that, Mihaela, and stay alive."

Elizabeth. Saloman's voice invaded her mind with all the ominous force of forked lightning. *They're here. It's time.*

Chapter Twenty

How many? Elizabeth asked urgently.

In spite of the cold shell he'd built, grief swamped Saloman. He couldn't prevent his sense of the world crumbling around him. Eleven from Budapest had betrayed him. And the incomers from Romania and Croatia were going not to him but to Luk. It was a bitter blow, and the odds were now powerfully stacked him against him. But he couldn't give in.

He showed Elizabeth a brief picture direct from his senses. *Luk and twenty-four vampires. More are coming this way.*

Twenty-four! My God, we can't do this! It's disastrous. We're hopelessly outnumbered."

It can *be done, Elizabeth. There is hope.* Saloman's brushed her agitated mind with his, a caress of tenderness, encouragement, and comfort, before he turned his thoughts elsewhere.

Angyalka.

It's happening, isn't it? Do you want us now?

Only as a last resort. If Saloman won out tonight, it was important he be seen to respect the hunters' wishes as much as possible. With a feeling of dread he despised in himself, he asked, *How many are with you?*

A few, Angyalka said evasively. Saloman closed his eyes. *Elek is here,* she added. And that at least was a grain of comfort in the ugly mess before him.

"Get up, Mihaela," Elizabeth breathed, scrambling to her feet and dragging the hunter with her. "They're here." Before she'd finished speaking she was already sprinting across the room to the reception desk, where Konrad and István sprawled at their ease. István lifted his head from the desk, blinking at her.

"It's now," she said urgently. "From the windows."

"The detectors," Konrad disputed, staring at his computer screen.

"Are slower than Saloman. Trust me."

István grabbed his stakes and leapt over the desk to join Mihaela. Aroused by the flurry of activity, Lazar and the other hunters threw off their sleeping bags and drew closer. Everyone was armed with a stake in one hand and a sword in the other; a belt or pouch full of more stakes hung around their waists.

Konrad came around from the desk to join the line of poised hunters, and twisted the computer monitor around to face them.

"Still no sign. What do you know, Elizabeth?"

"They'll come through the windows. One Ancient, twenty-four other vampires of assorted strength."

"Twenty-four? Oh, shit," Mihaela muttered. The monitor screen flashed red.

"Now," said Konrad grimly, and with the others, he turned to face the wall at the top of which the five long, narrow windows seemed to stare back at them blankly. "Stand back," he warned. "If they land on you with the force of that jump, you're dead."

"Guys," said István, "it's been good."

Oh, but it has; please don't let it end, Elizabeth thought in blind, pointless panic. The windows exploded inward, spraying glass at the waiting hunters. At almost exactly the same time, five vampires shot into the room like fearless children down a slide, surrounded by glistening haloes of crumbled, flying glass.

From behind Elizabeth, the air whooshed. Something—a piece of cloth or the edge of a boot—grazed past her ear, and even as Konrad shouted in warning, two tall figures landed in front of the hunter's line, facing the attacking vampires.

"I haven't been entirely honest with you," Elizabeth shouted. "Saloman is here with Dmitriu; they fight for us."

And then there was no time for more. The lead vampire resolved into Luk. Something burst into flames in his hand and was hurled over everyone's heads into the depths of the library, while more vampires dropped through the windows.

"Put out the fire!" Lazar yelled, but István had already pulled back from the line, running for the wall extinguisher.

As Elizabeth leapt forward, stake and sword raised to meet the onslaught, the number echoed in her mind with ever-increasing dread. *Two. There are only two of them, Saloman and Dmitriu. Maximilian has betrayed him again.*

Luk knew he was insane. It didn't bother him because it didn't make him careless. If anything, it made him obsessively care*ful*. He forced his followers to comb the area around the hunters' headquarters with him several times, checking with their eyes as well as their paranormal senses for Saloman, or for any other vampire who wasn't one of them. A couple were drifting through the town, unknown Romanians. Smirking, Luk sent them a telepathic beacon to guide them. But of Saloman's remaining loyal supporters, there was no sign.

"Good," he said, satisfied at last. "He hasn't cottoned on yet." From the roof opposite, he gazed down at the blank, doorless side wall of the hunters' building. Where the wall joined the pavement, a line of dull, oblong windows winked in the dim streetlight. The row of crowlike figures on either side of Luk gazed too, with a ferocious hunger that couldn't begin to approach his own. "So let's bring him."

With a glorious sense of freedom, Luk threw off his mask and lifted the protective cloak from his followers.

"Come, my children, let's hunt the hunters," he said with relish, and stepped off the roof. According to Maximilian, the hunters were relying on instruments that detected vampire presence. Right about now, they'd be shitting their smug, overconfident pants.

As his followers landed in a long, silent line beside him, he saw no reason to speak quietly. "Grayson, stick close to me; Maximilian and Timucin, you come in last, so keep checking for Saloman and his supporters. Let us bring death and destruction and the dawn of the new age that will devour us all!"

He wasn't quite sure where the last words came from, or what they meant. Grayson gave him a half-irritated, half-fearful look, which he ignored in favor of the task at hand. He stared at the window in front of his feet, which was only just large enough to let a grown man slide through horizontally, and with the power of his mind, he simply blew it in. The energy caught and spread like a virus, popping each window almost simultaneously, and with a cry of joy, Luk threw himself through, feet first, to create the doom of mankind and find his own.

Through the mist of falling glass, which seemed to sparkle in the hunters' lights as he shot into the room, he made out an unexpectedly poised line of humans. He smelled Elizabeth Silk. And then, even as he made his telepathic command to his next wave of followers to advance, he saw Saloman and Dmitriu leap over the hunters' heads and land squarely in front of him.

For an instant, he stared into his cousin's black, implacable eyes. Something rose up inside him that might have been rage or joy or a combination too confused to separate. *Fuck, but you're annoying.*

I know, said Saloman.

Luk laughed. *Then let it be now. Bring it on!* And summoning the fire, he hurled it from his hand deep into the core of the hunters' pride and joy. While the hunters panicked, Saloman and Elizabeth Silk both leapt for him. He sidestepped Saloman, reaching for the stake at his belt while with his sword he swiped off the nearest hunter's head.

Elizabeth yelled, a peculiar sound of agony and rage, cut off as suddenly as it began. And when Luk whirled around, it was Saloman's sword that clashed with his. Memory flashed, vivid and inconvenient. He knew that sword. He'd given it, and the bastard still wore it after what he'd done. In fury, he hacked, driving Saloman back with the sword and swiping viciously with the stake.

You're losing it all, Saloman. The library burns, the hunters are dying, damn their treacherous hearts, and your followers defect in scores—starting with your beloved Maximilian. Are you there yet, Maximilian?

I'm here, Maximilian said close beside him. *But Timucin isn't.*

Maximilian spun, leaping toward Grayson, who was plunging a stake toward Dmitriu's unprotected back, and struck hard and sure. Luk stumbled with shock, feeling Saloman's blade bite into his shoulder, barely comprehending that the dust of Maximilian's kill belonged not to Dmitriu but to Grayson, his last creation.

Now Dante isn't here either, Maximilian observed.

Thanks, said Dmitriu, already leaping onto a table after one of the Hungarian vampires.

You're welcome, Maximilian returned.

For an instant, grief almost undid Luk. Grayson was gone. Unthinkable. How had he let that happen? It forced him to disengage from Saloman, to jump back and take stock.

Grayson had awakened him with Saloman's blood

for his own ends. He'd taken advantage of Luk's weakness and confusion, and then of his strength. There was no love of his creator. And if Luk thought about it, as he did among the mayhem of the fight he'd begun, Luk felt no real love for his creation. In fact, he felt more emotion toward Maximilian, who was now fighting merrily along beside the enemy, damn him.

Oh, who cares? You were ever a treacherous bastard, Max! How well do you *trust him, Saloman?*

Implicitly, said Saloman, who'd obviously grasped that several of Luk's vampires were converging on the Awakener as instructed. Advancing at speed, he staked two of them at once. Elizabeth whirled and got another.

The hunters, though overwhelmingly outnumbered, were all battling with enough lethal fury to be dangerous. It was time to finish it before any more of his vampires died.

So fast that the humans wouldn't even have seen it, Luk leapt on Saloman. His cousin threw him off at once, with so much force that he dropped his sword. But that didn't matter; he'd made the touch, got the connection; and now, with fierce, vengeful satisfaction, he reached in and seized Saloman's mind.

By the time Cyn found the vampires, she was shaking with the feeling she'd called "malevolence" ever since she'd been old enough to know what the word meant. Here, on a respectable, quiet street in the middle of the night, the malevolence was overwhelming.

"There," she whispered, nodding farther down the road. A fight was already taking place. One man against another three. Except as three vanished in quick succession, she knew they hadn't been men.

"Wow," Pete said, awed. "Is he a vampire hunter?"

"No," John answered in a strange voice. "He's a vampire. He's talking to others inside that building. Telepathically."

"Can you hear them?" Rudy asked. "All of them? Do you know how many?"

"Lots," John said, tugging at his hair as though his head hurt, or he was trying to sort out the babble of voices. "They're trying to kill someone called the Awakener. Oh, shite, is that—"

"Elizabeth?" said Rudy. "Oh, yes. Let's go."

The sidewalk-level windows were broken, and from inside came the sounds of total carnage. Awkwardly, John got the ropes out of his backpack.

"Hurry," Cyn said, shivering, keeping her eyes fixed on the end of the street. "There are more coming." She'd be all right once the fighting started, but until then, all she could feel was the chill of evil.

"Let's go," Rudy said.

Saloman had stuck to his plan. Since Maximilian had agreed to go with Luk to keep track of events and to do what damage he could from that end, he and Dmitriu had entered the hunters' building early in the afternoon, so deeply masked that the staff they'd encountered had barely noticed them, let alone recognized them.

Even the business of breaking the shield enchantment to get in, and of building it again behind them, had been accomplished quickly and discreetly. In the library, they'd moved past all the researchers and librarians and taken up position at the very back of the cavernous room among the deepest shadows. So when the detectors were switched on and reset at five o'clock, they accepted him and Dmitriu as part of the environment. They remained silent, just as Elizabeth had hoped they would.

And although a couple of the hunters, especially Mihaela, had taken too many glances into the shadows, as if something there disturbed them, no one had truly seen them through Saloman's masking, because no one had truly had expected to. Apart from Elizabeth.

And at least he'd been able to give her a telepathic warning; with the detectors used to him and Dmitriu, Elizabeth hadn't been sure that they'd pick up any other vampire presence, so his own senses had been a very necessary part of the plan. When he and Dmitriu had emerged to face Luk's attack, there had been no time for the hunters to object.

Obeying his instructions, Maximilian and Dmitriu avoided tangling with Luk, and concentrated on his supporters. But clearly Luk had given instructions too, and those were to take out Elizabeth. Despite his trust in her new strength and abilities, her vulnerability scared him. He had to even the odds for her, and in his relief at achieving it, he'd turned his back on Luk.

Like taking candy from a baby, Luk mocked as Saloman froze in the grip of agony and humiliation, and the fear he hadn't been able to shake off in millennia of existence. *It gets you every time, and you never learn.*

Saloman made no telepathic reply. He couldn't.

"Saloman!" Elizabeth's voice, full of agony, told him she'd seen his situation. But this time, it was up to him to rescue her. He rode the pain, hanging on to one thought until, finally, Luk caught it.

I'm sapping your energy.

The pain loosened its grip as Luk instinctively drew back a little. But still he didn't release him. Instead, he drifted in front of Saloman, staring at him with pure, unadulterated hatred.

I've got enough, Luk sneered. *I'm stronger than before. And you're just as frightened.*

Saloman bared his teeth. "I like fear," he whispered. He sought it out at the epicenter of earthquakes, like the one in Peru just before he'd heard Luk's waking scream.

He took a step forward and Luk's eyes widened in shock. As Luk fought to tighten his grip once more, Saloman slammed his mind shut. He felt Luk's furious battering against it, but Saloman, staring deep into his cousin's red-tinged eyes, simply threw him out. Panicked, Luk stumbled backward and Saloman followed.

"Not this time, Luk. I choose who enters my mind, and you lost the privilege."

"When you killed me?" Luk screamed, swinging his fist faster than lightning into Saloman's face with enough force to break a human jaw. It slowed Saloman, but only for an instant. He thrust with his stake, drawing blood from Luk's arm as his cousin blocked the blow.

"No," Saloman said. "When you failed to knock." He thrust again, and Luk fell backward into the hunter István, who was fighting one of the Turkish vampires. "Now the door is locked. For good."

István whirled and caught his vampire opponent unaware by a backward thrust of the stake that turned him to dust. At the same time, from some hunter's instinct, well honed in many battles, he seemed to spot Luk's next move before he made it. After all, trapped between István's and Saloman's stakes, Luk had only one direction to go.

As Luk jumped, ensuring that any blow from Saloman's stake would miss his heart, István grabbed him around the waist, pinning both arms, presumably to keep him on the ground. It didn't work; Luk was too strong. He simply took István with him, and landed on top of one of the tall bookcases before shaking the hunter off like a dog dislodging a flea.

As Saloman whirled to face two charging vampires who were overdesperate to gain the power of an Ancient kill, he saw Luk kick István in the ribs, hard enough to send him spinning off the bookcase.

And then, most bizarrely of all, five humans jumped through the windows and rappelled down the library walls.

Blood dripped from Elizabeth's arm, trickling over her hand and between her fingers. It made the stake in her left hand slippery and hard to hold, and she'd already bungled one supposedly sure attempt on the heart of the vampire she fought. Of course, distraction didn't help. She'd seen Luk's mind-attack on Saloman, and her instinct to rush to his aid had allowed the vampire to slash her arm. That pain, she could live with, but it had been next to impossible to fight with the sudden agony in her head. It had to be Saloman's pain she was feeling, and along with her terror for him, it almost debilitated her.

Fortunately, it hadn't lasted long, though, and somehow, she'd managed to block the vampire, to defend from instinct until the pain lifted and Saloman was free. Another vampire, sensing an easy yet powerful kill, abandoned his fight with Lazar to join the one against her. Leaping high and kicking out, she floored him and finally dispatched her original attacker on the way back down to the ground. And, dropping to a crouch, she plunged the stake into the fallen vampire's heart before springing back to her feet, panting, and whirling to assess the next danger.

She took in the scene in a bare instant. The library was a mess. Tables and chairs had been upended and broken in the fight, some of the smaller bookcases overturned with books spilling out; Luk's fire hadn't caught enough to do much more damage than blacken one side of a bookcase, charring a row of books and singeing a few bindings before István had put it out. Since then, presumably, Luk had been kept too busy to summon any more fire.

Among the carnage lay a couple of wounded vampires, and the body of the dead hunter, Seb. There would be time enough to grieve for him later. Right now there was too much to do. Elizabeth fought on.

She had a glimpse of Saloman cutting a swath among the invading vampires, striking out with both hands in perfect time. His victims exploded into dust, and he strode on, repeating the maneuver with equal success before the enemy cottoned on and leapt back out of his way.

Elizabeth crashed her elbow back into the flesh of a fresh attacker and spun to meet him.

Apart from the lost Seb, the hunters were still on their feet, although bleeding. Lazar had blood all over his face, yet seemed to attack with a joy in battle that implied he'd been released rather than forced from his desk.

Near him, Mihaela plunged her stake and turned another vampire to dust. Though the numbers were still drastically against it, Elizabeth began to hope that maybe, just maybe, they could win in the end. Then Mihaela stepped back, almost touching a wounded vampire that lay at her feet. Elizabeth saw his sword arm twitch, and she yelled a warning to Mihaela. Hacking her own opponent to the ground, she sprinted across the room to help, but it was too late. The fallen vampire yanked on Mihaela's leg, bringing her crashing down to meet his bared teeth.

No! Elizabeth's agonized cry felt long and drawn-out; she didn't even know if she said it aloud. All she knew was, she could do nothing to stop this tragedy, and neither could the unbalanced, helpless Mihaela.

Incredibly, Mihaela landed on dust. Beside her, a capable hand withdrew the stake that had killed her attacker. Elizabeth skidded to a halt. Mihaela twisted to a crouch, staring up at her undead savior for the smallest instant and giving a curt nod. Maximilian, who had not betrayed Saloman again, straightened and turned away in search of fresh prey. It was a tiny incident in the carnage of battle, and yet as Elizabeth rejoined the fray, it bothered her, because of the expression in Mihaela's eyes as they'd encountered Maximilian's. The hunter who didn't fear death had looked frightened by her salvation.

Running next to help the sore-pressed Konrad, Elizabeth heard her name called and looked around wildly for its source. A row of people under the windows stood in wary, defensive postures, scanning the carnage before them.

"Elizabeth!" the woman's voice yelled again.

"Cyn?" Amazed, Elizabeth began to hack her way forward. *What the hell are you doing here?*

The thought formed involuntarily in her head. She certainly didn't expect a response. Yet a different voice said telepathically: *She's come to help. We all have.*

John Ramsay! Bloody hell! Emotion bubbled out of her as laughter, and she raised her voice with triumph. "Good news, guys! The cavalry is here! *Now* we can do this!"

For Cyn, the battle scene was a swirling, hacking, bloody mess that she could make no sense of. In the confusion, there was no way to tell who were the humans and who the vampires—except when they jumped. Yelling for Elizabeth had been a desperate attempt to find friends from enemies; but her joyous response lifted Cyn way beyond fear and indecision. Now they would make a difference.

They formed a wedge, as John had shown them, and fought their way toward Elizabeth. But it seemed the good guys were badly outnumbered, for a sudden, shocking attack from three sides broke up their wedge. Someone—she couldn't tell who—fell to the ground, and then Cyn was fighting for her life without time to pay attention to anyone else. She used her feet with brutality and, finding an opening, staked the vampire to dust. Whirling, she found another leaping toward her, far too fast to be human, and raised her stake once more. Without warning, it was wrenched from her hands. The vampire ran past and she thrust backward with her second stake at the one who'd interfered. She hit something hard and unyielding, and spun to ram the stake home.

She faced a tall, dark vampire with coal black eyes tinged with amber flame. With desperation, she thrust the stake with all her might. The vampire brushed it aside as if it were a mildly annoying fly.

"Know thine enemy," the vampire said dryly. "And protect the descendant."

"Rudy?" she blurted, looking wildly around her. She'd forgotten the descendant stuff that made Rudy so valuable a kill. But the vampire had already turned away, literally bumping into John, who froze, staring at him while around them battle raged.

"You're . . . you're . . ." John stammered.

"Saloman," said the vampire, and with a speed that blurred before Cyn's eyes, he staked two vampires rushing on their little scene.

Saloman himself. The overlord of all the other monsters. "Oh, shit," Cyn whispered, staring after his gracefully leaping body.

"It's a vampire war!" John yelled. "We're in the middle of a fucking civil war!"

Rudy and Cyn's cavalry was making a difference. Through sheer numbers, they were splitting up the enemy more and giving everyone a better chance.

Fighting on with new hope, almost on autopilot, Elizabeth caught sight of István dangling from the top of a tall bookcase, on which stood Luk, surveying the scene below him like a general. It was a long way for István to "dreep"—drop safely to the ground—but, dividing her attention, Elizabeth saw he had no such intention. Finding a foothold, he simply climbed up the shelves until he could jump up beside Luk and attack.

"Elizabeth!" he yelled through the noise of the fight, and she realized what he meant to do. Alone, he couldn't hope to kill Luk; but he could, possibly, push him off his perch for Elizabeth. Off balance, much as Mihaela had been, Luk would be an easier kill.

Luk laughed to see the hunter there, and Elizabeth began to get a bad feeling about this risky strategy. Worse, as she backed off from her latest opponent to do her bit, sharp pains prickled at her chest and sides, growing ever stronger, and it came to her that István was already hurt. It was there in his stiff movement, as he dodged Luk's swinging foot and parried the thrust of his sword. István was incredibly brave; she already knew that, but she'd never regarded him as foolhardy before.

He couldn't do this alone. Elizabeth reached for the shelves with one hand, glancing behind her to check on the battle's progress. Luk must have issued some telepathic order, for all his remaining vampires were disengaging and homing in on one target: Saloman.

"Oh, shit," Elizabeth whispered. Together they could weaken him, let enough of his blood for Luk to kill him. The hunters, baffled by the sudden maneuver, began to harry the vampires, but as they formed a circle around Saloman, each fighting a hunter with one hand and Saloman with the other, the damage was already being done.

Leaping back from the bookcase, she saw that István was employing a simple and possibly even effective measure, simply charging his damaged body into Luk's, too close for the sword to do much harm. Too close to the Ancient's teeth as well, but for the moment, he seemed to be avoiding that danger by coming in low.

Elizabeth hesitated no longer. Leaving István's bizarre battle for later, she ran to the circle surrounding Saloman. Dmitriu and Maximilian were there already, fighting side by side with the hunters. So was Rudy and Cyn's little group, although it was doubtful whether they knew why—they were simply trying to kill vampires, and for the moment that was enough.

Elizabeth's run felt like a battle charge. She even heard her voice yelling as she targeted her prey and leapt on him, killing the vampire instantly, more from surprise than skill. It gave Dmitriu next to her an extra opening to break through to Saloman's side, and the circle began to break.

Another fell under Saloman's merciless stake and, satisfied for the moment, Elizabeth sprinted back to István's struggle with Luk.

Luk teetered on the edge of the bookcase, locked in a grotesque embrace with István. It looked bad for the vampire, but even as Elizabeth ran to perform her part of István's plan, she realized with dread that Luk was laughing.

With a movement so sudden it blurred, he hauled István upward and sank his teeth into the hunter's throat. István continued to push, knowing, surely, that he would fall with Luk. An instant later, under Elizabeth's terrified gaze, Luk straightened, lifted the hunter high in his arms, and hurled him to the floor like a gnawed chicken bone.

István landed at Elizabeth's feet with a sickening crack.

The only scream she heard was her own as she fell to her knees beside him. Somewhere, she was aware of Luk jumping over their heads to land in the middle of the library floor, and the sudden flurry of movement as Saloman and the others homed in for the endgame; but what she chiefly felt was the agony of grief and her own guilt.

István's eyes were open and, astonishingly, he wasn't dead, for his eyelids flickered.

"István," she whispered. "Oh, God, István . . . Can you hear me? Where are you hurt?"

His eyes focused with obvious difficulty on her face, and she knew where he hurt. All over. The pain hit her like a wall in a high-speed car crash. She couldn't breathe; she couldn't move; nausea and dizziness flooded her, threatening unconsciousness. She fought it back, grasping István's helpless hand in utter pity for the pain of his cracked skull, his broken bones and ribs, and the weakness of his lost blood.

"I'm sorry, so sorry!" she exclaimed. She should have stayed with him, not given in at the wrong moment to her love for Saloman, who could, after all, take care of himself. Wrong decision this time. "Oh, God, no one should suffer this pain, István; I'd take it from you if I could. . . ."

István said, "I don't feel any pain." He sounded confused by this. "Have we won?"

Won? Who could possibly have won in this maelstrom of agony? She couldn't bear it. Her own voice filled her ears, crying out as wave after wave of pain engulfed her and grew, expanding and intensifying until there was nothing else. The staring faces of vampires from both sides, Mihaela's closer and white with fear, faded into black horror. And still it grew, whatever it was, hurling emotional and physical hurts so deep she wept in agony with them.

You couldn't fight destiny. This, then, was where all the prophecies led and ended for her. And there was no time, no more time. . . . Saloman's beloved face swam in front of her, wide-eyed with shock. She managed to grasp his arm and hold on, tried to speak, to tell him she loved him before she died. But the blackness took her too soon.

Chapter Twenty-one

It was sheer temper tantrum that caused Luk to throw the Hungarian hunter down like that, still alive and yet injured beyond repair. Saloman recognized it, because like Luk, he knew the battle was almost won. Only the outcome of the inevitable duel between the Ancients could change things now, and Saloman did not intend to lose.

As Elizabeth fell to her knees by the wounded hunter, Luk leapt off the bookcase to rejoin their interrupted duel.

There was a certain sense of déjà vu about fighting an angry, defiant Luk. He was still powerful and dangerous and more insane than ever, and still his friend, whom he must put out of his own misery before he caused any more for the world. Insanity was a blessing for him. A sane Luk would crumble with shame at what he had done in his rage. Saloman laid all that aside. It was tomorrow's pain. Tonight, he had a duty that he would not shirk.

He had no option but to defeat and kill Luk. If Luk killed Saloman, thus finally gaining the power of his true

Awakener, he would be unstoppable and the world's sufferings would be unimaginable. Everyone present must know that.

As his sword met Luk's, Saloman knew a sense of relief. It was almost over, and he could fight almost on instinct alone. And it would be a good fight. In his day, Luk had been the best. The tempo increased quickly, far beyond the speed the other vampires could achieve, and well beyond what the humans could easily see. Steel clashed on steel; stakes whizzed through the air; their bodies leapt and evaded, spun and thrust.

Because Luk was tired and not troubling to mask anything anymore, Saloman could sense when he tried to summon another fireball. He could even block it, although the distraction earned him a deep slice across the knuckles. Saloman licked them hastily to speed the healing process, leaping back as if to disengage and then, as Luk sensed the kill, plunging the stake straight at his cousin's heart.

It was Elizabeth's cry that froze them all in midfight. Penetrating the crashing, yelling mayhem like a knife through flesh, its preternatural, bloodcurdling agony seemed to paralyze everyone. Saloman's stake paused against Luk's heart. Luk's sword, already poised to strike Saloman's head, stilled. All around him, Saloman was aware, the fighting stopped in shock.

Elizabeth!

Ignoring the still very real danger from Luk, Saloman turned his back on his enemy and ran to her.

She knelt by István's side, holding the hunter's hand in both of hers. Tears streamed down her face, which was contorted in agony. She didn't even appear to be aware of the noise she made. Her arm and hand were bloody from some wound, no doubt painful but hardly enough to account for her obviously unbearable suffering.

"What's the matter with her?" Mihaela demanded, her voice too high with fear. "Saloman, I can't make her hear me!"

Crouching down beside Mihaela, he took Elizabeth's twisted, openmouthed face between his hands. Her pain-racked eyes seemed to focus on him. To his relief, her hand gripped his arm tight, as if holding on to her one salvation. Her lips moved, trying to speak. And then her eyes rolled up in her head and she slumped against him.

"Elizabeth!" Mihaela screamed.

At the same time, István whispered her name with a wonder that drew Saloman's stunned attention. István knew.

The Hungarian's gaze was riveted to Elizabeth's head, and despite his horrific injuries, there was no pain in those intelligent gray eyes. Saloman glanced at his own injured hand. It should be healing, but there was no sign now that any wound had ever been there.

A cut on Mihaela's cheek closed up as he watched it. Twisting around with Elizabeth still in his arms, Saloman watched the wounded vampires rise to their feet, saw Lazar touch his head as if surprised it didn't hurt.

Something like a wind seemed to blow through Saloman, lifting him and making him shiver at the same time.

"Elizabeth," he whispered. "My Elizabeth."

"What is it?" Mihaela demanded harshly. "Is she dead?"

Saloman smiled and stroked the beloved head.

"No," he said. "She isn't dead. She's a healer who's come into her gift and can't control it. She's taken all our pain into herself and caused much of the healing to begin. It rampaged out of control, as if she's taking on not just our pain but the world's."

"But she can't do that," Dmitriu said. "She'll die."

"No, she won't," Saloman said softly, reaching into her mind to soothe and block what she couldn't yet bear or manage. "No, she won't."

"Saloman," Maximilian warned, and he realized that Luk, who'd completely slipped his mind, was looming over him. He grabbed his dropped stake from some left-over battle instinct. Maximilian and Dmitriu stood on either side of Luk, holding their own stakes to his front and back.

Luk didn't appear to notice. His intense gaze was fixed on Elizabeth, or rather on the tableau of Elizabeth in Saloman's arms.

"The world is reborn," he intoned, in the voice of the visionary Saloman well remembered. "All is changed, and Saloman's dominant power eclipsed in this union that was always meant to be. The world shatters and forms again, never the same. The hour of the vampire is at hand and the world will be safe."

Abruptly, Luk sat down.

Dmitriu said, "What the fuck does that mean?"

And Maximilian laughed, a sound rare enough to bring a smile to Saloman's lips. Elizabeth stirred, and Saloman cradled her in his arms as he rose to his feet.

"It means this fight is ended," he said sternly. "Luk's challenge is over and all his followers will swear allegiance to me or die. This building is henceforth sacrosanct once more." He swept his gaze around the hunters. "I can't remove the knowledge of where it is; the secret can never be restored. But I can make it impossible for it to be entered by any without your permission."

"Including you?" Konrad demanded.

"No," said Saloman. "But I agree to knock first in the future."

"I think we're all glad you came without invitation," Lazar said reluctantly.

"Ambulance," Mihaela's voice interrupted, speaking into her mobile phone. "Urgently." Her attention was on István. "Will he be all right?"

It was impossible to tell whom the question was directed to. István said, "Yes." But Saloman, sensing in the hunter's body as he'd once sensed in Elizabeth's, was not so sure.

He said, "She's taken your pain and healed the

pierced lung that might have killed you. But your injuries are still severe."

Elizabeth's breath stirred his throat, making him shiver. She said huskily, "Who has?"

"You," Saloman said. "You."

After Lazar and the hunter Karoly had removed their colleague's decapitated body, the paramedics were allowed in to take István to the ambulance and to check out the walking wounded. Still dazed, Elizabeth watched, curiously detached and yet with every nerve ultrasensitive to her surroundings.

She wasn't dead; she wasn't dead at all.

Saloman sat on the floor by her side; and despite the human deaths and injuries, the battle was won and her friends were alive.

Saloman was scribbling something on a piece of paper, which he passed to Mihaela. "Those missing women. You might want to alert your police and paramedics to this address."

Mihaela's eyes widened. "How do you know?"

"Luk," Saloman said briefly, and without further questions, Mihaela got on her phone once more.

"Hey."

Elizabeth glanced up to see Rudy, Cyn, and John Ramsay. They crouched down facing her. Cyn said anxiously, "You really okay?"

"Sure!" Elizabeth shared her smile between the three of them and their remaining wounded colleague on the other side of the room. "I'm so sorry about your friend."

"It's the risk we're all prepared to take," Rudy said gruffly.

"I want to say thanks for coming, but it sounds so trivial, as if you turned up to a birthday party, instead of making the difference here. Without you, I doubt we'd have won this."

Cyn cast a glance of hatred at Saloman. "I'm still not sure what the hell 'this' was."

Mihaela said, "It's all right. The good guys won."

"Did they?" Cyn snapped.

Saloman smiled and stretched out his long legs among the fallen books.

"At a price," Konrad said bitterly from across the room. "Can I talk to you?"

As Rudy and Cyn moved away with Konrad, John hesitated. His gaze was riveted to Saloman's face. "You saved my life. In Afghanistan."

"I may have done. I didn't save them all."

John's lip twitched. "You're not *all* the bad guys, are you?"

"No," Elizabeth said quietly.

Dmitriu said, "You're telepathic. You've got the Ancient gene."

"What?" John said, baffled.

Saloman regarded Dmitriu with only slightly mocking pride. "I'm so glad to see you're taking up your new duties so quickly."

The library door clicked closed behind István and the paramedics, and as John, together with Rudy and Cyn, prepared to follow them, Elizabeth opened her mouth to release her flood of questions. But Dmitriu was before her.

"What about him?" he asked Saloman, jerking his head at the passive Luk, who still sat in the middle of the floor amid the carnage, apparently deep in thought.

Elizabeth slid her hand into Saloman's. Her hatred had vanished in understanding. "His pain was worse than anything," she said, low.

"I know."

Luk lifted his gaze. "I should never have been awakened."

"No," Saloman agreed.

"I would like to go back."

"I know."

"Will you do it now?"

"Not here," Saloman whispered, and Luk smiled. It

was a curiously sweet smile, allowing Elizabeth a glimpse of the true person he'd once been.

"No," Luk agreed. "Not here, now. I'm sorry, Saloman. It must be hard to be the last."

"It was." Saloman's fingers tightened on Elizabeth's, and with wonder, she realized she'd come to fill another emptiness for him.

Luk climbed to his feet. Saloman said, "Maximilian and Dmitriu will take you home. I have something to do before I can bring you peace."

Luk's strange eyes focused on Elizabeth. "From her will come the peace of the world," he said dreamily. "I like that."

He turned to go, Dmitriu by his side. Maximilian hesitated, then walked to Saloman. Unexpectedly, he dropped to his knees, took Saloman's hand, and kissed it. Elizabeth had the impression of some intense, unspoken communication between them. An instant later, he was walking on Luk's other side to the library door.

"Farewell," Saloman said softly. A human wouldn't have been able to hear over that distance, but Maximilian's nod showed that he did. It seemed that Maximilian was leaving again.

Mihaela, watching curiously from her sitting position against the wall, dragged her gaze back to Elizabeth. "Are you sure you shouldn't be going to the hospital too?"

"Oh, no," Elizabeth said hastily. Although she felt as weak as a newborn kitten, she couldn't bear the idea of a hospital, of parting from Saloman. "I've never felt better in my life. I just need to sleep."

Mihaela glanced at Saloman, as if for confirmation, then got to her feet. "Okay. I'm going to the hospital with István. Konrad?"

Konrad, moodily chewing his finger as he propped up a bookcase with his shoulder, straightened. "What about . . . ?" he began, with a jerk of one hand toward

Saloman, who would thus be left alone in the library with Elizabeth.

"He has spells to cast," Mihaela said dryly, catching Konrad's arm and dragging him with her. "Come on."

Elizabeth gazed around the carnage. "I wouldn't like to be the one to clear this up."

"It could have been worse."

"It could have been a lot worse," Elizabeth agreed fervently.

Saloman released her hand and stood, walking to the window wall, where he jumped and clung to the sill with one hand while reaching into the open space with the other. His voice intoned an enchantment that sparked visibly through the air to the broken windows on either side, and then he dropped back down.

"That should hold them in the short term."

"What happened to me?" Elizabeth blurted, because she could no longer wait to understand it.

Saloman walked back toward her. "You came into your potential. Which is the rare and powerful gift of healing. You tried to take the pain of the whole world and, not surprisingly, your brain shut down in protest."

With his foot, he cleared a space amid the carnage and crouched down beside her, taking her hand once more.

"It's been building in you, I think. What I mistook for telepathic sympathy was your not just feeling but *taking* other people's pain. John Ramsay, who so benefited from your brief visit. You thought it was just because you believed him when no one else did, but it was more than that. You helped him, physically and emotionally, and maybe even helped a few others on the side as you left the building. You didn't recognize or understand what you were doing, so you had no idea how to control it."

"That's the truth," Elizabeth said shakily.

"It would probably have been best for the gift to go

on growing gradually, but I suspect István's injury triggered its massive release and now you're stuck with it fully fledged."

"I felt so guilty," Elizabeth whispered, "because I went to you when I knew in my heart he needed my help more."

"He made his choice, and it almost worked too."

"I've been realizing what a wonderful person István is, and how much I like him. I couldn't bear his suffering. . . ."

"You did bear it," Saloman disputed. "And you kept him alive."

"Will he recover?" she asked eagerly.

"I don't know. But you can probably help."

Elizabeth gazed at him, awed and wondering. "I can do good in the world. Beyond killing bad vampires and—"

"And tempering my excesses?" Saloman suggested. "Yes. Yes, you can. This was the prophecy Luk saw all those years ago. He saw the woman as Tsigana, when in reality she was Tsigana's descendant, but he knew she would be with me. Elizabeth . . ."

He touched her face, her lips. "Your time is so short in this world. You have a gift now, a unique and wonderful gift that I cannot separate from you. I've rarely seen it so powerful in any of my people. So although I love you, I have to ask you again: Will you not consider eternity with me?"

She caught his hand against her lips, kissing it passionately. "I hardly consider anything else," she whispered. "I long for it, but I've been so afraid. . . ."

"Of what?"

"That I won't be Elizabeth anymore. That any good in me will be lost. That you won't love me anymore."

He carried their joined hands to his own mouth. "I will always love you. Turning you will not alter who you are. Not when I do it. Your soul remains. Everything that makes you Elizabeth will still be there, but stronger. It will make your healing powers easier to bear and to practice."

"And yet," she said, smiling through the ache in her throat. "I sense an 'and yet.'"

"And yet," he said, "you're still the sun to my night. I can't bear you to lose the sun."

Slowly, she let her forehead drop forward to his. "The sun doesn't make me Elizabeth."

He was very still. Elizabeth could almost hear the silence. "What do you mean?" he whispered.

She twisted her hands in his, clutching him closer. "Give me time, Saloman. I won't ask you today or tomorrow, or even this year, but I will do it."

He closed his eyes as if she'd kicked rather than pleased him. "As your duty to the world. Because of your gift."

"Yes," she said, bewildered. Something was leaking from the corner of his eye, frightening her.

Do vampires weep? she'd asked him once.

Yes, but I won't.

"Saloman." She touched his cheek with her fingertip and found blood. He was weeping blood. "It changes everything. Duty, yes, and desire to do it too. I feel all of that, but more than anything, do you not see it makes me your equal? Almost. It makes me worthy."

His eyes opened, spilling another stray drop of blood that he didn't seem to notice.

"I have something wonderful now," she whispered.

"You have always been wonderful."

"But with it, I can welcome eternity with you and have a chance—"

"A *chance*?" Abruptly, he pushed her back and leaned over her, his mouth so close to hers that one tilt of her head would bring them together. "Of love?"

"Of *keeping* your love."

"It doesn't work like that."

"How does it work?"

A half smile formed and died on his lips. "I don't know."

"I thought you knew everything."

"No, you didn't."

She made the tilt, brushing her lips against his and feeling the familiar electricity spark through her entire body. She felt the caress of his mind and opened to him.

"I can wait to turn you," he whispered against her lips. "I can even wait to love you. I never dreamed—" He broke off, drawing back to stare at her. His hand slid down from her cheek, over her breast, to her stomach, where it stilled. "Elizabeth. Oh, Elizabeth."

"What?" Suddenly frightened that after all this, he'd found the elusive illness, she grasped his wrist. "Is something wrong?"

He stared at his hand on her stomach and slowly lifted his gaze to her face. "Feel it. Reach inward with your mind. There is more than one life force in you. Touch it. Touch your womb."

"Touch my— Oh, God," she whispered. Seeking inside herself was difficult, but following his mind, she managed it. A tiny, budding life pulsed frailly within her, its pure, unformed spirit nestling in her own. A stunned, wild rush of love swept through her, embracing it and Saloman together.

"I have a child," she whispered, staring at Saloman through the tears spilling unchecked from her eyes. "We have a child. . . . How is it possible?"

"You're a rare being, Elizabeth Silk," he whispered. She had never seen his eyes, his whole face so intense. "Very few among the undead of my people ever bred. Our changed physiology made it almost impossible. Only as the living Ancients died out did an undead woman give birth for the first time. I believe it's only ever happened twice. But, it seems, between you and me lies some deep compatibility even I couldn't see." His hand caressed her stomach, and he smiled. "But Luk did."

"Luk?" Lost in the wonder that eclipsed everything else for her, she struggled to understand.

"This was the final part of his prophecy. From our union comes the peace of the world, our child who unites human and vampire in her being. My power is eclipsed."

She stared into his eyes. She'd never before seen them so warm or so excited. And so pleased with himself. He rose to his feet, lifting her in his arms with delicious tenderness.

"In you lies the world's greatest treasure," he said softly. "The first Ancient child to be conceived in two millennia."

ABOUT THE AUTHOR

Marie Treanor lives in Scotland with her eccentric husband and three much-too-smart children. Having grown bored with city life, she resides these days in a picturesque village by the sea. She has been writing stories since childhood and considers herself very privileged to be still doing so instead of working for her living. Her previous e-books include *Killing Joe*, which was an Amazon Kindle bestseller. In the Awakened by Blood novels, she is delighted to be able to bring together her long-standing loves of vampire stories and Gothic romance.

To find out more, please visit www.MarieTreanor.com or find her on Facebook.

Want to go back to the very beginning of
Saloman and Elizabeth's story?
Read on for an excerpt from
Marie Treanor's riveting

BLOOD ON SILK

Available now in print and eBook

The village Dmitriu had shown her on the map wasn't far, although the roads were dreadful. Grasping the steering wheel tighter to control the beat-up old car as it bumped over a major pothole, she felt something sting her right palm.

As soon as she could, she took her right hand off the wheel, almost expecting to find a squashed bee, but there was nothing except a welling pinprick of blood. Frowning, with one eye still on the atrocious road through the mountains, she brought her hand to her mouth and licked the wound.

"Ouch," she muttered. Something was stuck in there. She waited until reaching a relatively smooth stretch of road, then laid both hands together on the wheel and tried to pick it out. It pulled free with a pain sharp enough to make her wince. A thorn—a large rose thorn. She must have picked it up at Maria's without noticing until she'd driven it farther into her hand by gripping the wheel so hard. Blood oozed from it sluggishly.

"All I need," she muttered, licking it again before deciding to ignore the sharp pain. A thorn would hardly kill her, and she wanted to press on. Although the sun was going down, she couldn't resist the opportunity of at last finding some sort of context for the wretched Saloman character. Dmitriu's unexpected information had given her a new lease on life, banishing the lethargy she'd felt at Maria's. Besides, this was it: Sighesciu. . . .

It wasn't the prettiest village in these mountains. Despite the unspoiled natural scenery that surrounded it, Sighesciu itself looked run-down and poor. Leaning forward to peer farther up the hill, Elizabeth glimpsed a bulldozer and a mechanical digger. There were no signs of the ruined castle Dmitriu had spoken of, though. Taking the turn that appeared to lead up the hill toward the bulldozer, she let her mind linger on the enigmatic Dmitriu.

She'd been relieved that he hadn't suggested coming with her, had just sent her to the car for her map while he sat in the shade of Maria's vines to wait. There, he'd shown her the village and the hill and said that although he couldn't come right now, he might wander up there later to see how she got on.

Elizabeth wasn't quite sure how she felt about seeing him again. He was an intriguing character, apparently well educated despite his "peasant" style of dressing. She realized she'd no idea what he did for a living, although his manicured hands clearly showed that he wasn't a farmer. Insatiably curious, she wanted to know more about him—so long as it was all kept as platonic as their interaction that afternoon.

Her lips twisted into a smile and she laughed at herself. She was still harboring unrequited feelings for Richard, her PhD supervisor, who found her no more than an amusing curiosity. In any case, Elizabeth was smart enough to understand that half the attraction of Richard was his unattainability, if there was such a thing.

As she drew up to the top of the hill, she saw that the workmen were finishing for the day. Several cast her curious glances as they took off their hard hats and meandered past her battered old car. She'd bought it very cheaply in Budapest, but, although it didn't look like much, it had gotten her safely around many inaccessible and isolated villages in both Hungary and Romania, and she was almost growing fond of it.

Emerging into the gathering dusk, she wondered whether she'd left too late after all. She wouldn't be able to see so much if she had only a flashlight beam to work by. She might have to come back in the morning anyway. As it was, she had a bit of a drive ahead of her to the hotel at Bistriţa.

Casting that difficulty to one side, she looked around for someone to talk to. One man among those streaming back down the hill detached himself and called in Romanian, "Madam? Can I help you?"

"Thanks. I hope so! I was told there was a castle here."

The man took off his hard hat and gestured around him. Elizabeth took in the piles of stone and rubble scattered across the site.

"Ah."

"We leveled all that was left today, but there was nothing much to see anyway. Tomorrow we'll take away all the debris so we can begin building. Perhaps you've already reserved a house?"

"Oh, no. I don't live here. I'm just visiting."

The man laughed at that, as though the very idea of anyone looking like her—a pale-skinned northerner with untidy, strawberry blond hair; rather worn, old cropped jeans; a cheap sleeveless top; and a cotton hat dangling down her back from a string around her neck—could possibly be Romanian.

"These are holiday homes," he explained, "for foreigners who like our country."

"It's a very beautiful country," Elizabeth said with genuine appreciation. It was on the tip of her tongue to add that she couldn't afford luxury housing for foreigners, when it occurred to her that he might look on her request with more favor if he thought her a potential customer. After all, he appeared to be some kind of foreman or even manager.

She tried a smile and hoped it didn't look too guilty. "Would you mind if I stayed for a few minutes and looked around? Just to get a feel for the place and admire the views?"

He shrugged. "You're welcome. There are no gates to lock. Take as long as you like. Just be careful. We still have some old foundations to fill in, and some of them are pretty deep."

"I'll be careful," she assured him. "Thanks."

She made to pass on, but with obvious concern, he asked, "Are you hurt?"

She blinked, following his frowning gaze to the hem of her top, which now boasted a bright red, shapeless bloodstain. There was another smear across the leg of her jeans where she'd wiped her bleeding palm.

"Oh, no, it was just a rose thorn. I bleed easily, but it'll stop in a minute."

Satisfied, the man walked on, and Elizabeth began to pick her way over the rubble. Dmitriu had claimed there was a chapel here, and beneath it, a crypt. But neither was obvious at first glance.

Elizabeth rummaged in her bag until she found her flashlight. She was careful to hold it in her uninjured left hand, and shone the beam into the debris, looking for any carvings in the fallen stone, any lettering that might give her a clue. But if there had ever been anything, it had been obliterated by time and bulldozers.

She shivered as if someone had walked over her grave—instead of the other way around. But she couldn't quite laugh at herself. The hairs on the back of her neck stood up like hackles, and she spun around to see who was watching her.

No one. She was alone on the derelict site. Even the departing workmen had been more interested in their supper than in her.

What's the matter with you, Silk? she jeered at herself. *Vampires getting to you at last?*

Of course not. It was just that the sun seemed to set so quickly here, and this place did have an intriguing atmosphere. She *liked* atmospheres and had learned by experience that they could be useful guides. She preferred hard evidence, of course, but when that was lacking, sometimes you found something just by going with a hunch, a feeling.

Other times, you found nothing at all—like now.

Giving up, she spun around to head back to the car. Her foot slipped, and she flung out her right hand to save herself from falling. She winced as stones pressed into the thorn hole in her palm, and when she dragged herself upright, the flashlight flickered crazily across the tiny smears of blood on the stones. As another drip appeared, she brushed the dirt off her hand and thrust her palm at her mouth before following the beam of the flashlight to its end—a gap in the ground into which gravel and more rubble were already falling. That must have been where her foot slipped.

Elizabeth crouched down beside it, away from the bulk of the shifting ground, and shone her beam into the widening gap.

It was a room, like a crypt.

Excitement soared, drowning the last of her silly anxieties. She could make out rough carvings on the walls, perhaps angel figures. . . .

Elizabeth reached out with care and gave the rubble an encouraging push before leaping back to admire the effects. A little irresponsible, perhaps, but how else was she supposed to get in? She doubted her little avalanche was capable of damaging anything.

When the ground stilled, she edged forward. All seemed secure on this side of the wide hole. She knelt, trying to gauge the distance to the ground of the crypt. She was sure it was a crypt. It smelled musty and damp. If she were fanciful, she would have said it smelled of death, although any human remains would surely be long past the rotting stage. Maybe there were rats—not a nice thought. But she caught no scurrying creatures in the beam of her flashlight, and she thought she could lower herself down there without difficulty—"dreep," in the language of her childhood.

First, she rolled a fair-sized boulder to the gap and let it fall in. She might need it later to stand on to get herself out. Then, positioning herself, she gripped the side of the hole and let her feet slide through until she dangled. She let go and jumped the last foot or so to the ground.

It was an easy landing. Triumphant, she dragged the flashlight back out of her bag and shone it around the room. They *were* angels on the walls, worn with age but still remarkably fine for an out-of-the-way place like this. It made sense, she supposed. If this Saloman was important enough to have inspired so many legends, even after he'd been staked as a vampire, he would have been a rich, even princely, man.

The trouble was, there seemed to be no tomb—no markings on the wall to denote he was buried behind them, no tomb on the floor. There were just angels carved into the wall and broken stone steps that had once led up to the gap she'd almost fallen down, where the chapel used to be. It was exactly as Dmitriu had described.

Except for the lack of a body or any kind of inscription.

Bugger. He must have made it up too, just as Maria had done. He couldn't have known about this hidden room—it had obviously been sealed for centuries, and there was no evidence whatsoever that a chapel had ever stood above it.

So Saloman's origins remained elusive. But at least the angels were pretty. Elizabeth laid down her bag, pulled her camera out of it, and propped the flashlight on the bag to shine upward. Walking around the room, she photographed each angel in turn, changing the direction of the light as necessary. In the final corner, she stubbed her toe on something—rubble, she imagined, although her impatient glance could pick out nothing large enough. Ignoring it, she aimed the camera at the large angel above her head.

A shiver ran all the way up her spine to her neck, jerking the camera in her hand. She steadied it, irritated when a drop of blood from her hand distracted her.

"Whoever bled to death from a rose thorn?" she demanded, wiping her hand on her thigh again. Finally, she raised the camera and took the picture. And when she stepped back, she saw the sarcophagus right in front of her.

She blinked. "How the . . . ?" Perhaps her eyes had just gotten used to the particularly dark corner, but was the light really so poor that she'd missed *that*? Or was her observation so erratic? She must be *bloody* tired.

Grabbing up the flashlight, she shone it full on the stone sarcophagus. It was the size of a large man, its lid carved with a human figure in sharp relief, almost as if the corpse lay there looking at her.

As beautifully carved as the angels, it was a wonderful, detailed piece of art in its own right. She shone the flashlight from its booted legs upward over the long, open cloak, which revealed an ornate but empty sword belt. The emptiness might have been explained by the broken sword protruding from his stone chest; gory, yet tastefully done. So *this* must be the basis of the vampire legends.

She'd need an expert to date the carvings, of course, but late seventeenth century seemed about right. That meant she'd have to look for differences between the legends before and after Dmitriu's date of 1697. There were a lot of those for so young a man. She'd also need to reanalyze those stories set before his likely birth date, perhaps around 1670.

In fact, she needed to speak to Dmitriu again, and soon. She'd never expected to find anything as beautiful as this. . . .

She took one hasty snap before dropping the camera

back into her bag. Fascinated, she gazed down at the likeness of the man she now believed to be the legendary Saloman. The still, stone face appeared surprisingly youthful. With no martial beard or ridiculous mustache like Vlad the Impaler's, it was just a young, handsome countenance with deep-set, open eyes.

Why weren't his eyes closed? The irises and pupils of each were well delineated; they might even have been colored under the centuries of dust. Christ, he even had eyelashes, long and thick enough to be envied by most women.

But there was nothing else remotely feminine about this face. Its nose was long, slightly hooked, giving an impression of arrogance and predatory inclinations. On either side were cheekbones to die for, high and hollowed, and beneath, a pair of perfect, sculpted lips, full enough to speak of sensuality, firm enough to denote power and determination, and a strong, pointed chin. Long, thick hair lay in stone waves about his cloaked shoulders, and again Elizabeth could almost imagine that the dust covered black paint.

The sculptor seemed to have imbued a lot of character into that dead stone face, as if he'd known him well and liked him; yet he'd also captured a look of ruthlessness, an uncomfortable hardness that sat oddly with the faint, dust-caked lines of humor around his eyes and mouth. Well, he wasn't the first or the last bastard to have a sense of humor.

And besides, if he was a likable man and the true hero of some of the legends she'd listened to, why had he been killed in such a way? Where had the stories of atrocity come from? His enemies? He was a mirror of Vlad the Impaler, perhaps, except no one before Bram Stoker had made Dracula a vampire. The Saloman vampire stories were far older, and they came from natives.

There was a splash of discoloration beside his mouth. Frowning, she reached out and touched it. Wet—it was a drop of her blood.

"Oops."

But the carved face was so beautiful that she let her fingers linger, brushing against the cold, dusty, stone lips. Another drop of blood landed there, and she tried to scrub it off with her thumb. All that achieved was another drip and rather grotesquely red lips on the carving, so she yanked her guilty hand back and began to examine the rest of the sarcophagus.

It sat on a solid stone table, but it wasn't just the lid; it was the whole sarcophagus that was carved into the shape of a man, and she could find no hinges in the smooth stone. Perhaps the body was in the table underneath? Unless there were hinges or some kind of crack on the other side.

Leaning over the sarcophagus, she ran her fingers along its far side, but she felt only the detailed outlines of muscled arm and hip and thigh, so lovingly carved that just stroking them seemed intimate. She stretched farther so that her hair and jaw brushed against the cold stone of his face, and she felt along the table instead. It too appeared to be one solid piece of stone. So where the hell was the body?

Movement stirred her hair, almost like a lover's breath on her skin. Startled, she jerked up her head, but before she could leap away, or even see what was happening, something sharp pierced her neck and clamped down hard.

MARIE TREANOR'S

Blood Sin

is
"Sensual and thrilling."
—National Bestselling Author Michele Bardsley

Even if you stand in the light,
you can dwell in the dark.

Months after her dangerous encounter with vampire overlord Saloman, Scottish academic Elizabeth Silk is still trying to cope with both the demands of her ancestral bloodline—which marks her as a vampire hunter—and the overpowering desire she feels for the immortal she brought back from the grave. But she is not alone in her fascination with Saloman.

When Elizabeth tracks down a distant cousin from America, she learns he possesses an antique sword that has caught the interest of the Grand Master of the American hunters. It is the ancient and mystical sword of Saloman—a treasure of vast occult powers and a prize beyond measure to both vampires and humans. Now the race is on for possession of the sword.

Even as her enemies and allies shift their allegiances and battle for supremacy, Elizabeth must decide which will rule her own perilous fate: unwanted loyalty or unholy love.